"Look, it's a simple question. What was your job?"

"*Emperor.*"

"Emperor?"

"For a time, people used 'empress'—but that's not to my tastes."

The prison official made a note on his slate. "Emperor. Of what? This place?"

Georgiou looked up and around. "This space station doesn't exist in my universe. But it is in territory I conquered. Back in '53, I believe."

Frietas blinked. "Beg pardon—you said in your *universe?*"

"That's correct."

"You own a universe."

"A significant part of one." She frowned. "Or I *did*."

"You did." The interviewer smirked. "This should be rich. What happened?"

"I lost it. One of my rivals staged a coup."

"A shock, was it?"

"No, it was completely predictable." She coaxed forth a name that was acid to her mouth. "*Lorca.* I sent my daughter Michael to hunt him down—but she sided with him instead, and *that*, I should have predicted. Children make poor decisions."

"You're not the first to say that, I'm sure."

STAR TREK®
DISCOVERY

DIE STANDING

JOHN JACKSON MILLER

Based on *Star Trek*®
created by Gene Roddenberry
and
Star Trek: Discovery
created by Bryan Fuller & Alex Kurtzman

GALLERY BOOKS

New York London Toronto Sydney New Delhi

Gallery Books
An Imprint of Simon & Schuster, Inc.
1230 Avenue of the Americas
New York, NY 10020

First Gallery Books trade paperback edition July 2020

GALLERY BOOKS and colophon are registered trademarks
of Simon & Schuster, Inc.

For information about special discounts for bulk purchases,
please contact Simon & Schuster Special Sales at 1-866-506-1949
or business@simonandschuster.com.

The Simon & Schuster Speakers Bureau can bring authors
to your live event. For more information or to book an event,
contact the Simon & Schuster Speakers Bureau at 1-866-248-3049
or visit our website at www.simonspeakers.com.

10 9 8 7 6 5 4 3 2 1

Library of Congress Cataloging-in-Publication Data

Names: Miller, John Jackson, author.
Title: Die standing / John Jackson Miller.
Description: New York : Gallery Books, 2020. | Series: Star Trek: Discovery |
    "Based on Star Trek created by Gene Roddenberry and Star Trek: Discovery
    created by Bryan Fuller & Alex Kurtzman."
Identifiers: LCCN 2020008214 (print) | LCCN 2020008215 (ebook) |
    ISBN 9781982136291 (trade paperback) | ISBN 9781982136307 (ebook)
Subjects: GSAFD: Science Fiction.
Classification: LCC PS3613.I53858 D54 2020 (print) | LCC PS3613.I53858
    (ebook) | DDC 813/.6—dc23
LC record available at https://lccn.loc.gov/2020008214
LC ebook record available at https://lccn.loc.gov/2020008215

ISBN 978-1-9821-3629-1
ISBN 978-1-9821-3630-7 (ebook)

To Brent,
on catching a quarter century
of my misspellings

An emperor ought to die standing.

—Vespasian
June 23, AD 79
as reported by Suetonius,
The Lives of the Twelve Caesars

Historian's Note

The main events of this story begin in late 2257, after the conclusion of the Federation-Klingon War and Lieutenant James T. Kirk's assignment to the *U.S.S. Farragut.*

The Prime Universe events of the overture take place in 2233, during Philippa Georgiou's posting on *U.S.S. Archimedes.* The Mirror Universe events of the prologue take place more than twenty years later, in the weeks before the christening of *I.S.S. Charon* and Gabriel Lorca's betrayal of Emperor Georgiou.

Overture

THE OFFICER AND THE EMPEROR

With bronze as a mirror, one can correct his appearance; with history as a mirror, one can understand the rise and fall of a state. With good men as a mirror, one can see whether he is right or wrong . . .

> —EMPEROR TAIZONG OF TANG,
> Earth, 643

Never turn your back to a Terran, regardless of station for inside every one of us is an emperor waiting to rule. I started as an educator. The lesson I teach today: it only takes one Terran to turn reality upside down, and change the future . . .

> —EMPEROR HOSHI SATO,
> Terra, 2155

1

2233

U.S.S. Archimedes
Near the Tagantha System

"This isn't the *Kobayashi Maru*, Captain. This is real!"

"I know the difference," the captain snarled. "Now take your seat."

Lieutenant Philippa Georgiou sat down, but that didn't mean she would stand down. There were living beings on the freighter far ahead of *Starship Archimedes*, and they were in distress. The panic in the voices that had hailed her vessel sounded genuine—and the life signs the young officer was seeing on her display were waning.

That was reason enough to help, except for the added complication: where the freighter in question happened to be. Georgiou appealed to the navigator. "When will they reach the boundary?"

"The contact is eight hundred thousand kilometers inside the 2183 line," came the response. The dusky mess that was the Tagantha star system served as one point defining the border. "Freighter is still heading this way, but down to a crawl now."

"Gotcha," Captain Eagan said. "Keep watching—and hailing. Maybe they're just in a sleep cycle. I know what my life signs look like after a double shift."

A lot about Rodolfo Eagan rubbed Georgiou the wrong way; the worst was his way of trivializing important things. Dark eyes looked down as she fought for the right words. "Captain, they might not live long enough to reach the line."

"You don't know that." The fortyish Eagan clutched the

armrests of his command chair and leaned forward, squinting at the vessel on the main viewscreen. "We're at the absolute edge of sensor range given the dust out there. We can't even tell who they are from this distance."

"They've asked for help."

"But they won't tell us what's wrong." The captain looked back to Georgiou. "What we do know is the Federation agreed half a century ago not to approach space claimed by the natives of this region—no exceptions, not even for Good Samaritans. The residents do not want us there."

"Maybe they would, if we helped them." Georgiou looked up and gestured to the comm station. "It's possible that freighter is a visitor here, just like us. The language in the hail was Orion—and the ship looks like one of their older models."

"No sale, Lieutenant. The freighter in the *Kobayashi Maru* test looks convincing too—all the better to get you into trouble. Treaties are treaties. We're clearly at the heliopause here. Where this system begins, our options end."

All sorts of responses entered Georgiou's mind. That failing to act *also* wasn't the correct answer in the new-but-already-infamous test. Or that the so-called treaty with the locals was nothing of the sort: a real agreement would require one or more of the three reclusive but reportedly warp-capable powers to actually emerge from their interstellar hideaway to negotiate. It was nothing more than a unilateral declaration of borders, transmitted decades before from all three with an "or else" attached.

But Georgiou knew none of that was going to work on Eagan, who'd brought *Archimedes* to the region chasing a wayward comet. He wasn't a bad captain, but neither was he the one she was supposed to have. Starfleet had a habit of calling back officers for training in new technologies; it was the turn of the true captain of *Archimedes*. Eagan had spent most of his career in biology labs aboard research vessels that never left orbit, and his temporary posting aboard *Archimedes* had already exposed the extent to which he was ill-prepared to deal with the eventualities of deep space.

And matters of life and death.

"Help . . . us," crackled the low voice over the comm, sounding much weaker than before. *"You . . . must . . ."*

She watched Eagan as the words struck him—and as his return hails again went unanswered. He seemed shaken.

He isn't made of stone, she decided; *maybe he just needs some help.*

The captain turned to face her. "They tell me you do everything by the book, Lieutenant. So figure out a way to use it."

Georgiou pursed her lips—and thought. After a few moments, she perked up. "What if you don't cross the boundary with a ship?"

Eagan looked at her. "How's that again?"

"They'll be at the outer edge of transporter range soon."

"Ah, I gotcha. And no, they won't be—not at the rate they're slowing down."

"Then I'll beam as far as I can in an EVA suit and jet the rest of the way." Georgiou stood, forgetting Eagan's earlier order to stay seated. "I can at least check it out, Captain. If they're coming to us for help, maybe they just need a hand on the bridge who can fire the thrusters."

"A one-person cutting-out expedition?" Eagan looked back at her and scowled. "You're describing piracy. What if they don't *want* to cross the border?"

"I can ask. As long as there's still someone *to* ask."

"I don't think we can get away with that. It's an interstellar boundary. You're a Starfleet officer, a representative of the Federation—"

"I'll resign my commission," she said, shivering a little after she heard her own words. "For the day, anyway."

"A fig leaf won't work," Eagan said, more loudly. "Someone here has to press the control to beam you over there."

"I'll do it. I'm rated for the transporter."

"Right, because the last thing you want in a mutineer is someone who isn't checked out on the equipment." The captain didn't hide his amusement. "You're everything I was told you were, Lieutenant. If there were a medal for persistence, you'd—"

The navigator interrupted. "Orion freighter has come to a stop, Captain."

The voice on the comm, already softening, went silent.

Georgiou looked to the ship on the viewscreen—and back at Eagan.

"Go," he said, looking to the overhead in a hapless shrug. "Before I change my mind."

"Thank you, Captain!" Excited, she began walking. At the turbolift, she paused and turned. "Just to be clear, I have to resign in this plan."

"Forget that part. I don't need the bureaucratic hassle. Just be careful. If you wind up in the slave mines of wherever-it-is, don't say I didn't warn you!"

Engineering was one of Georgiou's areas of expertise, but even her talents had not been enough to get *Archimedes*' systems to transport her close to the stalled Orion ship. She'd had plenty of time while accelerating and then decelerating her jet pack to study the vessel, which had come to a stop in a hazy region of gas that made details difficult to resolve. She'd noted what looked like two exhaust vents ahead of the warp manifold—but those seemed odd, facing forward rather than aft. At another point, the bridge section had momentarily gone blurry, as if something had been expelled. Had there been a rupture, releasing the ship's atmosphere?

After landing on the vessel and manually cycling the airlocks, she understood why no one had answered her hails on approach. The ship's crew consisted of Orions, humans, and members of another species she didn't recognize, all with one thing in common. They were dead. If the hails had suggested that the occupants suffered lingering deaths, it was now apparent that many met their demise more quickly, expiring wherever they were. Some were still in their chairs, pained expressions frozen on their faces; others lay slumped on the decks. The shaft with the ladder had five bodies bunched in a clump at the bottom.

Horrific.

Her pace quickened. After checking the environmental seals on her spacesuit, she hurried to the bridge—and the comm system. Her public address message yielded no responses from anyone on board, so Georgiou put it to another use: calling *Archimedes.*

"I want you back immediately," Eagan said after hearing her report. *"No arguments this time."*

"Going by the book again, Captain, I need to get at least some information about what happened here." She'd first studied the air with her tricorder; she'd moved on to examining one of the corpses strewn across the bridge. "I can't return without knowing what my detox procedure should—"

Eagan interrupted. *"Lieutenant, look out!"*

Still kneeling, Georgiou had no idea exactly where she was supposed to look—until she saw the answer outside the ports. One vessel after another dropped out of warp, some arriving from aft, others appearing ahead. Commercial freighters, several of which bore gun emplacements: armed merchant ships. *No match for* Archimedes, she thought. But so many at once were likely to send Eagan into a paroxysm.

Indeed, the captain was emphatically repeating his call for her to get out when transporter effects shimmered all about. Bipedal figures in rust-colored environment suits surrounded her, their heads obscured by darkened faceplates. Georgiou stood, only to take a boot in her stomach from the nearest invader. She managed to keep from falling backward, but her tricorder clattered away on the deck.

A second assault came from behind. As ungainly as her spacesuit was, Georgiou was able to marshal a defense, turning and exploiting momentum to put her lunging attacker flat onto the deck. An additional figure joined the scrum, and Georgiou briefly caught a glimpse of the intruder who'd kicked her readying a weapon. She winced at the sound of disruptor fire—

—until she realized the shot had come, instead, from the weapon of another space-suited arrival, standing in the accessway to the bridge. His suit was different from the others', burgundy to their rust—and his disruptor blast, she saw, had been directed at the overhead. *"What goes on here?"* said a deep male voice, doubtlessly human.

"She was kneeling over a corpse!" The attacker who had started the fight, a female judging from her voice, gestured toward her.

"I had nothing to do with this," Georgiou said. "I'm here to help."

"To help yourself, you mean." The woman pointed her disruptor in Georgiou's face. *"Say good-bye!"*

2

Orion Derelict

The newcomer in the doorway laughed—a hearty bellow that echoed across the bridge. *"A looter? I don't think so, Zee. That's a Starfleet suit."*

"So?" the gun wielder snapped. *"Is that supposed to mean something?"*

"No, but this does," he said, tapping the barrel of his disruptor on the wings etched in gold relief on his left shoulder. *"Back off."*

At least I can tell who's boss, Georgiou thought as her attackers stepped away from her. The newcomer strode to the center of the bridge. If the insignia he wore wasn't familiar, the piece of equipment he held next was.

"Your tricorder," she said. "It's of Federation manufacture."

"A knock-off, actually. But imitate the best," he replied, consulting its results before putting it away. *"It tells me it's safe to do this."* Pressing a control on his collar, he removed his helmet to reveal a ruddy-skinned male of thirty or so with a mane of thick, black hair. Wide brown eyes looked past her to an object on the deck. "Give me her tricorder."

Georgiou stared at him as one of his companions reluctantly fetched the device and handed it to him. After a few moments' examination, he handed it to her. "Here you go."

Glancing at its readings, she tilted her head and looked at him. "You seem certain it's safe. Do you know what happened here?"

His nose twitched as he stepped between the bodies. "These poor souls will get pungent a bit later, but it's all right for now. And as for what happened—I can guess."

Whatever he guessed he did not immediately share. Instead, he looked over to the comm system, where Eagan was still chattering to no one: *". . . new contacts, be advised! We will not cross the boundary, but a Starfleet officer will be exiting the Orion ship and making her way toward* Archimedes *as her fuel allows."* A pause. *"Lieutenant Georgiou, do you hear that? This mercy mission is over!"*

The invaders' boss looked to Georgiou, intrigued. "You came here alone. This was your idea?"

"Coming here was my idea." She pointed to the comm panel. "Coming here alone was theirs."

"Interesting." He processed that for a moment. Then he made for the comm interface, where he worked the controls quickly. "*Archimedes,* is it? This is Trademaster Quintilian, currently aboard the *Jadama Rohn.* Those barges you're looking at are from the Veneti Corporation, licensed for commercial activity in this region. Your officer is unharmed, but do not approach. Repeat: do not approach." He flashed her a smile. "We'll sort this out in a minute."

"Finally, a response!" Eagan sounded flustered. *"Let me speak with Georgiou! I insist that you immediately—"*

"My word's good," Quintilian said, shutting off the comm. He turned to face her. "You know my name now—only one I've got. And I take it you're Georgiou."

"Philippa," she answered, without knowing why. "So you're not with the Triple Compact?"

"The—?" He thought for a moment. "Oh, yes—that's what the Federation calls the natives here." He chuckled. "That implies a *bit* more agreement than exists. I just call them the Troika."

"Troika it is." She studied her readings again. "These people suffered some kind of attack—I need a medical tricorder to tell. You're *sure* it's safe to breathe?"

"Calculating risks is my business." Quintilian stepped over and knelt beside a gray-bearded Orion corpse, already pale with death. With a gloved hand, he gently turned the figure's head from left to right. "I was afraid of that. It's old Vercer."

"You know him?"

"I did. Former pilot of ours who cut out on his own, with some friends. My convoy was in the neighborhood when his distress call went out. They were transporting something they shouldn't have—and it disagreed with them."

Her eyebrow went up. "A weapon of some kind?"

"It's a little more mundane—a recreational drug, highly toxic. I guess you could call it a weapon of self-destruction." He closed the Orion corpse's eyes and shook his head. "He was a friend, once. I hate to see this."

Georgiou frowned. "Successful drug smugglers don't often use their own product. Least of all an entire crew at once."

"These aren't drugs you're familiar with. The species of the Troika aren't built like humans—or Orions. Some of their 're-laxants' could kill you if you as much as got near an open vial. I'm thinking that happened here—probably belowdecks. But the substance is no longer active." He gestured to his companions, whose number had grown to nine as more had entered. "Go ahead, show her."

More helmets came off, revealing a mix of species: humans, Tellarites, Antarans—and a couple of Orions, who averted their gaze from the victims on the deck. Only the individual who had kicked Georgiou earlier remained helmeted, disruptor still in hand. *"Quintilian, this is none of her business."*

"I want her to see that it's not *our* business, Zee. I run a clean operation. We're not smugglers, and we're not pirates." He stood and looked to Georgiou, eyes earnest. "You've probably noticed already there's nothing to steal."

Okay. Convinced, she removed her helmet and took a breath.

Quintilian's face lit up, the man pleased to have won her trust.

"You're called Quintilian," she said. "As in the number?"

"As in the Roman." He turned toward the helm station and spoke over his shoulder. "An Earther, before your time. Rhetorician. Teacher of Pliny."

"The Elder or the Younger?"

He smiled to hear her say it. "You know, sometimes I forget." He sat behind the helm and started working the panel.

Georgiou read the logo on the shoulder of his spacesuit—and seeing the spelling, understood. "Veneti. The people who handled trade for England before Caesar's time."

He laughed. "See there, Zee? Somebody finally got it!" Quintilian looked back to Georgiou, clearly impressed. "My group does the same thing for the Troika. Trade between them—plus a little trade of my own with the outside. They consider it dirty work, fit only for the few aliens like us who already live in the neighborhood. I started with a single freighter ten years ago."

"Clearly you've expanded," Georgiou said, looking warily at the vessels holding position outside. "You've armed."

"Let's just say the place has personality. I can't tell sometimes if the locals closed the borders to protect themselves from you—or you from them." Quintilian returned his attention to the console. "Either way, this is their territory, and what happened to this ship is their business. They're going to want it. And they're going to want *you* gone."

The words alarmed Georgiou for a moment, until she felt the soft push of the thrusters. "You're taking me to *Archimedes*?"

"That sounds funny to hear out loud." He looked back to her, eyes alive. "Say, do you have a Greek history museum or something over there?"

"I . . ." she started. Another off-putting question in a room full of dead people. "Yes," she answered. "There's a display in our observation lounge devoted to his works—and of course, they're all in the library files. It's a science ship."

"Not really my line, but I like the history—and Earth's is always a good read. There's so much of it. I should make like a good human and go there someday." He faced the console. "But for now, I'm getting you to transporter range. The Casmarran sentry satellites at Tagantha have likely called all of this in already."

Georgiou noted the name. "The Troika species won't accept our help at all? What do they have against Starfleet?"

"It's not you," Quintilian said. "Well, it is you, but it's not *just* you. It's the whole neighborhood. Federation, Klingons, Gorn—when you folks come into conflict, it doesn't pay to pick a side. Or to be in the way."

"We would not infringe on a neutral's space."

"Yet here you are," Zee said, helmet-modulated voice flinty.

Quintilian gestured for his companion to simmer down. "Sorry—I guess you can see the opinion isn't limited to the natives." He stood and approached Georgiou. "I appreciate what you were trying to do, Lieutenant. It was already too late for these people."

Georgiou looked again at the bodies on the floor, being tagged and identified by Quintilian's crew. One used a marker to outline the locations of the fallen on the deck. It seemed such a sad end.

"You know, I'm not superstitious," she said. "But I saw the strangest thing as I was approaching."

"What's that?"

"The gases and dust here play tricks on the eye. But something shimmered for a second—as if the atmosphere was escaping the ship. Or maybe—"

"Maybe the souls?"

She blinked. "I didn't mean—"

"They'd be lucky to leave, then. Coleridge would have had them stay to work the ship."

Georgiou just stared at him. Who was this human, so far from Earth, yet knowing so much about it?

"It wouldn't be the strangest space tale I've heard." He offered his gloved hand, and she accepted the handshake.

"Thanks for checking on these folks, Philippa. We'll see the Troika learns what happened—and we'll leave you out of it."

"Until they're ready to talk to us."

"If not," he said, gripping her hand ever so slightly harder, "you can always talk to me."

U.S.S. Archimedes
DEPARTING THE TAGANTHA SYSTEM

Quintilian's word was good. She had been returned safely to her ship. Captain Eagan's relief at avoiding a confrontation had been immense, overwhelming any other detectible emotion. She suspected he was happy to see her home, yet still irritated over the incident she had nearly caused.

She regretted the Troika's standoffishness—and that she had been unable to bring back more data about the cause of the deaths. Her tricorder readings had found no toxins, but she had not been able to run full medical scans on the bodies. Quintilian's explanation, though, rang true with *Archimedes'* security chief, who had worked antipiracy missions elsewhere and knew the gamut of Orion activities.

She had been entering her thoughts about the day's events into her log when a personal subspace message arrived from Quintilian:

> *Thanks again for answering the distress call, Lieutenant. Not many would take a chance for strangers. I have some pull with the Troika; their space may be closed, but you're always welcome to visit me and the Veneti. You're the sort of Starfleet person they should meet.*
>
> *You seem to know your classics, so I am sending along something unlikely to be in your library—a facsimile of The Songs of Uthalla, a manuscript written by one of the last Orion emperors to his wife. Theirs was a high culture,*

once—I think you'll find it engaging. There's a ghost ship in there and everything.

Benediximus, Philippa—good fortune in your travels. You'll lead people one day, and they'll be better off for it.

Georgiou read the last line twice and sat back.

Notes from infatuated suitors were something she'd seen, including from those who were either erudite or pretended to be. But Quintilian seemed genuinely interested in her—and he had done what few others did, complimenting her job performance. Too many people she'd known in the Academy and Starfleet were obsessed with their own careers, unable to notice the growth of others.

And yet after the briefest of meetings, he seemed to understand what she needed to hear. A merchant, living in a place few humans were allowed to visit.

"You'll lead people one day, and they'll be better off for it." She didn't know whether to believe it or not—but who didn't like to see something like that?

I hope he's right.

3

I.S.S. *Hephaestus*
Near the Tagantha System
Mirror Universe

"All hail her imperial majesty, Emperor Philippa Georgiou Augustus Iaponius Centarus!"

Georgiou twirled, delivering a chop to the face of the gray-haired bridge officer outside the turbolift. His head slammed against the bulkhead—and she caught him on the rebound, throwing him to the deck. Another second found her boot planted firmly on his neck. "That's *Centarius*," she said.

His eyes bulged. "Yes, Majesty!"

She ground her heel in a twisting motion. "The Terran Empire honored Alpha Centauri by making it an early conquest. You dishonor my subjects by mangling their title."

"No! I—"

"Are you disagreeing with me?"

"*No . . .*"

He choked out her entire name a wrenching syllable at a time, bloody spittle flying from his mouth. Nearby, several members of her royal entourage—her imperial honor guard and select others—exited the adjacent turbolifts and headed for the darkened alcoves where they would wait until she needed them.

Like the bridge crew, they avoided looking directly at the altercation—but they definitely saw.

Good, she thought as she lifted her foot. She didn't care a whit for the Centaurans and their honor, but she did need to remind her people now and again that she was ready to defend her position at any moment, over any slight.

"If you want a picture of the future, imagine a boot stamping on a human face—forever." The wise Terran author who'd written those words had intended them as advice for emperors seeking the perfect government. As a matter of day-to-day motivation, however, Georgiou had found the neck a much better target, less likely to rupture and ruin one's clothing. Yes, as emperor, she could look any way she wanted without fear of judgment; she dressed to please only herself. But being outfitted by her servants took time—and time, criminally, was the one commodity she had no more of than any other person in the Empire. She had conquered many worlds, but there were so many yet to go.

If she could not give herself more years, she had to speed things along.

Fortunately, there were ways of doing that. Weapons of immense power existed everywhere; the Terrans had no monopoly on diabolical geniuses and infernal machines. Georgiou had to reach each and every weapon first and take them for herself, before they were wielded against the Empire or claimed by one of her rivals for use against her rule. Emperor Sato had seized power in exactly that manner with *U.S.S. Defiant*, a ship from an alternate future where the people were weak but their weapons were strong.

Now, someone had found a weapon in a forsaken corner of the Beta Quadrant. Georgiou wouldn't simply wait for it to be delivered to her, not with so many jackals about. She had to get it—and that required someone who knew the area.

"Where's our guide?" she asked Captain Maddox as she walked to the center of the bridge. "The new navigator?"

"Behind you," Maddox said, "trying to get his windpipe working."

"Oh," Georgiou said, looking back at the old officer she'd

accosted. He was still on his hands and knees. Realizing that her eyes were on him again, he rose and quickly staggered to his station.

"He was sent over from *Buran* by Lorca," Maddox said, distaste evident in his voice as he spoke his rival captain's name. "His record says he served aboard a ship of yours, long ago. I don't know if you even remember it: *Archimedes' Flame*."

Georgiou knew it well. The starship's name honored the parabolic mirror weapon created by a famed ancient Greek general who understood that war was science's only use. Her posting aboard it had been one more stepping-stone in her rise to power. The man before her rose and saluted. "I know you," she said. "You're Rudolfo Eagan."

"*Ro*—" The navigator quickly stopped, midcorrection. He cleared his throat. "Pleased you remember, Imperial Majesty."

"I remember I chose not to kill you when I took command from you." She coolly regarded what was left of him. "Did I make the right decision?"

He gulped, with apparent difficulty. "You saw I was better suited for another station, Imperial Majesty. I've served as a navigator and tactical officer faithfully on ships patrolling this region since."

"*This* region? What a disappointing way to serve the Empire."

The area was a backwater amid backwaters—territory no one had gone to the trouble to claim. The place had its privateers, but none of them had become rich; that spoke to a lack of anything worth stealing. And neither the Klingons nor the Gorn had seen much point in forming a defensive alliance with its residents, who seldom scurried out of their holes.

And it certainly looked like a hole. *Such an ugly sky*, she thought, surveying the mess on the main viewscreen. Multiple stars in close proximity had produced streams of ejecta, occasionally overlapping. A tangle of tangential matter: a Bok globule here, an emission nebula there. It was no wonder the Empire had skipped the area—

—until now. She glared at Eagan. "We're on the course I provided?"

"Yes, Majesty. We'll be in orbit around Tagantha in six minutes. It's the outermost Empire-facing system—the doorway to Troika space."

"*Troika?*" She'd heard the word before, but not in this context. "Explain."

"It's the local spacers' name for the three species who live here," Eagan said. "I've also heard them called the Three Hermits. They don't like visitors."

"I'm not interested in their likes."

"I can call up the invasion forces," Maddox said, looking back to her. "But I still don't know what you'd want with the place."

"You'll know when I tell you," she said. "*If* I tell you. Scan the coded frequencies—*all* of them."

"Very well. You heard the Emperor," he told his underlings. "Do it!"

Maddox worked well with her, she thought; he coveted her position as much as anyone, but he wasn't going to take his chance until he saw weakness. Before then, he was fully invested in her enlarging the Empire. She was seriously considering naming him captain of *Charon*, her new flagship, when it was completed.

"We're receiving a transmission on a coded channel," announced *Hephaestus*'s comm chief. "A repeating signal from a moving vessel, with your imperial signifier."

There it is, she thought. "Locate the source of the transmission and approach, full impulse."

"As you command." Eagan looked to her. "Note that it will require entering Troika space—"

"You're still talking." Feeling the impulse engines underway, Georgiou approached the comm station and addressed the officer there. "Shoo."

The emperor accessed the comm terminal and took a careful look. The transmission was immense, terabytes of nonsensical data, inscrutable to anyone without the emperor's personal decryption system. Georgiou entered her codes and watched the screen as the stream of data resolved itself into seven simple alphabetical characters:

WHIPSAW

"Whipsaw." *That's it.* The name her contact in the region had given for—*what? An invention? A discovery?*—that reportedly had the potential to change the political map of the galaxy. It was a word in Terran Standard, the name of an ancient logging tool later used as a torture device by the Canadian warlords once there were no trees left to cut.

This Whipsaw could cut down whole peoples, she'd been told. And it was aboard the ship that had sent the message. That was what the signal meant. Aboard and on its way to her, providing no one else learned of its—

"*Proximity alert!*" Eagan shouted.

She cleared the terminal display and stepped toward the main viewscreen. More than a dozen freighters outfitted with disruptor emplacements materialized in the space before *Hephaestus*, dropping out of warp. "What do we have here?"

Eagan spoke. "I've seen such vessels before on previous trips, Your Majesty. Merchant rabble. They generally warn us away."

"And you obeyed them?" Georgiou rolled her eyes. *Useless. I should have killed you when I had the chance.*

"We're being hailed," Maddox said. He looked to Georgiou. "Do we care?"

She did not—and didn't want to delay reaching the ship carrying Whipsaw, whatever it was. But neither did she want to reveal to her rivals on the bridge the importance of the thing she was after by breathlessly racing for it.

"Amuse me," she said, approaching a dais. A throne rose from the deck, and she took a seat. "On screen."

"Attention, Terran vessel. Be advised that you have entered—"

The human on screen stopped talking. The "merchant rabble" Georgiou had been told to expect were present behind him, hunched behind their leader's chair like the drooling gibbons they were—but their master was something else. He didn't wear the bangles and furs of a common trader; he looked almost respectable. Tanned and gray-bearded, he was a few years her senior—but he'd worn those years, and any difficulties of his life, well. He had the eyes of a much younger man—eyes that were currently wide with shock. *"You're the emperor!"*

"And you're scrumptious," Georgiou said, uncrossing her legs and leaning forward. "I like an older vintage now and again."

"I'm sorry. I expected someone important in a ship this size, but—" Recovered from his surprise, the merchant captain rose, only to take a knee. He clasped his hands and bowed his head. *"Hail to you, Philippa Georgiou Augustus Iaponius Centarius, Dominus of Qo'noS, Regina Andor, Overlord of Vulcan."*

"You see?" She looked all about *Hephaestus*'s bridge. "At least *someone* can get it right."

"Of course," the merchant continued, looking up. *"Your might is known far and wide."*

"Flattery will get you everywhere. I might even ask your name."

"I am Quintilian, of the Veneti."

Eagan spoke as Quintilian stood. "I've pulled up my notes on them, Your Majesty. A trading collective based in Hermit space."

"Troika space," Quintilian corrected. *"And that's the extent of our range. The Veneti handle trade between the three native species here, nothing more."*

"Ah, the Veneti," Georgiou said, smirking. "A classic. Caesar annihilated them when he took Britain."

Quintilian raised an eyebrow. *"I shouldn't be surprised that you know your emperors. But I'm here to avoid conflict—on behalf of myself and the Troika species."*

She leaned back, disappointed. Peacemakers bored her. "These are not your people. What do you care what happens to them?"

"Their way of life makes mine possible." Quintilian gestured broadly. *"The races here are exotic, Your Majesty—peculiar, and stubborn. You're not likely to get them to produce more than they do through . . . with your usual methods. But I work with people on the ground, who are used to dealing directly with me."*

Her tone grew icy. "Are you trying to sell me, merchant? I'm not in the habit of taking on motley bands as partners."

"I'm just trying to suggest another way," he said, letting the richness of his voice work on her. *"There were two Veneti, you know. The merchants I named my group for—but also a tribe in Italy."*

"Where Venice was. I'm not a fool."

"Rome absorbed them, without destroying them. You can do that too, Emperor. Work with us, and you can add to your power without laying waste to others—as you will most certainly have to do if you try to handle the species here directly. They will not cooperate."

"How refreshing. You seek to lecture me on governance as well as history." She sneered. "Tell me, Quintilian—or whatever your real name is—are there people on whom this act of yours actually works?"

"Act?"

"This *faux* erudition, in a tramp freighter captain. This joke of a protective fleet would be hard-pressed to fend off a ship of Klingon invalids. You don't have enough vessels—or pretty words—to drive me away."

"We're nobody's protectors. Our convoy just happened by, Your Maj—"

"However you reached this miserable place, you're still human. I can tell by how easily you lie." She waved indifferently. "But you're in luck, Mister Quadrillion. I don't need you—or your freakish alien friends. I'm after other game."

A ratty-looking white-haired Orion leaned over Quintilian's

shoulder, trying to get his attention. The master trader looked irritated. *"What is it, Vercer?"*

"New contact to aft. It's Jadama Rohn.*"*

Quintilian's eyes narrowed at that.

"We have that contact," Eagan said. "It's coming from beyond Tagantha—deeper within the territory."

Georgiou looked back to him. "Another one of these flyspecks?"

"Negative. It appears to be an Orion freighter. Older, different manufacture." Eagan looked up. "It's the contact we were closing on!"

The Whipsaw ship, she thought. Yes, her contact might well be transporting it to her via an Orion freighter. "What are the merchants doing?"

"They're at bay," Maddox said, glaring at the viewscreen. "They're just watching."

"Not anymore," Quintilian said, having overheard. He gave a hand gesture to his crew. *"You're a busy monarch—we won't take any more of your time. We'll get out of your way."* He bowed again. *"It has been a pleasure."*

"It almost was," Georgiou said, rising from her throne. "In another life, perhaps it would have been."

"Merchants powering up," Eagan called out.

"I don't think so." The emperor faced the old officer. "Eliminate them all—*now!*"

4

Georgiou didn't see Quintilian's jaw drop, but the shock was still on his and his companions' faces when she faced the screen again. *"We're withdrawing!"* he yelled. *"You don't have to do this."*

Eagan was now joined by tactical officers at either side, working with him to compute firing solutions. "They're turning to run—but won't get far," Maddox observed.

Outside the viewport, a disruptor blast lanced out from *Hephaestus*, striking one of the freighters amidships. It blossomed bright against the Taganthan stellar haze, prompting gleeful cackles from one of the shadowy alcoves to the rear of Georgiou's bridge. She didn't flinch; she already knew which member of her coterie-in-waiting the merriment had come from. As more blasts produced high-pitched laughter, she smirked at the chills it was sending through the bridge officers.

"We're trying to focus," Maddox grumbled, not looking directly at the alcove. "Is that noise necessary?"

"You have your crew, I have mine." In fact, they all belonged to her, but she was sure Maddox understood what she meant. "Tune it out, Captain. Get your people to focus."

They did. Another shot, another kill—and another and another. Quintilian was still on screen, shouting orders to the crew behind him. His convoy quickly disappearing, he looked back to Georgiou, hurt and betrayal in his eyes. *"Why are you doing this?"*

She shook her head. "For all your intellectual posturing, you seem to have forgotten the reason the Terran Empire does anything: *Because we can.*"

Quintilian's ship took a hit, instantly noticeable on screen as chaos erupted all around his bridge. A girder swung downward, smacking the old Orion he'd called Vercer squarely in the face. Alarmed, Quintilian rushed to cradle the man's form—only to gawk in horror as the Orion's head, barely connected, fell away to the deck. Startled, he let the rest of the corpse slip from his arms.

Another hoot from the alcove.

When Quintilian finally looked back at Georgiou, he showed her the green blood on his hands. *"He was like a father to me."*

"Family is overrated."

Fire and smoke rising behind him, Quintilian looked off to the side once before sitting, his jaw locked and his eyebrows joined in a stern frown. *"You'll regret this, Emperor. The poisoned chalice is a human concept—but we aren't the only ones who know how it works. Not by a long—"*

A blast from *Hephaestus* silenced him—and his image vanished from the screen, to be replaced by an exterior view showing the blazing debris of his vessel.

From the alcove, more hilarity—and from the bridge crew, shouts of success. Georgiou nodded quietly. She didn't mind keeping the gallery entertained, and while Quintilian had been a pretty thing, there were other pretty things in the universe, and more important matters at hand.

"Hail from the freighter," the comm officer said. "The ship he called *Jadama Rohn*. Sent openly—but addressed as before, with your imperial code."

Georgiou looked about. The Veneti were gone, but that didn't mean the coast was clear. "Scan in all directions for other vessels—including cloaked ones. Make sure we're alone."

Maddox peered at her. "What *is* this ship, Imperial Majesty?"

A look made him get to work.

"Nothing," Eagan said. "Nothing cloaked that we can detect. It's just us and them."

"Very well." Georgiou had waited long enough. "On-screen."

The Orion-built freighter had some Orions aboard, but it was the two figures in the adjoining command chairs that caught her eye. An older female and a younger male—both Caitians. The woman smiled. *"We meet again, Philippa—or should I say, Emperor."*

"S'satah, my old friend!" Georgiou warmed immediately. "You look just as I remember."

"You're too kind," came the response, half-spoken and half-purred. *"And you seem to have gotten a promotion. Well deserved, I say."*

"You would."

The Caitians were a species the Terrans hadn't seen much of—and that was a shame, because the few members Georgiou had encountered had proven exceptional as playthings. Who could resist a human cat? Georgiou knew that wasn't what they really were, of course, but a privilege of being Terran meant that she could value other beings strictly in terms of how they related to her own existence. Besides, the Caitians had almost certainly benefited as a species by their similarity to a human domestic pet, just as the ugliness of the Tellarite pig-men had made them more fun to kill.

S'satah in particular was a double delight: part pirate, part treasure hunter. She'd worked the Beta Quadrant for two decades as a privateer, striking alien races before the Terrans could. The mere hint of an imperial invasion drove many to panic, relocating their valuables and weapons to safety; that's when S'satah would hit them. Before becoming emperor, Georgiou had used the freelancer on many missions.

But the male Caitian seated beside her was someone new. He was burly and black furred, and his face seemed frozen in a scowl. "Who's the bad attitude?" Georgiou asked. "Don't tell me you've found someone new to take up with."

"Don't be disgusting," he hissed.

"Hush, P'rou." S'satah patted his wrist. "You'll have to excuse my son. You're his first emperor."

Georgiou marveled. "You have a son? I never knew you had children."

"Just one—he's only recently joined the trade. He's a good pilot."

"Refreshing to hear someone's child is good for something." The children of other Terran emperors had definitely not been, unless sponging on their wealth counted as a productive activity. The only decent argument for mentorship Georgiou knew existed in the form of her own adoptive child, Michael Burnham.

P'rou glared in her direction. "You destroyed the Veneti. That was never part of the plan!"

Georgiou didn't like explaining herself—a whelp was a whelp, no matter how strapping—but S'satah had earned her patience. "I didn't want them to interfere. Friends of yours?"

P'rou continued to glare. S'satah spoke for them. "They were targets. That's all they ever were—what passes for prey in this region. P'rou and I have hit them before."

"Then I have thinned out the herd. But I will make it worth your while. If you have what you say you have."

"I certainly do." She looked to her son. "Thrusters to one-quarter." She stood and faced Georgiou. "I have to go get it ready—but it's definitely worth the price. I can't wait for you to have it."

Georgiou couldn't wait either. Having seen quite enough of P'rou's grimace, she ordered the channel closed and snapped the fingers of her right hand. One of her black-clad attendants rushed from an alcove to her side. "Join the retrieval team in the transporter room," Georgiou said. "Identify the cargo and determine its capabilities."

The attendant responded by vanishing, transporting away to another deck. Her team would tell her within minutes if Whipsaw could be safely transported to *Hephaestus*; within an hour, they'd say if it was of any use at all.

Georgiou hoped to be able to reward S'satah for a good find, because the Caitian would not survive the alternatives. A dud weapon would merit death for wasting the emperor's time, of course—but something of immense power might also endanger the pirate. Operational security would demand it; already, her bridge crew had caught on to the game.

"It must be pretty important to bring us all this way," Maddox said after a few minutes' waiting. "I can't wait to hear about it."

Georgiou ignored his fishing attempt. "Just make sure no other vessels are anywhere near. In other words, do your duty."

Tense moments later, a signal arrived from *Jadama Rohn*—this one, a voice message from her attendant. *"Imperial Majesty, S'satah has shown us a cargo unit. It does not scan as containing explosive or any known harmful agents. We deem it safe to transport."*

"I'll follow in a few minutes," S'satah piped in, *"to explain it fully. It really is quite amazing."*

"It had better be," Georgiou said. She touched a control on the armrest of her throne. "Cargo transporter room, prepare to—"

A flash ahead of her caught her eye. Georgiou looked up to see two glowing masses on the main viewscreen, rocketing in parallel from *Hephaestus* across the short distance to *Jadama Rohn*. The instant she recognized them as photon torpedoes, the pair struck the freighter head-on. The flash of detonation triggered *Hephaestus*'s viewport filters; the shockwave from the point-blank shots in the murky medium surrounding Tagantha set off the starship's inertial dampers.

"Shields up!" Maddox yelled. "Someone's firing!"

"*We* fired, moron!" Georgiou leapt to her feet. "Lock down all weapons and begin scanning. Something may be left!"

"No life signs. Not the Caitians—nor your operatives," another officer responded.

"Who cares about them? The cargo! *Scan for the cargo!*"

It was no use. The torpedoes had annihilated every bit of physical evidence that *Jadama Rohn* had ever existed.

Georgiou spun and faced the trio at the tactical station. "Who fired those weapons?"

Startled by her yell as much as what had happened, the two officers on either side of Eagan recovered quickly and pointed to the older man. "He did it!"

His hands still clutching the console, Eagan appeared pale, the blood drained from his face. "I thought they were moving to attack!"

Georgiou raged. "What difference would that have made? That tiny ship, against *us*? I gave no order to fire!"

"Neither did I," Maddox said, needlessly. "Explain yourself, Eagan!"

Eagan stared at the emperor, frozen—until his expression changed. He tilted his head, and his mouth curled into a little smile. *"Gotcha."*

Maddox's security officers drew their swords and approached Eagan—but Georgiou gestured for them to hold position. She needed answers. "Why?"

"I can't believe you have to ask—*Lieutenant*." Eagan lifted his hands from the console and rubbed his neck. "I guess it's true what they say—you don't have to be a genius to be emperor."

"But why *that*?" she asked, trying to govern her wrath as she pointed to the main viewscreen, and the void where *Jadama Rohn* had been. "Answer. The agonizer booth will get it out of you, sure enough. What did you know about that ship?"

"You wanted it. That's enough." Standing tall for the first time all day, the former captain of *Archimedes' Flame* crossed his arms. "You took my ship, so I took one of yours. If I die, at least I die even."

Georgiou glared at him for several moments, deciding what she believed. When she did move, it was not to assault—but rather to walk back toward her throne. "Amazing. You actually accomplished something. You never amounted to anything, Eagan—but you have this." She looked back at him. "Congratulations. Revenge is the sweetest reward in life."

Maddox was impatient. "Let us take him, Imperial Majesty."

"Oh, no. Such a long time to nurse a wound—he should have his moment. Tell me, Eagan, when I took your ship, did it sting?"

"Did it sting?" Seemingly surprised to still be alive, Eagan laughed. "It festered! I was going somewhere, before you came along. But you left me alive. Your mistake." He took a step out from behind the tactical station. "Well, what are you waiting for? Go ahead and kill me, like you should have done before!"

"I have people for that," she said. Then, in a sound only a bit above a whisper, she added: "*Blackjack.*"

Eagan's eyes bulged at hearing the word—and the haunting echo of laughter, beginning again from the alcove. He turned one way, and then the other, searching for what everyone knew was approaching. "No—"

"*Yes!*" A black-clad figure yanked Eagan around by the collar of his tunic—and clubbed him with a metal baton, cackling as he did. The old man howled in pain, falling backward against the side of the tactical station. His attacker, a young blond human with deathly pale skin, pressed his advantage, getting into Eagan's face as he raised his eponymous weapon. "Blackjack, blackjack! Kill you like she should have!"

Georgiou watched with satisfaction as her agent did his work. A being that lived only to fight and kill, mentally conditioned by her scientists into the perfect assassin. Blackjack—his real name had never interested her—cared nothing for his own safety, turning bloodlust into blood on command. No security guard with a disruptor or sword had ever come close to being as deadly; there was no better companion in a fight.

And, oh, how his laughter terrorized those who heard it. It filled the bridge as he brought Eagan to the deck, smashing away. "She's got people for that! People for that!"

After thirty seconds, Georgiou was satisfied. "That's enough. The example is made."

"*Example. Example.*" A bloody mess, Blackjack continued clubbing as he sat astride Eagan's corpse. "*Example!*"

"*Blackjack!*"

Hearing her shout his name, the assassin pulled his weapon back to his chest. With one hand, he wiped his eyes—spattered with blood—and then he gingerly wiped down his truncheon. In his few lucid conversations with the emperor, he'd claimed the weapon had killed just about every historical figure ever assassinated; he knew, because it had told him so. Whatever the truth, Georgiou knew that contemplating the weapon calmed him down. He began chuckling softly, a wild animal no more.

"That's a man who enjoys his work," Maddox said, standing well apart. "Maybe a little too much. He's made a mess of my bridge."

"It isn't the first time," Georgiou said. "Nor will it be the last. You're responsible for staffing this vessel, Captain. Eagan's disloyalty reflects on you."

"Not me," Maddox said, putting up his hands. "He came from Lorca."

She frowned. Yes, she suspected Gabriel Lorca of having plotted against her—why should he be different from anyone else? His spies were legion. Had one aboard *Hephaestus* tipped him off that Whipsaw was valuable to her?

She didn't know—yet. But she did know what she would do now. "We've made a good start at depopulating this place, Captain. If the Troika species are uncomfortable with visitors, we should show them what true discomfort is like."

"Yes, Imperial Majesty!" Maddox smiled, quite obviously pleased at where she had directed her retribution. He saluted. "For the Empire!"

"Call me when the fun begins." She turned and strode off the bridge.

I.S.S. *Hephaestus*
Departing Troika Space

Georgiou had made good on her promise. Her two-week grand tour of destruction had proven that the species of the region were every bit as peculiar as Quintilian had claimed. But diversity, infinite or otherwise, was of no value to the Terran Empire—and she had found nothing else she wanted.

In particular, no trace of Whipsaw. If it was some weapon one of the Troika powers had developed, it had not been brought to bear against her—not even in their darkest hour. She could not believe it was a hoax: S'satah was as capable of deception as any mortal, but the Caitian was a utilitarian after her own heart. There would have been no profit to her in misleading her emperor.

Thwarting one, however, was a valuable end for many—and one in particular. In her chambers, Georgiou thought about her ally-turned-rival Lorca as she reread the latest message from the one person she did trust, currently on a mission to the Cawdor system:

> *I'm sorry you didn't find what you were looking for, Mother, but I think you're off base in suspecting Lorca. I know you think I'm too trusting of Gabriel, but you've got to have talented people working for you if you want your rule to last.*
>
> *Frankly, I've never understood how you can enjoy being emperor when you're constantly seeing threats around every corner—but you seem to thrive on it. I hope, for your sake, that's not a front. The crown would be a terrible curse otherwise.*
>
> *It's a big universe. I hope you'll get another chance at your superweapon—if that's what makes you happy. Until next we meet, good hunting.*

Georgiou frowned. *She calls him Gabriel.*

The emperor had never been comfortable with her adoptive daughter's admiration for her chief rival; she hoped it wouldn't become a problem. Because the purge would inevitably come. Either Lorca would strike, or Georgiou would—and only one of those choices guaranteed her survival.

She saw creation as it was. Filled with enemies, declared and secret, known and yet to be discovered. She would see them fall, every one. A being that wanted to share the universe with her could be her subject—or her victim. There was no third choice. No one would remember Quintilian, Eagan, or even Lorca—but her people would remember her, and what she did to them.

Georgiou had preferred ruling from the shadows; parades and statues were for those who had nothing left to accomplish. So many emperors, Terran and otherwise, had vanished into obscurity, leaving nothing behind but museum pieces. That would not be her. She would *never* stop fighting—and when it was time, when she had truly earned it, sentients everywhere would glorify her name. She was building the Terran Empire to be immortal; while it was hers, she would be too.

She would never give it up.

Ever.

Stage One
DEFIANCE

Few Terran emperors were more brutal or more mysterious than Philippa Georgiou. She conquered many worlds, taking titles from those she dominated—yet she preferred to be faceless to those she ruled. She made her presence felt across wide swaths of territory—yet few traces of her legacy survived the destruction of *I.S.S. Charon*.

It was as if she had simply vanished . . .

—SPOCK
The Stillborn Dynasty, 2267

5

Thionoga Detention Center
BETA QUADRANT
PRIME UNIVERSE

"You're a nothing! You're a zero! Whatever you were, you aren't anymore!"

The towering alien who had seized Georgiou's arm shook her hard. It was not the sort of greeting she, as emperor, had been accustomed to upon arriving aboard a space station—and she couldn't remember the name of her greeter's species, other than that she had eradicated a fair percentage of its population. But the giant had the advantage of surprise, as well as a hundred kilograms of mass.

Which it used now, hurling her violently to the landing bay deck, knocking the wind out of her.

"You keep your eyes *down* in Thionoga," the alien shouted, two mighty feet planted on either side of her as she lay flat on her back, trying to catch her breath. "Snotty little thing. I'm a sentry! You're trash. Look at me at your peril!"

"I wasn't looking at you," she said. "I was looking at *that*," she added, vision focused on a spot somewhere above. Distracted, the goliath's eyes followed; just enough distraction for her to act. Bracing her hands against the deck beneath her, Georgiou rolled back and kicked her legs upward, a springing move that brought her boots into crashing contact with the sentry's crotch.

She didn't know the creature's sex, nor care—but it definitely seemed to place some value over whatever it had down there, judging from the way it howled and doubled over. That gave her the chance to seize the sentry's collar with her left hand, delivering an open-palmed smash to its face with her right. Grabbing tufts of its bushy hair, she wrenched its head, throwing the brute off balance as she rolled in the opposite direction.

All before she was back on her feet.

Once she was upright, the melee began in earnest, as Big Nasty's twin joined in, followed by a couple of Nausicaans—likely also guards, judging by their uniforms. They were all targets for her, as she twirled among them, delivering kicks and chops to everyone she came near.

Three were collapsed on the deck when more sentries arrived, carrying long prods. Georgiou looked back to the shuttle that had brought her, only to see its Orion pilot and his disruptor-toting guards in the open hatchway. "What's wrong with you people?" he shouted. "Can't you handle a simple transfer?"

The first giant, one hand over a face gushing orange, pointed at her with the other. "She stuck her nose up at me—"

"I was trying to avoid your stench," Georgiou said.

"You broke my nose!"

"Believe me, I did you a favor!"

A group approached from across the bay: six guards toting tall silver staffs, the vanguard for a squat Denobulan in black. "What goes on here?" he asked.

The shuttle captain pointed to Georgiou. "This one's been giving us trouble since we picked her up. Even the Klingons didn't want her."

"That's a shame." The Denobulan seemed to be someone of standing, given the deference he received from the sentries; when he lifted a white-tipped baton, his silver-staffed phalanx sprang forward. They worked to encircle Georgiou, who quickly determined the electrical nature of their weapons.

"The Klingons have a name for these," the Denobulan said as they threatened her. "Painstiks. I expect they're self-explanatory."

Their effect certainly was, when a sentry lunged for her and she sidestepped, redirecting the guard and his weapon into the gut of one of his companions. An electrical shock rocked her victim, causing him to lose his weapon. She scooped it up—next wielding it both as a shocker and a bo staff to deliver harm to her assailants.

She had floored four of them when she saw the Denobulan advancing, his baton before him. Holding her longer staff in his face, she laughed. "Size matters, my little friend!"

"How droll." Unflinching, the Denobulan triggered something on his baton. A chilling blast of gas launched from its tip, striking Georgiou squarely in the face.

Blinded, she dropped her weapon and fell to the deck, coughing. "*That . . . was . . . no painstik!*"

"Life is full of surprises."

Still choking, Georgiou was barely able to notice the Denobulan walking up to her—and completely unable to do anything about it when he applied a hypospray to her neck. "Give her a minute—and then take her to accession." He spun and departed.

Georgiou's lungs cleared before her vision did. But this time, when she saw the sentries approaching, she felt no urge to do anything about it. Their arms under hers, they lifted her to her feet and marched with her toward a doorway off to the side.

Inside the hexagonal room, she saw the Denobulan settle down into a chair behind a large desk. Save for the side of the room she entered through, every wall had a closed turbolift door of a different color. The guards guided her to the only other furnishing in the room, a small bench across from the Denobulan's desk. They deposited her on it and departed.

"I am Frietas."

"You are alone," she said. That fact was clear, even if everything else still looked blurry. She turned her head toward the exit. "No manacles? No disruptors? I think I'm insulted."

"There's no need for theatrics." Frietas poured himself a steaming brew from a carafe. "The hypospray contained a fast-acting serum, which forces you to answer truthfully. And that

gas I dosed you with will keep you docile during the interview."
He stopped pouring and stared across at her. "It's standard
practice—don't give me any yap about your civil rights."

"I wouldn't dream of it."

"You wouldn't be in Thionoga if you had any rights left."
He gestured with his mug to the various turbolift doors. "This
meeting is about where we're going to put you."

"The green one is pretty." She loved how the portal seemed
to glisten as she watched. "I want to go there."

"I don't think that one's for you. It's for the mentally ill."
He opened a drawer and fished for a data slate.

"I killed someone, if that helps."

"So it says here." He read, "*Noor Engku, human murderer.*
Is that your real name?"

"No."

"It never is. And the real one?"

"Philippa Georgiou Augustus Iaponius Centarius."

"How's that again?"

She repeated it—haltingly, each word a carefully prepared
meal in her muddled state. "It's important to me that you get
it right."

"It's not important at all." Frietas referred to the data slate.
"This merchant you murdered to get here. Did he get your
name wrong?"

"No, he got it right."

"But you still killed him."

"And his whole fleet." She studied her fingernails, still
shimmering. "I don't recall how many ships he had, but I destroyed them all." She sniffed. "In cold blood. Do you have
that in there?"

"I don't see anything here about multiple killings. But it
doesn't matter. We don't get into the legal processes of the star
systems that send us prisoners. If you're here, your people want
you gone—but they won't pull the trigger. What you did was
enough to get you Thionoga."

"I thought you were trying to decide where I belong."

"Yes, but don't get the idea that any one part of this prison is softer than another. It's not a health spa. A perpetrator is a perpetrator."

She grinned. "I like the way you think."

"No, the reason we're categorizing you is to find out your skills."

"I kill people. I thought we'd gone over that."

"This is a penal colony. You must have seen the big asteroid the station's grappler has hold of. Our inmates do labor. Now, how would you describe what you were before you came here?"

"Ah." She clasped her hands and leaned back. "Apex predator."

"Enough nonsense. Did you have a title?"

"Many." She began to list them.

"Let's not start that again." He looked up, aggravated. "Look, it's a simple question. What was your *job*?"

"*Emperor.*"

"Emperor?"

"For a time, people used 'empress'—but that's not to my tastes."

The prison official made a note on his slate. "Emperor. Of what? This place?"

Georgiou looked up and around. "This space station doesn't exist in my universe. But it is in territory I conquered. Back in '53, I believe."

Frietas blinked. "Beg pardon—you said in your *universe*?"

"That's correct."

"You own a universe."

"A significant part of one." She frowned. "Or I *did*."

"You did." The interviewer smirked. "This should be rich. What happened?"

"I lost it. One of my rivals staged a coup."

"A shock, was it?"

"No, it was completely predictable." She coaxed forth a

name that was acid to her mouth. "*Lorca.* I sent my daughter Michael to hunt him down—but she sided with him instead, and *that*, I should have predicted. Children make poor decisions."

"You're not the first to say that, I'm sure." The Denobulan looked at her. "So I take it you were overthrown by this Orca."

"Lorca. No, he was blasted through a rift into this universe."

"Ah! And this is the person you killed?"

"No." Georgiou shrugged. "I mean, I *did* kill him, but he wasn't the merchant. Lorca returned to my universe, bringing a Starfleet vessel with him—"

"Starfleet just left one lying around."

"Patronize someone else. I'm being cooperative."

"Sorry. He came to your universe with a Starfleet vessel."

"Called *Discovery*. That's when I killed him—but not before I tortured him." She looked around. "You don't have any agonizer booths here, do you?"

"I'm not sure what you mean."

"Your warden would like them. They cut down on complaints."

"Well, maybe we'll look into that." His brow furrowed. "I'm not sure I follow your story. If you put down this rebel, you should still be emperor, right?"

"Unfortunately, the episode ended in the destruction of my starship. Whereupon my daughter—"

"Michael, the one who betrayed you."

"No, not her. The *other* Michael."

"You have two daughters named Michael?"

"In a sense. She's the Michael from *your* continuum—she came along when Lorca brought *Discovery* to my universe. And she took me back here."

"To this universe."

"Against my will."

Frietas pursed his lips before continuing. "I'm going to regret asking this, but this universe of yours—it's different?"

"Very much so." Georgiou yawned. "Do you know how you can tell that I'm not emperor here?"

"How?"

"You're still breathing."

He looked around. "Are you sure you're in the right facility?"

"I thought that's what you were here to decide."

He put down the data slate, frustrated. "They have to start sending me more information." He forced a smile. "I'm afraid there aren't any categories of labor on Thionoga that involve dictatorial rule."

"That's too bad." Reminded, she made a sad effort at snapping her fingers. "Oh, yes. I did have a job. I ran a nightclub."

"Service industry." He picked up the slate again. "Very good. Where was this club?"

"On Qo'noS."

"You lived on the Klingon homeworld?"

"Well, first I tried to destroy it."

"The nightclub?"

"No, the homeworld." She frowned. "It's a long story, and parts are classified. The Federation had given me my freedom, but it didn't mean anything; the Klingons weren't going to let me leave the planet. Once I knew I was stuck there, I decided to take over a business. For my own entertainment, as much as anything."

"I take it that mind-altering substances were on offer."

"I wouldn't be much of a host if there weren't."

Frietas raised his index finger. "*Now* it's making sense. You've been sampling your own wares."

"Only when things got boring. Which they did soon enough. It's hard to market vices on a planet where the natives' only hobby is beating the hell out of each other. Besides," she said, crinkling her nose, "Klingons stink."

He nodded. "We have a few here."

"Don't put me with them."

Frietas made another note. "Look, I get paid by the hour,

not by volume. I get to hear a lot of stories. Maybe you can use yours to entertain the perps down on brown level, while you're all sorting through the toxic recyclables." He set down the data slate and reached for a small panel of colored buttons on his desk. "There isn't a lot of joy down there. I'm sure they'll find your stories very—"

"Agent Georgiou!"

"Hold on," Georgiou said, rubbing at her temple. "Someone's talking to me."

"I know," Frietas said. *"I'm* talking to you!"

"Shh. It's the voice in my head." He gawked, baffled, as she listened to the implant in her right ear. "What is it?"

"I want you to shut up," responded a male human voice.

"This is an interview. I'm supposed to talk."

"Not like—"

"You're interrupting, Leland."

"Don't say my name!"

Frietas stared. "The voice in your head is named Leland?"

"That's right. He recruited me. And he's always bothering me."

"About operational security, you bet," Leland said. *"Next thing you know you'll be telling him about Section 31."*

"Oh," she said, reminded. "I hadn't gotten to that part!"

"Don't. I thought we'd inoculated you against truth serums."

"I am speaking to this individual of my own choice—which is the only reason I do anything." Georgiou looked to Frietas. "I apologize for my colleague's rudeness. Was there something else you wanted to ask?"

"No, I think I've got everything," he said, rising. He pressed a button on his desk console, and the green turbolift doors opened.

Georgiou looked at it. "The mental ward. I thought you said I didn't belong there?"

"I'm sold." He gestured to the guard inside the turbolift. "Take her away—and try not to get her name wrong."

6

Green Sector
Thionoga Detention Center

The Vulcan had lost a tooth. Georgiou stepped over it—and then over the bleeding Vulcan—as her jailer, another sweaty-faced Nausicaan, prodded her line of prisoners along the corridor. Up ahead, she saw the tooth-owner's likely assailant: a hairless alien guard, busy delivering a violent rebuke to one of her fellow green-clad prisoners.

"A refreshing approach to mental health," Georgiou mumbled so Leland could remotely hear. "The Federation is tied in with *this* place?"

"They helped found it," Leland said, *"along with a bunch of nonaligned powers out here in neutral space. The Federation can't make up its mind what to do with criminals, so it pretty much tries everything."*

What Terrans called punishment, Georgiou had learned, the Earthlings of this universe called "corrections." New methods for it were all the rage—as if anything could be more corrective than pain, and lots of it. But while revolutionary theorists like Tristan Adams had lately earned a lot of attention, Leland explained that the Federation still maintained its investment in Thionoga.

"It's the reason you and I can communicate," Leland said. *"We installed a lot of the tech here years ago—including the system linking your earpiece to our subspace relay."*

"And you kept a back door into the surveillance system, giving you a way to keep tabs on every political prisoner in the region, held by you or not."

"We figured it'd come in handy someday. Like today."

So predictable. The Federation managed to combine self-denial and hypocrisy in ways that both aggravated and amused Georgiou. Clearly, any government worthy of the name required a place where the criminal—or the simply inconvenient—could be smashed against bulkheads a few times a day. If the Federation's namby-pamby officials ever opened their eyes to the brutality that took place on Thionoga, she expected they'd burst with self-righteousness, immediately ending their participation. But by delegating the bothersome details to Leland and his team, they could remain blissfully blind.

If Leland had another name, Georgiou didn't know it. But she knew that the name of the group he led, Section 31, came from a portion of the Starfleet charter: evidently, the part that covered double-dealing and premature hair loss. The spymaster had shown up in her club on Qo'noS pretending to be a Trill, the disguise of choice for humans who wanted to look alien but didn't want to put too much effort into it. He'd offered her a chance to evade the Klingon dragnet in exchange for work—the assignment that had brought her to Thionoga.

Her cover story had required somebody to convict her of a crime; fortunately, her past was well stocked with routine incidents to which she could convincingly confess. She did so to a baffled magistrate for a mercantile league, who obliged her by putting her on the next prison transport. From recruitment to deployment was only a matter of days—but more than enough time for the emperor to decide that she hated Leland's guts.

"Looks like they're taking you to the mess hall," he said into her implant. *"Your chance should be coming up. Do you read me, agent?"*

"Don't call me that," Georgiou said, dabbing at her temple as she marched. "And if you keep yammering, I will dig this thing out of my ear and shove it down your throat."

"That's not much of a threat. The device is tiny."

"I didn't say I would let go of it."

"Nice. Focus."

She did, looking in on every prison cell her processional passed. After a time, Georgiou whispered, "Target negative. She's not here."

"You made it into the right section—congrats—but they keep her in solitary, except for meals."

"That doesn't sound very solitary."

"Take the opportunities when they come. And yours should be in about twenty meters."

Sure enough, rounding the corner, Georgiou beheld a menagerie of the galaxy's riffraff. Dozens of inmates, shackled as she was; many back from mining the asteroid Thionoga was attached to and all gorging themselves at long tables. Hogs at the trough—except for a small number of wretched individuals who lingered against the bulkheads and in corners, shrinking from the pandemonium. The others who'd been marching in line with her hurried toward the food, only to begin scuffling with those already there.

"Even in the mental ward, you've got to fight to eat," her Nausicaan escort said. "If you call this stuff food." He tugged the manacles she wore toward him and touched a control on them. A light went from red to blue. "You're checked in," he said. "Someone else will take you back to your cell later."

"Abandoning me?" she asked as he stepped away. "I'm heartbroken."

"I'm not. That stuff Frietas tranked you with is about to wear off. I saw what you did to the team in the landing bay."

"The logical thing would be for you to keep me drugged all the time."

"Get the Vulcans to arrest you if you want logic. All you can hurt here are the other inmates." He paused in the doorway and eyed her. "Something tells me you wouldn't mind that."

"I don't discriminate."

Actually, she did—and frequently. Thionoga was a genetic cesspool, populated by the trash of the universe. No Terran of any taste would wish to be in such a place, with these people, for longer than necessary. So she got on with it, fighting to ignore the smells and sounds as she scanned the dining hall.

There, she thought, noticing a small Tellarite female huddled in a corner. Her hands clutched together, the young woman rocked back and forth, quaking—the whole world evidently shut out.

Georgiou waited until an orderly brought out a steaming tureen. As other inmates crowded toward it, she made her way to the Tellarite's corner. She spoke. "Dess Glon Tah?"

The woman did not respond.

"Are you Dess Glon Tah?"

Nothing.

"I can't get a good look at her," Leland said. *"The imaging sensors are all facing the crowd."*

"That's what I'm for." Leaning down, Georgiou yanked at the woman's matted forelocks. She pulled upwards, forcing the Tellarite to stand and producing an anguished yowl. "So you do have a tongue," Georgiou said. "Speak to me."

"Leave me alone!"

"That'll do," Leland said. *"Voice print checks out. It's Dess."*

Georgiou pushed the Tellarite against the wall and spoke covertly. "You're with the Forest Circle movement?"

"I must be," came the tired response. "That's why they put me here."

"An environmental activist. They tell me that's a rare thing for the Tellarites here."

"It's rare for Tellarites anywhere," Dess grumbled. "But this shouldn't be happening. I'm a Federation citizen."

"Who was arrested outside the Federation."

"On Coridan V. I have no rights there. Or so they say." Dess slumped down the bulkhead and returned to her head-down stance. "Now go away."

Georgiou turned her head to survey the room. Nobody had noticed the conversation. "This is who you want?" she asked

Leland quietly. "I can't believe she's worth the trouble. Barely more than a child."

"That 'child' was charged with trespass and willful destruction," Leland said. *"The mining guild buried her here."*

"If she interfered with my mining operations, I might too. But the Tellarites are part of your little club. You can't get her out?"

"Ambassador Gav runs interference for a lot of their dilithium mining operations. Admitting that Dess is in Thionoga would force the Federation Council into a confrontation with the Tellarites it doesn't want."

"You're such cowards."

"Harmony in the ranks is a priority right now. We've just finished a war that a lot of our allies say was started by a human who defied orders!"

Georgiou didn't need to be reminded of the story—and the role her and Burnham's doubles had played in it. Studying the exits, she announced that her chance had arrived.

Leland agreed. *"Go for it."*

Georgiou knelt down beside Dess and spoke quickly. "Listen closely, girl. I'm a—" She checked herself. "I work with your friends. I'm here to get you out."

Dess looked up, eyes bleary. "What?"

"I said, I'm here to rescue you. There's a supply shuttle waiting. The pilot's left the cargo hatch unlocked, with a nice spot in the hold for us."

The young woman didn't understand. "Who are you?"

"That's not important."

"I don't believe you."

"Believe *this*." Georgiou held up her manacled wrists before Dess. "Leland: be useful."

"Done." A remote command sent through the mainframe caused Georgiou's cuffs to deactivate. They snapped open and fell from her wrists. She quickly reached for Dess's manacles and read Leland the number labeled on them. A second later, the Tellarite's hands were free.

Astonished, Dess rubbed her wrists. "How'd you do that? They've had those on me for weeks." She perked up. "They say I'm crazy, that I'm dangerous!"

"What you are is *loud*." Georgiou studied her for several moments, before rising. "Hang on to those manacles and wait here—while I make some more noise."

A cheer from the inmates heralded the arrival of another huge tureen. "More slop, vermin!" the Ktarian cook yelled. "Fill your mugs and fill your bellies!"

Georgiou stepped between inmates at a table and snatched a metal mug. "Hey!" shouted its owner.

"Sorry," she said, advancing on the cook. "Yoo-hoo!"

The cook's head snapped toward her. "Wait your turn, human!"

"Don't think I will," she said, swinging the mug and smashing the Ktarian in the face with it. The cook reeled but did not drop his steaming vat. Georgiou sidestepped him—and a good shove sent him and the tureen barreling into the hungry queue. Within seconds half a dozen inmates were tangled with him on the deck, covered in scalding gruel.

Spinning, she grabbed one inmate after another, pushing them toward the pile and preventing anyone from rising. The sentries stationed nearby went for the scrum, not for her—and quickly slipped and were pulled under. The other diners got into the act, hurling dinnerware and dinner alike.

Georgiou hustled from the fray. "It's begun," she said aloud to herself. "Too bad there's no war cry for a fight involving food."

"*Matter of fact,*" Leland replied, "*this universe has one.*"

"That doesn't surprise me."

Dess, on the other hand, *was* startled by the events—still cringing and clutching the deactivated manacles. Georgiou delivered a roundhouse kick to an advancing guard before rejoining the activist. "Come on, girl. Let's go!"

Georgiou shoved Dess toward the kitchen, pausing briefly

to deal with another couple of sentries. A third appeared while Georgiou's back was turned—only to receive a smashing blow in the face from someone else: Dess, wielding a metal tray.

"I've been wanting to do that for weeks," she said.

"Hope you enjoyed it." Georgiou pointed to the manacles Dess had dropped in order to pick up the platter. "I said, bring those." Seemingly unsure why she needed to, Dess retrieved the cuffs.

Georgiou directed her through another aperture. *"Left and then right,"* Leland called out, guiding the pair through corridors to a stairwell. *"There's a spoke of the station connecting your wing to the cargo shuttlebay."*

The pair made good time toward it—surprising Georgiou, who might have expected Dess to be worse for her ordeal. With youth came resilience. Leland's coaching helped, directing the two away from advancing sentries; the couple that couldn't be avoided, Georgiou made short work of. Nobody had wielded a disruptor against her, so she didn't yet have one of her own— but it hadn't mattered. Thionoga's brutes weren't accustomed to people who fought back.

Soon, Georgiou and Dess emerged from a passageway onto a catwalk suspended over a landing bay. *"Your ride's down there,"* Leland said. Georgiou spotted the shuttle in question on the deck down below. *"There's a ladder at the far end of the catwalk, just before engineering storage."*

"That's what I wanted to hear," Georgiou said. She turned to Dess, who was looking down at the ships. "You're almost there. Ready?"

The Tellarite gushed with glee. "Whoever you are, I don't know how to thank you!"

"More to do first. Manacles."

"Uh—here," Dess said. She passed them to Georgiou. "Are you going to put them on me? Pose as a guard?"

"Don't be ridiculous." Georgiou stuffed them into her waistband. "I have a better plan. Climb that railing."

Puzzled, Dess nonetheless complied. "Like this?" Feet on a lower part of the railing, the Tellarite looked out over the landing bay, a great height off the deck. "Won't they see me?"

"I need a distraction. You're it." Abruptly, Georgiou grabbed Dess by her collar and backside and hurled the young woman headlong over the railing. The Tellarite screamed as she fell—all the way down, until her body caromed off the side of a gantry and smashed into a pair of unsuspecting workers.

Georgiou looked over the side at the spectacle. "Huh. I was hoping to see her bounce."

"*Wait!*" Leland called out. "*What did I just see?*"

Georgiou ignored him as she rushed up ahead to her real destination, the engineering substation. It didn't take long for her to find what she was looking for. She opened a panel on a console and began fishing.

"*What happened to Dess? What did you do?*"

"Nothing that wasn't going to happen," Georgiou said, finding the relay she was looking for within the mass of ODN cabling. "Nothing she didn't deserve."

"*What?*"

"That girl wasn't a prisoner," she said as she pulled out the manacles Dess had saved. "Tellarites have disgusting skin under the best of circumstances—but those wrists were baby smooth. She said she'd been in those cuffs for weeks."

"*That doesn't mean anything! She's scared, she's disoriented!*"

"She's pretty damn muscular for someone who can't get fed," Georgiou said, talking even as she used a tool to expose the manacles' electroshock coils. "And she's never been to the Coridan system. The dilithium's on the third planet. I should know—I reduced it to its mantle supplying my ships."

"*That's still no reason to—*"

"But what really gave you away was the environmental front. Iaponius is literally my middle name—I know Japanese. And one of a number of ways to say Forest Circle is . . . *Kobayashi Maru.*"

Leland went quiet for a moment. Finally: *"Too cute, huh?"*

"By half."

The spymaster laughed. *"You're good."*

"I'm gone." Georgiou's patience was at an end. "I'm not some cadet to be tested. I won't be manhandled and drugged to prove myself." She finished wiring the manacles to the cabling. "This pulse will direct back into the surveillance systems. It should knock out your ability to see and hear me for a while—and it will shut you the hell up." She smirked. "That's the best part, actually."

"Wait! You can't do this—"

"I can do anything. I quit."

7

Red Sector

Since reaching the stars, the Terran Empire had grasped ever outward. Yet even as it seized far-flung worlds, many of its rulers turned inward—and backward. Every moderately successful monarch, general, or revolutionary in Earth's history had been claimed as an antecedent by one Terran emperor or another, whether or not a familial tie really existed. If it bolstered one's legitimacy to invoke kinship to Alexander, Shaka, Rommel, or Khan, why not? Every little bit helped.

As emperor, Georgiou had drawn on her share of historical names—but unlike many of her predecessors, she also had studied their ideas. It did not impugn her intelligence to draw upon the tactics of another, especially not when that other was long dead. By using the best ideas, she made them her own; making them *solely* hers was the job of the historians commanded to cultivate her legend.

Nobody in either universe, for example, had definitive creatorship of the Thirty-Six Stratagems of ancient China. Some attributed them to Sun Tzu, while others considered them an amalgamation of warfare tactics passed down orally. Georgiou had claimed them as hers early on; her ancestral homeland on the Malay peninsula wasn't exactly next door, but most of her subjects didn't know the difference. And the teachings were, after all these centuries, useful—even for someone escaping an interstellar prison.

"*Hún shuǐ mō yú,*" she recited to herself as she crept out from a maintenance accessway. *Disturb the water and catch a fish.* She had disturbed many ponds on Thionoga in the two hours since ditching Dess, causing chaos on a tremendous scale. It was easier than she'd imagined possible—because while her mission had been a sham, the space station had turned out to be a real prison, one that had sublet part of its facility to Section 31 for Leland's game. The second Georgiou stepped out of the path he had plotted for her and into the rest of the facility, one opportunity for mischief after another had come her way.

There were the Blue and Orange Sectors, made indistinguishable to their workers after she deactivated the lighting. There was the delicious misdirection in cargo bay three, where she'd powered up a space tug she could never have escaped in and debarked the second it started moving. It had slammed into a parked chemical hauler, setting the whole deck on fire. That emergency made possible her masterstroke in Violet Sector, repeated since in Tan and Red: convincing the prison blocks' command computers to open every cell in the area. The inmates, no fools, had obliged by running amok.

"Almost too much fun to stop," she said aloud, delighted not to hear a response from Leland. Then again, it was hard to hear anything over the sirens—especially here, in Red Sector's command center. The staffers having long since decamped to a more secure location, she had no difficulty finding an unattended terminal. The trouble was searching for one that hadn't been smashed.

Finally reaching one in working order, she assessed her location and looked for a likely escape vessel—a warp-capable ship that wasn't a prop left by Leland. Only one fit the bill, well away from her position. *Another gauntlet to run—of course.*

She gnawed her lip on realizing there was no way around a simple fact: she would need help. She wasn't going to be able to steal a ship *and* open the landing bay doors *and* hold off her pursuers all alone. The last problem was the biggest. Even with the disasters rumbling through Thionoga, there were just too many sentries roaming about—whose number, she had seen, occasionally included officers in Section 31 uniforms. She needed help—or a force amplifier.

She walked around a bank of terminals. A disruptor sat on the deck, still beside the body of a guard the mob had cold-cocked. It was a sign of how well the revolt was going that the rioters had ignored the weapon. By now, they had plenty. Georgiou knelt and reached for it—

—only to pause. She hadn't killed anyone in her escape. Not yet, anyway. She'd broken jaws and limbs and shattered a lot of egos. But Dess was alive; Georgiou had heard her howling after her impact. So far, nothing she'd inflicted on anyone was beyond the medical science of a universe of softies who flinched at the suffering of others. Georgiou had no compunctions, of course, but she knew if she started killing now, she might be sentenced to Thionoga—or a prison that actually functioned—for real.

And the Michael Burnham of this continuum certainly wouldn't approve.

But neither was she present to object.

So be it, Georgiou thought. She needed no excuse to rid the universe—any universe—of people who didn't matter, of those who stood in her way. It was the answer she was heading toward all along, and it was also logical. Even amid the chaos, escape would require more than just tricks or—

"*Come on! Was that the best you've got?*"

Georgiou grabbed the disruptor and looked up. Down the corridor leading to the command center, a sandy-haired human male in a red prison jumpsuit stood at a crossing, taunting someone down another passageway. Even amid the klaxons, his voice carried far. "Oh, look at the big bad guard of Red Sector," he called out with a heavy Irish accent. "Bo Peep has lost his sheep!"

"Shut up, you!" A burly Nausicaan in a guard uniform charged into the intersection. The prisoner stood his ground, assuming a boxing stance. The pair engaged. For several seconds, the human held his own—until the Nausicaan, who had weight and reach on his side, landed a haymaker that knocked him to the deck.

But the human didn't stay there. The prisoner rose, wiping blood on his sleeve. "That all you've got?"

Enraged, his opponent lunged. The man hustled out of the way—and then leapt on the guard's back, grabbing a handful of hair in each fist. "I've had my fill of running," the once-captive declared. "Give me a ride!"

The Nausicaan howled at the hair pull—and wrestled violently, trying to shed his rider. "Get off me!"

"Not a chance!"

Then the bloody-faced prisoner laughed, loudly and maniacally.

Georgiou nearly lost her balance. "*Blackjack!*"

The lumbering pair came too near a metal support beam, giving the human rider a chance to slam the guard's head against it. One painful-sounding crack later, and the prisoner was on his backside on the deck, having fallen from the collapsed Nausicaan. The human bellowed with laughter, delighted by his spin. "Next time, I'll bring me a saddle!"

Georgiou gripped the disruptor tightly as she stepped slowly toward the entrance to the corridor, mesmerized. An Andorian prisoner entered the hallway and looked down at the unconscious guard. "Looks like you taught old Graff a lesson. He deserved it!"

"He's a good fellow, just doing his job," the giggler said, getting up. "But I so enjoyed it."

"You're wasting time," the Andorian replied. "Too many guards downstairs. I'm going back to Blue Sector. I'll take my chances in the dark."

"Well, go your way, then! I'll be laughing when you try to escape aboard a garbage scow."

"It'll beat being in a cell with you!" The Andorian headed off.

"I think I've been insulted," the human said to no one. Only then did he spy Georgiou. "Oh! I didn't see you there."

She nearly took a step back as he approached. If he was the man she knew—or a version of him—who knew what crimes he might be in for? But he seemed amiable. He wiped the remaining blood from his face with his hand. "Green Sector, are you?"

Georgiou looked down at her prison-issue uniform. "Obviously."

"Hmm. You're not right in the head. Did they break you? Or did you have a screw loose when they brought you in?"

Georgiou stared blankly. "You don't recognize me." *What am I saying?* "I mean—of course you don't. You wouldn't."

"Oh, you poor confused soul." He pointed at her. "You know, I don't mind if you are a wee bit daft—we all are. But I do mind that bit of menace you're holding there."

She looked down and realized she had trained the disruptor on him. She'd done it instinctively on hearing his laugh—and hadn't moved it since. She lowered it. "I meant nothing."

"Of course." He smiled and outstretched his arms to either side. "This silly place is all the excuse you need. I'd pick up a gun too—but I don't like them much."

No, you never did. Too neat.

"Are you lost?" he asked. "How about a name?"

"Georgiou."

"That's a fine one. Regal as can be."

"And you're *him*."

"I am as me as I can be." He'd just started chuckling when a sound from up the corridor startled him. "Looks like our hosts don't like the redecorating that's been going on. So if you don't mind, I think I'd better be on the move." He started toward one of the exits—only to look back. "If you'll promise not to be shooting that, you can come along."

"Okay."

Almost numb with surprise, Georgiou followed. It was always good practice to keep a serial killer ahead of you.

In her own universe, Blackjack barely knew Georgiou's name—or anyone else's. He'd been a terror in his younger life: a skilled pilot and engineer with an insatiable taste for cruelty and homicide. Those weren't drawbacks in her world, but they had made him the target of a couple of cadets who'd sought revenge. They'd left him for dead: beaten, broken, and bloodied—yet still somehow smiling.

She'd found him then. She had no recollection of what his name had been—only that she'd seen a possible asset. Her people had reassembled him, omitting a few damaged and needless bits of brain associated with morality and self-preservation. Training and conditioning had made Blackjack the perfect instrument of brutality, a wild animal that killed on command. Terran records officially listed him as deceased; he had later brought that condition to many of her rivals.

The corridor reached an end, and this Blackjack contemplated two sealed doorways on either side. He stepped to the one on the right. "Main tower access. Ah, you're the one."

She remembered the map she'd seen—and spoke up. "That's the wrong way. We need to escape."

"I already have escaped," he said, starting to fiddle with the door's electronic lock. "I figure it's about an hour before the goons take over again. Enough time for me to find the warden's larder. I don't know what you call her species, but word is she likes a good Irish whiskey."

"You drink?"

"I know what you're going to say. It's an old stereotype. Far from it. What I love is fun—chemistry and nationality be damned."

"Wait," Georgiou said, stepping beside the door to speak

to him as he worked. It was as close as she'd gotten to him, and she didn't know how he'd respond. "The way on the left goes to a landing bay with a shuttle that'll get me out of here. Both of us, if we work together."

"You learned that at the control center, did you?" He smirked. "That's all fine for you, but I'm staying."

"What?"

"I mean, I don't mind getting out and running around right now. I love a good tumble and it's some new scenery. But I'm not leaving Thionoga. I'm guilty. I'm serving my time."

Little surprised Georgiou; this did. She gawked at him. "Look, I have to get out of here, and I can't do it alone."

"I'm sure you're very nice, Georgia—"

"Georgiou."

"—and when they've got you sane, you'll be right as rain. I'll be glad to know you. But there's a bottle of single pot still here and it's calling my name." He hit on the right combination of controls, and the door opened.

She frowned. "*Blackjack!*"

"I'd say 'bingo,' but whatever word you prefer." Halfway through the portal, he paused to look back at her. "You could share a sip with me, you know. Cracked or not, you are a comely thing."

Without thinking, she struck him hard in the face, causing his head to smack against the side of the hatchway. She tensed up immediately: the Blackjack she knew would never have said such a thing, but neither would he have tolerated the blow. This man hadn't been conditioned to respect her authority.

Instead, he just blinked. "Whoa," he said, blood flowing anew from his mouth as he said it. He wiggled one of his lower front teeth, which gave way.

She watched as he flicked it to the deck. "I didn't mean—"

"Don't worry yourself. I get 'em knocked out all the time—just not here yet. I'd always assumed it'd be a sentry that'd do the trick." Then his eyes darted to the ceiling, as if figuring. "Ten minutes. This is the earliest I've ever been smacked by a woman."

"Don't be an ass." She tugged at his collar and pulled him back into the corridor. Section 31 and Thionoga's guards wouldn't be at bay forever; it was time to take another tack. "Listen. If you don't help me get to that shuttle, they'll kill me."

"Who?"

"The people who run this place!"

"You *are* daft. There's no capital punishment here. It's why Thionoga exists."

"It exists for governments to do away with troublesome people," Georgiou said. "And mine doesn't want me around."

"Hmph." He crossed his arms. Then he eyed her. "What are you in for, again?"

"Nothing."

He scratched his chin. "Chivalry *and* justice. There are days I could go for that. But I'm still not sure—"

"In the process you'll get to pummel a significant percentage of Thionoga's sentry corps."

"Oh, you're singing my song."

"And those who stand with me will become my servants in the afterlife."

He snorted—and smiled. "Georgie, you are my kind of barmy. All right, then." He put up a finger. "But I'll only help you board. Then you're off."

"Whatever." She turned back to face the portal on the left. "Looks like the same mechanism."

"Allow me," he said, stepping past her toward the controls before she could object. "We'll just say the other door was practice for—"

Before he touched the panel, the automatic door slid open, revealing Frietas, Georgiou's interrogator from before. The Denobulan appeared to have traversed a war zone. His clothing was a shambles, and his fist clutched the baton he'd used to waylay Georgiou earlier. He was clearly not expecting to see her again, or here. "*You!*"

He lifted the baton to defend himself, but it was too late. Georgiou delivered a high kick to Frietas's chin. He crashed backward to the deck, losing his weapon; she caught it in mid-descent.

It was her companion's turn to gawk. "You're sure you need my help?"

"I'm sure. Here," she said, shoving the baton into his hand. "You don't like guns. I'm betting this is more your speed."

As she stepped over the fallen guard, he contemplated the weapon. "Huh."

She looked back, fascinated at the spell the thing had over him. *Maybe this universe isn't so different, after all.* But time was wasting. "Are you coming or not?" He was still spellbound. "*Jack!*"

"Sorry," he said, snapping out of it. "And it's Sean." He cracked a bloody-mouthed smile. "Most people call me *Finnegan.*"

8

One of the stranger commercial concepts in ancient Terran history was the life insurance policy. It didn't provide for an elder's estate after death; rather, it protected parents against the significantly more dire prospect that their offspring might fail to achieve power. Little was worse than realizing one's progeny had no ambition or ability; in such a dark moment, it was good to know one could be compensated for investing so many years in useless sacks of flesh.

As with most concepts, "life insurance" had once meant something different in Starfleet's universe, and Georgiou believed she had acquired her own policy in Finnegan. Thirty minutes into their traverse of Thionoga, he'd quickly found his way into the bodyguard role his counterpart served, running ahead as her blocker. She was perfectly able to take care of herself, of course, but why waste effort? Finnegan had bowled over so many along the way that she hadn't even needed to shoot anyone. He wasn't a behemoth—or a big man at all—but he seemed suffused with energy that was ever directed outward. Every bit Blackjack's equal as a brawler, Finnegan took to it with abandon and glee.

He might not be everyone's nightmare, but she was pretty sure he was someone's. *He's a chaos demon.*

And maybe he was trainable. "The truncheon," she said as they went. "You're armed. Act like it!"

"Right," he said, swinging the baton. He'd used it more to disarm than anything. That was fine for the black-clad Section 31 agents they'd met, who seemed intent only on her capture, but the humiliated and harassed Thionoga guards were riled, brandishing fewer electroshock staffs and more disruptors.

Finnegan's approach made her wonder how many murders he was imprisoned for, and how he had perpetrated them. The man clearly wasn't the sadist she knew; not once did he attempt to drive his baton through the eye sockets of any of the sentries he bowled over. He was formidable and useful, but she did not fear him.

But he did make her uncomfortable, especially in one area.

"We're almost there," Finnegan said, leading her down the hallway she'd located on the map. "Parting will be such sweet sorrow," he said, glancing back to give her a wink. "Maybe I'll see you off with a kiss."

Georgiou shuddered. In the less frenetic moments, Finnegan had made similar quips that he probably considered flirtatious—pedestrian come-ons that she'd otherwise have disdained. Instead, they made her skin crawl. Georgiou had as open a mind about physical relations as any Terran—more so, in fact. But if the Blackjack of her universe had urges, only homicide could satisfy them. Sean Finnegan was young and not unattractive, but she still reacted to him as if he were Blackjack's double.

At the end of the corridor, three guards pounced on Finnegan. She had to engage, this time, knocking out the one who got past him while he dealt with the other two.

He looked back. "Don't tell me I let one get through."

"You're slipping. Winded?"

"Never." But his hair was mussed.

"There's the ladder."

Earlier, Georgiou had located a dome atop one of Thionoga station's upper spurs. From the lower levels, she could tell that it served as a receiving area for VIPs, presenting visitors—and, she imagined, auditors from participating governments—a picture of the station that was not only sanitized, but elegant.

It also had something else, according to the central computer: the warden's yacht.

Stepping off the top rung of the ladder, she saw the vessel. It sat across a wide expanse of landing bay, complete with large ports looking out into space. The place seemed uninhabited as she entered the chamber; unsurprising, given the chaos elsewhere.

"The station has disruptor turrets," Georgiou said. "But they'll never fire on the warden's ship."

"Aye," Finnegan responded. "On a day like today, she might be fleeing in it."

"I don't think they'd shoot at it in any event. The ship's too valuable," she said, admiring its lines and elegant design. It would be a nice ship to explore a new universe in. She pointed to the right. "I'm betting the spacedoor controls are in that cubicle."

"I'm on it." He paused and turned to her. "It's been a joy. Should we say our good-byes now?" He smiled, new gap in his teeth fully evident. "We could always drink a toast. I could go back and get that bottle."

"Do and I'll break it over your skull." Georgiou was already moving toward the yacht. "The spacedoors."

"Right!"

Georgiou had only gotten partway to her destination when a human figure stepped out of the yacht. Bald and square jawed, he looked coolly down on her. "Agent."

"*Leland.*" She approached the bottom of the yacht's landing ramp, disruptor still in hand. "What a pleasure to hear your voice again."

He looked past her. "Looks like you've made a friend."

"He's come in handy," she said, eyes and weapon fixed on the spymaster. "Get off my ride."

Leland gestured and called out, "Hey! What's your name, pal?"

"What's it to you?" Finnegan replied—and in that instant, Georgiou saw that he had turned back from the cubicle and was approaching. He waved his truncheon threateningly. "You leave her alone!"

Georgiou nearly spat. "I told you to open the doors!"

"After you're safely aboard." Finnegan glared at Leland. "She says her people put her here to kill her."

Leland seemed amused. "Did she?"

"Are you one of them?" Finnegan asked. "You look like the sort of snake who'd jail a poor woman for nothing. Now, let her pass!"

"I was already going to," Leland said, strolling casually down. He regarded Finnegan. "We've been able to get enough surveillance running to see your act. You're quite the slugger. Academy trained?"

"Champ five years in a row."

"That many? I guess graduating's hard for a future prisoner."

"What can I say? I loved being an upperclassman."

Already atop the ramp, Georgiou turned, intending to close the hatch. Instead, she saw Leland raise his fists. "I won a bout or two myself, champ. Care to give it a try?"

Finnegan laughed heartily and threw his baton to the deck. "I'll have you seeing stars without looking out the window." He and Leland squared off. "Two falls out of three?"

"*You idiot!*" Georgiou shouted at Finnegan. "Can't you see he's trying to delay you? Go open the spacedoors, before I shoot the both of—"

Dozens of meters away, the doors to a turbolift opened, discharging a half dozen black-clad Section 31 security operatives. Leland unclenched his fists and backed off from Finnegan. "Sorry, I don't really fight. I've got people for that."

Enough! Disgusted, Georgiou stepped backward, reaching inside for the control to seal the yacht—

—only to feel her muscles go limp. Darkness enveloped her and she pitched forward, tumbling down the ramp.

For her entire time as emperor, she had guarded against a blade in the back. She had never thought to expect a pinch to the neck.

Georgiou felt as if she had only been out for a few minutes when she opened her eyes. An enormous female Vulcan in Section 31 security garb loomed above her. "Philippa," Leland called out, "I don't think you've met Sydia, my chief of security."

"I . . . think I just did," Georgiou replied.

"Well, I *did* say I brought people with me."

Emerging from her haze, Georgiou realized the situation was much changed. Finnegan was far across the deck, hands behind his head and facedown as Section 31 officers and Thionoga sentries argued over him. Georgiou had members of both groups training their weapons on her as well.

"I should have shot you people when I had the chance."

Sydia didn't respond. Instead, she wrenched her prisoner to an upright seated position on the deck and handcuffed her. No give to these manacles, Georgiou found—and, she suspected, no secret code to deactivate them. The security chief then brought Georgiou to her feet, where she saw Leland engaged in a heated disagreement with even more Thionoga personnel.

Georgiou spoke up. "All this for me? I hope I haven't caused any inconvenience."

One of the quarrelers, she saw, was Frietas, visibly bruised from their earlier encounter. He nearly leapt out of his skin when he saw her. "She's awake! Sedate her before she blows the station up!"

Leland tried to calm him. "Your administrators and my organization have an understanding. The operation may have gotten a little out of hand, but—"

"Out of hand?" Frietas raved. "Three sectors are still afire—and the mental ward's mounted an organized insurrection! You've set Thionoga back a hundred years!"

One of Sydia's comrades approached her with something—and moments later, the Vulcan stepped toward Frietas. "I'm told this is your baton, sir."

The Denobulan grabbed for his weapon—and still rattled, pointed it in Georgiou's face. After a moment of futility, he checked a reading at its base. "The tranquilizing gas is exhausted. Someone's been using it!"

"Yeah, that was our brawler over there," Leland said, gesturing to the crowd around Finnegan. "When we closed in on him, he picked up the baton from the wrong end and accidentally gassed himself in the face. I guess he didn't know it did that." He rubbed the back of his head and shrugged. "Look, he's yours. We'll just take her and get out of your way."

"Oh, no!" Frietas shook the baton before Leland. "I speak for the warden when I say our people will want both prisoners—and probably some of you!" Several of the prison guards who'd been watching Georgiou redirected their weapons toward Leland's team.

Sydia snapped to attention, interposing herself between Leland and the sentries. "Instructions?"

He had some—which he spoke into his communicator. "This is Leland. Extract the team—plus Georgiou." He made a little salute to Frietas. "Bye."

Then he waited. And waited.

Eyes narrowing, Leland made another call. "I said extract the team. Confirm receipt of order."

When no response came, Georgiou's lips curled upward. "Problems?"

Leland gestured for Sydia. "Go look out the port. See if our ship's still there."

Sydia left his side with reluctance. Moments later, she responded, "It is still docked to the station."

"Then why can't—" He looked to Sydia. "Are the station's shields up?"

"They haven't worked for hours," Frietas said. He pointed at Georgiou. "Guess why!"

He motioned for the sentries to approach Georgiou, causing Leland to step in front of her. The lack of response from his starship clearly having unnerved him, he gestured for calm. "Look, it's been a complicated day. Let's work something out."

"Step aside. There's a thousand prison cells on this station. We can find room for all of you if we have to—"

"New arrival!" shouted Sydia from her lookout position. All eyes turned to the large window, beyond which a Federation starship approached. Unusually for a Starfleet vessel, it had four nacelles, two atop and two below, further astern. "*Nimitz* class!"

"They've come to bail you out," Georgiou said. "We won't be cellmates after all."

"Maybe." Leland stared at the port and the still-distant arrival. "Depends on who it is."

"What does it matter?"

"I guess you wouldn't know. The *Nimitzes* are favorites of admirals. *Europa* had been Brett Anderson's flagship—it was one of the first losses in the Klingon War." He ruminated. "There's only a few possibilities, some of them better than—"

Sydia spoke again. "It's *Pacifica*!"

"Oh," Leland said, his normally controlled face showing just the hint of alarm. He lifted his communicator again. "I guess we'd better get ready for a hail."

Glowing materialization effects announced several new arrivals on the now-crowded deck. Their number included *Pacifica* security officers, led by someone Georgiou knew well.

From both worlds.

"Admiral Cornwell," Leland said, straightening. "I wasn't expecting you. What brings you to the neighborhood?"

"Start by asking the person whose neighborhood you've just ruined," Katrina Cornwell said. The dark-haired woman stepped to one side—and revealed the Rigelian female who had just materialized behind her. "I think you know Warden Ohtak?"

"Warden!" Frietas said, brightening. "I'm so happy you're safe."

"The admiral beamed me off Thionoga five minutes ago," Ohtak said, "when my control center fell."

Her remark startled Leland, who looked at Cornwell. "You didn't just drop out of warp?"

"We've been stationed in the debris field," Cornwell said, "until we got the warden's distress call. Aren't you the one who's supposed to know everything?"

"Stationed nearby," Leland repeated, digesting.

Cornwell's voice was stern. "Admiral Patar and her colleagues in Intelligence may run your section, Captain Leland, but you're still part of Starfleet. And Starfleet tries to keep an eye out for biological weapons."

"Biological weapons?" Leland looked around and shrugged. "I don't know what you're talking about."

"She means *me*, you imbecile!" Georgiou stepped near. "You were watching me—but she was watching *you*. Starfleet doesn't trust its own spies."

"Hey, wait a second." Leland put up his hands innocently, eyes darting to the many Thionoga personnel in earshot. "I don't know what you mean. We're just a security team, running a training operation."

"Oh, give it a rest," Georgiou snapped. "Thionoga is renting you space for your black site. I think they know you're not here making instructional vids."

Ohtak jabbed a finger at Leland. "You won't be doing anything anymore. This facility is a disaster—and it's all your fault!"

"Starfleet will make good," Cornwell promised. "This is better discussed elsewhere." She gestured to Georgiou. "I assume you have no objections to our taking this prisoner?"

"I absolutely insist," Ohtak said.

Frietas pointed in the opposite direction. "What about the other one?"

"What other one?" the admiral asked.

Georgiou looked to see that Sydia and the Thionoga guards had Finnegan on his feet. His hands bound behind him, Finnegan was marched toward the gathering before the yacht. The gas from Frietas's weapon seemed to have calmed him, as it had Georgiou, making his grin seem even more dopey—if that were possible.

And when he saw Cornwell, he bubbled with glee. "Well, hello there!"

She turned—and dropped the communicator she was holding. "*Sean Finnegan?*"

"Kitty, my girl, it's been an age!"

Georgiou and Leland looked at each other. *Kitty?*

"He's one of ours," Ohtak said, clapping her hand on his shoulder. "Take her, but he stays. He's got a sentence here— and he's just added to it."

Cornwell was still stricken with surprise. "What—what did he do?"

"He helped me," Georgiou replied dryly. "That ought to be crime enough in your world."

Finnegan looked downcast. "I guess it's good-bye after all, Georgie."

It was Leland and Cornwell's turn to look at one another. "*Georgie?*" she said.

"I've decided to let that one go," Georgiou said. "For old times' sake."

"Old times?" Cornwell recovered her composure—and then her communicator. "*Pacifica*, I have a party to beam out."

"*Now, Admiral?*"

"Before things get any stranger."

9

Starfleet didn't believe in agonizer booths, but Georgiou thought it seemed to subscribe to the theory behind them. The luxurious quarters she'd first been imprisoned in aboard *Discovery* were an aberration; Starfleet's vessels, including that one, regularly confined people behind energy shields in small spaces. And while there might not be regular bouts of electrocution, they inflicted discomfort in other ways. Brig furnishings were either devoid of taste or missing altogether. Food was served in her cell, presented without imagination or attention to theme. And the prison uniforms were nothing special. Thionoga's, but without the parasites.

And when it came to a certain form of torture, Starfleet had the Terran Empire licked. It allowed visitors. Plenty of them. Since Georgiou's sudden departure from Thionoga, they hadn't left her alone. Nine different interviewers had come to see her: some working for Cornwell and something called the Federation Security Agency, others working for Starfleet Intelligence, mostly Section 31. The latter were easily identifiable, as they never gave their names. Who did they think they were fooling?

So she was not surprised when her dinner, such as it was, was interrupted by workers who placed a small table and two chairs just outside her cell, right beside the force field. But when she saw Cornwell and Leland arrive from different directions, she began to hope the parade of visitors might be nearing an end.

"Just a second," Georgiou said, standing from the small table and chair provided to her for dining. She pushed the table right to the force field, so as to almost adjoin the one on the other side—except for the energy barrier. She smiled with satisfaction and scooted her chair to the table. "Now, we can pretend we're one big family."

Cornwell looked to Leland, who stood, stoic. When she took her chair, he followed suit. Both produced data slates, which they placed before them on the surface.

Georgiou feigned rapt attention. "Are you going to tell me stories? I do love entertainments at dinner."

Cornwell spoke without looking up. "We've been investigating events on Thionoga in parallel. I assume you figured that from all the interrogators."

"No, nobody's been here."

"As near as I understand it, Leland visited you on Qo'noS several days ago to . . ." She paused, as if about to say something unpalatable. "To *recruit you* for Section 31. Leland then staged a training exercise at the black site on Thionoga—"

"There are no black sites," Leland said, eyes not moving from his data slate.

"An exercise at an internment facility where the Federation has *guest privileges*," Cornwell pronounced. When Leland had no objection, she continued. "A test of your abilities as a potential agent."

"And as *I* understand it," Leland said, reading, "operatives for Klingon Emperor L'Rell alerted the Federation that I had removed you from Qo'noS, which led to their alerting Starfleet Command. Then, despite the fact that there was never any objection to my plans from Admiral Patar—"

"Who is not the only overseer of Section 31," Cornwell interjected.

"—Admiral Cornwell requested and received permission to reroute *Pacifica* to *spy* on us."

"Which the Federation Security Agency demanded—because of *who she is*."

Georgiou clasped her hands together. "This *is* entertaining. Are you going to talk like this all night?"

Cornwell ignored her. "The Federation only ever wanted Section 31 to keep tabs on the emperor. They never wanted you to run a salvage operation."

"That hurts," Georgiou said.

"Now Thionoga is trying to salvage its entire facility—and the agent you had posing as Dess has had to have five bones repaired. All because of Section 31's bright idea—and its lack of foresight." The admiral put down her slate and stared at Leland. "I thought you were in the business of predicting everything."

Leland gestured at his own slate. "We sure as hell didn't predict that one guy—that Finnegan. Starfleet didn't even know he was there, or why."

Georgiou piped up, "Isn't it refreshing when your top spy doesn't know something? It must give you such a feeling of confidence."

Leland ignored her and scrolled through the list on his slate. "Finnegan's record—it's something else." He looked keenly at Cornwell. "How did *you* know him?"

Cornwell waved dismissively. "Sean's grandmother lived next door to my family—he visited during the summers. My folks would give him odd jobs."

"I see," Leland said, referring to his data slate. "Got into Starfleet Academy the first time on a captain's choice—those recommendations are always confidential. You?"

The admiral scowled. "I don't see how that's what you should be asking right now."

Leland put up his hand. "You're right." He turned to Georgiou. "The more important question is how *you* knew him—and that he was there."

"Ah, another interrogation." Georgiou turned her gaze to the unpalatable green things on her plate, which she began moving around with her fingers. "No truth serum this time? You mean I can play coy and protect my reputation as a diabolical genius?"

"Do we *need* a truth serum?"

"No," Georgiou said. "Lies are for amusement—and for people trying to achieve power. I already have it."

Cornwell corrected her. "You mean, you *had* it."

"That's your opinion. I see this as one more realm to conquer."

Leland tried to get her back on track. "Finnegan."

Georgiou flicked a pea with her index finger and watched it flash off the force field. Satisfied, she did it again.

"Finnegan," Cornwell implored.

"Oh, all right," Georgiou said. "I didn't know he was there. But I would have tried to find him if I had. He has skills in my world."

Leland checked his notes. "He said you called him Blackjack."

"A masterpiece of Terran workmanship. He kills for pleasure—but also on command. I determined a pathological murderer might come in handy in escaping."

Cornwell's eyes went wide. "Murderer?" She looked to Leland. "What was he in for?"

"I'm—uh, still trying to find that out. Thionoga's records say his original judgment was sealed by the government that charged him. I've tried to ask since, but they're not returning hails right now."

The admiral shook her head. "Sean's a lot of things, but he's no serial killer."

"He would've been more useful to me if he had been," Georgiou said, flicking another legume. "But it's not Finnegan's fault he's less than he could be. He'd never met *me* before."

Cornwell stared at her. "That's . . . very generous?"

"He was a great asset, though, and one I might be willing to train again. But he may need the lobotomy, like we gave Blackjack."

"A *what?*"

"A surgical practice—I'm surprised you haven't heard of it. Michael told me you were a psychiatrist." Georgiou studied the back of her hand. "You try to fix the mentally unfit. My people looked for ways to use them."

"There is no 'unfit,'" Cornwell said, growing cross. "And I don't even *want* to know what you do with them."

"Are you certain? I think you all get a vicarious thrill from hearing what you might be capable of, in other circumstances." She indicated Leland. "I know *he* does."

Leland didn't take the bait. "Back to Finnegan. You just stumbled across someone who is, in your own world, your chief assassin?"

"I didn't say he was my chief." She added a thought. "He did *kill* the chief . . ."

Leland shook his head. "She knew him. It's too much co-incidence."

"Do you think I had a mole in Thionoga, or in Section 31? Or both?" Georgiou smiled. "No wonder you wanted to hire me. I'm apparently quite intrepid."

Cornwell looked to Leland. "It could be a chance meeting. Burnham says these coincidences tended to happen when they were in the Terrans' universe—however many different events separate our realm from theirs, people tend to cross paths with others they know. Or even themselves."

Leland frowned. "I don't like it. It's not logical."

"Poor spy boy," Georgiou said. "Creation refuses to fit into the neat little box you have for it." She had noticed the phenomenon, herself, certainly—and was beginning not to question it. She looked to Cornwell. "Take you, admiral head-shrinker. Your counterpart works for my cousin."

"Doing what?"

"Hopefully not my cousin. Alexander has invented acts that have no names even in my world." Georgiou's nose wrinkled at the thought of her vile relative. "But he is also a strutting popinjay—a complete imbecile. 'My' Cornwell is probably kept busy enough making sure he doesn't set his palace on fire."

Cornwell stared for a moment, and then blinked. Georgiou had found people were always fascinated to know what they were.

"What about Leland?" Cornwell asked. "Is he there?"

Georgiou nodded. "He debases himself for currency outside a Martian mining compound. Normally, I wouldn't have heard of such a person, but there's a disease named for him."

Leland gave an exasperated sigh. "She does this. This is the fifth different biography she's given for me."

"I thought you didn't lie," Cornwell said.

"This is for fun," Georgiou replied. "And because one of the stories I've told has been true, he's now going to be driving himself crazy wondering which one it is."

"Don't count on it," he grumbled.

"I think I've heard enough," Cornwell said. "Section 31's test was a bust, Leland, because the whole recruitment was a bust. From what I understand, she never took the job seriously, nor your mission."

"I certainly did," Georgiou said. "I even selected an alias. Your spies use them, don't they?"

Leland rolled his eyes. "We were not going to call you Divinity Churchmouse."

"Wasn't it innocent-sounding enough? I really don't know. Where I come from—"

"Yes, yes. They eat kittens for breakfast."

"No, not breakfast."

Cornwell forged ahead. "It all comes back to this: that you should never have been recruited in the first place."

Georgiou leered at her. "*You* recruited me first, Admiral. Starfleet gave me the captain's chair of *Discovery*."

"When the Federation was on the brink of defeat, ready to try anything. It was almost a dreadful mistake. Burnham and *Discovery* saved us from violating our core principles."

Georgiou winced with nausea, not all pretend. "You also

gave me a token signifying my freedom—which you knew would be completely useless while I was on Qo'noS. You knew L'Rell would keep me penned up. I suspect it was your first official request to her." She chortled. "You introduced me to the *Discovery* crew as having escaped from a Klingon prison. Little did they know that was where they were delivering me."

Leland kept pressing his case. "The emperor has skills, Admiral. She has knowledge—of places that exist in both universes that we haven't yet gotten to see. We can use her."

"She's using *you*," Cornwell said. "Can't you see this has always been about escape for her?"

Leland shook his head—and then turned his gaze toward Georgiou. "Is she right? You were really just trying to get away?"

"Qo'noS was getting boring," the emperor said. "But I wasn't about to trade one prison for another. Even that pretend one of yours."

"But there's so much you can do with us."

"*For* you. Not for me." Georgiou turned her plate upside down.

"It's the Terran mind," Cornwell said. "She's never worked a day in her life for anyone else. Why should she do it for you?"

Georgiou sneered. "Especially for a so-called secret organization that has its own ID badges—and whose leader takes orders from a *computer program*!"

Cornwell's eyes darted to Leland, who shuffled uncomfortably in his seat. "I don't know what you're talking about."

Georgiou rolled her eyes. "This again." She looked to the admiral. "For someone who lies for a living, he's got the worst 'nonchalant' face I've ever seen. He couldn't keep a newt undercover."

Cornwell watched her—and then glanced at Leland. "It sounds like she knows."

"We hadn't told her anything about that yet," he said. "I swear!"

"I got it out of one of your underlings," Georgiou said. "The homely one. You all lack the imagination to think of anything truly diabolical, so you farm it out to an algorithm. Or me. What do they call it, 'Control'?"

Leland put up his hands. "I've never—"

"Save it. The name fits perfectly. You're all starved for leadership here in this universe, but no one will step up. So you have to invent something to think for you." She rolled her eyes. "You're almost not worth the trouble to conquer. I could just reprogram the machine and you'd all serve me."

Cornwell flinched. "Could she do that?"

"No!" Leland put up his hands. "She doesn't even know the first—"

"I was an engineer, among other things. But relax," Georgiou said. "Sneaking in and subverting is no way to start an empire. That's no fun at all."

"All right," Cornwell said. "We know what you were and where you came from. You'd be cautious, too, in our place, if someone like you appeared."

"Don't presume what I would have done. I was on the lookout for secret weapons all the time," Georgiou said. Then, idly lifting her plate, she decided to engage the matter. "But if someone *did* come to my universe—someone who was smarter, craftier, and deadlier than anyone else around? I would have killed that person. Immediately, before she ruined everything. But *you* won't. And that's why the Federation will fall."

"To you?"

"To me—or to the Klingons, or to someone."

"Section 31 exists to prevent that," Leland said. "We think of things that the Federation Council would never—"

Georgiou moved suddenly, slinging the plate at Leland. It flashed noisily against the force field, causing both her visitors to stand—and Leland's chair to crash backward as he drew his phaser.

Georgiou clasped her hands on the edge of the table and

stared right into the weapon. "Deactivate the force field. Set that to kill and fire." Her focus didn't waver. "If you really exist to protect the Federation, then you have to do it."

He stared at her, spellbound.

"*Do it! And stop wasting my time.*"

Cornwell's eyes darted from Leland to her. "And if he did deactivate the field, you'd flip that table up into his face, blocking the shot. Then you'd kill us both and escape. And that wouldn't help the Federation at all, would it?"

"It would sure help *me*."

Cornwell spoke coolly. "You're just a big bundle of hate, aren't you?" She retrieved her chair and sat down. "Such rage. Do I need to find you a counselor? Someone to hurry you along through your stages? You seem to be stuck on anger."

Georgiou glared. "What are you talking about?"

"Stages of grief," Cornwell replied, picking up her slate and speaking matter-of-factly. "It was an old psychological construct. More of an aid to understanding than an actual progression."

Seeing Leland holster his weapon, Georgiou knew her gambit had failed. She leaned back in her chair. "We have such a model too—for coping with the loss of status."

Cornwell raised an eyebrow. "This should be good."

Georgiou reeled them off. "*Defiance. Murder. Plundering. Destruction.* And my favorite: *Vengeance.*"

"You've got to be kidding."

"One: refuse to accept your defeat," Georgiou said. "Two: kill someone, *anyone*, who bars your way. Three: take what you need in order to build your power anew. Four: lay waste to all your enemy's works."

"And five?" Leland asked.

"Leave nothing of him but a stain on your palace floor."

He smirked. "Come to think of it, it does sound a bit therapeutic."

Georgiou crossed her arms and shrugged. "When you're

wronged, who else should defend you, if you refuse? Either you take the power, or you take the punishment."

Cornwell shook her head. "*Who hurt you?*"

Leland gawked. "You're going to psychoanalyze a whole universe, Doctor?"

"That's *Admiral*. And no, I only was really asking about one person. But one's enough—and I've seen enough." She stood and looked down at the seated Georgiou. "We took you on once when the Federation was in dire straits—and you nearly made us regret it. I don't care what special skills or point of view you have. Letting you loose on the universe was bad enough. Giving you an intel job would be putting a phaser in your hands."

"I don't need a phaser. You might have seen."

"It was a metaphor. Here's another. You're an invasive species, Philippa—a threat to the ecosystem. L'Rell knew that better than anyone. It's why the Klingons did such a good job keeping you cooped up. But the Federation isn't willing to give them the job again."

Leland volunteered, "What she knows is still useful. Section 31 could hold her."

"I trust you only marginally more than I trust her," Cornwell said. "If you have a problem, have Patar take it up with Starfleet Command. But the Federation Security Agency has its own powers, and it agrees with me. *Discovery* kept a future Klingon emperor in the brig for weeks. I'm betting *Pacifica* can hold a Terran one indefinitely."

Leland put up his hands. "Let's discuss—"

"It's done." Cornwell waved her data slate before Leland. "And one more thing. This Thionoga place is clearly not somewhere the Federation needs to be sending any more business to—covert or otherwise. I'll see the judicial authorities get a report on that place!"

The admiral stood, stopping in the doorway just long enough to look back with incredulity. "*Divinity Churchmouse?*"

After Cornwell departed, Leland mumbled, "That report will get lost."

Georgiou chuckled. "I almost appreciate the boldness of your hypocrisy, Leland. Very Terran. But you'll never take it to the next level." Then her smile dissipated. "I don't suppose your machinations extend to finding a way to get me out of this place?"

Leland let out a deep breath. "The Federation's terrified of you. I can't imagine any situation that would make them release you."

"I forgot—*your computer* does all your imagining for you." She stood. "Now unless you can find me some real food, get the hell out of my throne room. No more audiences today."

10

Shuttlecraft *Leizu*
BETA QUADRANT

"So those medals of yours," the bearded pilot asked the Trill woman. "Are they really gold?"

"You know, I've never asked."

"Are you wearing one now? I mean, under the uniform."

Emony Dax tried to let an exasperated sigh serve as her answer. When the pilot didn't stop staring, she said, "That's a no."

"Just curious."

When Lieutenant Kubisiak still didn't look away, she threw up her hands and retreated to the rear of the shuttlecraft. *That's a no too.*

Having spent most of her young life on display, Emony had discovered that fame produced different responses in those she encountered. Some, like *Leizu*'s pilot, fawned over her, asking about this Olympiad or that one, plumbing for gossip about the other athletes, and generally getting overfamiliar. Her long experience dealing with such people meant they usually weren't more than a nuisance.

Another group of people, however, was trickier. Its members assumed gymnastics was all she knew, dismissing her potential to do anything else. *Leizu*'s other passengers certainly had started with that view—and it was harder to take, because what people thought of her intellect had never mattered before. Emony's physical feats did the talking for her.

For most of her life, that was more than enough; critically, it had brought her to the attention of the Trill Symbiosis Commission. The Dax symbiont, having resided inside legislator

Lela and mathematician Tobin, had longed to be paired with someone more physically active. Emony fit that bill perfectly.

Receiving the symbiont felt at first like a reward—but it turned into a blessing. Beyond what she gained from accessing Dax's wisdom and experience, Emony found the joining enhanced her skills, keeping her competitive far longer than her age should have allowed.

And that was the problem. Modern medicine, diets, and training regimens had made it possible for athletes of many species to compete well into their adult lives. But whether Trill, human, or something else, gymnasts started their careers young. It didn't matter that Emony's body was up to the challenge; she had no interest in taking honors away from rivals who were now half her age, especially when the symbiont was giving her an advantage. It didn't matter that the Trills had never revealed the existence of the symbionts to outsiders; *she* knew, and so did Dax, who understood her trepidation. Its curiosity satisfied, the symbiont agreed it was time for a change. The 2256 Olympiad had been her last.

Emony had first thought of going into medical research years earlier, when visiting a university in North America to judge a competition. She'd encountered a young medical student there, whose unconcealed interest in her made *Leizu*'s pilot seem like a smooth operator. But Leonard McCoy had also thought highly of her intelligence, poring over texts with her in an antiquarian bookstore on the Oxford town square. "If you ever get out of this racket," he said in his Mississippi drawl, "consider medicine."

She had—only to find, to her chagrin, that doctors needed to start early too. The Dax symbiont had more years of experience than any being she'd ever met, but it was the wrong kind of knowledge. Starfleet hadn't panned out, and neither had her other offers. The best she could manage was signing up with a team of civilian researchers looking into a subject she knew something about: astrokinesiology.

How sojourns in different gravities and atmospheres affected physical mobility was something Starfleet was keenly interested in. Since the subjects of study were always on the move, it fell to mobile research efforts like hers to go to *them*. After nearly a year of voyaging from one far-flung Starfleet vessel to another, Dax felt she'd made the jump from athletics to academics. But she'd never fully convinced her companions on the team—

—and her boss was a lost cause. Rodolfo Eagan didn't look up from his data slate as she entered the shuttle's lab area. "There you are, Dax. Did you enjoy chatting up the new pilot?"

"Time of my life."

"Another fan, I suppose. Must be nice to be recognized for something."

"So I've heard."

A long-range warp-capable shuttlecraft detached to Eagan's team, *Leizu* had picked up a new pilot every other starbase stop; she'd barely gotten to know any of them. And she'd also stopped waiting for Eagan to give her something useful to do.

He looked up at her, his nose wrinkling. "I need to tell the pilot to watch the antimatter intermix in chamber two," the gray-haired man said. "We'll make better time."

"I can do it."

"Better if I do." Eagan stood and headed forward. "It's pretty involved. Dax, see if Garber and Winnock need you to proofread their reports."

"Aye, Captain."

That was what he wanted to be called. As a Starfleet officer years earlier, Eagan had led science vessels like *Hipparchus* and *Archimedes,* though only on an interim basis; he'd never achieved a command of his own beyond small survey ships. He'd since retired and returned to his original calling, heading research efforts—but from the way he ran his people, he clearly still thought he belonged on a bridge, and that anyone younger was a rank plebe. Doctor Winnock, previously the beleaguered rookie before Dax came along, had put it best: "People never really leave the captain's chair; they travel with their own."

Garber, the other of the team's research physicians, handed her a data slate. "Sixteen files this time. Just see how it reads; don't worry about the technical stuff."

"But I want to worry about it."

He smiled. "I know. Just don't let it slow you down."

She'd gotten more support in single days from Garber and Winnock than she'd gotten from Eagan all tour—though often it just took the form of sympathy.

"You're still feeling like a glorified courier?" Winnock asked.

"And not sure where the glory comes in." Dax was going to elaborate, but Eagan barged back in on his way aft, causing her to step back.

"We're coming out of warp in a few minutes," he said. "Let's get set quicker this time. Our subject is a big starship, four hundred people—we'll need to work fast." He began pulling cases from a locker. "This is a type-one protocol, basic as it gets. They've been studying a volcanic planet for a while now, so there may be physiological differences between the ground teams and their previous baselines." He turned his head. "Dax!"

She was still just a meter away. "Present."

"Take these." He began piling medical sample cases into her arms. He pointed toward the cockpit. "When whatshis-face—"

"Kubisiak."

"—when Kubisiak there lands, I want you out following the doctors wherever they go."

She acquiesced. The routine hadn't changed once in eighteen stops, yet Eagan felt the need to explain it to her each time.

"This would go faster if they just beamed you aboard their starship and then to the planet. But you've got your *thing*," Eagan said, hitting the last word with annoyance.

Dax's "thing" was a reluctance to be transported aboard Starfleet's top-of-the-line ships; she had no idea whether their advanced sensor systems would identify that she was carrying a symbiont. None of the Trills knew for sure whether that was a possibility, and it remained a worry for a people who liked their privacy. It had also punctured her original Starfleet hopes.

Eagan swore. "I *knew* I forgot to ask something. Dax, put all that down and tell the pilot to add something to his hail. The type-one test reactants are sensitive. We need atmospheric pressure readings for every site we're visiting."

"Check."

Unable to find a place to stow her cargo, Dax just carried it forward to the cockpit. She plopped the mountain of cases on the copilot's chair beside Kubisiak. He smiled at her. "Missed me, did you?"

If someone gave me a phaser, I wouldn't. "Captain Eagan—"

"Is no captain—unless you count those twelve minutes the year I was born." Kubisiak rolled his eyes. "What's his lordship want now?"

"Planetside data. He needs—"

A jolt went through *Leizu* as the ship dropped out of warp before a red planet with volcanic features. "Look at it yourself. Tycho IV dead ahead."

And the starship orbiting it: *U.S.S. Farragut.*

"She's big," Dax said, spellbound.

"*Constitution* class. Some buddies of mine serve on her—Drake, Gilhooley, Morwood." Kubisiak adjusted the shuttle's course. "I was just about to hail."

Dax nodded. Then she focused on something in the nearer space before *Farragut.* "What's that?"

It was a thing without shape: a will-of-the-wisp, a smudge in space swirling its way through the void above Tycho IV.

Shapeless, but not aimless. It was headed for *Farragut.*

"What the hell is that thing?" Dax asked again.

"I don't know—but it doesn't look good at all," Kubisiak

said. He pointed to sensor data on the cockpit monitor. "*Farragut*'s aware of it. They just scanned it, see?"

"It's moving faster," Dax said. She leaned in closer, not believing what she was about to say. "It's like the scan *aggravated* it."

Eagan appeared in the cockpit behind her. "What's going on? What did *Farragut* say?"

Dax pointed. "That thing's going after the ship."

As Eagan gawked, trying to make sense of what he was seeing, Kubisiak slapped the console and shouted, "What's wrong with *Farragut*? Shoot, already!"

Phaser fire finally did come from the starship—but it was too late. The cloud was upon it, first billowing across the saucer section, and then sinking in, as if it were being absorbed.

Eagan shook his head. "That's not right." He headed toward the copilot's chair, forcing Dax to quickly relocate the sample kits to the deck at her feet. Eagan worked the comm controls. "*Farragut*, this is shuttlecraft *Leizu*, civilian research group. What's your condition?"

Static. And then—screams.

"*—killing us! It's killing us!*"

Eagan's breath caught. "What do you mean?"

"*The cloud! We need doctors—but it's already struck sickbay!*"

Eagan gaped at the sight of the ship—seemingly peaceful against the backdrop of Tycho IV. He seemed spellbound. "Sir," Dax said.

He didn't respond. When he didn't respond a second time, she reached past him and touched the comm control. "We have doctors aboard, *Farragut*. Do you want us to dock?"

"*No, keep your distance!*" came the shouted reply. And then, after a pained couple of moments: "*Yes. Yes! We'll beam them over.*"

Eagan blinked. Reevaluating the situation, he reentered the conversation. "We'll go to the departure pad aft. It'll be three to transport, *Farragut*."

Dax straightened. "I'll tell the doctors we're going."

Eagan grabbed her arm. "I'm the third. You stay."

"But people are hurt—"

"I've had Starfleet training, you haven't."

"Then you'd better take me too," Kubisiak said, producing his phaser from underneath the seat. "I'm security when I'm not a taxi driver."

"Gotcha. You see?" Eagan said to her. "Someone's got to stay." He released her and reached for the cases on the deck. "Pilot, help bring these. They could come in handy."

"Aye."

Dax watched, helpless, as Eagan and Kubisiak gathered their goods and piled out of the cockpit. Leaving her alone with the planet, the starship, and the blinking comm panel.

Silent, but for the screams.

11

Dax had spent the last year telling herself that Starfleet hadn't worked out. In truth, she'd washed out. Too old to seriously vie for the highly competitive medical program, she'd done the initial weeks of training for the regular service—only to realize that her recruiting officers had only been interested in her celebrity. They'd wanted her to serve a public relations role, attracting cadets Starfleet wanted more than it wanted her.

A show pony, to use a term she'd learned from McCoy. She'd departed then. The Dax symbiont found Starfleet service intriguing, but that life would have to wait for another host.

But in the shuttle watching *Farragut*, Dax had found herself wishing that she'd stayed in just a bit longer, to pick up more skills. And she found herself aching for all those aboard the starship, people who might have been her comrades had things worked differently.

The cloud had departed. Or vanished. Or both. Dax had waited for an interminable hour, alone and unable to raise *Farragut* or her team on the comm. Then, she'd seen the vapor-like object emerge from a part of the starship's hull—not the same place where it had entered. It moved as if it were a living thing, yet nothing in *Leizu*'s computer archives described anything similar.

Then it was simply gone, as if it had always been a trick of the light.

She'd acted at that point, orders and consequences be

damned. Emony had never flown a shuttle before, much less piloted one into a landing bay. All that would have come later, had she stayed in Starfleet. But her preceding host Tobin had worked as an engineer, and had the hand-eye coordination needed for magic tricks; combining those skills with a forgiving piloting system and Emony's dogged focus, she'd stuck the landing.

Yet nothing in the lives of either of Dax's previous hosts prepared her for what she saw in *Farragut*'s halls. Death everywhere. Officers and enlisted alike had dropped where they'd stood, their faces and lips a ghastly blue. She'd remembered to wear an oxygen mask on the way out, but nothing could make her breathe normally. Not here.

The survivors she'd found were all panicked, and none of them were making much sense. She'd been able to piece together what had happened early on: For some reason, the officer at the weapons station—a rookie like her, she'd heard—had failed to fire on the cloud in time when it approached *Farragut*. It had traveled the halls and vents of the ship then, wreaking havoc and killing those unlucky enough to be in its path. Details of what had happened weren't entirely clear beyond that, but one thing was certain: Garrovick was dead, along with roughly half his crew.

And so, she discovered, was most of her team.

She had tracked them to the deck that main sickbay was on. Evidence was everywhere of the desperate defense that had been waged against the invading cloud; the anteroom to the clinic was barricaded with bodies, all in the same condition. One belonged to Kubisiak. His phaser still clutched in his withered hand, the pilot seemed to look up from the deck in a twisted expression of horror.

Garber and Winnock she found sprawled over patients. Rolling them over, she wondered if the *Farragut* officers they'd tended to had even been alive at the time. No matter: her colleagues had given their all, dying in the service of others, and that fit with everything she knew about them.

That left only one other missing from her party—her supervisor. But before she could search for Eagan, he came to her, his sagging frame supported by a dark-skinned older human in a blue uniform. Eagan's face was drained of color and his body was nearly limp, and yet his dangling hands clutched the handles of two medical cases.

Dax rushed to his side. "Sir!" She peeled off her oxygen mask, trying to get him to respond.

"*Dax?*" he mumbled, his eyes unfocused. "Take . . . these."

She tried to peel the cases from him, only to find that his grip was so tight she had to force his hands open.

"Set me . . . down, Ananke," Eagan rasped.

She recognized the name as belonging to *Farragut*'s medical officer; she'd corresponded with the man remotely in preparation for the study. He did as he was asked, resting Eagan's body in one of the few clear spaces on the deck. All the biobeds were in use, none by the living. Ananke directed Dax to bring a wet sponge.

"People reported a sickly sweet smell—and then collapsed," he said. "There's not a red blood cell left in any of the dead."

"What . . . what would *do* that?"

"*It* did." Taking the sponge, Ananke wiped Eagan's forehead. "He was the last person to encounter it before it withdrew. I don't think it finished what it was trying to do to him."

Dax brightened. "Then maybe he'll be okay."

Eagan groaned. "It . . . got me . . . *enough.*"

"Try to relax, Rudy," Ananke said. "I can't hit you with any more stimulants."

"Not . . . important," Eagan said. He called for Dax—and then squinted at her, upset, when she appeared, empty-handed. "I told you . . . take the cases . . ."

She'd set them down nearby. She gestured. "They're right there, sir."

"No," he said, attempting to lift his right hand. She reached for it—and tried not to recoil when it felt like half-thawed meat. "I said . . . *take the cases!* With you, in the shuttle!"

Turning back to the containers, Dax realized they were the diagnostic packs they'd intended to use at Tycho IV to test for the presence of local organisms that might impact their surveys.

"Both the kits have been exposed to the—to the whatever it was," Ananke said. "Eagan risked everything to get them into its path." The *Farragut* officer added handfuls of petri dishes to each case. "I'm enclosing tissue samples we've taken from the deceased—and I'll send my report to your shuttle. We can't spare a soul right now."

Dax understood. She stared at the cases. "Where should I take them?"

"One to Starbase 23, for sure," Ananke said. "It's close, and they'll have a proper quarantine facility for sample intake, in case there's some plague involved here."

Dax gulped. She guessed she was already exposed to whatever it was. But there was no worrying about that now. "I'll take care of it." Then she looked again. "And the other case?"

"Also . . . to the starbase," Eagan said, straining. "The Import . . . Inspection Service office. Understand?"

Dax wasn't sure she did, but she agreed anyway.

"They'll . . . want to see samples . . . firsthand. Tell them . . . *Eagan wants to get them to Leland.* Got it?"

"Leland," she said, memorizing. Then she did a double-take. "Wait. You want me to take medical samples to an *import office*?"

Eagan reached for her with his other hand and pulled himself feebly toward her. "If this . . . is what I think . . ." He lost focus and struggled to find words. "I'm depending . . . on you," he finally said. "*Go.*"

Dax looked to Ananke—and back to her boss. "Aye, Captain."

Eagan's hand slipped from hers and he sagged flat to the deck. His labored breaths ceased.

Ananke knelt and checked for vital signs with a tricorder. After a few moments, he lowered his gaze. "One hundred percent mortality rate." Ananke closed Eagan's eyes.

"Is it okay that I take these?" Dax asked, one case under each arm. "I'm not really a doctor." She wasn't even sure she could fly a shuttle through warp without the computer's help.

"You're on Rudy's team," Ananke said. "You've got clearance on medical matters." He gestured around him. "And I don't think we're going to run out of tissues to sample." He drew forth his communicator and flipped it open. "Ananke to bridge."

A weary human voice answered. *"Kirk here."*

"Clear shuttlecraft *Leizu* departure to Starbase 23, priority one, medical."

"Of course. Bridge out."

Ananke closed the communicator and stared at it. "That's the young man who didn't fire in time," he said. Seeing Dax waiting on his word, the doctor turned to face her. "Please," he implored, "see this through, for the sake of all who died."

"And lived," she said.

"No, I don't think anything will get us over today." He looked again at the communicator. "And some of us will have more trouble than others."

Stage Two
MURDER

You'll never be better than the people you work with. Look at Emperor Georgiou, back in the day. She surrounded herself with the worst of the worst, a wretched lot. One was a grinning madman who laughed gleefully as he murdered people.

A while ago, I found out he was my countryman. I didn't like being called "Smiley" so much after that . . .

—General Miles O'Brien
Road to Rebellion, 2375

12

It's like I'm invisible, Dax thought.

The Starfleet admiral and the human named Leland had been talking past each other since they had met at either side of the briefing table, grave-looking entourages in tow. Dax had been seated at the end, her back to the screen showing the visuals from *Farragut* that were part of Ananke's report. She was more than happy not to look at those again.

But four hours into the scheduled thirty-minute briefing between Federation officials, Starfleet, and whatever Leland was, Dax had begun to think back fondly on all the Olympic panels that had judged her over the years. Those meetings were neither organized nor rational, but at least when they argued over her, she was out of earshot. Now, Dax was hearing female pronouns left and right in the crosstalk, and understanding neither what the others were talking about, nor why she was being discussed so heatedly. She was just a courier, the bringer of bad news.

But as news went, it didn't get much worse.

The last hours had been a whirlwind. The nature of Eagan's research project had required a fast shuttlecraft, handy for zipping between the various starships whose crews were under study. That had more than served Dax in the emergency: *Leizu* had arrived from *Farragut* in short order, once she'd figured out the automatic navigation system.

At Starbase 23, she'd provided Eagan's samples and Ananke's report to the Federation without delay. Its officials had been grateful in the extreme. Starfleet had heard from *Farragut* via subspace, of course, but its recovery vessels were still getting underway to

Tycho IV. It was entirely possible something else bad might yet happen to the starship; she preferred not to think about it.

If the Federation had been deeply concerned, the Import Inspection Service's response was another matter. A receptionist in the featureless office had told her Leland was not on the base, after first denying that anyone by that name worked there. The worker had then asked her for her case of samples anyway. Dax had declined, insisting on hanging on to it until she could fulfill Eagan's exact dying order. She'd retired to the Federation-supplied quarters for an exhausted catnap—

—only to awake to find the case was empty. In fact, on examination, she realized the whole container had been replaced by one that was nearly identical. No work appeared to go on in the Import Inspection Service offices, but it apparently was so interested in her baggage it was willing to send someone to break, enter, and supply a duplicate case.

Leland did arrive, the next morning, in a vessel traveling alongside *Pacifica*, the Starfleet flagship of Admiral Cornwell. The woman had treated her with kindness and compassion, completely sympathetic about Dax's ordeal. Leland, for his part, had been more clinical, though not entirely detached; his speech seemed to quicken with every mention of the cloud.

The Cloud—now described in documentation with a capital letter—had been mentioned interminably in the meeting since. There was the fact that it appeared to have changed its chemical makeup even in the seconds between Eagan's and Ananke's readings. And the fact that in the main, it seemed composed of dikironium, a substance that should not exist in nature. And that it could not possibly be alive, though it gave all evidence of having feasted on its victims' blood.

Most jarring to Dax: the news that something like it might have been seen once before, a quarter-century earlier. Yet nobody had done anything about it, then or since.

That was the point where they lost her, with the Federation

officials, Starfleet officers, and Leland's black-clad support staff talking back and forth.

"... *no way to know if these incidents were connected without more data* ..."

"... *why couldn't it be a Klingon doomsday device, since we were willing to do the same to them* ..."

"... *could never ever find the* Jadama Rohn *if we wanted to, given where it went* ..."

"... *treaties are made to be broken—especially against a threat like this* ..."

"... *publicizing could start a panic* ..."

"... *she isn't the same person at all* ..."

"... *she's the perfect candidate* ..."

"... *she's untrained, untrustworthy* ..."

"... *she* ..."

"... *she* ..."

"... *she* ..."

Dax slapped the table. "Enough!"

The officials stopped midsentence and stared at her.

"You keep talking about me like I'm not here," Dax said. "Stop it!"

Leland flinched, seeming puzzled to be addressed by her at all. "We weren't talking about you."

"Well, you're sure not talking *to* me!" She turned and gestured to the horrors on screen. "Two hundred people are dead—doesn't that mean anything to you?"

"*Certainly,*" said the one person attending the meeting via hologram: a dark-haired Vulcan Federation official whose name she'd never caught. "*Their deaths mean a great deal. This discussion is about what to do next.*"

Cornwell opened her hands wide. "Emony, the person we were arguing about isn't you. There's someone who might—I repeat, *might*—be able to get us more information about what happened. But we don't really trust her."

Dax was flabbergasted. "What, is she incompetent?"

Leland chortled. "Oh, she's more than competent."

"She's a handful," a Starfleet officer said.

"Of plutonium," another added.

The person poses a threat," the holographic Vulcan said. *"She cannot be trusted not to flee. And if she did discover the Cloud's origins, I would not trust her with that information either."*

"We manage risk," Leland said, gesturing to his team. "We wouldn't send her alone. We'd watch her."

"Like on Thionoga?" Cornwell asked. "You had sensors all over that place and a thousand guards."

He frowned at her. "If we're going to start *this* again—"

"*I said, stop!*" Dax faced the image of the Vulcan. "This woman. Can she find out something that would prevent *that* from happening again?" She pointed to the screen. "Can she?"

The Vulcan clasped his hands. *"It is improbable."*

"But there's a chance?"

"Small."

"Then that's enough. Get her." She faced Leland. "They want you to surround her with a team. Do it."

She paused, momentarily startled at the extent to which she'd taken over a roomful of people, evidently authorities in their fields.

And then she said something she wasn't expecting to say. "Once you've done that—you put *me* on the team."

Leland raised his hands and smirked. "Whoa. Absolutely not."

Cornwell looked to her, again kindly. "I'm not sure, Emony. I understand wanting to help, but that's not your area of expertise."

"Yeah, no balance beam where we're going," Leland interjected.

Dax smoldered at that—and proceeded to count on her fingers. "Rodolfo Eagan. Mae Winnock. Vihaan Garber. People I've spent the better part of the year working with. Even Kubisiak, the pilot. They were counting on me to make sure you found out about this, to make sure you made certain that this never happened again. Those people—and everyone else aboard *Farragut*. So, no. I'm not going to let this go, not now. I will see it through."

Leland picked up his data slate and faced the others. "I think we need to move on."

"*No*," she said, standing up. "Yes, you're right. I'm Emony Dax—a gymnast. But I'm also a four-time gold medalist. A hundred billion people I've never met can name everyone I've ever dated. I'm sure if I go to the civilian section of this starbase and call a press conference about going back into competition, I could get on the feed of every journalist in the quadrant."

The Vulcan raised an eyebrow. *"What . . . would you say?"*

"That the spacelanes aren't safe—because they aren't. Because they're being traversed by a killer cloud, waiting to drink people dry." She put her hands on the table and spoke emphatically. "Wait. Did I say *a* cloud? Maybe there are dozens of them!"

"We don't know that," Cornwell said.

"You don't know that there aren't. I've heard that much here today. And what will people think if I tell them that the Federation wants to keep this whole thing a secret?"

Leland and his companions looked at one another. He set his jaw and stared at her. "You won't do that."

"Are you going to stop me?" She stared at him. "Oh, I forget. You break into people's quarters. Who *are* you, anyway?" She'd never seen Starfleet officers in black before, nor their special badges. "If you're going, I'm going too. I sure as hell don't have anything better to do. The Cloud ate my job!"

Quiet fell—and her energy spent, she sat down, staring forward.

Cornwell regarded her, before looking to the Vulcan. "Ambassador, a team could work. Dax could be on it—as an observer."

"*The Federation will require more insurance than that,*" he replied. "*If you're deploying the emperor, she must be escorted by people who know who she is, and what she's capable of.*"

"We'll have people," Leland volunteered.

"*Not just Section 31. The Federation Security Agency must be represented.*"

"Babysitters," Leland grumbled. He looked to the ceiling. "She'll never tolerate it."

"She'll deal—or else," Cornwell said. She looked thoughtful for a moment. "I think I can find some people, Ambassador."

Leland looked to her, his eyes narrowing. "Who are you thinking of?"

"You worry about your own people." The admiral faced Dax. "Emony, are you sure this is what you want?"

Dax nodded—only to turn to the ambassador. "Wait. Did you just say '*emperor*'?"

13

Regrets, to a Terran, were alien things. When the entire basis of a society rested upon the right of the individual to act arbitrarily at any moment, most people did exactly that.

It wasn't conducive to societal stability, of course; without the Empire serving to channel ambitions, anarchy would result. But it was helpful to mental health, Georgiou thought. The only frustrated people were the ones out of power, and they kept themselves busy trying to do something about it. Everyone else in her universe would have little use for Admiral Cornwell and her counselor ilk. Nothing beat melancholia like bacchanalia.

The days in solitary since the admiral's sole visit, however, had been enough to make Georgiou regret her parting comments to Leland. She'd asked that nobody else bother her—and nobody had, with even her meals being transported in and out. Cornwell had evidently decided that Georgiou was capable of tricking even the most dedicated jailer into opening her force field through one ruse or another. It was a nice show of respect, but it had severely limited her options.

So, when Leland returned—with a lithe blonde in a Section 31 uniform in tow—Georgiou took immediate interest. "I'm back," he said, standing in front of her cell.

"No admiral, I see." Georgiou picked up her chair, spun it one hundred eighty degrees, and straddled it before the energy field, as if prepared to get the latest gossip. "Have you brought me a roommate? Or is this ingenue another one of Cornwell's therapists?"

"I'm Emony Dax," the woman replied. "I'm—uh, working with Leland."

"Another little girl," Georgiou said. "Did you get her from the same place you found your alleged leader of the Forest Circle? The one I threw off the catwalk?"

Alarmed, Dax looked to Leland. "*What?*"

"His agent. His plant on Thionoga," Georgiou said. "I threw her onto the hull of a starship. She broke a few bones, easily repaired." She looked Dax up and down. "You're wiry. I bet you'd fare better."

A little unnerved, Dax glanced at Leland before looking back at Georgiou. "They, uh, told me what your story was, er—"

"Emperor."

"*Emperor.* It's kind of unbelievable."

"*I'm* unbelievable. Believe me." Georgiou clasped her hands. "But I'll give you this: you do make for a better Trill than Leland did. You may even be the genuine article. Although I didn't know too many of your kind where I came from."

Eyes down, Dax spoke cautiously. "What—what do your people know about Trills?"

"That you still exist, which means something. It helps that you're a lot more attractive than a lot of the aliens out there. It's an evolutionary aid not to be gruesome. You also mind your own business better than just about any race we've encountered."

"Another helpful trait, I guess."

"Or maybe you all just have something to hide." She looked keenly at the woman, who had gone pale. "You're always acting *furtive* about something."

Leland seemed to notice Dax's discomfort. "Ignore her. I told you, she likes to intimidate everybody she meets."

"Everyone needs a hobby," Georgiou said. "No matter. I suppose you must be important, for Cornwell to come racing back to Starbase 23."

Leland regarded her coolly. "What makes you think we did that?"

"The ship changed headings quickly a couple of days ago, and it was unplanned," Georgiou said. "There's a little miss in the inertial dampers that happens when your vessels drop out of warp suddenly—only an engineer would feel it. My people solved that problem in capital ships a while ago. I'm surprised you're not as far along."

Leland frowned. "I'll make a note of that. But how—"

"The food they transport into my cell got fresher yesterday—though not necessarily better. Your shipboard arboretums aren't large enough to raise vegetables to waste on prisoners."

"But how did you know it was Starbase *23*?" Dax asked.

Georgiou smiled primly. Leland glared at Dax and said, "She didn't know. You just told her!"

Dax blanched   and the emperor chuckled. "I already knew she wasn't Section 31, Leland. She doesn't have the sullen look that says she's lost faith in everything she's ever believed in. She also has too much hair."

He ignored her. "I've brought her here on special assignment. She's the only survivor of a team that . . . ran into some trouble."

"Is that so?" Georgiou couldn't believe such a little slip of a girl had done anything. "What did you do, my dear—hide in a cargo unit?"

"You don't need the details," he said. "We're here for yours." Leland got down to business. "What do you know of the Troika? The astropolitical entity, I mean."

The question was out of nowhere, and Georgiou leaned forward with interest. "Why do you want to know?"

"Why do you refuse to answer?"

"Because the information will cost you."

"What's your price?"

Georgiou stood and began pacing. "Since our little dinner earlier this month, I haven't left the brig once. At least at Thionoga I got to walk to the mess hall."

Leland snorted. "Yeah, we know what happened next."

"Exactly what you wanted to happen—up to a point. The vaunted security apparatus of a Federation starship ought to be able to figure out a way to let me take a lap around the saucer section."

The spymaster considered it. "I'll see what I can do. Good enough?"

She shook her head and gestured to her table, now bare. "As long as you're bringing in food from the starbase, get me something from the executive kitchen. I know your brass doesn't eat the same garbage they give the enlisted."

"Is that it?"

"No, but until you get me a wine list it'll have to do." She stopped pacing and looked directly at them. "I *destroyed* the Troika. Not too long ago."

Leland's eyes widened. "One of your fleets did it?"

"Yes, but under my direct command. I enjoyed that one. They were in a real armpit of the Beta Quadrant—even the Klingons didn't want it. But we weren't going to allow a bunch of weirdos to declare their territory off-limits."

Leland looked to Dax. "I told you she'd have gotten in."

"That's right," Georgiou said, studying her fingernails. "Three species, all different, all bizarre. I enslaved one, massacred another, annihilated the third. It was barely worth it—they had nothing worth taking. But they defended every meter of the place like it hid buried treasure." She smiled. "It's so much better when they put up a fight."

Dax frowned. "You're happy—because people you conquered fought back?"

"They should melt away like the Trills, you mean? Cooperating and keeping their mouths shut?" Georgiou snorted with derision. "The Troika at least earned my respect." She peered at Leland. "How is it that you know nothing about them?"

"Who said that?"

"You did, when you asked me."

"The Federation's had an agreement for decades not to broach the borders of Troika space," Leland said. "The little we know about them came from an encounter with a human merchant who's allowed to work the area, years ago. That's who gave us the name Troika."

"Ah, yes. Quadrillion."

"Quintilian," Leland replied, startled. "You know him?"

"Know him? I killed him." She looked to Dax, who seemed all out of stunned expressions. "He's the reason I know the Troika name, too, as a matter of fact."

Leland laughed. "Now *that's* something."

Georgiou's eyes narrowed. "What?"

"Because he taught that name to you *here* too." He turned his data slate toward her. "To *our* Georgiou, I mean. She's the one who made contact, back in 2233."

"Another one of my droll coincidences. Well, I certainly hope I slept with him. He was a man who made an impression. I'm sure the younger version of him was delectable."

"It was a brief meeting," Leland said. "But it began a long correspondence between the two—"

"That's no fun."

"—giving us most of what little we know about the Troika. And that relationship is the reason we're here."

It dawned on Georgiou that Leland had more on his mind than just information gathering—and Dax, shuffling uncomfortably, confirmed it when she asked Leland, "Can I just tell her?"

"You'd better not," Leland said, continuing in what Georgiou regarded to be his let-me-handle-this voice. "Section 31 has reason to believe that there is information in Troika space that would be useful."

"Thanks, that isn't vague at all." Georgiou studied Dax. "And it relates to what happened to *you*, I suppose."

Leland kept talking. "We want to insert a team of investigators, but we're unaware of their detection capabilities—and are concerned that abrogating the treaty might be counterproductive at this moment."

"Because it's astride what is now border space between the Federation and Klingon territory, and you're afraid of pushing these neutrals to the other side—especially when your peace is based on blackmail." Georgiou stared at him, exasperated. "This would work so much faster if you simply told me everything."

"You wouldn't respect that."

"I don't respect you now."

"Well, I'll tell you this: as far as we know, only one person has the ability to get the Troika to accept visitors—Quintilian. And there's only one visitor he'll accept: Philippa Georgiou."

That amused her. "Apparently my counterpart made an impression too. I wouldn't have thought she had it in her."

Dax looked confused. "Isn't she *you*?"

"She's a shadow. A specter. A lesser version who was never taught to go after what she wanted. And she died stupidly." Georgiou looked to Leland. "You're sure of this invitation?"

"Quintilian's been asking her to visit for years, in the messages she showed Starfleet Command."

"And also in the messages she didn't show them," Georgiou said. "I'm sure you've seen those too."

"Something like that."

Georgiou ruminated. There was a way to escape in this, certainly—but she had to be sure the offer was legitimate. She wouldn't put it past Leland to run another charade, just for sport. "Quintilian wouldn't know that your Georgiou was dead?"

"The messages show he was only communicating with her when his fleet would pop out from Troika space for one reason or another. But as far as we can tell, nobody's emerged from Troika space for more than a peek since the war began. They may not even know it's over."

"So I would make the contact, posing as her—and lead your team."

Leland chortled. "You'd go. Not lead. And you wouldn't be alone. You'd ask to bring a delegation."

Full of people to keep an eye on me, she thought. She looked over his shoulder. "Where's Cornwell? I can't imagine she'd allow this at all, presuming she has anything to say about it."

"She does get a say—but I won't get into that," Leland said. "We'd want to go within a week."

"Are you in?" Dax asked.

"I'll consider it." Georgiou gestured around the cell. "I have a busy schedule here, you know." Then she looked back at Dax. "I admit I can't imagine what *you* might have been involved in to cause them to drop everything and do this. You're no spy—and you're far too fit to be one of Leland's dreary analysts."

"I was a gymnast," Dax said. "In the Olympics."

"Ah, yes. I've heard of those. We have games, too, for the emperor. But the stakes for the participants are quite a bit higher."

14

Thionoga Detention Center

As soon as Sean Finnegan pushed his ore cart into the light of the space station's processing center, his workday immediately brightened. "Ah, Kitty, you're a sight for sore eyes!"

"That's *admiral*," Cornwell said, advancing across the factory floor toward him. "And I'm surprised you can see anything with that swelling."

"Oh, this?" Finnegan wiped the rock dust from his hand onto his tunic and pointed to his face. "I got into a wee scrap with the garda this morning."

She frowned. "One guard did that to you?"

"Not one. The *garda*. You know, the whole detail."

The admiral looked with alarm at the sentries stationed around, all of whom were paying Finnegan at least some attention.

"They said I might be getting a guest, but I never imagined you'd come back." He looked at his shabby uniform. "Sorry I didn't have a chance to clean up."

The admiral then turned to the companion she'd entered with: no less a figure than Warden Ohtak, who appeared discomfited by Finnegan's state. Cornwell addressed her sternly. "I'm going to want to speak with him alone."

"We're not letting him out of our sight again," Ohtak said.

"Are you afraid of what he'll tell me about this place? From what I can already see, he's been badly abused."

"Actually, *he's* been the one picking fights with the guards," the warden said. "We've finally got surveillance back online after your debacle. You can see for yourself."

"S'truth," Finnegan said, shrugging. "But you're right. I'd

rather not talk about this last dustup with the warden here." He glanced at Uhtak. "Begging your pardon, ma'am."

The warden threw up her hands and shouted for the guards to give Finnegan and the admiral some space. His work foreman was the last to retire. "Talk fast. You still have a quota to make!"

"Up your arse!"

Before the Tellarite could respond, Cornwell took Finnegan by the elbow and guided him away from the others.

It was a relief to get away from the cart. He'd spent all day inside the asteroid Thionoga was attached to, chopping for dilithium ore while standing atop gravity plating; the sort of precision work that couldn't be done with machines.

Reaching the shadows beneath one of the ore processing units, she located one of the first-aid kits and found him something for his face. "You were going to tell me why you would pick a fight with an entire detail?"

Finnegan looked back at the warden, now distant, and chuckled. "Well, to tell the truth, I was a bit fluthered, if you know what I mean."

"I don't."

"Langers. You know, ossified." He peered at her. "I can't believe you didn't pick up a word or two when you were in Ireland."

"I must not have been going to the right places." But the admiral caught his drift. "How is it you manage to be inebriated while in prison?"

Finnegan chuckled. "Thionoga has a lot of artisans, you might say." He knelt forward and spoke covertly. "It turns out the native breads they pass out to the Orions ferment in the saliva of Tellarites."

Cornwell winced. "And you drink it?"

"I sure wouldn't. That's disgusting."

"I agree."

"But the Nausicaans have a liking for it." Finnegan jabbed

his thumb back in Ohtak's direction. "Including the trustees who stock the warden's pantry. They're happy, I'm happy." He grinned, satisfied. "It really does take all kinds."

Cornwell finished tending to his bruise. "You are, as ever, a spectacle."

"That's what your *da* used to call me." He grinned, his missing front tooth in evidence. Then he considered for a moment. "Would it help if I told you they won't medicate my injuries here, and that the drink eases the pain?"

"Would it be the truth if you told me that?"

"Would telling the truth get me out of here?"

"Not on its own." Cornwell put away the hypospray and pulled a data slate from the pouch slung over her arm. "You can't believe how long it took for us to sort out exactly who'd put you here, and why."

"I admit I'm a bit hazy about it now."

"You punched an alien prince in the face."

Finnegan's eyes widened. "Ah, that's right."

Cornwell read from the slate. "Apparently since your last dismissal from Starfleet, you've had a variety of odd jobs—including working security for the ceremonial heads of state of Troyius. They dumped you here after you broke the crown prince's jaw."

"Well, now, to be fair, he had it coming to him. A man shouldn't commit to a contest, no matter what his station, if he's going to be a sore loser."

"What contest?"

Finnegan scratched his head. "There was drinking—and I know it had to do with large pieces of furniture and a window." He raised his index fingers. "There was definitely some fire involved."

"That explains the pictures of the palace," Cornwell said, shivering as she dismissed the file from her data slate. "How'd you come to this, Sean? No one's ever had any problem with your performance of your duties. You were the top of your class—competent at just about anything we assigned to you."

"Competent? That's all they've said?" He laughed and gestured to his ore cart. "Ask the foreman. I get done early."

"That's the problem. You always had too much time on your hands. At Starfleet Academy, you were a one-cadet hazing committee."

"Someone had to do it."

"No, they didn't," Cornwell said. "We don't have hazing committees, Sean."

He chortled. "Are you telling me you want a Starfleet Academy where no one ever tests the cadets' mettle? Sees whether they can survive a little ribbing?"

"Yes, Sean, I am telling you that." Cornwell grabbed his collar and bared her teeth at him. "That's *exactly* what we want. No more brawling!"

"You think Shiner Hendrix would be captain already if I hadn't knocked him around a bit? Or that Guiler fellow? Or Stovall?"

"Have you noticed that *you're* not a captain? Have you wondered why? I'll give you a minute if you need to work it out, but someone at the top of his class really shouldn't need it."

"I was tops, wasn't I?"

"For five years. Most people are out in—" She released him and turned away. "Never mind. It's useless."

Finnegan watched her for a moment, and then stared down into his ore cart. He and doing the right thing had never gotten along for more than a few days at a time. Thionoga was, by far, the worst place he'd wound up; maybe the universe was telling him something in bringing Kitty to him.

He looked to her. "I want to say, I do appreciate your looking after me all these years."

Cornwell glared back at him—and then softened. "Well, your grandmother was more than a neighbor. Before you were born, my mother wasn't around a lot. Your nana was very good to me."

"Rest her soul," Finnegan said. "I loved staying with her. It probably helped me survive past age ten."

She chuckled. "I always imagined you had a lot of brothers back home and roughhoused all the time."

"Sisters, and they could sure deliver a punch. Those summers were like a time-out." He looked down and sighed. "I've never really thanked you for sending all the messages over the years—you know, the ones to get me back into the Academy, and then back into Starfleet. You've given me more chances than I deserve."

He looked up after a moment, to see Cornwell staring at him, evaluating. "Well, I may have something else."

Finnegan's heart leapt. "Oh, if you could get me into Starfleet again!"

She put up her hands. "I never said—"

"You're so right about the others passing me by. You know who I saw a ways back? Little Jimmy Kirk! I ran into him on Earth—I think he was avoiding me." He cracked a gap-toothed smile. "He told me he got *Farragut*. I told him he needed to eat less alien food."

"What?"

"*Farragut*. It sounds like a digestive complaint." Seeing her react with revulsion, he added: "It's a joke."

Cornwell finally understood. "No, you wouldn't have heard. Not in here."

"Heard?" Finnegan's smile broke. "What, did Jimmy make captain already? That's really . . . well, *soon*." He shook his head. "Maybe it was that last punch in the gut for luck."

"Sean, just shut up." Cornwell called up something new on her data slate and turned it toward him. "Shut up and look."

Finnegan cast his eyes on the imagery—and the breath went out of him. The halls of a proud starship, strewn with uniformed bodies. The face of every corpse shown in close-up was blue and contorted. "This is *Farragut*? What the devil happened?"

"We're only now getting recovery vessels out to her. Much of what we know comes to us from a civilian medical researcher who was first on the scene," the admiral said. "There was an invasive cloud that attacked—"

"A cloud? A cloud of what?"

"Dikironium is the main substance detected. But the cloud acted as if it was alive. It sought out the crew—and drained them of their red blood cells."

Finnegan framed furtively through the images. "Is he alive?"

"Who, Kirk?"

"Yes!"

"He's one of the survivors. But they all had a rough time of it." Cornwell nearly had to pry the data slate out of Finnegan's hand. "As a matter of fact, Sean, what happened to *Farragut* is the reason I returned here."

That baffled him. "You can't be so down on recruits you'd look for replacements in Thionoga."

"That's not it. The Federation has a problem, and we need your help. You have a connection . . ."

She paused, leaving him puzzled. "Unless you're in the market for pre-chewed bread, I'm not sure what else I can do."

"It's more who you are than what you can do. I mean, the Federation needs *you* to do something, but—" Cornwell stopped again and touched her forehead. "This is so frustrating."

Seeing her unease, Finnegan raised his palms upward. "This is Little Sean here—you know, the fast study? You used to say I could learn anything in five minutes. Just take it from the top."

She gestured to the slate. "We've only seen victims like these once before. Twenty-five years ago, on a trading ship called *Jadama Rohn*. And the person who saw them was Philippa Georgiou."

Finnegan recognized the name. "That woman I helped the other day called herself Georgiou."

"That's right."

Something new occurred to him. "*Philippa*, though. Wasn't there a captain by that name?" Focusing, he spoke with more assurance. "Yeah. Won the Star Cross."

"There was. She died in the war."

"Hate to hear that. I never met her—I've been in and out of service . . ." Then he scratched his head. "What, is there some connection between these two? Are they related?"

"We need to take this up someplace else," she said, waving for the warden to approach. As they waited, she eyed him. "This is going to be a little complicated. You are sober now, aren't you?"

"I don't know. What time is it?"

15

Shuttlecraft *Doolittle*

Kitty, you're diabolical, Finnegan thought. She'd had him figured out years earlier—and she'd also devised a way to keep him quiet for much of the flight from Thionoga. Waiting aboard *Doolittle* had been a Starfleet medic who knew dentistry, and who had spent the past half hour replacing the tooth Finnegan had lost to Georgiou days earlier.

The medic stepped back. "It's a perfect fit."

"You're a saint." Finnegan bit down a couple of times. "They say the dentist at Thionoga learned his trade from a Klingon who skins wild *targ*s with a dull spoon. I'm not sure what a *targ* is, but I gave it a pass." He shook the medic's hand. "I owe you a drink, friend."

"Just stay safe. I've seen rugby players with more original equipment." The medic retreated to the rear of the shuttle. Finnegan stretched and headed for the cockpit.

"Good as new?" Cornwell asked from the pilot's seat as the stars flew by.

"Good enough. Handy you had that fellow along." He claimed the chair beside her. "Shall I take it again from the top, teach?"

"*Admiral.* And yes."

"So you're telling me this woman who looks like Philippa Georgiou *is* her—but from a different universe, where she's an evil emperor."

"Was," Cornwell said.

"Was evil?"

"Was an emperor. We don't know if she's still evil."

"And in this other world, I'm her loyal lapdog."

"Deadly assassin. But yes. Someone she trusted."

Finnegan sat back in the navigator's chair and rubbed his temples. "And I thought my head was hurting before."

Cornwell had worked quickly. The Federation had fixed things with the Troyius royal family, leading to his speedy release from Thionoga. He was certain Warden Ohtak was probably celebrating his departure still—and discovering she had fewer bottles of her favorite spirits than she thought she had.

For Finnegan's part, he needed a drink.

"Our Georgiou," Cornwell said, using a nomenclature they'd resorted to repeatedly, "only had a basic tricorder when she boarded *Jadama Rohn*. But later on she analyzed the data and interpolated a malady that matches what we saw on *Farragut*. She also thought she saw a cloud—and both those things she reported to her commanding officer."

"And that's the officer you said that recognized it on *Farragut*."

"Right. And before Eagan died, he dispatched a member of his team to alert both the Federation and Section 31."

"*Those* guys," Finnegan grumbled.

"Yes, those guys." Cornwell looked away from the controls. "You know about Section 31?"

"They turfed me out after four weeks a few years ago."

"How were you even in?"

"One of your recommendations caught the attention of a recruiter who needed someone that had an in with the Antaran embassy."

"On Vulcan—where you'd done some security work."

"I was supposed to sneak back into the embassy and look for . . ." Finnegan paused, remembering. "Well, let's just say it's best if we don't go to wherever Antarans come from." He thought for a moment. "Or Vulcan."

Cornwell sighed. "It's a wonder my recommendations count for anything anymore."

Finnegan could tell the admiral had gone back and forth

repeatedly about bringing him in. He hastened to sound useful. "I think I actually get it. You can't trust this woman, but you have to. And you think she might accept me helping her, because I was this ally of hers from the other side."

"Leland's going to pair her up with veteran agents. That's what the Federation Security Agency wants too." Her jaw clenched. "I don't think that'll fly. She'll ditch them on general principle. But from the little surveillance Thionoga still had working—and from what you said—it's clear she likes you." Cornwell paused. "Maybe that's too strong a word. She'll tolerate you."

"Because she thinks I'm Crackerjack."

"*Blackjack.* Like the game."

"Ah, yes. We played it back at the Academy. But I'll tell you, I'm more partial to ones where you drink. The cards just get in the way."

"You *have* to stop saying things like that," Cornwell said. She soldiered on. "From the interviews we've done, we get the impression her Blackjack is someone who's ruthless, efficient, and trusted—though maybe not a talker."

"She already knows I'm not that person. How hard should I try to be the guy she wants me to be? Should I snarl and spit and break things?"

"Do whatever's necessary—within reason. This is a psychological play, Sean. I figured we needed options."

"Well, she may opt not to accept me." He pointed to his replaced tooth. "She did that, remember?"

The shuttle jolted as it dropped from warp. Finnegan spotted the large Starfleet vessel up ahead. He oohed. "*Nimitz* class. Yours?"

"She's called *Pacifica*. We got a double play-on-words there—for the water planet, and also Nimitz, who commanded in the Pacific." She patted the console. "Her shuttles are named after Pacific aviators."

"That's a relief. I thought *Doolittle* was a remark on my career so far."

U.S.S. Pacifica

The Section 31 operations trainer paced around Georgiou's desk, the only one in the onboard center. "Let's try again," the Andorian said in a flinty voice. "What do we do when we need to inform your controller of your location and no encrypted subspace link is available?"

"I stand up and rip off those stupid antennae," Georgiou replied. "Then I shove them up your nostrils for daring to include yourself in the royal *we.*"

The trainer threw his data slate to the deck in disgust. "Teaching you is impossible! You haven't the slightest interest in becoming a useful asset. And that's exactly what I'm going to tell Leland!"

"Give him my love," Georgiou called out as the Andorian stormed into the hall.

The second the door behind him sealed, her gaze fell upon the data slate, still on the deck. Casting her eyes about, she knelt and reached for it—

—only to have it disappear, carried away by a transporter beam.

Typical, she thought. They hadn't stopped watching her, even after releasing her from the brig and putting her back into a Section 31 uniform. And she was sure they wouldn't stop, not while she was still aboard Cornwell's starship.

It was bad enough that Georgiou had been forced to endure a crash course in Section 31's operations for the second time in a few weeks. What made it worse was that she'd also once again had Federation Security Agency officials breathing down her neck, interrupting her "studies" at irregular intervals to evaluate the potential threat she posed. And whenever those sessions ended, a Section 31 analyst was sure to be along, grilling her for her every memory of the Troika.

The greatest insult was that it was all another deceit. The

Trill couldn't possibly have been part of anything important for Section 31; if Emony Dax were any greener, she'd be an Orion. The whole thing, Georgiou had decided, was all about one thing and one thing only. The real reason Leland—and possibly his digital overlord, Control—had taken such an interest in her: the future. *Their* future.

For years, Georgiou had known about the Federation's universe from the records brought to the Terran Empire in 2155 by Hoshi Sato. She, who named herself empress when she realized what immense power she had; she, who changed her title to "emperor" when she understood she never again needed to care what any male thought. Georgiou had chosen her "Iaponius" name to suggest a connection to Sato's homeland.

The records about the Federation's universe found aboard *Defiant* went to 2268, about a decade ahead. Starfleet and the Federation knew from Michael Burnham that some traveler from their future had gone to Georgiou's past, but the emperor doubted *Discovery*'s crew had shared many more details than that. Georgiou supported that caution. It wouldn't do to warn *Defiant* away from its date with destiny if it meant unpredictable results for her own existence. It was a good bet, however, that Section 31 and Leland knew at least as much as the Federation did, if not more. She suspected he'd been more involved with time-travel research than he'd been letting on. It was all a farce. Leland wanted her around for what she knew, not what she could do—and he had figured she'd be more likely to spill her guts outside a prison cell.

It would help if I really did know the future, Georgiou thought. But her secret fact—and current grief—was that as emperor, she hadn't studied the alternate historical records in depth. She'd been busy consolidating power—and the *Defiant* files, so long the reward for new emperors, had already lost much of their value. What had mattered in her universe was the immense power of *Defiant* itself, and the technological

secrets its records held; knowledge about locations and species not yet visited in her universe also had been useful. But
most of that information had already been acted upon by her
predecessors. Its impact could be seen both in the Empire's
starships and the map of imperial territory; conquests already
made. "The good stuff," to use an expression of her universe's
Lorca, was gone.

What remained was trivia, mostly for entertainment purposes. There was little actionable intelligence in the fact that
the Klingon Empire attacked the Federation in this universe.
Sure, it might have underscored that the species was a potential
threat, but Terran emperors had started addressing that years
before.

Leland, of course, didn't know any of that. She'd had some
fun, suggesting, sometimes with no more than a raised eyebrow, that she knew more about the future than she actually
did. But whatever amusement that might have held for her had
long since been exhausted. Something had to give, and soon.

The door to the training center whisked open, admitting
a meek-looking human years her senior. She'd dealt with him
before: Pettigrew, a Federation observer charged with indoctri-
nating her in their beliefs.

She sighed. "Now what? Shall I recite the pledge to the
flag?"

Pettigrew looked around the featureless room. "What flag?"

"The one in all our hearts."

He grinned. "Starfleet has oaths. We don't. But I have
something here that might qualify." He placed his data slate on
her desk. "A ceremony recently took place on Earth, following
the events of the Klingon War. It may teach you better than I
could."

Georgiou rolled her eyes—and then froze as she cast them
onto the small screen.

Michael!

Pettigrew noted her interest. "In this room, you can cast

it to the surrounding screens." He touched a control on the slate, and instantly Georgiou found herself sitting in Starfleet Headquarters, watching Cornwell preside over a presentation ceremony to the *Discovery* crew. Around and behind her, cadets and VIPs listened with rapt attention to Michael Burnham as she pontificated.

"—will not take shortcuts on the path to righteousness," Burnham said. *"No, we will not break the rules that protect us from our basest instincts. No, we will not allow desperation to destroy moral authority."*

"I'm told you know this young woman," Pettigrew said. "She sees our ideals clearly."

Georgiou tried to tune him out.

"Some say that in life there are no second chances," Burnham said. *"Experience tells me that this is true. But we can only look forward."*

The emperor smoldered. She had not heard from this universe's Burnham at all since they parted company in the underground temple of Molor. Georgiou wondered if Leland or Cornwell had shared anything about her present situation with Michael. Whatever the answer, the doppelgänger of her adopted daughter hadn't contacted her. Why should she? Gallivanting across the galaxy had to be much more fun.

And now, here she was, addressing the faithful, assuring them of their—and her—righteousness. She'd even said the word.

"—we will continue exploring. Discovering new worlds, new civilizations. Yes, that is the United Federation of Planets."

"But it is not the Terran Empire," Georgiou silently replied.

"Yes. That is Starfleet."

"Section 31 not included."

"Yes, that is who we are—and who we will always be."

But it is not me—and it never will be. Georgiou's anger rose. Wrath, at Leland, at Cornwell, at the Federation. At Michael, for bringing her to this misbegotten universe. And abandoning her to it.

She was done. It was time to go. Time to leave.

Time to kill somebody.

Pettigrew saw that she was lost in thought. "A wonderful speech, wasn't it?"

She looked at the old man—and then the data slate on the desk before her. Her mind churned. Then, she smiled at him. "It *is* wonderful. Please, let's listen to it again. More closely, this time . . ."

16

The man named Leland laughed so hard tears came to his eyes. He tried to speak but couldn't. Finnegan put his hand on the guy's shoulder and joined in the glee. He had no idea what the Section 31 chief was on, but he figured it had to be good.

"I'm sorry," Leland said, when he finally could speak. "I thought you said the Federation gave you one of its slots on the mission team."

"Ah," Finnegan said, a finger to the air. "The *admiral* did."

Leland nearly broke out again at that, before quickly regaining composure. "I'm sure she had her reasons. Glad I bumped into you." He looked down at what Finnegan was carrying. "Sorry I jostled your, uh—"

"Popcorn," Finnegan said, displaying the container he'd special-ordered from the galley. "Part of the training."

"Of course."

"Want some?"

"I'll pass."

Finnegan had another thought and withdrew his hand from Leland's shoulder. "Er—sorry for nearly bashing you at Thionoga."

"Don't sweat it." He patted Finnegan on the back. "Welcome to the team, Sean."

"Good to be aboard!"

The bald man continued up the corridor, pausing once to look back at Finnegan before heading around a corner. More laughter wafted down the hallway.

There's a jolly fellow, Finnegan thought. *Section 31 must be a happy place to work after all.*

He'd been working, too, since his arrival aboard *Pacifica*—though he remained a bit murky about what his title was. He knew he hadn't been reinstated to Starfleet; as near as he could figure, he was a civilian specialist, seconded to Section 31. It didn't have the sound of a long-term career, to be sure, but it was easier on the back than hauling ore.

Finnegan entered a turbolift, popcorn bucket in hand, ready to get back to his workplace for the afternoon. He nodded absently to the other passenger, an ensign. Then he stared at the ceiling and began to mumble: "Think like a murderer. Think like a murderer. Think like a murderer."

"Excuse me?" the ensign asked, looking up at him.

"How's that?"

"I thought you said, 'Think like a murderer.'"

"Ah, right," Finnegan said. He smiled and indicated his bucket. "You see, I'm on assignment. That was advice from the admiral."

"*Our* admiral?"

"Yes, I . . ." Finnegan paused. "You know, I think it's probably classified." He gave the ensign a wink. "Official secrets and all."

"Of—of course," the ensign stammered.

The turbolift stopped and the doors opened. "That's my stop," Finnegan said. "I'll be seeing you!"

"Uh, yeah." Out of the corner of his eye, Finnegan could see the ensign leaning out of the open turbolift, looking after him. It was nice that people were interested in him, but he had work to do.

Think like a murderer, he said to himself as he walked to his destination. *Think like a murderer.*

Kitty Cornwell had indeed said those words, as he'd begun his training that morning. "Georgiou is much more likely to accept you if you're more like her henchman was," she said. "And that means you'll be better able to keep tabs on her for us in the field." That had made sense to him, although he was unclear on exactly *how* he'd report in on her. But Cornwell had clearly thought he could pull it off. Georgiou didn't know why he was imprisoned at Thionoga, so he could play it any way he wanted.

The problem was that while Finnegan was great at mischief—ask any cadet at the Academy—evil, he wasn't. He was able to summon enough menace to frighten, certainly. But that was always in the name of a good laugh, even if he was the only one who laughed about it.

Both the Federation and Section 31 wanted the investigative mission into the *Farragut* Cloud to begin yesterday, and Cornwell had a full slate of meetings about it scheduled with the other prospective members of the team. But while she wasn't able to proctor him this afternoon, she had given him a suggestion: watch old movies.

All through the day in the darkness of *Pacifica*'s small theater, he'd screened parts of many different productions, every one steeped in malice. Most had been produced on Earth between the First and the Third World Wars; people then seemed to have a taste for the macabre. Maybe it was the shadow of death constantly hanging over them. But there were also snippets of scripted entertainments from other worlds, each one a crash education in Thinking Evil.

Reentering the theater and reclaiming his seat, he put his feet up and called for the computer to pick up where it had left off. As the room darkened and the images resumed, he sighed. Somewhere between Iago and the Mad Scourge of Tellar Prime he'd not only gotten the gist, but started to despair of the whole idea.

What kind of place was Georgiou's realm, anyway, if everyone walked around dragging their knuckles and hating all day? And how was it even possible that their Finnegan was a vicious wretch? He knew himself to be a prankster, no more. Didn't their Sean have sisters, a grandmother, a neighbor like Cornwell to keep him from turning into this "Blackjack" character?

Maybe he did, he thought. *But maybe they're bad people too.* That was agonizing to think about.

"Damn it, that's enough," he said, straightening in his chair. "I've seen plenty. Computer, end playback."

"Working." The images on screen disappeared, leaving him in the dark.

He rolled his eyes. "You forgot the lights."

Nothing.

"Computer, lights!"

When there was still no action after a few seconds, he let out a deep breath. He hadn't found a voice-recognition system in years that couldn't get his accent; that *Pacifica* had one was startling, and a bit unnerving.

But not as unnerving as the next thing he noticed: the kernels in the bucket in his lap starting to float upward, little blobs in the blackness. He quickly released the tub to grasp at them—only to have the container tumble away, pinwheeling corn everywhere.

Now I'm floating too, he realized. *Oh, Kitty. They've given you a lemon. Your big ship's a disaster.*

Darkness notwithstanding, Finnegan saw his duty clearly, regardless of his role: engineering needed his knowledge—if not a good talking to. If they were all like that stammering kid in the turbolift, they probably thought artificial gravity came from a can.

Bouncing off the overhead as he felt his way toward the door, it occurred to him that at the very least, this was one calamity they couldn't pin on him.

Section 31 Vessel *NCIA-93*
Alongside *Pacifica*

Emony Dax knew how to work with people she disliked. Many of the coaches Emony had learned from thought that motivation meant keeping their athletes in a state of perpetual fear.

Some of the academics Tobin knew were so arrogant they couldn't finish a sentence without an insult or a slight. But Emony had always been able to muddle through, finding a way to cooperate. She'd done everything poor Eagan had ever asked, understanding that his experience was worthy of respect, even if his attitude wasn't.

Her brief time with Section 31, however, had put her amiability to the test. The agents aboard *NCIA-93*—a drab name for a forbidding vessel—had been downright unfriendly, looking upon her as an invader in their secret society. Nobody had even explained to her what the ship's name stood for. Leland tolerated her for what she knew but lapsed into patronizing without a thought. And while Dax wasn't expecting cheer from a Vulcan, his henchwoman Sydia had never said more than a five-word sentence to her. And every one of those had begun with "do not."

"Do not look at that," Sydia said of the console before Dax's chair in the command center.

"They said I could wait here."

"Do not tell her that," Sydia said to an aide.

Someone guided the Trill to a chair facing a wall. Dax didn't care. She had ten minutes before her respite—shuttling back to *Pacifica*, where Leland and Cornwell were set to brief the entire team headed for Troika space. The admiral, at least, was pleasant. But Dax wasn't looking forward to seeing Emperor Georgiou again: by far, the worst possible coworker she could imagine.

She'd almost resigned after learning of Georgiou's origins, and the crazy-land she was said to be from. A "mirror universe" where alternate versions of people acted in venal ways? It sounded bizarre, macabre, impossible—and Dax came from a people who secretly implanted symbionts in their bodies. Nothing in her or any of her predecessors' histories readied her for the concept—and no briefing could have ever prepared her for meeting Georgiou.

In their meetings, Georgiou had treated Dax to conde-scending comments, shocking statements, and occasionally, licentious innuendos that made her skin crawl. She could see why Leland and Cornwell considered the emperor a possible asset: she was clearly one of the most intelligent beings Dax had ever met. But every interaction had ended with the Trill harbor-ing the same thought: *Why didn't I get to meet the nice one?*

It didn't matter. Georgiou was the only person who could help prevent another *Farragut*—and that had energized Dax. She'd done plenty of gymnastic routines where levels of dif-ficulty had been added. She had to cope, to contend—and she had to make sure that the emperor would help. Whatever else Georgiou wanted out of her existence on this side of the mirror, that had to be nonnegotiable.

Dax looked at the time. Her transport to the meeting was past due. She stood and approached Sydia, who was busy at another station. "Weren't they supposed to call me when the shuttle was ready?"

"Do not—" the Vulcan started, hiding her console screen. Then her head tilted, and she stepped to another station. "Something is wrong with *Pacifica*."

"What is it?"

"Power dips. To start with."

"We can't shuttle over?"

Sydia glared at her. "*Pacifica*'s bay doors cannot open with-out power."

Another Section 31 officer called out that the ship wasn't responding to hails.

Dax grew alarmed. She'd been through this before. "Can we transport people there? Are their shields up?"

Sydia stared. "Life-support only."

Dax's breath quickened. The Cloud couldn't have followed her, could it?

She had to find out—and this time, she'd need to use the method of transit she'd so often avoided. She'd just have to hope for the best that it wouldn't reveal her species' secret. Heading for the turbolift, she called back. "Sydia, I'm going to the transporter room. If they don't send me to *Pacifica*, I'm going to come back here and ask you a question a minute for the rest of your life!"

17

Georgiou swam, a shark in the night. *Pacifica* was her ocean, its Jefferies tubes the underwater rivers connecting lakes and inlets as she made her way toward the only bay she cared about. Thionoga had been a dry run, by comparison. Now she had brought one of Starfleet's most advanced vessels to heel using nothing but a pair of night-vision goggles and the one asset that had never failed her: the stupidity of others.

Or rather, one person in particular. Harmon Pettigrew, tutor in Federation civics and gasbag-in-chief.

She had intended to kill him, an hour earlier in the training center. She had planned to smash his data slate against the composite surface of her desk, after which she would have impaled one of the device's shards in his neck. He would have lived long enough for his biometric scans to be useful in getting the two of them out of the locked training area, but surveillance would have caught it, giving her mere seconds to get anywhere. As satisfying as his death would have been, she'd decided to look for another way.

Instead, Georgiou had appealed to the old fool's vanity, declaring, after the third replay of Burnham's pablum, that an epiphany was at hand. His words had swayed her, and so had those in the speech; she was on her way to becoming a good and productive member of Federation society, and a diligent and trustworthy agent for Section 31. She only needed time. Time to meditate on Burnham's words; time in which no others would intrude upon her thoughts as she contemplated her new path. She needed privacy—

—and, oh, yes, the data slate, so she could continue watching the interminable ceremony. The boob had immediately agreed, never realizing that his device was still tied into the training center's visualization tools; neither had he remembered to log out from his VIP priority access to the starship's systems.

That was all an engineer of Georgiou's caliber needed. It had been an easy matter to huddle up in her chair, pretending to watch the speech when, instead, she had hacked her way into the main computer of *Pacifica*. The work had required more finesse than her sabotages at Thionoga; it didn't surprise her that Starfleet systems were better prepared against cyberattack than those of some unaffiliated prison for civilians. But introducing malicious code into a closed system was a freshman course among the Terrans—and she was far from a novice.

And it helped that the code had already been written for her. She only wished she could be present when they figured out where she'd gotten it from.

The important thing was that it worked. In short order, she had blunted the surveillance threat while also generating enough emergencies to get everyone the hell out of her way. The lights were out, of course: that classic from Thionoga was worth a repeat. Killing the gravity was another must. She had added the flourish of random restarts of those systems on certain sections of the ship, boosting gravity to Jupiter-cloudtop levels long enough to smack the hell out of anyone trying to get oriented.

Then came the targeted attacks on the people *Pacifica* would be deploying against her. She treated main engineering to a series of false readings from the warp core; not enough to force people to evacuate the ship, but enough to keep them chasing gremlins in the dark. Starfleet's vaunted security personnel were given something different to worry about, as the main computer took note of wherever they were and began speaking in urgent Klingon in adjacent rooms.

Cornwell and Leland she'd just locked in their conference room, listening to a screech from the main computer so loud as to make calling for help difficult. It was a lesser fate than, say, beaming them into space, but she'd only had forty minutes.

Since then, it had been an easy matter to avoid *Pacifica*'s crew as they blundered about with their portable lighting; those without, she had simply floated past, sneaking by along the overhead. Nobody was looking for her, so far as she knew, but she couldn't count on that being the case forever. Fortunately, her destination wasn't far.

Shuttlebay dead ahead. Georgiou lifted her goggles long enough to check the data slate taped around her forearm. She'd used it as her guide and command center, purposefully tripping the ship's sensors on momentarily in areas when she needed intel. It told her that the cargo deck and attached shuttlebay remained nearly deserted. That was good. While she'd left those areas in the dark, she'd kept gravity functioning there, figuring that things floating around and bumping about wouldn't be good for her prospective escape vehicle, whichever one she chose.

Georgiou replaced the goggles and opened the hatch before her. True to her expectations, the cargo area was a canyon of black pillars when she peeked inside. Crates and cylinders stacked to twice her height, all still sitting on the deck. She grasped the doorframe and reoriented herself before stepping gingerly down into artificial gravity.

She popped off the goggles and cast them away. After several seconds to adjust to the darkness, she thought she saw a bit of light here and there behind the obstacles; since there were ports in the bulkhead facing outward, she assumed she was seeing starlight.

Still, she wasn't going to take any chances.

"Illuminate cargo deck and shuttlebay ten percent," she told the data slate. It responded, giving her just enough light to see something that she'd first noted weeks earlier on a pass through *Discovery*'s corridors: an emergency cabinet, positioned partway up the bulkhead. She'd made a beeline for one earlier when her journey began, obtaining the night-vision goggles it held before directing the computer to seal every other locker aboard *Pacifica*, lest its occupants get the same idea.

She opened this one with a smashing high kick. The door swung open, revealing more goggles, an oxygen mask, a first-aid kit, and a communicator. She wasn't interested in any of those.

"Here we are," she said aloud, admiring the phaser in the low light. She'd avoided taking one from the earlier cabinet, for fear *Pacifica* had some tracking system on its weapons that wasn't visible through the main computer; that would be just the sort of thing Starfleet would have. But now, there was no stopping her. Not when she was this close to—

Georgiou froze. She sniffed the air. Something was burning. Phaser in hand, she began to turn—only to step back, startled, when a torch-bearing figure emerged from behind a column of cargo containers. "*Boo!*"

"Get back!" Georgiou stuck the phaser in the face of the new arrival—a face, she now saw in the firelight, that was contorted with laughter.

"I thought that was you, Georgie! Nobody can kick a door open like you."

"*Blackjack?*"

"Finnegan, Blackjack—your choice," he said. His torch, she noticed, was a bunch of chemical-soaked rags twisted around a half-meter-long lug wrench. "We have to stop meeting like this."

She was still reeling. *Blackjack? Now?* "What are you doing here?"

"Looking for trouble—you know me." He brought the flame below and before his face, grinning evilly in the light. "You *do* know me, don't you?"

"No, I mean what are you doing *here*? I thought they kept you on Thionoga."

"Oh, that. Cornwell got me out and brought me here,"

Finnegan said. "I used to be Starfleet, you know. There's some secret mission—she thought you might be happier if I was on the team." Torch in hand, he wandered the stacks of cargo, a troll in the forest. "Besides, Thionoga didn't want to keep me there any longer. They know what I can do. Pretty soon I'd get around to doing it."

"Cornwell said you were no murderer."

"Ah, but she just knows what I was convicted of." He smiled back at her. "She doesn't know what I was *guilty* of."

She stared at him. "New tooth."

He clicked his teeth together and gave a little growl. "Helps to have 'em when I'm hungry. I get testy when I get hungry." He leered at her. "But they tell me you know that."

"How do you mean?"

"I mean they told me about who you are—and where you're from." He bowed theatrically. "Never met an emperor before."

"The news is certainly getting around."

"They also told me who *I* am. Where you're from, I mean."

"And what did you think of that?"

He laughed. "It's crazy." Then he began balancing the base of the lug wrench on his open palm, looking up at the flame as his makeshift torch teetered back and forth.

Georgiou had anticipated a lot of eventualities in her escape, but finding Blackjack again wasn't one. It seemed plausible that Cornwell might have brought him in; the Federation and Section 31 had certainly recruited a lot of other people to work on her. But she didn't remember any menace in Finnegan's voice or demeanor back on Thionoga, and what she was hearing from him now was certainly not like the Blackjack she knew. His manner was—what? More playful? Mocking?

Maybe this is just what he was like before the surgery.

"Normally you can't set things on fire on a starship," he said, grasping the wrench again to end its teetering. "Definitely something wrong above decks. Bet it feels like old times."

Georgiou had no time to relive anything. She began making her way through the aisles. "Allow me," Finnegan said, hurrying ahead and lighting her way.

"Why are you really in the cargo hold?"

"It was the only place I could find with gravity." He looked to her. "What—uh, what are *you* doing here?"

"Same old, same old." She waved the phaser before her. "I'm leaving. But this time, I won't be needing you to mess with any space doors." She gestured toward the data slate. "I'm taking care of it myself."

He stood, motionless. "Where to this time?"

"Same as before. Anywhere else." On the starboard side of the storage area, something caught her eye. She stepped quickly to the port, where she saw *NCIA-93* hovering stationary off the starboard bow: Leland's ship.

She'd known it was there, of course; she'd even spent time on it between her recruitment on Qo'noS and her deployment to the prison ship that took her to Thionoga. What she didn't fully know was what its armaments were. Distracting *Pacifica*'s crew was one thing; she was reasonably certain her sabotage would give her a window during which it could not fire on her. But Leland's ship type had appeared in no records she'd ever seen, and she had never been allowed to visit the bridge. She doubted she'd be able to simply fly a shuttle past it.

Then she remembered the man behind her. "You were Starfleet?" she asked.

"That's right. Jack of all trades."

"Your shuttles aren't armed—but I know they can be."

"Simple stuff," Finnegan replied. "We switch in equipment pods—I used to be able to mount one in under five minutes." He rested his free hand against a cargo container. "Nothing a smart person can't do on his own!"

"Control your fire," she said.

"Okay, there is that—fire control's from the back station. Shuttle pilot can't do that."

"No, I mean control your fire," Georgiou said, gesturing indifferently to his torch as she stepped past. In the seconds it took for Finnegan to realize what she meant, the rags on his wrench, burnt through, tumbled from it. They singed his wrist on the way down, causing him to swear—and then to angrily stomp on them after they hit the deck.

She looked back at him. He sure wasn't Blackjack, she decided, but he was probably right about the fire control systems. The Terran Empire didn't even make an unarmed shuttle; Starfleet, on the other hand, existed under the delusion that it was not a military organization, ignoring basic necessities in the process.

She would not. "Blackjack!"

Nursing his wrist, he looked up. "Huh?"

"They want you to shadow me? So shadow me."

"You mean—?"

"I need your help after all. Come on, before I change my mind."

"Whatever you say, Your Highness!"

"And keep the wrench. You look good holding it."

18

"*Admiral on the bridge!*"

"Not intentionally," Cornwell said, stepping into the command well of the Section 31 vessel. She and Leland had just been transported across from *Pacifica* after an interminable period during which the two were locked, weightless, in the dark with several colleagues. "That's the last time I let you talk me into using a briefing room without a window. Or a comm."

"If you could make calls out," Leland said, "it wouldn't be a secure room."

"It certainly secured us." Cornwell had seldom seen Leland flustered, but the ordeal had definitely unnerved him. She could relate, having transferred her own flag to *NCIA-93* only after it became apparent no fix for *Pacifica* was coming quickly. "Do you have any idea what's happened?"

Sydia pointed to several screens showing readouts from the ship. Many sections were blinking or black, indicating that the only systems still working on *Pacifica* related to autonomic features like life support. "We have never seen such a disruption of user control outside a test environment."

That jolted Cornwell. "You mean you've seen it *inside* a test environment?"

Leland's eyes fixed as she said that—and then he and Sydia looked at each other. "You don't think—"

Sydia went to another console and called up some information. "It seems," she said gravely after a moment, "that there has been unauthorized access to Pandora's Box."

"*To what?*" Cornwell said.

"No, no," Leland said, shoving past Sydia to sit at the station. "That can't be right." But after a minute at the controls, he clapped his hands on his scalp. "She did it." Mesmerized, he pushed himself back. "*Damned if she didn't do it!*"

"Georgiou did what?" the admiral demanded.

Leland stepped away from the terminal and pointed. "My developer team belowdecks runs simulations to game out Starfleet's response to cyber threats. They're always designing new malware packages. Apparently one of our guests must have known they were here."

Sydia pointed to a notation on another screen. "It looks like the files were first accessed when she was aboard, between Qo'noS and Thionoga. A back door was inserted into the system, accessible via subspace."

Leland acknowledged. "And this says a Federation official with priority clearance opened a channel downloading it to *Pacifica* an hour ago. Know anybody who would do that?"

Cornwell had heard enough. "Where's Georgiou now?"

"Our sensor sweeps have been unable to tell," Sydia said. "We are not even certain she is on *Pacifica*."

"We're one of two starships parked in deep space. She's either there or here. Find her. She's either got a ride coming, or she's going to find one."

Standing before his people, Leland swallowed his pride. "Do what the admiral says."

As the humbled bridge crew turned back to their stations, Cornwell stepped nearer to Leland and his aide and spoke in low tones. "This is ridiculous. Not only did Section 31 build a means to disable one of Starfleet's own ships—but she stole it while she was training for your loyalty test!"

"Perhaps," Sydia said, "we did not give her enough to do."

U.S.S. *Pacifica*

Doolittle. Chennault. Hanson. Reading the shuttle names as she passed them, Georgiou had seen another of Starfleet's little hypocrisies. Finnegan had mentioned they were named for military aviators, a peculiar choice for an alleged peacetime organization. She'd brought it up earlier when one of her trainers had explained who the original Farragut was. The ridiculous justification was that they were all voyagers by sea or air who had acted with distinction; the martial nature of those acts was secondary. She'd laughed then. *I'll just bet they don't honor anyone who was on the losing side.*

At last, she came to the shuttle she'd been hoping to find. "Here it is. *Boyington.*" She gestured to Finnegan, who was tailing her with a service vehicle. "You've brought the wrench. Have at it."

"With pleasure," he said.

"Try it with speed." He'd taken his damn sweet time finding the weapons pod and loading it onto the crawler; now, as he backed the machine toward the shuttle's snub nose, she wondered how committed he was. Three times already, he'd stopped to ask her questions that didn't need answering, usually with some malicious twist thrown in. She couldn't tell whether he was trying to delay her, to establish his bona fides as her ally, or both—but she was unconcerned about capture. She'd used the data slate to trigger a new round of convulsions for *Pacifica*, thanks to the programs she'd discovered during her time on *NCIA-93*.

"Why this shuttle again?" Finnegan asked as he hefted the weapons pod into position.

"*Boyington*'s the one they intended for our expedition," Georgiou said. "It's long range, warp capable—and is fully stocked with what you people consider food."

"And drink, I hope."

She ignored him. "We ought to be able to make the Alpha Quadrant in a few days. Have you ever heard of the Badlands?"

"Sounds like a fun vacation spot in your world."

"It's a good place to not be found—and it hasn't been tainted by the Federation yet. There are worlds ripe for the plucking, ready for a leader."

Wrench in hand, Finnegan paused in his work. "You're really looking to become an emperor again?"

"I never stopped being one. Now hurry up. I have places to go and worlds to—"

"*I can't believe this!*"

Georgiou spun, phaser in hand—and saw Emony Dax standing outside the open doorway to *Boyington*. The emperor raised an eyebrow and lowered the weapon. "Ah, our little lurker comes forth. The sensors had said someone else might be here."

Dax walked toward her. "Leland's been beaming people aboard in various places, trying to help out. I asked to be sent to the shuttlebay." The young woman's eyes were wide in the low light. "Looks like it was the right call. Did I just hear you say you're going to leave?"

"Why ask questions you already know the answer to?" Georgiou had grown tired of delays. "Blackjack, are you done yet?"

Finnegan was not. In fact, she saw that he had stepped back from the shuttle's prow entirely. He dropped the wrench on the deck, flicked the sweat from his hair, and smiled broadly at Dax. "Well, hello there!"

"Not now," Georgiou said, grabbing her forehead.

"I don't think we've met. I'm Sean Finnegan."

The angry Trill barely took her eyes off Georgiou to look at him. "Hi," she said, distracted. "Emony Dax."

"*Emony Dax!*" Finnegan smacked his hands together. "I knew you looked familiar! Me and the cadets used to bet on your gym meets."

Dax did a mild double take. "You'd *bet*?"

"Well, it was more of a drinking game, but—" Finnegan wiped the grease from his hand onto his shirt and extended it toward her as he approached. "I am a fan!"

Georgiou rolled her eyes. "Are you going to finish the work? I have places to go!"

"Yes," Dax said. "To Troika space—with us!"

Finnegan balled his fists with enthusiasm. "You're on the mission too? This gets better all the time!"

Fine! Georgiou pushed past him, disgusted. The weapons pod only needed a few more turns of the wrench. She set down the phaser and retrieved the tool from the deck.

"You're on Leland's team?" Dax asked Finnegan.

"Cornwell brought me in. But yeah."

"Then you've got to stop her. She's trying to escape!"

"Not trying hard enough, apparently," Georgiou said, crouching to turn the remaining bolts.

Finnegan cupped his hand to his mouth and spoke to Dax. "They told me to stick with her," he half whispered. "I've been trying to slow her down, but she's dead set on going."

"I can hear you," Georgiou called out. It didn't stop them from talking, but at least her suspicions were confirmed.

"You can't let her go," Dax said. "Leland says she's the key to the whole mission. You've got to stop her!"

Work completed, Georgiou rose—and stepped toward the pair. She faced Dax. "Little thing, nobody stops me. Ever. And I am not going on your stupid mission. I never was." She turned toward Finnegan. "As for you—you're as disappointing as everyone I've met in this universe. Maybe more so. Blackjack was an artist. And he did what he was told."

Looking into her cold eyes, Finnegan swallowed. "You know what I think," he said. "Obedience is overrated. But I will follow an order now and again—from the right folks." He seized the data slate on her wrist and undid the tape, freeing it. "Let's go have a nice talk with them."

So aggravating, Georgiou thought. "Very well," she said, spinning—and smashing Finnegan in the face with the business end of the wrench. He tumbled backward, blood flying. She watched as he slammed into the deck.

"Huh," she said, kicking his motionless form. "I've always wondered what that felt like. No wonder Blackjack enjoyed it." She bent over to retrieve the fallen data slate—

—and looked into the muzzle of the phaser she'd set down earlier. Dax pointed the weapon like the head of a snake she wanted kept far from her person. "Stop right there!"

Forgetting the data slate, Georgiou sneered at her. "Oh, you aren't serious."

Dax stepped backward in the direction of the shuttlecraft's open doorway. "I'm going to do what I should have done before. I'm going to call Leland. I'll bet the comm system still works in there!"

Georgiou's lips curled upward. "Ah. You *aren't* serious." Clutching the wrench, she stepped toward Dax, menace in every move.

"Stay where you are. Or I'll stun you."

"How fun! I only had it set to kill." Georgiou stopped walking. "Go ahead and change it. I'll wait."

Dax glanced down at the weapon—only to look more closely at it. She seemed puzzled.

"Oh, you *are* green." Georgiou chuckled. "Doesn't come with instructions, does it?"

Giving up, Dax pointed it again. "I don't have to change it. Stay back!"

"You won't kill me because of your mission—and you can't kill me, because you're a child. But I'm not a child—and I don't care about your mission." She took a step forward.

"I said *stop*!" Dax fired the phaser. The warning shot sizzled harmlessly overhead.

"You're not convincing me." Georgiou saw Dax look back at the shuttle entrance, a few steps behind her. Athlete or not, if the Trill bolted for the inside, Georgiou knew she'd catch her. "You'd better shoot me, dear."

Her face racked with fear, Dax fired again. Closer, this time.

Georgiou kept stalking toward her. "Run, rabbit. I'll wring your neck."

"What is *wrong* with you?" Dax yelled. "Don't you know what this is about? Don't you care?"

The emperor paused her approach. "What are you talking about?"

"I'm talking about the mission. Why you're here. Why we're doing this. I'm talking about *Farragut!*"

The name was out of nowhere—but Georgiou had heard it before. "The starship?"

"Of course the starship!" Dax spoke frenetically. "It was struck by a cloud that killed half the people aboard!"

Section 31 had never told Georgiou the truth about anything—but Dax seemed to be sickeningly earnest. And what she was saying shocked her. "Wait. What kind of cloud?"

"We think it was alive. It passed through bulkheads, traveled independently through space," Dax said. "It went after people—and drained their red blood cells!"

"*A blood devil?*"

"Call it what you want—it was horrible!"

A blood devil! Georgiou's mind reeled. She had heard of the creature in the Beta Quadrant lore she'd studied. An ancient menace, considered mythological. No evidence of one had ever been found. Was it possible people in the Federation's universe had never heard of one?

Then it dawned on her. The Federation *had* heard of one. "The cloud—it's the reason for this mission?"

"Of course it is!" Dax said. "It killed people on *Farragut* the same way people died on the freighter your double encountered at the edge of Troika space years ago. The *Jadama Rohn.*"

"Captain Georgiou?"

"She was a lieutenant then—but yes. That's why we need you—and that's why we're going. To find that ship, to explore the connection. To keep it from happening again!"

Georgiou's breath caught. *Jadama Rohn* was the freighter her old ally S'satah had been flying when she was delivering to *Hephaestus* the secret weapon she'd discovered in Troika space.

Whipsaw was a blood devil!

In a flash, she saw it all. If S'satah had found a blood devil—and been able to contain it in such a way that Georgiou's team from *Hephaestus* hadn't initially been able to detect it—then it was possible that it could be controlled.

And if it could be controlled—and if there were more specimens where S'satah found hers—then Whipsaw might mean for Georgiou here far more than it would have in her universe. If Dax's account was accurate, *Farragut*'s fate proved that Starfleet had no defense against the clouds, once deployed.

"Do they know where the—where the cloud that struck *Farragut* went?"

"No," Dax said. "I saw it emerge directly from the hull of the ship and vanish. Almost as if it had teleported or something."

The wrench fell from Georgiou's hand, clanking against the deck. *Teleportation! Passing through bulkheads! What* couldn't *it do?*

She calculated. So there was a blood devil loose in the Beta Quadrant—but there was no telling where it had gone, nor how to attract it. No wonder Section 31 and the Federation had turned to the past, and the slender reed of their Georgiou's *Jadama Rohn* encounter, for a lead. The emperor didn't quite understand how the same ship could have appeared a quarter century earlier in connection with the blood devil—but that was something that could be discovered.

But only if she went.

Fortunately, there was already a mission heading in that direction.

Still under Dax's panicked, watchful eyes, Georgiou turned. Finnegan was alive and on his hands and knees. His fingers fumbled with his red-drenched mouth—and he flicked a tooth to the deck. "Same damn one."

Georgiou looked at it—and him—and then raised her hands before Dax. "You've convinced me."

Dax's eyes goggled. "I did *what*?"

The older woman edged backward toward the resting place of the data slate. "I'll go with you—but we need to agree that this never happened."

"We *what*?" Finnegan blurted.

Cautious of the jittery Dax, Georgiou carefully knelt and toggled the data slate. After she issued a few commands, the lighting in the shuttlebay returned to full brightness.

"What's she doing?" Dax asked.

"You've got me," Finnegan replied.

Georgiou stood. "Computer, get me the bridge."

A puzzled voice echoed through the chamber. *"Bridge here."*

"I've managed to defeat the malware incursion," she said, brushing herself off. "Your systems should be returning to normal."

"Who is this?"

She licked her lips and winked at the others. "This is *Agent* Georgiou."

19

> *". . . a delight to hear from you, Philippa—I'd grown worried when I hadn't in so long. And what a surprise your request was. Yes, of course—I can't wait to see you in person after all these years. Forthcoming will be instructions for entering Troika space as a special guest of the Veneti . . ."*

Georgiou finished reading the message on screen and sat back in her chair in the conference room. It was as simple as that: all she'd had to do was message Quintilian using the channel he'd shared with her counterpart a quarter century earlier. The merchant's response had arrived within an hour.

The day before, in the shuttlebay, Georgiou had considered dispensing with Dax and heading for Troika space alone. That had only lasted for a moment. Without Finnegan to operate fire control, she hadn't thought much of her chances of getting past *NCIA-93*. Acquiescing, she'd decided, would lead her to the same destination. And it looked like it was going to—though there had certainly been recriminations aplenty in between.

Cornwell entered with Dax in tow. "This room again," the admiral said, nearly groaning.

"Try leaving the door open this time," Georgiou said with a smile. It paid to be helpful.

The others sat. "We've decided to agree, for the sake of the mission, that yesterday's problems never happened—"

"No commendation for resolving them?" the emperor asked. "*Tsk-tsk.* Terrible how Starfleet treats Samaritans."

Dax looked to Cornwell. "What's a Samaritan?"

"In our universe, someone who helped a robbery victim,"

the admiral said. "I'm sure she'll say in hers it was somebody who helped the robbers." Cornwell took a look at her data slate. "This report says we're just about done with the repairs from yesterday—"

Georgiou reached outward. "Oh, can I see?"

"Hell, no." The admiral pulled the data slate closer. "Mister Pettigrew has been placed on leave by the Federation Security Agency and is on his way back to Earth aboard *Doolittle*."

"Apparently *Do-Nothing* wasn't available," Georgiou said.

"You see, that's something that has to stop," Cornwell said, putting the slate down. "This is never going to work if you don't start treating the people you work with better."

"More lessons in comportment. Who will be my master of etiquette once we're parted, Admiral? Is that Leland's hidden specialty?" The door opened, and the man himself entered. She waved. "Speak of the devil and he shall appear."

Leland led Finnegan and Sydia inside and gestured for them to take seats. He gave a wary look to the door when it closed behind him.

"Sure that's wise?" Georgiou asked. "Don't you want a communicator in case you get stuck? Or perhaps sandwiches?"

"Pandora's Box is locked down," he said, sitting. "We've stripped out code to render its applications inactive."

"You shouldn't have had them in the first place," Cornwell said.

"They were designed as a test of Starfleet security protocols." He nodded to Georgiou. "You could say our agent tested them."

Cornwell sighed, disgusted.

Leland forged on. "Now that we're here, we have a new issue. Quintilian's attachment noted that the Troika powers have only cleared him for three outsider guests."

"Three?" Cornwell was astonished. "We'd planned for a team of nine."

"All to keep an eye on little old me." Georgiou rolled her eyes. "I don't like crowds."

"Apparently," Leland continued, "the three native species really only intended for him to allow in one person—but because each agreed to one visitor, he took it to mean he got three total. I get the sense he has to wheedle and politic to keep his franchise over there." He looked to Georgiou. "Did he ever say why the Troika allows foreign traders to act as their delivery service?"

"I'm still going through their correspondence," Georgiou said. There was years of it, all provided to her that morning for her research. "Every time they get near anything useful they veer off into discussing Vulcan poetry or the Han dynasty. They once did a whole exchange on the economic reforms of Charlemagne. I have to read it in short sections or I get too excited."

"Read it all. You have to *be* Captain Georgiou to make this work. Quintilian claimed not to know for sure what had really befallen *Jadama Rohn* in 2233, but he indicated in later messages that the ship still existed."

Cornwell appeared fretful. "But sending only three people. Which three?"

Leland pointed. "Well, Agent Georgiou, of course." He nodded to Dax. "Emony gets a slot because of her . . . previous bargain."

Impressed, Georgiou looked to the Trill. "Did you make a deal, dear? Good for you!"

Dax simply shuddered. The young woman had been wary of Georgiou since the shuttlebay incident.

"That leaves one more slot," Leland said. "I'm thinking Sydia."

"Just us girls," Georgiou said. "We'll paint the Troika red."

Cornwell slapped the table. "No, no. That's two slots for Section 31. The Federation Council insists on an observer."

"You're counting Georgiou as one of our slots?" Leland asked, alarmed.

"She's your agent, isn't she?"

Sydia clasped her hands and faced forward. "Admiral, I assure you, my loyalties are both to the Federation and to Section 31. I can serve both."

"No," Cornwell said. She faced Georgiou. "And she's already established she's going to make life hell for whoever else we send."

Dax grew agitated. "The clock is running. Quintilian's expecting us now. Can't we decide?"

Finnegan, uncharacteristically silent until now, spoke up. "You know, I could still go."

The others looked to him, some surprised he was still there.

"I'm not this evil henchman of hers," he continued. "But we do get on. You know, apart from the blood and the bashing."

"You *like* the blood and the bashing," Georgiou said.

Finnegan didn't crack a smile for a change. "I've heard from people who've heard from Jimmy Kirk. Some of our friends are gone—and the rest went through hell."

"I was there," Dax said somberly.

"Well, if I can keep it from happening again, I still want to try. An evil cloud's not a fair fight."

Georgiou considered. She didn't really care who went with her; it would all end the same, with her finding Whipsaw and reclaiming her empire. Finnegan seemed highly unlikely to interfere with that end. "He's acceptable," she finally said. A meager endorsement, for sure, but she figured anything more enthusiastic would be suspect.

Leland eyed her—and then Finnegan. "Okay with me," he said.

Cornwell studied Finnegan for long moments, before nodding. "All right, Sean." She toggled a control on her data slate, throwing a star map onto the large screen before them. "Where's the insertion point?"

Leland didn't need to consult his notes. "Quintilian's instructions said Tagantha. It's where *Archimedes* ran into him years ago."

"That's nearest to the Casmarrans," Georgiou said, putting stress on the second syllable of the name. Seeing blanks on the others' faces, she added, "One of the Troika races."

Cornwell and Leland looked at each other. "Did we know the names of any of the species before now?" the admiral asked.

The spymaster indicated the emperor. "We knew *she* did—but she wouldn't say. But that's why we—"

"Yes, yes, I'm the guide to the hidden kingdoms." Georgiou looked to Cornwell. "What else?"

"We'll follow the original plan, with you entering via a Starfleet shuttle, like Captain Georgiou would have. I guess you've seen it—*Boyington*."

Dax nodded. "I've checked the shuttle—it's ready to go." She looked to the admiral. "Who was Boyington?"

"Aviator. One of the Flying Tigers who unofficially assisted China in World War II before the United States was involved."

"Sounds covert," Leland said. "I like it."

"Once war broke out, he led a squadron called the Black Sheep."

Finnegan chuckled. "Okay, now you're *definitely* trying to tell us something."

"That I won't deny," Cornwell said. "They had been Boyington's Bastards, but they wouldn't print that in the newspapers."

Georgiou sighed. "I don't know what I'll do without these little historical insights."

"We're more interested in yours," Cornwell said. She stood. "Leland's ship will shadow you to Troika space and park outside, waiting for word." She looked down across the table. "I'm dead serious, Your Highness. The Cloud hasn't struck again—but nobody doubts it will, and the only defense is finding out its origins. If you betray us again, we'll make your last couple of imprisonments seem like days at the spa."

"Very Terran. Maybe I could get to like you people after all."

"Dismissed. Get to work." Cornwell marched out, with

Dax and Sydia following. Leland lingered, making notes on his data slate.

Finnegan and Georgiou rose from their chairs at the same time. "I guess we'll be working together," he said, "so no hard feelings."

Leland looked up, his interest piqued. "What exactly happened?"

"Just a friendly tiff."

"I hit him in the face with a wrench," Georgiou said.

Finnegan rubbed his jaw—and then felt inside his mouth. "That reminds me. I need to get to sickbay. Cornwell's dentist was going to fix me up again, but I missed him earlier."

Leland stopped Finnegan before he could exit. "You know, you could come over to our ship. Our doc does good work. She'll fix you right up."

Finnegan gave a gap toothed grin. "Thank you, brother. I owe you a drink." A beat. "You think I could have a drink first?"

Leland smirked. "I'm sure we could arrange that."

"Then I'm definitely going." He waved and departed.

As Finnegan ambled off, Leland turned to Georgiou. "You're really going to play nice this time?"

She crossed her arms. "I'm unaccustomed to having my word questioned."

"I've stuck my neck out for you."

"Yes, thanks for all your kind assistance." Passing him in the doorway, she paused and touched his cheek. "It's a shame that in my universe you were dissected by Klingons and served to their livestock."

He closed his eyes and shook his head. "*Please* stop doing that."

Stage Three
PLUNDERING

Enjoy all the riches you can today, because eternal life is over rated. I once met someone who was a thousand years old—a Casmarran, last survivor of a race slaughtered a century ago by Emperor Georgiou. She didn't spare him to show mercy. Is there any greater punishment than wandering forever, with your whole world gone?

—Ezri Tigan
From a message to the Intendent, 2372

20

In one of the languages of Georgiou's homeworld, the term
déjà vu meant "already seen," while another concept, *déjà vécu*,
referred to a more chronic and unnerving phenomenon: the
persistent feeling that whole sequences of events had been lived
through before.

If many more people hopped between universes, Georgiou
figured someone would need to ask the French to come up
with some new terms. She'd longed for something to call the
knowledge—not the feeling, but the *certainty*—of having seen
something before, only in her reality. Then there was the extended version, having the same experiences over again, only in
a slightly different context. That one, while more annoying, at
least offered her an advantage: she usually knew what was coming next.

It was happening again as *Boyington* exited the gaseous
mess of the Taganthan System to head deeper into Troika space.
In her universe, the first sentry vessels from a Troika power had
appeared within minutes after her annihilation of Quintilian's
flotilla and the destruction of *Jadama Rohn*; there hadn't been
time to clear the traitor Eagan's body from the deck before the
fireworks started. Here, again, as if on cue, a half dozen ships
appeared far ahead, spinning through space toward her.

Or, to be more precise, *rolling*.

"Weird ships," Finnegan said from the pilot's seat. "Like
starfish on a skewer."

"They're Casmarran," Georgiou responded from behind.
"Get used to the way they look. You'll see a lot of it." It was a

visual theme with the Casmarrans; six broad five-pronged as-
terisks connected through the center by a tall central stalk. The
gold-colored vehicles spun on their long axes through space,
their spokes nearly a blur. Propulsion came from jets mounted
on small hubs at either end of the axles.

In the copilot's seat where she'd been practicing piloting,
Dax gawked. "Bizarre. They're like those spiked things Trill
farmers use to punch holes in the soil. *Aerators.*"

"These will punch holes in our hull, if we let them."

Dax quickly stood and gestured to Georgiou. "Maybe *you'd*
better sit here."

"Don't worry yourself. Sit."

Georgiou adjusted her collar. For the second time in
recent history, Cornwell had provided her with a Starfleet
captain's uniform; the emperor had worn her first one aboard
Discovery. It was far too drab for her tastes and not nearly
comfortable enough, but it conveyed some authority—
especially as Leland had decided it would be best for Finnegan
and Dax to dress as her lieutenant and ensign, respectively.
The titles were a sham, but Finnegan nonetheless had relished
being in uniform again.

He looked back to Georgiou. The Casmarran vessels were
still distant, but approaching fast. "They don't look too happy
to see us. Sure you don't want to tend the guns?"

"Your Captain Georgiou would never shoot first. You don't
want me to break character so soon, do you?"

"It'd still be nice to shoot second."

Dax bit her lip. "Enough. I'm hailing them."

Georgiou looked away in boredom. "You're wasting your
time."

She did it anyway. "This is Ensign Emony Dax, of the
Starfleet shuttlecraft *Boyington*, on a peaceful mission at the
invitation of—"

"Unauthorized," came the answer in crisp Federation Standard over the comm.

Dax said, "But I'm escorting a person who—"

"*Unauthorized.*"

"We've covered that. Do you know how to reach—"

"*Unauthorized. Unauthorized. Unauthorized. Unauthorized.*"

"Not big on the vocabulary, our Casmarrans." Finnegan frowned. "Sounds like a canned response. Is there anybody even aboard those things?"

Georgiou knew the answer. "A sole Casmarran, ensconced within the spine. We found that out when we cracked one of the ships open."

Dax stared. "How do they not get dizzy traveling like that?"

"Their bodies have sophisticated and redundant balancing structures."

"How do you know?"

"We found out when we cracked a *Casmarran* open."

Wincing, Dax looked to Finnegan. "How much of the stuff she says is real, do you think?"

"I've stopped asking," he replied.

Georgiou smirked. Now that Finnegan knew what she was—and now that she knew what he *wasn't*—he'd grown a bit more reserved where the emperor was concerned. Dax, meanwhile, had stiffened her approach toward her. That was something of a surprise to Georgiou, who'd thought the Trill would refuse to be around her at all following the episode in the shuttlebay. *Maybe there's more to her than I thought.*

Finnegan pointed to a shining star in space, the place where the sentry vessels had originated from. "There. That fella matches the coordinates Quintilian sent you."

"Then that's your destination," Georgiou replied. It had been her first stop, in her realm. "A quick warp."

Dax nervously looked at the Casmarran vessels, growing in perspective every second that passed. "They don't look willing to get out of the way."

Finnegan smiled. "Watch and learn, Emony." He worked the controls, banking *Boyington* into a steep curve. The Casmarrans responded, altering direction—only to scatter as he threw the shuttle into two consecutive dramatic turns. It was enough. "Hold on," he said, punching a control. *Boyington* snapped into warp—

—and dropped out three seconds later, awash in light. Not from the formerly distant star; rather, it reflected off the large orb filling its forward port.

"That's . . . unique looking," Dax said.

The Casmarran obsession with fives and sixes was expressed topographically on the cloudless planet, with what appeared to be high, bright-colored mountain ranges dividing the surface into darker regions within enormous pentagons and hexagons.

Finnegan gawked. "I think I just found the football I lost as a kid."

Georgiou knew what she was looking at, recalling it from the Terran invasion. The white ranges dividing the polygonal segments of Casmarra's surface, she already knew, weren't mountains at all, but rather artificial structures. Massive alabaster cities sat at the vertices where the depressions joined; the kilometers-wide walls dividing them were just more urbanity, wrapping around the planet and separating it into different zones.

Those zones were riven with pits, the broad expanses almost completely denuded of resources. Casmarra was a place that had been mined out long ago, with the only hint of what the surface might have originally looked like appearing in the area that Quintilian had told them to approach.

"There's where we were directed," she said, pointing to a pentagonal spread of emerald and azure many hundreds of kilometers across. "The Casmarrans call it the Alien Region."

The beauty of the area as seen from orbit startled Dax. "Normally people give the outsiders the worst land."

"Quintilian talks about it in his correspondence—says the

Casmarrans would have ripped up the area long ago had he not bartered for it in exchange for his services." Georgiou nodded. "That's where he said to go."

"But he was supposed to meet us by now," Dax said.

"Well, somebody's coming," Finnegan replied, pointing to the Casmarran vessels streaming upward from the planet toward them. Identical to the ones they'd just evaded, in all but one respect: number. "It's a whole swarm of the boyos."

And more approaching from orbit behind, Georgiou realized from the scans.

Dax fretted. "You're *sure* we were invited?"

Georgiou frowned. "Hail him."

Quintilian's message had promised safe transit and had provided the suggested route for their passage—but he had prefaced it by saying he'd need to guide them in. He hadn't said anything about what to do if he was a no show.

Earpiece in place, Dax frenetically punched commands into her console. "I keep sending messages on the frequency Quintilian gave us. Nothing. And all I get from the Casmarrans is more of the same one-word answers." She looked back to Georgiou. "Should we turn around?"

"No. Stay the path to the end." She pointed over Finnegan's shoulder to the Alien Region. "Take us down."

Finnegan turned the vessel in that direction—only to find that move matched by the incoming Casmarrans. Spooked by the ships swarming toward them, Dax looked urgently at him. "Something's clearly wrong, Sean. We shouldn't stay—"

"Who's the captain here?" Georgiou asked, showing off the pips on her Starfleet insignia.

"Those aren't real," Dax said. She pointed outside at the approaching vessels. "Those are. Look, Leland's running silent outside the boundary. We could go back—"

"And so much for your poor dead friends drained by the Cloud," Georgiou said. "They'll just have to be satisfied with your good intentions."

"Stop riding me." Dax pointed to the readout from the scanner. "I meant we can call Quintilian again and find out—"

Something clanged off the underside of the shuttle. A second later, another sound.

"Did they just rake the hull?" Finnegan asked. "You said they punched holes."

"That's what they tried with me," Georgiou said.

"How'd you stop them?"

"I brought a fleet of battle cruisers."

Finnegan looked to Dax. "So that's the problem. I left my battle cruisers in my other pants this morning."

A third close encounter made it clear the vessels weren't trying to puncture *Boyington*; rather, they were anchoring to it. And doing something else, they realized, as the lights went out inside the shuttle. Finnegan and Dax watched with alarm as the displays on their consoles blinked and went dark.

"That's flight control," Finnegan said. He leaned back, done for now.

More Casmarran vessels passed near the shuttle; the sequel was more metallic sounds, then grinding. Georgiou felt a sudden lightness—and then realized the cause. The gravity plating no longer worked.

"This feels familiar," Dax said, clutching her armrests. "I guess the high-heeled boot is on the other foot."

As seconds passed, ever more of Finnegan's "skewered starfish" arrived outside, clustering around the vehicle. Dax looked to Georgiou. "You really don't have a plan? You're just going to let this happen?"

She didn't respond. She was deep in thought, reflecting on the messages she'd read that had gone between her counterpart and Quintilian. He'd mentioned that the Casmarrans had taken possession of *Jadama Rohn* after its crew died—and she'd definitely remembered seeing factories and landing facilities on the world below, before destroying them.

"If they wanted to decompress the shuttle," she said, "they'd have done it by now. They're preparing to move us."

Finnegan agreed. "They're joining up," he said, peering outside. "Building a structure."

Dax's eyes widened. "Did you see them do this before?"

"No," Georgiou said. She watched as a final addition to the macabre frame around the shuttle blotted out the last bit of light from outside. "We never left enough Casmarrans alive to do something like this."

"That settles it," Finnegan said, stretching. "We're definitely in the wrong universe."

Georgiou nodded. *I feel that way every day.*

21

Vertex 22
CASMARRA

"Unauthorized. Unauthorized. Unauthorized."

"You said that," Finnegan said to the tall Casmarran before them on the landing platform.

"I think it's saying it once for each of us," Dax said.

"How egalitarian," Georgiou observed. "Almost as sickening as their bodies."

Before stepping onto the tarmac, the emperor had warned her companions of the sulfurous smell exuded by the Casmarrans. She hadn't bothered to prepare them for what they *looked* like, however; it hardly seemed necessary. They looked exactly like the ships they flew.

"They're like walking hydrae," Dax had said on first encountering them. While the Casmarrans appeared to range from one to three meters tall, every one of the golden-hued creatures was configured the same way: a central trunk, surrounded by six levels of five limbs each. Some arms were more prehensile than others, almost able to function as tentacles. The lowest level of arms sat flush with the ground, gripping it as if with suction—turning each Casmarran into a temporary tree.

But only briefly, for the beings astonished the new arrivals with their nimbleness. Some traversed short distances by skittering. Others curved their trunks completely over such that their topmost armatures touched the ground, becoming their bases. Georgiou had seen several climbing to the landing platform in this manner. Where metal springs on a staircase could only "walk" downward, gravity seemed no impediment for the Casmarrans.

And the strangest behavior of all could be seen below the landing platform, on the many broad statue-lined thoroughfares that crisscrossed the Casmarran city. Just as their spaceships had "rolled" through space, so the creatures propelled themselves, tumbling laterally along their highways. "Like wheels on a steamboat," Finnegan had said.

The rote nature of the Casmarrans' speech, observed earlier by Finnegan, had a simple explanation: they had no mouths—or any other perceptible sensory organs at all. The dissections performed by her imperial scientists suggested they might use a sonar of some kind. Artificial speech came from small blue boxes banded around the Casmarrans' midsections, between the third and fourth clusters of arms. Only certain Casmarrans had them; Dax had guessed that implied some kind of status.

The Casmarrans had certainly exercised dominance over *Boyington*'s occupants in short order. Their exit from the shuttle had been compulsory. The Casmarrans had unsealed the vehicle on their own, at which point the smaller vessels that had wrapped around it had activated their engines, shaking it until Georgiou, Finnegan, and Dax had emerged.

Since then, ever more Casmarrans had crowded onto the landing platform. They evidently understood what phasers were; Finnegan's had been plucked from his hand by one of the larger specimens' spongy limbs the second he hit the tarmac. Georgiou still had hers, tucked safely inside her waistband. Any Casmarran that went looking for it would lose a tendril.

Dax looked back with concern at the creatures filing in and out of *Boyington*, strewing the expedition's precious supplies everywhere. When Finnegan moved to prevent one from dumping out his duffel, a larger Casmarran had interceded. *"Unauthorized."*

"We're from the Federation," Dax said to the speaker. "We're looking for information on what may have happened years ago to—"

"Unauthorized."

"The air's a bit thin here," Finnegan said. "I could swear he said 'unauthorized.'"

Dax's brow furrowed. "I wish I could get through to them."

"Do a handstand," Georgiou said. "That's how they get around."

A loud clattering sound came from *Boyington*, and more supplies fell tumbling out of the hatch. Casmarrans crowded over the goods, tearing articles of clothing apart with their appendages.

"They seem a bit peeved," Finnegan said.

Georgiou was losing patience. "There's nothing wrong with them a well-placed meteor wouldn't cure."

"Funny."

"I wasn't trying to be." She pointed to the sky, where a couple of little moons were visible in the twilight. "We directed one of those onto the planet. The whole atmosphere burned off in a matter of hours."

Dax glowered at her. "You *annihilated* these people?"

"'People' is stretching it, don't you think? And no—I left one alive. It annoyed me."

"Annoyed you how?"

"It came to me to beg for its people—but it got my name wrong."

Dax looked disgusted. "You have a perfectly horrible answer for everything, don't you?"

"Experience, my dear. You could live three lives and not see the wretched things I've seen."

Then she saw something else: the approach of an aerial vehicle. Across the platform, milling Casmarrans moved out of the way to give it room to land. Moments later, Georgiou could tell the airship was disgorging passengers, but too many Casmarrans were standing about to permit her a clear look.

It was another couple of minutes before the barricade of golden creatures parted, permitting the approach of an entourage whose members walked on two feet. Five disruptor-toting Orions stepped forward first, taking station in front of the Federation visitors.

"Good to see you," Finnegan said, offering his hand. "I hope you fellas are better conversationalists."

"Hands on your head!" the Orion he'd spoken to shouted.

Dax complied within a second; Finnegan, reluctantly, followed suit once he figured out the score. But Georgiou did not. She was dumbfounded by the arrival of two more figures who were not Orions. Indeed, they were the only Caitians she'd known to be in Troika space.

S'satah! And her giant of a son—what was his name? She admitted she didn't remember. But here they were. Her pirate ally and adult son, back from the dead. It was becoming a regular occurrence for her—and yet one that remained unnerving.

S'satah's son saw Georgiou and stormed toward her. "You!"

"Yes, me." Georgiou blinked. "Have we met?" It was a genuine question: in this universe, she had no idea.

"Put your hands up!"

The Orion guards on either side of her pointed their disruptors at her head. Looking about and calculating her odds, Georgiou slowly raised her hands. The Orions took hold of her wrists, allowing S'satah's son to frisk her.

"Aha!" he said as he felt the phaser she was hiding in her waistband.

She eyed him as he fished for it. "Careful. Some people don't like that."

"*Shut up!*"

"Step aside, P'rou," said a softer voice. "Let me at her." Over his shoulder, Georgiou saw S'satah approach. The petite woman looked nothing like the pirate queen she'd remembered; she was dressed in formal business attire, with none of the gaudy jewelry she wore in the emperor's universe. She carried a briefcase under one arm, and a data slate under the other.

Interesting, Georgiou thought. *Have we gone straight, in this universe?*

S'satah's eyes locked on hers—and the woman hissed. "I can't believe you'd come here!"

"Yet here I am." Out of the corner of her eye, Georgiou could see Dax and Finnegan staring at her, puzzled. The emperor shared the feeling. She hadn't remembered anything from Captain Georgiou's records that indicated that her counterpart had met S'satah before. But there were other matters at hand— and she decided to play her role as intended. "We've come a long way. Is this how the Casmarrans greet a diplomatic delegation?"

S'satah spat on the ground. "They don't accept them, and you know it."

"What *else* am I supposed to know?"

"Quiet." S'satah spun on her heel and strutted over to one of the Casmarrans wearing a blue speech device. The being towered over the privateer-turned-businesswoman, but S'satah showed no indication of discomfort. "Recognize," she said.

"Authorized," it responded. *"Authorized Factor."*

"Greeting-statement, Manager Xornatta."

"Greeting-statement, Authorized Factor S'satah."

Finnegan whooped. "More words! I knew they were holding out."

S'satah ignored him—and gestured to Georgiou. "Intruder, Federation-type."

"Intruder, Federation-type," the Casmarran repeated.

"Vessel located-platform, convey location-impound, Vertex Two-Two."

"Concur." The Casmarran waggled its limbs at a nearby companion. *"Convey vessel, Federation-type."*

Seconds after the command, Georgiou heard behind her the whirr-snap *Boyington*'s hatch made when it closed. The Casmarran vessels that had adhered to it fired their rockets, lifting the shuttle into the sky. Finnegan was alarmed. "Hold on, there! That's ours!"

"The Casmarrans are impounding it," S'satah said, "like they do all vessels that stray into Troika space. They don't want you here."

"Taking our ride is a damn funny way to get us to leave."

"Your companion talks too much," P'rou declared. He stepped over to Finnegan and got into the human's face, using his more massive frame to intimidate. "Talk some more now. I dare you."

"I had a cute little cat once," Finnegan said. "She had breath about like yours too."

P'rou punched Finnegan in the gut.

"No!" Dax said. She looked urgently to Georgiou, who responded with the slightest shake of her head. It was important to see what these people were about before retaliating.

Doubling over, Finnegan coughed for several seconds before looking up at Georgiou. "They . . . *did* ask me . . . to talk more . . ."

"That was their first mistake," the emperor replied. She looked over to S'satah. "Your second mistake is interfering with me, and my business."

S'satah looked surprised for a moment to hear such stern words. "Since when do Starfleet captains talk tough?"

"A year in a Klingon prison camp will have that effect." That was the cover story they'd come up with on *Discovery*.

"Tragic. The fact remains you *have* no business here. You're violating a treaty—"

"Which is barely a treaty, as I read it. It was a unilateral declaration of borders. The Federation and Starfleet respected them—but that doesn't mean they accepted them, then or for all time."

At that, several of the box-wearing Casmarrans grew more animated—and those without the implements responded, drumming their limbs on the surface of the platform and creating a low rumble. Eyes wide, S'satah gestured to them. "You're lucky they don't fully understand our words," she said.

"They're aware of how badly your damned war with the Kling-ons went. If the Federation thinks to make a puppet out of Casmarra—"

"That's not what the Federation does," Dax said.

"Oh, really?"

"Planets join of their own accord."

"Because they're terrified of the Klingons," S'satah said. "Or the Gorn, or someone else. Your 'members' are just fod-der, buffers for your enemies to trounce. Well, the Casmarrans want no part of you, the Klingons, or anyone else. They're not going to be a front in your next war!"

"Look," Finnegan said, holding his midsection, "this is all a mistake. We had an invitation."

S'satah stopped—and turned her eyes back on Georgiou. "You had an *invite*?" She smoldered. "Yes. Yes, of course *he'd* do that. I should have thought he'd know better."

P'rou snarled. "I'd be happy to go tell him he made a mis-take."

"Yes, where is he?" Georgiou asked. "Quintilian. That's who we're discussing. Isn't it, S'satah?"

The Caitian sneered. "I should be honored that the high-and-mighty Captain Georgiou knows my name."

"I've been a lot higher than this." Georgiou kept her eyes focused on S'satah. "My question. Where is he?"

"He can't help you, if that's what you mean. Quintilian is a guest here—and his franchise is only in space. There's only one offworlder with a license to manufacture on this planet, and that's me." Then a grin came across her face. "And that's not all."

S'satah turned and again addressed the Casmarran she'd spoken with before. "Amendment, Manager Xornatta. Remand bipedal intruders, Federation-type, to S'satah, authorized factor."

The Casmarran repeated her statement in full.

P'rou stepped back over and jabbed Georgiou's phaser under her nose. "She's just gotten authorization for us to kill you. Right here, right now."

Still holding his gut, Finnegan blanched with pain. "Why do *you* get to do it? Don't they get their stalks dirty?"

"They'd rather not," S'satah said. "That's why the traders are the first line to keep you people out—that's a duty that comes with the franchise. Alien security planetside here is licensed to us. And managed by P'rou."

Dax's eyes went wide. "You can't just kill us!"

"Says who?" S'satah stalked past her. "This is Troika space! There's no Federation consulate here for you to run crying to." She looked back to Georgiou. "And *your* death was sealed as soon as I saw you."

Again with the particular hatred, Georgiou thought. "How, again, did I earn this venom?"

P'rou threatened her with the phaser. "You ruined my life! Both of ours, with your accursed advice!"

S'satah bared her teeth. "Do you know how long it's taken us to recover? To get some semblance of success in our lives? And now here you come—"

"I'll kill them all," P'rou snarled. "*But her first!*"

Georgiou had heard enough. She started to say something—only to release a gasp. Her eyes rolling back into her head, she slumped downward in a faint, startling P'rou.

"Philippa!" Dax called out. She looked to S'satah. "Help her."

"We're about to kill her," the Caitian said. "Why should we do anything—"

She never finished her statement. Crumpled on the tarmac at P'rou's feet, Georgiou took the opportunity to reach for a weapon the Caitian had not found, a long silver knife secreted in her right boot. It found a home in P'rou's massive left shin, causing him to drop his phaser and howl with pain.

As he reached for the gushing wound, she grabbed his collar and yanked downward. He pitched forward, much as the guard who had accosted her back on Thionoga had—only this time, she tumbled willingly with him, reaching, in the process, for the knife lodged in his leg. When the two were upright again, she was fully behind P'rou, with the scruff of his neck in one hand and the blood-soaked blade held to his carotid artery.

"Shoot her!" P'rou yelled.

"Then we both die," Georgiou said.

"*Don't shoot! Don't shoot!*" S'satah called out to the Orions.

It became clear in a moment who the guards took orders from. Pressing the knife to P'rou's neck, Georgiou looked about, unsure of her next play. The Casmarrans whirled about, clearly agitated by the action. Georgiou shouted her demand. "Tell them to return our shuttle!"

"They won't do it," S'satah said. "You're disturbing their order. They'd kill all of us before they let you leave!"

P'rou raged. "Mother, shoot this thing!"

"P'rou, shut up!" S'satah stepped toward Dax, still under gunpoint by the Orions. She took one of their disruptors and waved it between Dax and Finnegan. "Let my son go! Or should I kill one of these?"

"I don't care," Georgiou said, tugging at P'rou's head. "Do it. Pick whichever. They're nothing to me."

"*What?*" Dax shouted. "Are you really going to let her do this?"

Finnegan raised a finger in a point of order. "You know, they did say they were going to kill us anyway."

She looked daggers at him. "Sean, shut up."

"Sorry."

All around, the Casmarrans swayed and stomped, their unease brought to a crescendo. Only Georgiou realized it might not be anxiety affecting them when she caught a glimmer from the sky.

"Look behind you," Georgiou said.

S'satah's eyes filled with anger. "What kind of fool do you think I am?"

"I'd love to take time to answer that," she said. "But we're about to have company."

The Casmarran sun glinted off a cargo vessel, descending

from the sky in the north. And not just one. A whole series of freighters, approaching the city and setting the natives into paroxysms of movement. Several Casmarrans quivered festively in place; others quickly cleared the landing area where *Boyington* had been parked to make room.

"Recognize those?" Georgiou asked P'rou. She certainly knew them. She'd destroyed what she suspected was the same fleet back in her own realm. "The Veneti."

"Damn it," he said, massive shoulders sagging.

The Casmarran that S'satah had conferred with, Xornatta, approached her. *"Authorized Factor S'satah, belay."*

S'satah looked up at the being, alarmed. "Question belay!"

"Convoy observed. Authorized Trader Quintilian."

She slapped her hand on her chest. "Security franchise authorized, S'satah! Federation-bipeds remanded!"

"Quintilian communication," Xornatta said, a pair of limbs curling to indicate the Casmarran's blue box. *"Oast import arrived."* The next line carried added emphasis. *"Food import arrived!"*

"Is that box a receiver?" Finnegan asked.

"I think it is," Georgiou said. "And unless I miss my guess, I think the Casmarrans have just gotten a better offer."

S'satah looked angrily at the descending lead vehicle—and at Georgiou. Finally, she called out to her guards. "Belay."

"No!" P'rou howled. But the Orions stepped back—allowing Dax to quickly reach for the phaser the Caitian had dropped.

"Put it on kill, my dear," Georgiou said. "I taught you how, back on the shuttle. No more of that warning-shot business from the landing bay."

Dax's eyes were wide with panic. "You shut up too."

Seeing S'satah's people in abeyance, Georgiou called Finnegan over to where she still had P'rou under her control. "You want a free jab at this one before I let him run back to Mama? You'll enjoy it."

"No," Finnegan replied. "I only like fair fights."

"I've seen you go either way," she said. "You're wasting fairness on his kind. Struts and snarls, but if the odds aren't entirely in his favor, he hides under the furniture."

"You'll pay for this!" P'rou shouted.

She cooed in his ear. "Poor impotent little kitty. Go hide under something." Then she released him and stepped back.

The Caitian scrambled to his feet, favoring the uninjured leg. Returning to his mother's side, he looked back to his former captives—and the descending freighter. "We should stay to finish this, Mother. I know you don't want to have to see *him*, but—"

"If I see His Highness Quintilian now, there *will* be shooting."

P'rou snorted. "What would be wrong with that?"

She tugged his arm. "We're going." She shot a look back to Georgiou. "You should too. Set foot anywhere else on my planet, and you'll regret it."

"Your planet?" Georgiou gestured to the Casmarrans waiting in anticipation of the freighter. "I thought this was *their* planet."

S'satah gave her a nasty look any Terran would have been proud of.

22

Alien Region

Quintilian, it had turned out, was not on the lead freighter that had landed in *Boyington*'s former resting place. Instead, he'd sent an aerial vehicle with instructions to bring Georgiou and her companions to his estate. That Quintilian's people possessed transporter technology was something Starfleet had known since Lieutenant Georgiou's first encounter with the Veneti, back on *Jadama Rohn* years earlier, but the emperor had a good idea why the trader sent the antigrav flier. He wanted to show off.

The aircar was one common to the Orion colonies, Finnegan had said—but nicer, with a luxurious interior and broad, ceiling-to-floor ports allowing its passengers a panoramic view. Through them, Georgiou saw the pentagonal territory known as the Alien Region unfold beneath her, all described by Quintilian's chatty personal pilot: Phylla, an Orion woman of advancing years.

S'satah's factories, abutting the raised plateaus between the Casmarran metropolises. Grimmer locales, homes to the non-native workers she employed. And, across a lake of lustrous blue, the lush, rolling hills that were home to Quintilian's estate.

"Tallacoe," Phylla said with evident pride. "Boss named it for the legendary home of one of my people's greatest emperors."

"The Orions have an empire?" Finnegan asked.

"*Had*," Dax said. "Many centuries ago."

"Then I'd say it's pretty much gone to seed since then." He glanced to Georgiou. "But then, empires are tough things to stay on top of."

She ignored him. Her eyes were fixed outside and down

below, where they saw the same things over and over again: *Money. Wealth.* And, unusually, something she never saw much of on Terra, even in the richest estates: *Class.*

That was because, between the fountains and the vineyards, between the gardens and the marble, there was no attempt to simply knock off the famous statues and architecture of great civilizations. Rather, there appeared to be a restrained effort to draw upon the elements that gave those things beauty, creating a look that recalled the greatness of the past without duplicating it.

And somehow, the trappings of Quintilian's modern commercial enterprise were able to exist here without seeming out of place. Magnificent round structures sat at several locations, hubs for tree-lined boulevards; only when she saw a freighter descending into one of the building's open rooftops did she realize she was looking at a warehouse. The facilities were conspicuous, even as their function was not.

Georgiou peered at the pilot. "I see many Orions working below. Why would they be ruled by a human?"

Phylla looked back. "Quintilian's the best boss we've ever had. He runs a tight operation—no drugs, no thievery, no gambling allowed. Veneti employees are housed in Tallacoe rather than S'satah's slums, as long as they stay out of trouble."

"This is a closed society," Dax said. "How did so many of you come here?"

"Veneti ships make a few trips each year to trade beyond Troika space. The natives won't trade with the outside, but we still need technology, and the Alien Region likes its imports. The ships always bring back a few folks who want to escape somewhere. Like me," Phylla said. "I'd have never been a pilot among my people." She winked at the women.

"Would you look at that?" Finnegan said, gawking at the largest structure in the region.

"The Pinnacle at Tallacoe," Phylla said. "Just like in the old tapestries. Took twenty years to build—the master just moved in a couple of years ago. It's a beauty."

Georgiou had to agree. It was an ancient setting for a modern age, half resembling the engravings she'd seen of the Hanging Gardens of Babylon. Her cousin Alexander had once tried to duplicate that possibly mythical palace, without much success; his sensibilities were as limited as his good sense.

With the Pinnacle, Quintilian had succeeded.

Tiered gardens climbed to the heavens, framed by waterfalls that seemed not in the least artificial. The airship climbed, too, swooping around marbled columns draped in clinging vines, spiraling upward to the topmost level. In that broad space of sky sat a carpet of green, lined by a wall laden with multicolored flowers and broken only once to create an overlook for an observatory. Within the plaza, she saw a Romanesque fountain feeding a twenty-meter-wide pool—and fronting a modest three-story villa that looked better suited for a Tuscan hilltop than for Troika space.

"Here we are," Phylla said. "Domus Quintiliana." The pilot set the airship down in a clearing between the fountain and the building and released her passengers. "If you'd like a closer look at anything while you're here, don't hesitate to ask. I'm at your service—when the master of the house doesn't need me, that is."

Georgiou and the others had only been outside for a second when she lifted off, quickly removing her discordant bit of technology from the scene.

And then—peace. Peace in the late afternoon sun, broken only by the splashing of the fountain and occasionally by chirps or a caw from a small structure nearby. Movement in a netted window suggested it was an aviary for Earth birds.

"Nice. But weird," Dax said.

"Well," Finnegan said, "it beats a punch in the gut." He strolled over to the fountain, sat, and took off his shoes. A moment later, he was sitting on the rim, soaking his feet. "You think those vineyards are for wine?"

Georgiou nodded. Quintilian's hobby as a vintner had

come up in his messages to her counterpart; he must have even gotten a bottle out to her sometime, because he'd asked her if she'd enjoyed it in one of their last exchanges.

Dax looked at her. "What should we do now?"

The emperor had already decided. She was partway to the door of the villa when she heard a high whine behind her. She turned to see a transporter effect before the fountain. Finnegan tried quickly to stand, lost his footing, and splashed into the pool.

The light subsided, revealing the man she'd met—and killed—a couple of years before. He looked better than he had in her universe. Still the gray fox, tanned and healthy, but with finer clothing, including a burgundy cape that came to his knees. He held an ornate golden walking stick—which he let fall to the ground the instant his brown eyes saw Georgiou. "Philippa!" he declared, stepping toward her. "I can't tell you how good it is to see you."

She closed the distance and took his outstretched hands. *How huggy are we?* she wondered as he brought her toward him for an embrace. She got her answer soon enough. It was long and full, his hands around her hips rather than her shoulders. And when they finally drew apart, he looked directly into her eyes and whispered, "Together at last."

They kissed, an event that the emperor welcomed, even as she had a thought so amusing it nearly broke the mood: *Why, Captain Georgiou, you old dog. You've had a secret love all this time.*

She drew back. "I thank you for the invitation."

"As do we," said Dax, alongside Finnegan.

Quintilian glanced at them—and then Georgiou. "Who have you brought us?"

Georgiou suppressed a chuckle. "This is my aide, Ensign Emony Dax."

The man looked to the Trill, his eyes swiftly widening with recognition. "Not *the Olympian?*"

Dax smiled awkwardly. "You can't tell me you've heard of me way out here."

"Nonsense." He separated from Georgiou and stepped over to take the shorter woman's hand. "If seeing my estate didn't tell you as much, I'm sure your captain would have: I'm a fanatic when it comes to the old ways. Not just of my own people, but others'—though I'm ashamed to admit I don't know much about the Trills. But the Olympics were one of ancient Earth's greatest inventions."

He kissed her hand, prompting Dax to shoot an astonished look to Georgiou.

Behind them, the third member of Georgiou's party clambered out of the fountain, barefoot and dripping. "And I'm Lieutenant Sean Finnegan," he said, waddling over.

"Uh-huh," Quintilian replied. He immediately redirected his gaze to Georgiou and Dax. "My apologies for my late arrival," he said, starting to walk about, favoring his right leg very slightly. "We were on a trading mission when I got your message. I don't normally go with the traders anymore, but the harvest is always a big haul. It's paid for half of what you see around here—and the land it's on."

"Your home is beautiful," Dax said.

"I agree," said Georgiou, and she did.

"So glad you like it," Quintilian replied. "Not that I'm surprised—a lot of the ideas I put into Tallacoe came from our talks. You have an unerring taste." He waved to the west. "There's a whole grotto down below there that's loosely based on the pictures you sent me of the shrines of Vulcan."

Georgiou nodded, feeling a bit of discomfort as she did. *Maybe I should have studied their correspondences more closely.*

"My etiquette's terrible," he said, as if sensing some unease. "You don't need a tour after your travels. There'll be time for that. You'll stay here, of course."

Donning his shoes, Finnegan brightened. "That's good, because those walking celery stalks stole our shuttlecraft."

Quintilian acknowledged that he'd already heard. "I have my people checking into that. And speaking of my people . . ." Trailing off, he clapped his hands and looked past Georgiou to the villa. "*Gnaeus!* See if our guests need help with anything!"

"That's the thing. We don't really have any—" Dax said, starting to turn. She stopped in midsentence when she saw the lumbering hulk emerging from the doorway to the villa.

Gnaeus—which Quintilian had pronounced with the first letter sounded—was a brown mass of muscle two meters tall. A leathery two-armed torso any human bodybuilder would be proud of trundled about not on legs, but what Georgiou could only consider to be organic tank treads. Muscular wave motions within the creature's abdominal base propelled it about like a gastropod—but more speedily than any snail ever moved.

"A Dromax," Georgiou said.

"Of the Dromax, from the Dromax system," Quintilian responded, seemingly unsurprised she knew the name.

Georgiou did know it, because the Dromax had been the most vicious fighters she'd faced in Troika space. Somewhere underneath the recessed carapace that served as a head was a mind for violence—which suited them nicely, as a living tank interested in song and oratory would have been a waste of evolution's craft. In fact, she had never heard one speak at all, having gotten the species name years earlier from S'satah—the friendly S'satah, *her* S'satah.

So she was surprised when Gnaeus addressed her. *"Greetings, honored guests of the master,"* he said, a male human voice emanating from a red box mounted around its midsection.

"Gnaeus is the true master," Quintilian said, "master of the estate when I'm away. Dromax never sleep. He's the only one of his kind up here on the Pinnacle, so he likes receiving guests. As do I."

Finnegan stared, mouth open, at the creature, his second strange alien of the day. He pointed to a discoloration on the

Dromax's gut—a pair of large, blackened crescents tattooed below the voice box. "He's got moons on his belly!"

Dax glared. "Don't be rude, Sean!"

"It's not a problem. It's an identifier in their culture," Quintilian said. He stepped over and clapped his hand on the shoulder of the creature. "It's why I named him Gnaeus. It's a praenomen—a given name—meaning 'birthmark.'"

"I am that I am," Gnaeus responded in a voice that was both booming and sedate. *"I am not offended."*

Georgiou thought that was good for Finnegan, as she'd seen video of Dromax tearing Terran foot soldiers limb from limb. That had convinced her to enslave the species upon their defeat.

Gnaeus retrieved Quintilian's walking stick and offered it to him. Georgiou took note again of the older man's slight limp.

"It's nothing," he said, noting her gaze. "Touch of inflammation from an old injury. Flares up a little when I'm going from planet to planet."

As Dax explained that she'd been part of a project studying exactly that, Gnaeus moved to address Georgiou. *"You will please follow,"* the Dromax said, turning for the house. Quintilian gestured to the door.

Finnegan stepped forward quickly and walked beside the magnate. "The captain tells me you're fond of wine."

"Oh, yes," Quintilian said, suddenly seeing something of interest in him. "Some of our recent vintages here have been truly remarkable. Are you an oenophile?"

"I like a taste now and again." He shot a wink back at Georgiou and put his hand on Quintilian's shoulder. "Tell me, do you have anything for broken ribs?"

The two men entered, chatting away, while Georgiou's progress inside was halted by Dax, who pulled at her sleeve and took her aside. The Trill seemed dazzled. She whispered, "Who *is* this guy?"

"He's my boyfriend. Didn't you read the briefing?"

23

Domus Quintiliana

"More wine?" Quintilian asked, eyes glistening in the candlelight.

"More of everything," Georgiou said, offering her glass.

Reclining on the dining couch beside hers, he gestured for a servant to open another bottle. "More for the lady of Tallacoe."

"I'm surprised there is no one by that title already," she said, not minding the appellation. She'd seen humans and Orions working in the villa: all young and fit, if wearing significantly more than those she employed in her nightclub on Qo'noS. But the couch by her host's side had been placed there specifically for the dinner. "All this is too much to enjoy alone," she said.

"Well, you know me," her host said, taking the bottle. "Married to the business." He poured for her. "Say when."

"Always." She smiled, glad to be wearing something besides her stuffy Starfleet uniform. His servants had found wardrobes in the villa for all of them, and hers right away; she found the black evening gown fit perfectly. It was good to be in her element again—or, at least, in an adjacent box on the periodic table.

Dinner had been a nine-course meal, so far, served to them as they reclined in the manner of ancient Roman nobles. It was, by a long stretch, the most sumptuous repast she'd enjoyed since being transported off *I.S.S. Charon.* The emperor knew from Quintilian's correspondences with Captain Georgiou that he admired in equal measure the ascetics of the past and the great leaders who liked a flourish of excess. Both found expression in his home: the simple furnishings of his dining room, accented by the truly magnificent fare upon it.

"What's this dish?" Dax asked, already halfway through it as she asked.

"Sautéed grellion stalks, straight from the fields of Oast," he said. "You can't get it any fresher—we just brought it in today."

"Oast?" Georgiou asked.

"Third part of the Troika." He grinned. "I know, I've probably never mentioned that name before. It's kind of a reflex. Think the other species here are reclusive? They're galactic travelers compared to the Oastlings."

She nodded. She'd never known the proper name of the place; just that her scouts had recommended bombing the hell out of it. And she had.

Gnaeus, standing at attention with arms crossed near the eastern entrance, abruptly turned and exited through it. Quintilian saw that and looked down the hallway on the opposite side of the room. "I should amend what I just said. There are two Oastlings who've ventured far, alone among their people. And here they are!"

Georgiou and her companions looked to the western hallway. Previously darkened, it now contained a flickering, like torchlight. What emerged from the corridor, however, were no bearers carrying flame. Rather, two spindly beings entered, each with two arms and five legs. And in place of heads, bulbous light-giving ellipsoids sat atop their necks like squashed bubbles.

"Step forward, Pyramis," Quintilian said. "You, too, Thisbe. Let my guests look at you."

Georgiou did indeed look. She'd only seen Oastlings imaged from orbit; the sight had been enough for her to conclude such grotesques had nothing to offer to Terrans. In person, they were uglier still. As the nearer one approached, she saw its head was a transparent membrane inside which bioelectricity appeared to crackle within a dark cloud of gas. Georgiou squinted but could see no other structures inside.

Could any being have a gaseous brain?

"Pyramis and Thisbe are only the second and third Oastlings who've ever left the fold, to my knowledge," Quintilian said. "They're more than just my connection to a very private people. They help keep me organized."

Thisbe nodded to Quintilian—and inside her head, visible to all, clouds whirled and swirled. Slowly, glowing straight lines took shape, gaining texture and, finally, color. Finnegan gaped at the three-dimensional image. "That's our shuttle!"

"That's right. I asked for an update," Quintilian said. Spying a data slate in Thisbe's clutches, he gestured for her to approach. He took it and read. "That's where I thought it was."

Finnegan's ears perked up. "Where is it?"

"It's gone to impound in Vertex 22." He looked up. "That's what they call the cities that sit between the geometric regions. I've tried to get them to adopt something more creative, but the Casmarrans do things their own way."

"Can you help us get it back?" Dax asked.

"Maybe, but not for a while. They're going over it, inspecting it for antigens. You may have noticed they're a touch antsy about outsiders."

"They let *you* live here," Finnegan said.

"All the outsiders are limited to this sector—and Dromax aren't allowed off Tallacoe's grounds."

"What of those two?" Georgiou asked, nodding to the Oastlings.

"They're not welcome at all—but I paid for this space. I do what I want. They never leave the building, so it isn't a problem." He handed back the data slate. "Thank you, Thisbe. You too, Pyramis. You may go."

As they shimmered off, Georgiou asked, "I take it you named *them*, too?"

He smiled. "Many Oastlings don't have names, as you and I would understand them; they mostly communicate through those pictograms. Theirs is a culture I'd love to know more about, but I get the impression they don't think any of us are ready for it."

"Thisbe and Pyramis. Another European legend?"

"Babylonian. Though the best-known account comes to us from Ovid, a Roman."

"Lovers, I take it?"

Quintilian looked at her and smiled. "They snuck each other notes through a wall."

She laughed at that.

"I figured you'd get the joke. I'd considered Heloise and Abelard, but they don't really fit my motif."

Finnegan's glass having been drained yet again, he placed it upon a servant's tray with a clink and wiped his face with the back of his hand. "You know quite a bit about quite a bit, Mister Sextillion. Don't you ever get ribbed by the other merchants?"

"These days, most of them work for me, so I have a lot of time to read and learn—and most of what I get comes from outside." He nodded to Georgiou. "Your captain has sent me some wonderful texts over the years. With a few exceptions, the Troika species tend not to have much in the way of narrative history; they're constantly reinventing their worlds, every day a new one. But for everyone else, I think the whole galaxy would be better served by a more robust understanding of the lessons of the past."

He stood from his couch and walked along the edge of the room, gesturing to the paintings on the wall. All depicted historical scenes from various planets. He stopped before one, an icon depicting a scowling Klingon. "For example," he said, gesturing, "from what I've been able to gather from the news that's filtered in, the entire Klingon War seems to come from a fundamental misunderstanding of the stories of Kahless."

Georgiou raised an eyebrow. "How so?"

"T'Kuvma set his whole doctrine on the idea that the Federation threatened Klingon identity—that its very existence might cause their empire to come apart. But the true Kahless knew otherwise. His first precept of the *qeS'a'*, in fact, drew upon the story of the feuding warriors of Kopf's Cliff, who ultimately needed one another when the fires came. I can see a day when the Empire might need to rally to the Federation's aid, or vice versa."

"Preposterous!" the emperor said, in a manner more hers than Captain Georgiou's.

"I'm sorry—I forgot. I'd heard you were imprisoned." He walked back over to her and knelt, placing his glass on the floor and his hand on her wrist. "I'm sure that must have been a difficult time for you."

"You're forgiven," she said, more relieved that he hadn't caught her break in character. As delightful as dinner had been, a shot at Whipsaw was the reason she had gone this far.

"Just the ravings of a man with too much time on his hands," Quintilian said. "It's a shame there isn't a true descendant of Kahless around to set them straight." He took up his glass again and drained it.

Dax looked to Georgiou—and then spoke. "Mister Quintilian, there's another reason we're here."

"Oh?" He turned to face her.

"When the two of you met years ago, there was a freighter in distress: *Jadama Rohn*. What happened to it?"

Quintilian set down his glass and scratched his beard. "Why would you want to know about that?"

Georgiou quickly interrupted. "What she *means* is—she was wondering if the captain had been provided for." She shot Dax a look that said *"Patience."*

"Vercer?" He looked down and chuckled lightly. "Good old Vercer. I haven't thought about him in years."

Georgiou nodded. "Your early messages talked about how he'd been your mentor. I'd mentioned it all to Dax," she said, "and how he'd died. You know, transporting drugs so dangerous they killed his entire crew." She glared at the Trill. "Dax was wondering whether his family had been provided for."

"Indeed?" He looked to the young woman. "What's your interest?"

"Well," Dax said, quickly improvising, "I work with an agency that provides relief to the families of victims of war—and also the families of those who've lost their lives to the drug trade."

"In this galaxy," he said, "there's often no distinction."

"Right. When the captain told me what had happened, I just thought to ask. Because he was your friend, and it sounded so bad."

Georgiou watched Quintilian. Dax had scrambled—but it appeared to have worked. "That's very benevolent of you, thank you." He shook his head. "That was twenty-five years ago, now. His children are grown—not in my employ, if they stayed in Troika space at all."

So there were children, Georgiou noted. "I don't suppose there's any way to find out at this point."

"I can't imagine." He thought for a moment. "The only person in my circle that ever gets down there is Phylla."

The pilot. She'd fished for a bit more, and caught something. She decided to quickly change the subject—

—but Finnegan beat her to it by standing and attempting to offer a toast to Quintilian. It was only an attempt, because in the process, his glass leapt from his hand, sailing end over end. He reached over for it and lost his balance, falling backward over his couch. Two seconds later the floor had two new occupants: a shattered glass on one side of the furnishing, and Finnegan on the other.

Already standing, Quintilian rushed to his side. As other servers approached, the blitzed Finnegan muttered, "A very fine vintage."

"Have Gnaeus call for the doctor," Quintilian ordered. "He just fixed your ribs a couple of hours ago, Lieutenant. I think you overdid it too soon."

Finnegan stared blearily at his benefactor. "I . . . don't want you to think . . . I drink to excess because I'm Irish."

"Of course not. That kind of thinking went out centuries ago."

"I drink to excess . . . because I haven't accomplished what I want. And because . . . I'm going to be forty."

Dax gawked. "In a dozen years!"

"A responsible officer . . . plans ahead." Finnegan looked back over his shoulder as Quintilian's servants moved him down the hall.

Their master began to follow. "I'd better see that he makes it to his room," Quintilian said. He looked to Georgiou. "Nightcap later?"

"Of course," Georgiou said. As soon as the room had emptied, she hopped up and walked over to Dax, who had just risen. "What was that?" she asked in a hushed voice.

"What was what?"

"Asking about *Jadama Rohn*!"

The Trill was baffled. "It's why we're here, remember? We need to find out whether how those people died was connected to the cloud on *Farragut*. Why can't I just ask him?"

"Keep your voice down!" She pulled Dax aside to the corner. There wasn't any obvious sign of surveillance equipment, but she didn't think there would be in a place designed for artistic appeal. "We both read Lieutenant Georgiou's after-action report—the one she revised after she'd diagnosed the deaths. There's no drug known, illicit or otherwise, that consumes red blood cells."

"Then, or now. Right."

"So either one exists in this region, and he was telling the truth—or something else happened to the ship, and he didn't want me—I mean, *her*—knowing about it. Which means we've got to tread carefully. If he didn't want us knowing then—"

Dax nodded. "I guess I hadn't thought that through."

"No, you didn't. We've got a lead now." She looked to the doorway, where she thought for a second she saw the hint of a shimmering glow. After an instant, it vanished. "Act normal— and go to bed. It's time for me to go to work."

24

Domus Quintiliana
CASMARRA

Work, for Georgiou, meant trying to get a few more facts about *Jadama Rohn*—and the possible blood devil—out of Quintilian in a way she'd known she would enjoy: seduction. She'd been interested since seeing him from the bridge of *Hephaestus*, but that, of course, was not to be. Or so she'd thought. One seldom had a second shot with a person after you reduced them to atoms.

The wardrobe in her quarters was fully stocked with apparel suitable to the occasion; however busy he claimed he was, Quintilian was clearly no monk. She had changed her mind about what to wear—or not—several times, trying to calibrate between her desires and what the mogul's relationship with Captain Georgiou might have been. Once settling on something, she'd lit the candles in her room and waited.

And waited.

Over the next hour and a half, she changed clothes five times, with her choices alternating between more conservative and less so. On one hand, she was angry about being stood up; on the other, she felt less like wasting time once he did appear.

When he didn't show by the two-hour mark, only the rage remained. It was a good thing so many of her rivals died aboard *Charon*; if any had ever somehow heard about a mere mortal standing up the emperor, her reign would have immediately ended.

Screw Section 31, the Federation, and blood-eating clouds of all kinds—this is war!

She reached beside the bed for one of the candlesticks and

discarded the nub of wax, already burnt low. There was some weight to the holder. A good heave at the mirror would do double duty, attracting attention and giving her shards with which to cut the man's throat when he arrived. She had it in hand when a knock came at the door.

"There's nobody home!" she yelled.

"*Madam, you are requested in the specularium.*" The low voice belonged to the Dromax, Gnaeus.

"Why should I go to—" she sputtered. "To the what?" It didn't sound good.

"*It is the observatory. Master Quintilian has something he wants you to see.*"

"Now?"

"*Yes, the observatory works best at night,*" Gnaeus said, without a hint of satire. "*It is across the lawn, so consider the temperature.*"

Blood still boiling, she tossed the candlestick onto the floor and found a kimono. It didn't go with what she was already wearing at all—but as she yanked the obi tight, she knew he'd never find that out. He'd be lucky if she didn't throw him off the side of his damn citadel.

She arrived at the weathered brick building at the edge of the rooftop terrace only after padding, barefoot, across the lawn. The fluffy pair of house shoes in her room had offended her by existing; besides, she had her fury to keep her warm against the Casmarran night.

She found him not inside the structure, but on a patio at the far side, perched right at the yawning edge and overlooking much of the Alien Region far below. Quintilian's attention was high above as he hunched over an ancient telescope, making adjustments by the light of the moons and the stars.

Arriving nearby, she cleared her throat, determined to keep her thoughts to herself until she could find words so sharp, so acidic, that they would flay his skin from the bone.

He spoke without looking back. "Have you ever been to Capri?"

What?

"Tiberius built a villa to each of the gods there," he said, still peering into the eyepiece. "The richest is Villa Jovis, perched at the highest place on the island." He gestured outward. "Tiberius's behavior there was pretty horrible. Unspeakable, in fact. There are even rumors that he threw unwelcome guests over the walls, to die horribly on the way down."

Glad to hear my idea is sound.

"The whole residence was on an artificial terrace, sort of like I have here. It was excavated at the orders of someone named Mussolini. Maybe you've heard of him."

Heard of him? We had a starship class named for him.

"At the promontory, they found the Specularium—an observatory the emperor had built for his astrologer, Thrasyllus of Mendes." He turned to gesture to the structure around and behind him. "No one's clear on what it looked like; the place was in ruins even before the Third World War. But I think it looked very much like this." He looked to her for the first time. "Tiberius died at Villa Jovis, in fact."

"Did he freeze his ass off?"

Quintilian stared at Georgiou—and then laughed, long and hard.

She delighted to hear it, in spite of her anger. "I was thinking of throwing you over the edge, just now. You misled me."

"No, I just didn't tell you where the nightcap would be." He stepped to the shadows and retrieved a bottle and a pair of long-stemmed glasses. "I'm sorry. Business intervened. Apparently Zattah's got the Casmarrans pretty riled up about my asking you here."

She took the glass. "Zattah? Not S'satah?"

"I could never get the Caitian consonants down. Besides," he said as he poured, "Zattah was one of the great emperor-consorts of the Orion Empire. She built the first Tallacoe, in fact."

"She and P'rou were . . . not too welcoming. You heard what P'rou did to my lieutenant."

"Well, Finneran is fine now." He looked to her. "Finnegan?"

"It really doesn't matter."

"I take it he's a bit of a brawler. He asked to wrestle a few falls with Gnaeus."

"And how would that go?"

He chuckled. "Medical science can only fix so much."

She drank, knowing that *Terran* medical science had made Finnegan into a much better man. Or a better weapon, at least.

Quintilian shook his head. "I'm sorry about what P'rou did. I'm afraid that's more about me."

"How so?"

"I've known him most of his life. He's an émigré here, like everyone else—his mother fled to join us when he was just a toddler. She tended to handle surface trading for us; she's a good linguist, and helped develop those voice boxes the Casmarrans and the Dromax use. P'rou, meanwhile, was always aboard our ships. You could say the Veneti helped raise him."

"But?"

Quintilian looked away. "As soon as he came of age, he wanted more responsibilities. He was good at it. He was on his way to being master trader—the post I used to have before I declared myself semi-retired. But as a captain, he treated his crews abominably."

"If they're refugees too, they've probably seen worse."

"That's not how I want to run the Veneti. We're a haven from that—from many things." He shook his head. "I couldn't have P'rou mistreating others. So I relieved him of his duties."

"And his mother left your services, too."

"Not entirely because of that, but—" Quintilian waved his hand. "Well, you know all the rest."

No, I don't, Georgiou thought.

He placed his empty glass on the ground. "I'm so rude. Come look!"

She didn't know what he meant until she saw him step to the telescope. She really wasn't interested; her opinion of the ugliness of the sky in Troika space hadn't changed, and she wasn't in the mood. "I don't really feel like—"

"I know what a lover of astronomy you are. Please, be my guest."

Grudgingly—and remembering which Philippa Georgiou she was supposed to be—she stepped to his side and studied the awkward contraption until she found the eyepiece. "Right here?" she asked.

"You're such a kidder. Take a look."

She did, wondering why her counterpart—or anyone else—bothered to use such an outdated means of studying the skies. But when he spoke, she realized that there was a point to looking.

"That's Dromax," he said, referring to the colorless glob in the eyepiece and the swarm of satellites surrounding it. "An enormous gas giant with dozens of huge moons, tearing themselves apart whenever they get near one another. A metaphor for the Dromax themselves, constantly warring."

Georgiou nodded. She'd interrupted their wars to enslave the race.

"I'd show you Oast, but it's enveloped in an absorption nebula."

She remembered. They were a bugger for her scouts to find—and once she'd decided to eliminate the species, her fleet had simply fired torpedoes at every gravity source within.

He stepped closer to the edge and gestured downward to his facilities on the surface. "They were all isolated from everyone, even each other. The Veneti helped give them a classic triangular trading structure. The Casmarrans are great manufacturers, but they need raw materials—that's something the Dromax have in abundance. The Dromax, in return, get weapons and machinery for their wars."

"You're a war profiteer?"

"I'm a shipping firm. If my people didn't carry the Casmar-rans' goods, someone else would."

"And the Casmarrans make out either way."

"They do all right, but it's not only about greed. By pro-longing the wars between the Dromax, the Casmarrans ensure they don't have any trouble from them."

Self-interest was something Georgiou understood. That Quintilian had also turned it to his advantage spoke well of him in her book.

He crossed his arms. "You've seen what both parties get out of the deal from the Oastlings—food, and lots of it. Neither the Casmarrans or the Dromax are much for farming—and while you can't see it, Oast's sun makes the Oastling planet the breadbasket of the Troika."

"And what do the Oastlings get?" Georgiou asked.

"They get left alone."

Georgiou understood that too. "So it isn't real trade. They're vassals, bartering for their protection."

"It's not as simple as that—there's more to them than meets the eye. But, yes, they do love their privacy. And are will-ing to accept what it costs." He crossed his arms and looked to the sky. "Everything I need, Philippa—everything these people need—is right here."

She studied him. Welling with pride, and not in the least tired at this hour. He had accomplished something, though it had apparently taken most of a lifetime. She expected he had done the same in her reality, for all the good it had done any of them. She doubted any alliance between the Troika species was even possible; they were just too strange, too different. And it would not have made any difference in stopping the Terran onslaught.

But this Quintilian didn't know that, and he seemed happy. The rewards here were just so different, she thought. On arriv-ing amid the Klingon War, she'd initially thought this universe wasn't much different from her own; violence spoke and power was all. The merchant she'd seen on *Hephaestus*'s screen might have made for a plaything for a couple of days, but nothing more: he was somebody who'd chosen not to fight for dominance. A trader was a traitor to himself: a coward. The man before her, though, was something more. Might he have succeeded, had he followed a different path?

And could she ever succeed in his?

She blinked. *Whipsaw. Blood devils. Focus.*

She stepped to his side. This wasn't quite the place for a seduction—and it certainly wasn't the weather for it. But even under these stars, she could get things rolling, and start coaxing out some more vital information later. She grasped his arm and pulled closer for warmth. His hands and body were colder than she'd expected, but she intended to change that. "Have you ever told me your real name?"

He smirked. "You don't like Quintilian?"

"It sounds like you found it in an old history text."

"That I did. I was reading a lot in those days." He nodded. "First name was Quin. Last doesn't matter—that life was nothing to me."

"I have known my share of orphans." *And made a few too.*

"Oh, that's right," he said, remembering something and pulling back. "How is Michael, by the way?"

She did a double take. "Burnham?"

"Of course Burnham. You're so proud of her. She made it through the war, I hope?"

Georgiou answered carefully, but truthfully. "I saw her at the end."

"That's good. I think we both take in orphans, hoping to find homes for them in our service." He shook his head. "Didn't work with P'rou, though."

"Nobody's perfect."

"Well, give her my best. And tell her I hope to see her again."

"Of course." Georgiou tried to curl up closer to him. "I'll—"

She stopped and looked up at him. "Did you say '*again*'?"

He nodded. "Of course. Five years ago, remember?"

"I . . ."

He parted from her and stepped to the telescope. "That was when you brought me this."

Georgiou stared at him, afraid she would start babbling. "Yes. I brought you that when I visited five years ago."

I visited five years ago?

"I was sorry you both had to depart so abruptly, but I know Starfleet's leave situation. *Shenzhou* needed you." He looked up at the moons. "My business needs me bright and early tomorrow. But I'd like you and your friends to join me later in the morning, and I'll show you around the operation."

He clapped his hands, and Gnaeus emerged from the interior of the observatory. "Yes, sir?"

"See that the captain gets back to her quarters."

She stared. "To my quarters."

"Yeah," he said. He stepped back closer to her and put his hand under her chin. "I'd suggest a different destination, but I remember what you said last time."

"What I said last time."

"I didn't want to push—I know how you feel about that."

Her eyes goggled. "We've . . . been corresponding for a quarter of a century—and you're afraid of moving too fast?"

"Well, one of us was. I just want you to be sure," he said, kissing her on the forehead. "Good night." He disappeared back into the observatory.

Gnaeus remained on the balcony. "Your chambers, madam?"

You're lucky I'm very confused right now, she thought as she stormed past him. It was all she could do not to make like Tiberius and throw the headless thing over the edge.

25

Tallacoe

"Why the hell didn't Section 31 tell me I'd been here before?" the emperor asked. "I mean, that *she'd* been here before!"

In a distribution-center alcove out of earshot from Quintilian's tour group, Dax looked at Georgiou and shrugged. "I don't know why they didn't tell you. I haven't thought of anything new since the last time you asked." She added more softly, "But five minutes is a long time."

Georgiou clenched her fists and turned away.

She had slept in the most comfortable bed she'd known since *I.S.S. Charon*, yet she had risen enraged—and also alone, which only added to her fury. After taking breakfast in her quarters, she'd belatedly joined Quintilian's tour of the shipping facilities on his estate. Thereupon she fell, silently screaming, into a sea of disquisitions into the varied lading practices of freighters.

"—*the same freighters on the Oast–Dromax runs can be used on the Dromax–Casmarra runs, but they have to be disinfected once here to make sure no toxins from the Dromaxian ores survive to the next time it hauls food. Now, over here—*"

Were it not for Quintilian's silken voice, the emperor would have fled entirely—that, and the fact that the man had found himself constantly interrupted by aides needing advice. Those interludes had given Georgiou ample chances to rant not-so-quietly to Dax.

"Leland sent me here with practically a gigaquad of correspondence between the two of them, telling me to act like the captain," Georgiou said. "They told me how she sips her tea, how she wears her hair, and drilled into me her whole service record, so I wouldn't trip up. Yet nobody bothered to tell me that she'd actually *visited* the place. *And she even brought Michael!*"

"Didn't you say Burnham's off on assignment with *Discovery*? Maybe they never got the chance to ask her about it." Dax shrugged. "Maybe they didn't know about the whole thing."

"Leland acts like he knows everything. How could he *not* know?"

"Well, he didn't know this. Or maybe he had a reason not to tell you." Dax pursed her lips and frowned. "But that doesn't make a lot of sense either."

Georgiou added her own grimace. None of her Terran captains were allowed to go running around free from surveillance whenever they felt like it; there was too much danger of revolt. She kept them under watch at all times, usually with her chief of security, Joann Owosekun, providing reports that detailed every minute spent, every light-year traveled. But the emperor didn't know how Starfleet worked. "Can a captain just hare off to a forbidden zone?"

"I don't know. I'm not Starfleet." Seeing the third member of their party off chatting with Quintilian's pilot, Dax had an idea. "Finnegan!"

His head snapped toward her at the sound of his name. "Emony!"

Georgiou rolled her eyes as he hustled over. Finnegan had reportedly appeared right on schedule for the tour, energized and none the worse for the previous day's injuries and night's festivities. Blackjack had been resilient, too, but his pain receptors had been surgically deadened. How Finnegan managed remained a mystery to her.

Dax took him aside. "Is it possible for a Starfleet captain to just vanish for a week?"

"You mean off the bridge, when encountering some kind of alien menace? Some mysterious power, is that it?"

Georgiou glared. "She means vanish on their time off, you dolt."

"Ah," he said. "It's a simple matter, a simple matter indeed. On shore leave, you can do any blessed thing you want. I'd imagine a captain could go a lot farther—get into even more trouble, if you know what I mean."

Dax and Georgiou looked at each other.

He smiled, his eyes alight. "I'll tell you, I once hopped a tramp freighter for a weekend just to spend fifteen minutes on Risa." He kissed his fingers. "But what a fifteen minutes."

"Ew," Dax said.

Georgiou agreed. "She means you can go now."

Finnegan shot her a sidelong glance. "You'll be a happier person if you try the coffee. The Oast Roast works wonders." Then he ambled back to the group.

Dax began figuring. "The captain and Burnham were both on *Shenzhou*, and Georgiou had a standing invitation. But would she really risk violating a treaty just to visit a friend?"

"Doubtful," the emperor said. "She was sickeningly obedient." She ruminated for a moment. *If it were for an assignation, would she bring Michael as chaperone?*

There was no answering that. She threw up her hands.

Dax paid note. "I don't think I've seen you like this. You're—well, you're flustered."

"I don't like surprises."

"Well, I'm sorry I gave you one by talking out of turn at dinner last night. This is all new to me," Dax said. "I figured we were here investigating, but I guess there's a distinction between police work and intelligence work."

"They're one and the same in my world. We stuff you in a box and shoot electricity through your body until you talk."

"Uh-huh. Sure, whatever you say."

The emperor had found she could no longer reliably get a reaction out of Dax by talking about the brutalities of the Terran Empire. Georgiou decided to take that as a positive development. Dax wasn't any more necessary to her plans than Finnegan was, but keeping company with someone who cringed at her every comment was so dull.

She saw several workshops along the corridor of the facility. A lumbering Dromax exited one, nearly bumping into her. *"Excuse me, madam,"* it said, enunciating through the red voice box on its midsection.

"You're excused."

"I am glad. The day is pleasant. I must return to my security duties."

As polite as Gnaeus, she thought, though she noted it had a different-shaped marking on its gut. The Dromax trundled off, making her wonder how they could be the same species she'd seen fighting in the video Captain Maddox had presented, the one that convinced her they needed to be enslaved.

Then she heard an identical Dromax voice emanate from the workshop. *"Stop touching me, imbecile!"*

She peeked around the corner. Another Dromax stood there before one of Quintilian's uniformed workers, ranting obscenely as the human tinkered with the voice box. "It'll just be a quick adjustment."

"Quick! I've seen quicker corpses," the Dromax said. It had yet another different belly marking. Shifting, it noticed Georgiou. *"What the hell do you want?"*

"Just saying hello," she said.

"It's bad enough my general sent me to work here among stinking sacks of flesh. I have to deal with constant interruptions!"

The human worker apologized. "Sorry, Captain. The Dromax communicate with one another through several methods, including minuscule changes in body temperature at various locations. The translator's sensors have to be adjusted regularly to sync with Quintilian's preferred vocabset."

"Why are you telling this to—" the Dromax started to say. Something the technician did caused its tone to alter: *"—an*

honored guest of ours, interrupting her tour? Please excuse us, and enjoy your day at Tallacoo."

Georgiou grinned. "I sure will." *If only all my minions had had similar gadgets to adjust.*

Rejoining the group, she saw Quintilian return from his conferences alongside an Orion woman whose hair was almost entirely white. "Sorry," he said, leaning against his regal walking stick, "but the schoolmaster had a great idea."

"School?" Georgiou asked.

"For the children of the shipping workers," the schoolmaster replied. "We always have a fete day after the harvest is delivered. The students have several athletic competitions planned for Master Trader Quintilian's benefit this afternoon. Tumbling, dance, gymnastics." She clasped her hands and faced Dax. "He sent over videos of one of your performances this morning; I showed them to the kids. They'd be absolutely delighted if you'd judge their competition, and maybe say a few words."

The request had caught Dax completely off guard. She looked to Georgiou. "I'm here on Starfleet business—"

"She would be absolutely delighted to judge your event." Georgiou patted Dax on the back. "I can do without you for one afternoon, Ensign."

"Wonderful!" the schoolmaster said.

Quintilian smiled at Georgiou. "It's kind of a command performance. You can watch from my box at the arena."

She stepped toward him and straightened his collar. "I appreciate the invitation, but I think I'll take your pilot up on that offer to look around some more. I'm sure my companions will be in good hands with you."

"Dinner, then?"

"Marvelous." She touched his cheek. "I'll see you later."

Beaming, Quintilian stepped away to confer with the schoolmaster—and seconds later, Dax sidled up to her. "What did you just do?" the Trill asked under her breath, teeth clenched.

"What do you mean?"

"I mean I've judged so many damn competitions I want to smother myself under the next mat I see. I didn't come on this mission to do it again!"

"No, you came on this mission to find *Jadama Rohn*. And I'm not going to be able to do that unless I can get away. You just keep your eyes on Quintilian."

"Hmm. I'll admit that's not a hard thing to do," Dax said, looking over at the man. He seemed confident and magnificent in his industrial element. "He sure is something. Did you get your nightcap?"

"I could have used a night*gown*. He had me stand on a ledge in the middle of the night for an hour so he could show me his telescope."

"I'm guessing that's not a euphemism."

"Tragically, no."

26

Alien Region
CASMARRA

Phylla and her aircar had been easy for Georgiou to find; both were within the structure Quintilian's group had been touring. The pilot had seemed delighted that her offer had been accepted—up until the point in the low-altitude flight when Georgiou had surprised her by asking to visit the factory slums outside Tallacoe's walls.

Georgiou's first cover story, that she was seeking a companion of Quintilian's that she had met years ago, had left Phylla worried and skeptical. Anyone her boss still wanted to know still had a job with him, and thus lived within the confines of Tallacoe—even the retirees were provided for. Georgiou had then played the Starfleet card. "The Federation is interested in issuing Quintilian its highest civilian honor for an act of rescue in neutral space many years earlier. We just need to speak to a witness."

Suddenly happy to help, Phylla had deposited her near an Alien Region bar frequented by Quintilian's former rivals. Unwilling to leave her aircar in that neighborhood, she'd left Georgiou with a communicator and many words of warning. "If I don't hear from you in three hours, I'm coming back with every Dromax in Tallacoe. If anything happens to you, the boss will have my hide!"

It had taken her little time to discover why caution was in order. Quintilian's successes had long ago given him a near monopoly in shipping; the few rival operations had dwindled to a sorry bunch of idlers hanging around the tavern, waiting for whatever scraps of work came their way from S'satah and her factories. Outsiders were suspect and unwelcome.

Georgiou had expected as much that morning, selecting her ensemble from what she considered her wardrobe's "Proletariat Collection," bland coveralls perfect for a day touring the holdings. Quintilian had approved—but more importantly, the outfit had helped her blend in. To a point: she had only been forced to pummel two people to get the information she needed. Captain Vercer's children had indeed emigrated offworld, but he had other relations about.

The trail ultimately led her to a shabby hovel near the western reaches of the Alien Region, in the shadow of the great wall of Casmarran urbanity that separated the area from the next one beyond. Her information hadn't been very specific; no alley here would ever get a name. But she had found a name etched beside the door to a dilapidated apartment. The letters in Orion were so weathered they were barely visible, but she could make out what they said:

HOME OF VERCER AND JADAMA

Jadama. As in Jadama Rohn*!*

The door was made of cheap metal; she hadn't seen an automatic door anywhere in the region. It was bent, having been kicked in a time or two; its lock didn't catch. When no one answered her knock, Georgiou let herself in, certain that the groaning hinges would alert anyone inside.

She was right. No sooner had she stepped into the filthy anteroom than a shrill female voice called out from behind a tattered curtain. *"Get out of here!"*

Avoiding trash on the floor, Georgiou worked her way along the inner walls, heading toward the aperture. She was nearly to it when a disruptor blast sizzled through the curtain, the blast's energy terminating against the wall by the entrance. Looking back, she saw several blast marks all over the wall, ranging from the floor to the ceiling.

Lots of intruders—or a poor shot. Maybe both.

"Get out! Nothing left to take!"

"Your curtain is on fire," Georgiou shouted.

"Damn it!"

Another blast—and the wall she was leaning against vibrated. That shot had missed the doorway entirely, impacting inside the shooter's room. Georgiou played a hunch. "I'm going to put out the fire," she said. "I don't want you to shoot me."

Two more shots, both ripping through the burning drapery. Then . . .

"Okay."

No fool, Georgiou grabbed a poker from the fireplace and used it to reach toward the curtain. She gathered it in and pulled it from its pinnings, which gave way easily. Seconds after stomping the flames out, she waved the poker before the doorway. When the motion prompted no further firing, she spoke. "I know you're blind, Jadama."

"What of it? We all have problems!"

"I may be able to help you with yours. But you must not shoot me."

A beat. "All right."

Georgiou peeked around the corner and saw her: an old white-haired Orion woman curled up in an ancient chair, disruptor pistol tightly clenched. The din of the gunfire past, she could now hear tinkling music coming from a player somewhere.

"That's 'The Dance of the Whirligigs,'" she said, easing into the room. "I've heard it."

"What daughter of Orion hasn't?" The old woman frowned. "Who are you?"

Seeing a plaster face mask on the side table near the woman's chair, Georgiou decided on an answer. "A friend of your husband's. You are Jadama, correct?"

The woman nodded—and for a second, her face brightened. Then her expression turned sour. "I know that voice."

Georgiou stopped in the middle of the room. "Have we met before?"

"You know we have," Jadama said. "You came around here, a few years ago, asking questions. You and your friend."

Michael, Georgiou thought. If she and her counterpart had come here, it could only have been for one reason. She quickly settled on an approach. "We talked about your husband, back then. About Captain Vercer. I'm here to follow up."

Placing the disruptor on her table, Jadama reached for the plaster mask. Her eyes teared up. "Vercer is dead and gone. Why don't you leave me alone?"

"I'd just like to know about his final assignment. His—"

"*Get out!*" Jadama clutched the mask to her chest and began fumbling again for the disruptor.

Georgiou pounced across the remaining distance for it, laying her hand upon the weapon even as Jadama did. In the act, the table tumbled, sending the weapon to the floor. The emperor went down with it. This universe's Michael wouldn't approve of her struggling for an elderly person's weapon, but Georgiou wasn't about to get shot by—

"*Auntie!*" called a voice from outside. "Are you all right? It's Junah!"

"Junah, come quickly!" Jadama called.

A younger Orion female in work fatigues appeared in the doorway and saw Georgiou kneeling on the floor beside the table. The grubby-faced woman reached into her satchel. "Get away from her!"

Not about to have another weapon pulled on her, Georgiou grasped Jadama's disruptor from the floor and spun. "Don't do that."

Eyes widening, Junah raised her hands away from the satchel and lifted them to the air. "There's nothing to take, can't you tell?" she said. "Just the gun. It's her only protection from people like you!"

Georgiou played another hunch. Sidearm still in one hand, she lifted the table back into place with the other. "There was a fire," she said, nodding to the missing curtain. "I put it out.

Ask your aunt." She looked to Jadama. "I came to visit. Tell her."

Holding tightly to the plaster mask, Jadama choked back tears. "She's one of those who came around before—about Vercer!"

Junah's eyes narrowed with recognition. "Yeah, you."

Georgiou stared back. "Yeah, me."

"I told you to get out the last time you were here." Then she began looking around the hovel. "Where's your partner this time?"

"I came alone."

"That's half of a right decision. Leave."

Seeing how overwrought Jadama was—and that Junah seemed to know something—Georgiou landed on a compromise. "I will—if *you'll* talk to me."

Still fearful for her aunt's safety, Junah relented. "Out there."

Georgiou stepped into the anteroom with the younger woman and placed the disruptor on the shelf behind her. She expected she could take out Junah a dozen different ways; the weapon was worth more set aside, as a show of good faith. "Now. Captain Vercer."

"Isn't it enough you bothered us before? My uncle is dead. Vercer died before I was even born."

That startled Georgiou a little. Life in the Alien Region had aged Junah.

"But you know of how he died?"

"Of course—as much as anyone knows." Junah stepped over to the smoldering curtain and knelt. "What did you expect my aunt to tell you that she didn't before?"

"What she told me before would be a start."

Junah looked up at her, surprised. "Don't you remember?"

"The friend I was with—she took the notes. Those notes went with her after we left."

"Parted company, huh?" Junah rose and started to shake

out the curtain. "I'm not surprised. Nobody can keep a job on this planet."

"Unless they're working for Quintilian."

Junah laughed. "*Especially* if they're working for Quintilian!"

Georgiou sensed an opening. "That was where it started, right?" She strained to recall the events detailed in Lieutenant Georgiou's report about her encounter. "Vercer had lost his job with the Veneti. That's why he was operating on his own, with *Jadama Rohn*. Named for your aunt?"

"*Rohn* means 'dear.' It was his ship originally; Quintilian bought it when he was starting up the Veneti. When Uncle Vercer broke away, he put all his earnings into buying it back. After . . . *the incident*, Quintilian's people flew it back to orbit—where the Casmarrans confiscated it as a possible biological hazard."

Georgiou's breath quickened. *Biological hazard? Now we're getting somewhere!* She ran her finger against the dust on the shelf. "Did they find out what had happened on board?"

"Everyone died!"

"I mean, did they find out why? Was it drugs—or something else?"

"It wasn't drugs!" Jadama shouted from the other room.

"Her ears work fine," Junah said, smirking. "But she swore it to your face then. Uncle Vercer ran a clean operation."

"You . . . both seem certain of that."

Deciding the curtain was a loss, Junah folded it and stepped to the open window. She leaned out, threw it into the street with the rest of the trash, and turned back to Georgiou. "Look, after he broke ties with Quintilian, things were tight. But he'd gotten another client."

"What client?"

"I don't know. But he told my aunt that the one job would pay for their entire year."

"He was in the Tagantha System when his ship was found. You don't know where he was going? Where he'd come from?"

"How should I know?" She gestured back to Jadama's

room. "She didn't, either. He never said. That made it all the worse, not knowing."

Georgiou thought for a moment. "The Casmarrans took the ship. Where?"

"Impound station. Right over there in Vertex 22, in fact. Quintilian gave them a report, so I guess that was the nearest place." Junah walked to the basin that passed for a kitchen and sighed. "For years, Jadama and her kids tried to get it back, to get some value out of it—but the Casmarrans said nobody would want a plague ship. It's still there, for all I know."

Maybe with my shuttle parked right beside? Satisfied, Georgiou stepped to the shelf and picked up the disruptor. She gestured with the weapon as she approached the exit. "I'll leave your aunt's disruptor in the street—someplace the scum who live here won't find it." She stopped in the doorway and turned to face Junah. "Present company excepted, of course. You've both been very helpful." She paused. "I'm not exactly sure I can arrange a reward for you—"

"Don't do us any favors." Then Junah looked up, her attention drawn to something behind Georgiou's shoulder. "*You*, on the other hand . . ."

Before Georgiou could react, a burst of energy at her back sent her flying forward into the hovel. She knew a low-powered stun blast when she felt one; nothing else fired point-blank was survivable. But she did lose hold of the disruptor and was in no shape to fight when a pair of Orion toughs collected her off the floor. They turned her to face the shooter.

"We meet again," P'rou said. He pointed his weapon at her. "Five different people tipped us off. Three at the bar, one in the street—and just now, her, through the window."

When trashing the curtain, Georgiou remembered. *I'm such a fool.*

"I'm Junah—and I know who you are," her betrayer said to P'rou. "I don't want the reward she offered, but I'll take one from you."

P'rou gestured to one of his partners. "A worthwhile transaction. Pay her something."

"And one more thing," Junah said as P'rou's toughs dragged Georgiou to the door. "Make sure she doesn't come back. I'm sick of seeing her."

The Caitian released a growl, smiling all the while. "It'll be my pleasure."

27

Alien Region
CASMARRA

Leland had wanted Georgiou to play secret agent. In her universe, that recalled images from old Terran video dramas where heroic masterminds fought to prevent scurrilous enemy spies from interfering with their plans for domination. No children ever wanted to play the spies, who usually died horrible and deserved deaths, often staged with exotic creative flourishes.

Those were all in fiction, of course, something busy Terrans seldom had time to bother with. They were too busy making their dreams a reality. It was in that spirit that Georgiou had agreed to work as Section 31's infiltrator in Troika space: because of the potential reward, a weapon with which her empire could be created anew. The prospect for a theatrical demise wasn't on her sensor screen.

P'rou, on the other hand, had clearly watched too much of something, if his choice of lairs was any indication. After her capture at Jadama's home, the Caitian and his thugs had carted Georgiou to a near-abandoned factory close by in the Alien Region. For half an hour, the emperor had lain strapped to a metal table in a shabby old foundry, now rumbling reluctantly to life. Smelting equipment and molds were all about; the only light came from kilns being relit.

"Sorry to keep you waiting," P'rou said, returning from a control station on the other side of a partition. "We only operate this place when we have enough ore—it takes some time to restart. And I didn't want to send you off before my mother saw you."

"Always thinking of Mommy," Georgiou said.

The bruiser moved to strike her—only to stop, his fist centimeters shy of her face. "No, better you remain pristine until we're ready."

"You'd better not wait around too long. I'll be missed."

"You won't be found." He held up the communicator Phylla had provided; it had been wrested from her before she could use it. "I turned off its homing device back at the flat."

Georgiou exhaled. The building stank of charred metal. Her place of restraint offered her full view of the high ceiling, where giant vats hung suspended from railings. Some were being pumped full of water, clearly part of some cooling system. Other containers, parked outside an enormous furnace, awaited something far more threatening.

P'rou saw where she was looking. "We're melting kironium now. You'll get a closer look soon enough."

The name gave her pause. "Kironium? I didn't think that was found in nature."

"That's *di*-kironium. Kironium's rare, but Troika space is lousy with it. Everywhere but here, that is. The Casmarrans dug all theirs up centuries ago."

Another connection, Georgiou thought. Dikironium, Dax had said, was detected as a component of the cloud that had beset *Farragut.* She eyed the jet-black vats, beginning their automated move into the furnace. "What exactly does kironium do?"

"To flesh? You're going to find out."

"As long as we're waiting, indulge me."

He snorted. "Kironium is good for only one thing: it pleases the stinking Casmarrans. It replaces tin in kironium bronze; they can't get enough of the stuff. Something in the alloy triggers their pleasure receptors."

Georgiou had seen the statues everywhere. "So their art gives them a high."

"Or something. It's pretty to look at, and the Dromax still have plenty of ore. If the Troika ever threw the gates open to the galaxy, they could probably move a lot."

"They don't want to do that?"

"Some things are more important than wealth," he said. "Mother says you Starfleet people poison everything you touch." He glanced at the kiln, its safety barriers keeping in most of the blazing heat but releasing a fair amount of light. "The Casmarrans are great at manufacturing, but they despise high temperatures. That's given us a business here. All the hot work goes to outsiders."

"Like you," she said. "I'm not surprised. You're a parasite, living on the fringes. Never going for the real chance."

Newly enraged, P'rou advanced toward her again—

—only to turn when he heard his mother's voice: "*Where is she?*"

"Right where you want her." He stepped aside to admit S'satah, again dressed as if she'd come from a business meeting.

Hovering over Georgiou, S'satah looked her prisoner up and down, feline eyes flaring with glee in the light of the glowing furnaces. "Wonderful. It's not even my birthday."

"We celebrated your birthday once," Georgiou responded. "As I recall, *you* were the one in restraints."

"Stop talking nonsense."

"Ah, yes. I was thinking of someone who was more fun."

Bewildered by the comments, S'satah held up a comm. "You were a fool to come here." Her expression turned quizzical. "P'rou's message said you were asking about Captain Vercer."

"Looking up an old friend."

"Old friend?" S'satah laughed. "You're the one who found him dead!"

Georgiou's eyebrow arched. "Who told you that?"

"Nobody needed to tell me," S'satah said. "I was there!"

The emperor's eyes narrowed as she tried to remember all the details from her counterpart's report. "There was no Caitian aboard that day."

"Says you. I was in a spacesuit. You couldn't see my face—

but I stuck a disruptor in yours." S'satah did so again, now. "Remember?"

The emperor did not, but there was no explaining that. There had, however, been mention in Lieutenant Georgiou's notes of the person who'd threatened her. "There was someone Quintilian called Zee." She looked up. "*Zattah?*"

S'satah laughed derisively. "He was always renaming people. The world's his toybox and we're his playthings." Venom dripped from the Caitian's voice.

I get it now. "Were *you* his plaything, S'satah?"

The woman slapped her with her free hand.

"I'll take that as a yes."

S'satah stepped back and pointed outward, in the general direction of Tallacoe. "That place beside him was mine! The job of master trader was going to be P'rou's!" She jabbed a furry finger at Georgiou. "But all those years, he kept messaging you. Again and again. You don't think I knew? He didn't even hide that he was doing it. He'd even get up from our bed to contact you!"

"Then you definitely aren't the woman I knew," Georgiou said. "She was more distracting."

P'rou balled his fist. "Let me at her!"

S'satah was about to—but then she held him back. "Wait a minute," she said, glancing at her son. "She's Starfleet."

"You have a grasp of the obvious," Georgiou droned.

"So she's got a pretty uniform back in her luggage. What of it?" P'rou asked his mother.

"So why would she risk her neck asking around here?" S'satah loomed over her again. "Why do *you* care about Vercer? About *Jadama Rohn?*"

"You know Starfleet. Driven by curiosity," Georgiou said. "And we're all bleeding hearts. A gerbil dies across the galaxy, we send an inquest team."

"But twenty-five years later?" S'satah tilted her head. "Or was that also why you were here five years ago?"

"You used to be a sport, S'satah. Let's torture each other and find out what we all know."

S'satah glowered at her—and then looked to the furnace, where a vat of white-hot kironium bronze emerged. Noisy motors above the overhead track carried it, suspended, out over the work floor. "P'rou, what's going on?"

P'rou smiled. "I thought we'd send Quintilian a nice statue."

"A gift to commemorate old times?" S'satah grinned. "I like it."

Georgiou had suspected all along that was the plan. "It won't work. My body will burn—or melt. You'll have nothing but a messy metal lump. Believe me: I know whereof I speak."

"Then we'll send him a messy lump," S'satah said. "With a recording of its creation."

Georgiou strained at her bonds, to no avail. Her head turned, she saw mother and son step partway across the foundry floor. Three of his four Orion henchmen were gathered, anxiously awaiting what was sure to be a grisly spectacle. Preparing her comm unit to record the emperor's death, S'satah asked, "Who's running the show?"

"Wemmis." P'rou pointed to the booth that held the control station. He cupped his hands and shouted to be heard over the machinery. "We're in position, Wemmis. Let it rip!"

After a moment, the enormous overhead vats went into action, trundling along. Georgiou's exertions took on greater urgency. Vats crossed beneath one another in midair, changing direction and heading toward her.

As gears ground, P'rou looked up. "Wait!" His call only barely audible to the struggling Georgiou over the din, no one in the control cabin heard it at all—or, at least, nothing changed in the motions of the vats overhead. P'rou shouted at the booth. "Wemmis! What's going on?"

A static-ridden message came over the public address system. *"There's a problem in the mrflfnff!"*

S'satah looked to her son. "In the what?" she asked.

"There's a problem in mrflfnff!*"*

P'rou started toward the booth. "That's the wrong vat. And the wrong way. *Wemmis!"*

"Sorry, he's not home," boomed an accented human voice over the public address system. *"Bath night!"*

S'satah looked up and saw the hinged bottom to the vat directly over her head opening. She screamed—only to be literally drowned out as thousands of liters of machine-chilled water pummeled her and P'rou's goons.

"Mother!" Seeing S'satah and his companions flattened beneath the still-cascading torrent, P'rou dashed toward them. Realizing they were choking but alive, he pivoted to charge back toward the booth. He didn't get but a step before he ran into what the restrained Georgiou had already seen: a large metal bar swinging at his face, wielded by a grinning human.

"You should've gone for the shower!" his assailant shouted, the words covering a sickening crack, as metal met fur. P'rou tumbled backward, unconscious, into the coursing puddle that held his cohorts.

Georgiou called out, "Finnegan!"

Finnegan doubled over in laughter, dropping the crowbar with a clang. "Never thought I'd get to use the bucket trick on duty!"

"Finnegan, you moron. *The vats!"*

He looked up and saw what she did: the herky-jerky transit of a molten-metal-filled vat, splashing superheated liquid as it made its way toward her. "Whoops."

He ran to her side—not what she wanted him to do. "Go turn it off!" she said.

"I was lucky to turn it on!" Unable to pull loose her restraints, he glanced up at the approaching vat before running back across the foundry floor.

Georgiou saw there was no way he could get there in time. "What are you doing? Come back here!"

"Make up your mind!"

Finnegan had just passed the pile of coughing prank victims when he spied the disruptor S'satah had dropped. He snagged it and headed back to Georgiou.

"At the base," she said, pointing to where the metal straps holding her down were connected. Finnegan knelt, trying to figure out where to shoot.

"Oh, bloody hell," he cried. He stood and took aim. Not at the vat itself—or S'satah and her Orions, trying to regain their feet. Instead, he targeted something much farther away: the overhead motor controlling the vats. His shot struck something mechanical, causing the vat to jerk to a halt, spilling a drizzle of molten alloy that just missed Georgiou's table.

The danger wasn't over, she saw: the motor was still running, somehow, gears grinding away even though its burden made no progress. Finnegan adjusted the disruptor and fired once at the connection locking the strap holding her arms. Georgiou sat up immediately, seized the weapon from him, and directed his attention back to her drenched captors. "Stop them!"

While she reached around the table to target the straps holding her legs, Finnegan ran back across the floor and found the crowbar—just steps short of a rising Orion. Finnegan swung again, causing the male to fall backward across a crawling S'satah.

"Ha ha!" he shouted, waving the crowbar in a fencer's riposte. "*En garde!*"

"*Run, you fool!*"

He looked back to see the shouter: Georgiou, standing free—and pointing. Pointing at the track suspended from the ceiling, where the damaged motor, having finally decided which direction it wanted to turn, slung the vat of kironium bronze on a headlong trip to the far side of the foundry floor. In seconds, the vat violently reached the end of its possible journey—and, with nowhere left to go, dumped its contents. The superheated metal blossomed onto the floor, showering nearby equipment and setting off a chain reaction of explosions.

Finnegan made a panicked dash in Georgiou's direction, while S'satah and her Orions gathered up the fallen P'rou. "Run!"

Georgiou took aim with the disruptor at her former captors, but there was no time to change the setting, much less shoot. Not when the track structures all around the foundry started their own groaning collapse, spilling water and alloy as they descended. Instead, she grabbed Phylla's comm unit from the floor where P'rou had dropped it and fled, following Finnegan into the street.

The foundry burned and churned, exploding as the pair bolted through the alleys. They were three blocks away when the din subsided.

There, winded and leaning against the back wall of a slum, Georgiou looked at him in amazement. And when Finnegan's breath returned enough for him to double over with riotous laugher, she did something she'd never thought she would.

She joined him.

When the elation subsided, she finally asked, "What are you doing here?"

"I saw that you were trying to sneak off with that pilot lady. What's-her-name? Pillow."

"Phylla," Georgiou corrected. "I didn't sneak off. I had Quintilian's okay."

"But you left without me or Dax."

Wiping sweat from her hair, she regained her cool. "Why would I need either one of you?"

"I'm assigned to watch you. They said you'd try to ditch me."

"Perhaps it's because you belong in a ditch," she said, reaching for the pager. She cracked it open and reconnected the power source. "You're not Blackjack. You're of no use to me."

"Seems like I was a lot of use back there."

She closed the pager and activated it. "I had things fully under control."

"Didn't look like it."

She wasn't going to argue that point. She walked briskly past him, knowing Phylla would need room to land. But she stopped and turned when a different question occurred to her. "How did you even know where I was?" She held up the pager. "This wasn't working—and I haven't had my ear implant since Thionoga. Leland didn't give you some way to track me, did he?"

"I wish he had—it would've been easier." He pointed to the sky. "I hitched a ride on the roof of your aircar."

You what? Georgiou looked to the sky. "We were in the air for half an hour."

"It was a bit brisk, I'll admit." He flexed his fingers. "Rough on the knuckles too. I'm just glad it wasn't raining."

Looking up again, she saw the aircar approach. Yes, Phylla would have stayed in the area—and definitely would have seen the conflagration. It was just possible that someone might perch atop the vehicle, she saw—but one question eluded her. "Why would you do something like that?"

He shrugged. "It's my job."

She took a full step backward. A willingness to risk his neck insanely in the performance of his duties? *That's Blackjack.*

Then she did a double take. "Wait. I was ambushed earlier. Why didn't you help me then?"

"To be honest, I stepped away for a bit. I'd seen you stop in that pub and I figured I'd be a poor guest to visit and not pay my respects. Then I see they're dragging you down the street." His expression grew thoughtful. "In retrospect, I probably should've mentioned I don't have the local currency *before* I opened my tab."

She rolled her eyes. *That's Finnegan.*

Phylla landed ahead at an intersection. Georgiou waved him toward the vehicle. "Let's go. I don't know how much of this I want to get back to Quintilian."

Finnegan looked at the black plume of smoke rising in the north. "I have a feeling he'll find out."

"I'll think on it."

Then he followed her. "Hey, can I ride inside this time?"

"I'll think on that too."

28

Domus Quintiliana
CASMARRA

Quintilian had indeed learned about the disaster at the foundry, and Georgiou's proximity to it; she had expected there was little chance that Phylla would not have reported back to her boss at some point. But the pilot had also evidently shared Georgiou's cover story about a possible Federation award for him, and while it had not fully satisfied his curiosity regarding her whereabouts, he had pressed her no further about it.

Dax, meanwhile, was fit to be tied, having kept Quintilian busy all day, talking first with the schoolchildren and then going with him on a tour of the estate's artwork. Through whispers over another exquisitely indulgent dinner, the Trill had learned a little of Georgiou and Finnegan's adventures—and the emperor discovered that Dax had been forced into some evasion tactics of her own.

"I'm just glad you showed up," Dax had said. "The longer the day went, the more he flirted with me."

Georgiou had been more impressed than offended. "He certainly is ambitious. He must be twice your age."

"That's what *he* thinks," Dax muttered.

Georgiou chortled. "What do you mean by that?"

"Oh, nothing," she said, fumble-mouthing a little. "It's just when you're famous, you get a lot of experience deflecting unwanted attention."

What Dax had not wanted, Georgiou certainly desired—and not just because she refused to be supplanted in the mogul's imagination. If S'satah was to be believed, Quintilian had evidently been in a relationship during much of the time he was corresponding with Captain Georgiou—and he was apparently keeping his romantic options open now as well. She imagined that either of those things might have been off-putting to her counterpart, but neither offended her in the least. Knowing there was a libertine behind that polished exterior made the emperor feel more akin to him, not less.

And so, having many more questions that needed answers, Georgiou made sure her evening walk with Quintilian ended not at the observatory, but rather the highest place on the estate: his bedchambers on the villa's top floor. As a Casmarran moon rose outside in the cloudless sky, its light washed across a bed strewn with mangled sheets, but empty of occupants. The couple sat on the floor, leaning against the bed as they took a rest and watched the moonrise.

"I'm so glad this finally happened," Quintilian said, reaching backward to retrieve his champagne glass from the table. "It was worth the wait."

"Twenty-five years?" She chuckled. "I suppose that's praise." She clinked her glass to his. "I was surprised last night didn't end here."

"Well," he said after taking a sip, "I remembered the last time you were here. You were more reserved. You're almost a different person."

"Is that a problem?"

"Not at all. But I was worried that I'd offended you then."

Georgiou seized the opening. "How do *you* remember that visit?"

"I remember being surprised when you asked to see me, after twenty years. I remember a lot of walks with you, while Michael was touring around. And then I remember the day when she came back and whisked you out for the afternoon."

Georgiou feigned recollection as she took another drink.

"You packed up your shuttle pretty quickly after that. You'd said Starfleet had summoned you back, but my people never detected any transmissions."

Then you were looking for them. "In my position," she said cautiously, "there are things I can't always share." She needed a subject change. "You've never spoken much about where you came from."

"There isn't much to say. My parents were prospectors. I was born in one of those little colonies the Federation warned people about starting—too far from Starfleet's protection, but close enough that we assumed we'd get it anyway."

"Which colony?"

"It no longer exists. You know those little brushfire wars that would happen between the Federation and the Klingons, like Donatu V? We got invaded—wasn't even by the Klingons, but one of their slave-species proxies. That's what happened to my knee—got crushed under debris."

"It doesn't seem to have stopped you."

"Still flares up a little—we didn't exactly have access to good care at the time." He looked out the open balcony doors to the moon. "My parents put me on a freighter to safety while they stayed to fight." He cast his eyes downward. "I was eight."

She didn't bother asking what had happened to them.

"I kicked around on merchant ships for a while that's how I met Vercer. He'd heard there were shipping contracts to be had between the Troika species, safe from the outside world. You know the rest."

"Not all," she said. "There's S'satah's part in your story. Or, should I say, Zee's."

She didn't explain—and it turned out she didn't need to. He stared at the glass, nodding. "How'd you find out?"

"I'm perceptive like that."

"Well, I guess she wasn't very welcoming when you showed up five years ago. She certainly didn't like me sending her and P'rou immediately on assignment. I was just trying to avoid a collision."

"And it was after that when you fired P'rou—and S'satah left." She stared at him. "Did I have anything to do with that?"

"Which part?"

"Pick one."

"Zee and I kept company out of convenience. In the beginning it wasn't something I thought was worth mentioning to you. As the years went on, I figured it was too late. At the same time, she was acting like P'rou should become my heir—and that I should put up with whatever antics he had in mind. She was Agrippina to my Claudius."

"And P'rou was Nero."

He grinned. "I've always loved that you can relate on these things. You definitely saw there was a problem five years ago, but I liked that you never told me to get rid of him. You just talked about Starfleet, and how ships could and should be run. It made me want to raise the bar." He straightened. "And yes, drumming him out meant she went too."

You don't sound too disappointed.

"*You*, on the other hand," he said, "would make a fine master trader."

"That's one I've never heard before."

"I'm serious." He gripped her hand. His grasp again felt cooler than she'd expected, but it soon warmed up. "You've told me all about your work—not just your adventures, but how you handle problems. And how you cultivate those you think are talented, like Burnham. So when you're ready to retire, I'm sure I can find a place for you."

Georgiou pulled her hand back. Innuendo, she appreciated—but the offer was meant for someone else.

He watched her stand. "What's wrong?"

"Nothing." She fished through the sheets for a wrap. "After the last few months I've had, this place has been marvelous. The food, the . . . *accoutrements*—have been just what I needed. I could stay for years."

He stood up. "I thought that was what I was offering."

She donned her kimono. "Shall I be frank?"

"Surely."

She stepped to the open balcony doors. It was a warmer night than the one before. "It's not a growth proposition. You're doing okay—but the prospects in this region are limited."

Quintilian looked about the lavish room. "I'm doing pretty well!"

Georgiou disagreed. "You're at the mercy of your client states. Any of them can pull your trading franchise on a whim. And you're only allowed to trade your own manufactures outside Troika space. Your growth is permanently stunted."

Seeing she was serious, he found a robe and put it on. "The idea is to keep them safe, preserving what already exists here." He joined her on the balcony. "And they get a say, you know. I'm not an emperor."

She stifled a laugh.

He noticed. "What?"

"You spend an inordinate amount of time thinking about them. Emperors and empires."

"That's not exactly experience."

"You've even named yourself for one."

He pointed to the air. "No, he was an educator. Marcus Fabius Quintilianus. Brilliant man; Vespasian made him a consul in the years after Nero."

"I must have been thinking of another universe. My point remains."

Quintilian nudged her playfully. "Seriously, what would you do if you *were* emperor?"

"Emperor," she repeated, her hair tousled by the breeze. "Not Captain Georgiou. Emperor."

"That's right."

She paced across the balcony. "Acting not in the interest of Starfleet or the Federation, but of the Veneti, and the Troika species."

"Sure. Humans, Klingons—all other alliances are immaterial. What do you think?"

"As emperor," she said, turning, "I see many possibilities.

Your intent has been to protect these strange species from a galaxy of beings who are not like them, and who would use their resources and territory for their own purposes. But to succeed, you *will* have to use them for your purposes, in a way you've never done."

He leaned back against the doorjamb and crossed his arms in evident interest. "Tell me more."

She stepped to the railing and pointed in the direction of the hangars. "The Veneti freighters have little rock-shooter cannons. I would upgrade them. They can become serious warships without adding significantly to the vessels' masses or their energy needs." She turned back to face him. "Once I've done that, I'd maximize what I get from the species themselves."

He chuckled. "Were you at dinner? I've already gotten quite a lot."

"You're skimming off the top, like a trader," she said, filling the last word with disdain. "An emperor *plunders*. An emperor would see how easily the Veneti freighters move around in Troika space—and would see opportunities."

"Like?"

She pointed to the star directly overhead, one that he'd shown her the night before. "First, the Dromax. You say they're warlike and multiply quickly. They have to be brought under your control first." Clenching her fists, she paced again. "I would spare a few freighters for kamikaze duty, landing in tactical centers bearing high explosives. In the chaos following detonation, my next wave lands, bearing commandos."

"Bearing *what*?" He laughed, plainly amused by her flight of fancy. "Where's this army coming from?"

She pointed down from the balcony. "My warehouse workers, just as my merchants are my navy. They'll be enough—until the Dromax are brought to heel. You've said they multiply quickly. *They're* your shock forces."

Mesmerized, he nodded. "Draft the conquered. Like Alexander"

"Then back to Casmarra. The economy will be in collapse without the Dromax military market. I bomb S'satah's facilities and declare *myself* the market for Casmarra's munitions."

His eyes widened at that. "*Kill* her?"

"She was willing to do it to me when I landed." She didn't mention the foundry. "Only then do I mop up the Oastlings. The fear they have for the other powers is mutual—otherwise the Dromax certainly would have invaded. But I'll have both the Casmarrans and Dromax on my side, and can quickly take whatever's necessary."

Quintilian, who had begun listening with bemusement, was no longer smiling—but neither did he appear horrified. "Then what?"

"I no longer need worry about trading internally for profit—or about the locals' fears about opening up to outside trade." She looked to the sky and spread her arms wide. "I open the doors, trading with neighboring neutral systems until I see which are most vulnerable, ripe for takeover using the tactic I used with the Dromax."

"That won't work with the Federation and the Klingons."

"That, I will have prepared for. There are a host of weapons which may be employed—once manufactured. *Or found.*"

He stared at her. In a lower voice, he said, "Then what?"

"Repeat." She faced him. "Repeat, and rule."

For several seconds, he watched her, dumbfounded. Georgiou worried for a moment. She'd broken character, showed him something she hadn't intended to. She wasn't sure how he'd respond.

Then he started laughing. "It almost sounds like you've done this before."

She smiled—and stepped back inside. "Where's that bottle?"

———

They continued celebrating each other's existence far into the night. If he exhausted more easily than she expected given his years, he returned to the game again and again—repeatedly calling down for wine and sweets between their more private activities. It was, for Georgiou, like a time out of a dream.

So much so that when a dream began for her, she couldn't tell that she had fallen asleep.

She was on Terra, in the training center, practicing—no, watching *others* practice fighting. Young people. Herself—and San. Her beloved, long-dead San.

The emperor stepped toward them, wondering why she hadn't been noticed yet. When San delivered a kick that put her younger self onto the floor, Georgiou stepped over to offer words of encouragement—and a hand.

"Get up! The floor may be comfortable, but you can't stay down forever." She knelt closer. "Open your eyes!"

Her younger self did that—revealing, in place of eyeballs, two dark oval bubbles, gases swirling within.

Just like the Oastlings' heads.

"You don't belong here," Young Georgiou said in a voice not human.

Georgiou swiveled to see San approaching, with the same eyes—plus lightning. *"You don't belong here,"* he chanted.

She turned again—and put her hands to her ears to shut out their words. But they pierced her brain, and she felt her entire existence peeling away. She screamed, but no sound could blot out what they were saying.

Georgiou snapped up in bed, sweating. But even as she panted with exhaustion, somehow she knew the truth: she was just in another dream.

29

Domus Quintiliana
CASMARRA

"You've been asleep all day!" Dax said.

Georgiou yawned. "Aren't you going to ask me about my night?"

"Spare me. I think I know all I want to know."

Georgiou had awakened with the sun on the horizon; the fact that it was going down at the time had been a surprise to her. Her revels had contributed to her long slumber, surely—and then there was the dream, as strange as any side effect she'd ever experienced from a chemical, alcohol or otherwise.

Quintilian had long since exited his chambers. For some time, she'd lingered there, studying his mirror and personal effects. None of the indicators of vanity in an older man: no telltale wig stands, no color for his salt-and-pepper beard. All else was normal, like a hypospray containing what appeared to be a vitamin supplement. She did see a container of rouge, which matched the trace amount on her fingertips; she didn't judge him for that. He wasn't likely to keep his tan aboard starships.

After a quick predinner breakfast rustled up for her by the servants in Quintilian's villa, she'd found Dax reading in the building's library. It was a smaller version of an enormous structure she'd seen on her tour the day before—and it didn't take Georgiou long to realize the Trill gymnast had been figuratively bouncing off its walls for hours.

"What's *wrong* with you?" Dax asked in anger.

"What's wrong with *you*?"

"That's easy. I'm on a mission, remember? And I haven't been able to do anything."

"It's important to know one's limitations." Georgiou exited the library.

Dax stormed after her into a drawing room. "I'm serious," she said in a hurried whisper. "You and Finnegan nearly got yourselves killed trying to find out where *Jadama Rohn* was. It's in the Vertex 22 impound. We should go."

"In my own time," Georgiou said. Since the previous evening, sleuthing for secret weapons had lost its urgency. "If Vercer's niece was right, it was moved there twenty-five years ago. It's not going anywhere."

Dax grabbed the taller woman by the arm and turned her. "What about *Farragut*?"

"What about it? I don't think the Cloud is coming back for the other half."

"You don't know that." Dax scowled. "I think you just want a few more days of being treated like a queen."

"Why shouldn't I? You know what I was robbed of." Georgiou forcibly removed Dax's hand from her arm. "You should sympathize. You were famous across the stars—and now you're nobody. Take the spoils where you can get them."

She marched into one of the galleries, leaving Dax behind—and attracting the attention of Quintilian, who was conferring with Pyramis and Thisbe. Standing before a wall lined with busts of emperors from many planets' histories, he beamed when he saw Georgiou. "We'll take this up again later," he said, and the Oastlings quickly withdrew.

"I thought I heard you arguing with someone," he said as Georgiou accepted his embrace. He looked toward the door to the drawing room, where Dax had been. "Having a problem in the ranks?"

"Just an impatient child who doesn't like to wait."

"Well, some things are worth waiting for. A very long time," he said, kissing her. Then, his hands still on her arms, he held her out so he could look closely at her.

"What?"

"Nothing," he said, drinking her in. "I just see you in a whole new light." He shook his head, smiling all the while. "I never imagined."

"I have that effect on people," she said. But the depth of his gaze made her wonder if it was something other than their relationship status that had changed.

"I have an incoming call from the Casmarran interlocutor," he said, stepping back. "Dull business, I'm sure. But I'll see you for a late dinner. The larders are still full from Oast—and my cook has promised some amazing things." He cupped his hand to whisper. "Don't tell anyone, but we save the best stuff for ourselves!"

"The only logical thing to do."

He kissed her and went on his way, another ornate cane in hand.

Georgiou looked back at him, heading purposefully into the sliver of the universe he ruled—and began to wonder. She'd been intending to build her base anew in the Federation's universe. Conquest had to begin somewhere and had to start with something. In her reality, she'd have thought nothing of killing Quintilian and supplanting him, plundering his estate and putting it to her own ends. But even though the opportunities in this region of space were limited, he seemed to know how to get the absolute most out of them. Good help was hard to find; smart help was even more difficult.

And all that, plus eyes like his?

The emperor had taken lovers aplenty in her time, but the nature of Terran existence cast the bonds between individuals into a purely utilitarian light. As much as his letters to Captain Georgiou had dripped sentimentality, the man she'd met had seemed to be morally malleable—willing to take an opportunity when he saw it. She could live with that. Such a person could be a companion in a real sense: none of the communion-of-spirits business this universe's Burnham had mentioned. With Quintilian, she could envision an alliance, both military and commercial. The personal was just a plus.

She had never wanted to be part of Section 31. Weaponizing a blood devil—if that was what Whipsaw indeed was—only had been under consideration as a means to an end. She'd already laid out for Quintilian a master plan for his domain, and he hadn't objected. It made perfect sense to her: the Veneti would need never worry again about trading internally for profit, and he could open the Troika up to external trade whenever he desired—picking vulnerable neighboring systems off and repeating the process.

Again, and again, until, eventually: *Terra firma. Terra eterna.*

She surveyed the busts of emperors in the gallery. Mostly males, but not all; a fair mix of humans, Orions, Klingons, and others. Which, she wondered, would be removed to make room for her image? Or would she have them all removed?

"Excuse me."

She turned to see Gnaeus in the doorway. "What?"

"The Master Trader requests your presence in his study."

"Which one?"

"I will lead you. But he says it would be better if you changed into your Starfleet uniform."

Georgiou's eyes narrowed. What could possibly require her attention—and in that thing?

"Give me a minute," she said.

Gnaeus was waiting at the foot of the staircase when she returned, dressed again as she had been when she landed on Casmarra. She followed the hulking creature down several corridors. Turning one last corner, she saw Finnegan in the hall wearing his Starfleet uniform and looking concerned.

"Georgie," he said, his hands clasped.

"Don't call me that," she said.

"I'm afraid we're being called to the headmaster's office. It's happened to me a time or ten."

"We'll see." She dismissed Gnaeus and headed inside, Finnegan in tow.

Quintilian stood amid a large study, holding a data slate and speaking to a Casmarran whose image was projected on the far wall. "Manager Xornatta, I don't like to hear lies spread about my guests," Quintilian said. Seeing Georgiou and Finnegan, he motioned for them to enter along the side of the room, out of sight of whatever was projecting his image. "Specify damage."

"Authorized Factor S'satah element-damage," Xornatta said, the Casmarran's limbs taut. *"Causation intruders, Federation-type."*

"Correlation, not causation." Quintilian looked searchingly. "And what's this about something of S'satah's? I still don't understand."

S'satah entered the picture, dwarfed beside the Casmarran. *"What the manager means is that your so-called guests sabotaged one of our vital factories."*

"Vital?" Quintilian looked at his data slate. "If you're talking about the foundry that burned yesterday, my information is it was rarely operational. And so old it could have gone up on its own."

"That's not what happened—and that's not what the Casmarrans think." S'satah addressed Quintilian coolly. *"More than a dozen witnesses outside saw your friends running from the explosion."*

"Witnesses who live in your slums, working for you," he replied. "You're going to have to try harder than that."

"There's also surveillance imagery. Not just ours—it's from one of the Casmarrans' satellites, tasked to look at the Alien Region. You're here at the natives' invitation, Quintilian. And Georgiou and her lackeys are here at yours. You sent saboteurs—"

Finnegan had heard enough. He stepped beside Quintilian and spoke to the screen. "My captain was abducted. I was trying to save her!"

"Ah, there's one of the criminals now," she said to the Casmarran. *"This one broke the jaw of my son—and the fire he and his captain began caused serious burns to dozens of our employees."*

Quintilian looked quizzically at Georgiou. She hadn't mentioned to him what had happened, intent on keeping her

investigations into *Jadama Rohn* to herself. She felt obligated
to step in—and did. "Tell the Casmarran chieftain what really
happened," she said. "You abducted me off the street. Finnegan
saved me. There were no employees present—just your thugs.
And no one was burnt. I saw you all escape."

"*Nonsense.*" S'satah glowered. "*I warned the manager that
your allowing guests in their space would cause nothing but trouble, Quintilian. It's plain who you meant the trouble for.*"

Quintilian shrugged. "We're not in the same business at all,
Zee—"

"*Don't call me that!*"

"I mean there's no motive. And these officers have no
motive."

Finnegan put his hand to his face. "Did I really break
P'rou's jaw?" He looked pale. "I didn't mean to hit him that
hard."

Quintilian and Georgiou gave Finnegan looks that said
his remarks were not helpful—and S'satah seized on them immediately. "*There you go—a confession.*" She faced Xornatta and
issued a request. "*Remand bipedal intruders, Federation-type, to
S'satah, authorized factor!*"

Georgiou had heard that demand before. Quintilian interceded. "Belay request. Shipping Factor Quintilian, appeal
remand."

Xornatta's limbs rotated around its central stalk, a visual
that almost suggested gears turning to the humans. At last
it declared, "*Authorized Carrier Quintilian, expel intruders,
Federation-type.*"

"Expulsion isn't enough," S'satah said. "*I want them.*"

"Expulsion is too much," Quintilian replied. "And too
many. There are three guests. One does not stand accused." He
rephrased it for Xornatta.

"*Expel intruders, quantity two,*" Xornatta ruled.

Georgiou stood by Quintilian's side. "And if he doesn't?"
she asked.

"Conditional action, Authorized Carrier Quintilian . . . deauthorized."

Quintilian nearly sputtered. "You'd revoke my franchise?" He was incredulous. "Where would you get your food from? Your raw materials?"

S'satah crossed her arms. Her face beamed. *"I have plenty of your former employees ready to step in—on my behalf."*

Quintilian spoke cooly. "This is all personal for you."

"Of course." She glared at Georgiou. *"The order is given. Two of them are expelled."*

The Casmarran agreed. *"Concluding-statement, Authorized Carrier Quintilian."* The transmission ended.

Quintilian stood motionless for several moments. "They really have let her get to them." He faced Georgiou. "She always had a better touch with the Casmarrans."

"She's making a power play," Georgiou said. "Don't let her."

"I don't have a lot of choice. Xornatta's word is law on this planet." He scratched his beard. "But there are ways to work the law. Two of you have to leave, but Xornatta didn't say which two."

Finnegan blinked. "Wasn't it obvious? She and I would have to go."

"The Casmarrans are very literal, very precise. I only have to deliver two expulsions. And I would decide whom." Quintilian looked to Georgiou. "I would get your input as captain, of course."

"Of course," Georgiou said. It wasn't the way she had intended for it to happen, but she would be rid of her babysitters once and for all. A shame, in Finnegan's case, as he had just become useful.

He seemed bereft. "I'm supposed to stick by you."

"The people who gave that command are not in charge here." She pointed to the door. "You can give them my regards—when you and Dax reach them."

The young man stared at her—and his shoulders slumped. "I guess you win. It's been fun."

"We'll put you on the next freighter out," Quintilian said, satisfaction with the result overruling his unease over what had just transpired. "The Casmarrans this morning returned some of your things they'd taken from you the other day. Gnaeus will bring them to you."

"Aye. I'll go tell Dax." Finnegan departed.

Georgiou watched him go. If she wasn't committed to staying before, she was now. She turned to Quintilian. "Didn't you say something about a late dinner?"

Georgiou's third luxurious repast in as many nights rivaled for sheer gluttony any meal she could recall from the Terran Empire. Part of it was that there were two fewer guests to share the food—but also, Quintilian seemed to want to celebrate, regardless of the earlier smackdown.

"I'll devise ways to repay S'satah," Georgiou said. "Nothing too harsh. But an insult like that before the natives cannot be allowed to stand. It undermines their respect for you."

Quintilian grinned. "I just love this side of you. We have many things to talk about." He raised his glass. "I'm looking forward to it."

Georgiou raised hers as well—but through the glass, she saw something she didn't want to. A figure, waving to her silently from the hallway. "Excuse me," she said, getting up. "I won't be long."

She met Finnegan in the darkened corridor. "Gnaeus was supposed to have taken you to your flight. What are you doing here?"

"We've got a new problem," he replied. "You remember that aircar Phylla took us around in?"

"Did she catch you trying to climb on top of it again?"

"I couldn't if I wanted to. It's gone. Dax stole it."

30

Vertex 22 Impound Station
CASMARRA

The Casmarran guard's limbs extended to their full length, blocking Dax's way. *"Intruder, Federation-type, opposition-intent. Authorization-demand!"*

"Belay opposition," she said, adjusting the small device in her hand. "Authorization imminent."

Since her competition days, Dax had been an early riser. That had been the case today. Neither Finnegan nor Georgiou had been awake when a Casmarran flier had arrived at Domus Quintiliana, bearing a crateful of items the creatures had looted from *Boyington* for examination. So Dax had been the first to find among the returned items their tricorders, personal comm units, and—importantly—universal translator units.

Lela Dax had been a Trill legislator of long standing; reading complicated texts had been part of her stock in trade. So, too, was she accustomed to the sublanguage that was peculiar to the law: the formal vocabulary used, as well as the protocols for when specific words should be spoken.

During her long wait for Georgiou that day in the library, Emony Dax had put some of her predecessor's skills to work. She'd studied a twenty-year-old text authored by none other than S'satah, the Caitian who had accosted her. The topic: technology-assisted communications with Casmarrans. Drawing upon her understanding of forms of address, Dax had made enough sense of it to run the text's attached audio file through the universal translator's new heuristic recognition mode. It was the latest in Starfleet technology; even Quintilian wouldn't have been able to trade for it yet. It might even have still been restricted to Section 31.

But it had allowed her now to say, "I'm on an authorized assignment from S'satah, the licensed manufacturer, to inspect records relating to a past impound." And to hear her words repeated as *"Objective-authorized, referent Authorized-Factor S'satah, Vertex-22 Impound specimen data directive."*

"Objection. Intruder Federation-type."

"Oh, this," she said, referring to her uniform. "That's part of the assignment. I am with S'satah and P'rou." She pointed to her freckles. "You see? Spots, just like a cat."

She wanted to kick herself for the last little joke as she heard the words translated; they were sure to confuse the Casmarran. But the guardian drew back its limbs. *"Authorized objective, Visitor, Caitian-type."* It allowed her to pass.

Dax breathed a little easier and proceeded up the wide corridor. The interior of the Casmarran structure seemed like something from a living cave; the walls of the hallways were shaped with a waxy, organic tan-colored material, while the floor seemed almost crystalline. Perhaps to help the Casmarrans, who made better time by rolling, she reasoned.

She'd had no idea where the impound station was in Vertex 22, but that had turned out to be the simple part. She'd seen what had happened to *Boyington*. She'd seen a way not only to have the Casmarrans show her where the station was, but to take her there personally. She just needed a vehicle for them to impound. The aircar was an obvious choice. She'd watched Phylla operate it, of course; she'd also spent a couple of hours reading up on texts on how to fly one.

There had followed, earlier that evening, a hair-raising flight from Tallacoe to the Casmarran city, which she first overshot; her problem thereafter had been not colliding with the many structures around. Fortunately, the species' obsession with statuary led to many parks, meaning that all she struck while trying to brake the aircar were exotic-shaped lumps of bronze. As broad as the natives liked their promenades, they'd never designed for a Tiill on her first suborbital flight.

Phylla's beloved aircar would never fly again on its own, but that had actually worked out for the best. Casmarran fliers had enveloped the wreck just as they had done with *Boyington*, lifting off into the air bound for the impound station, none of them aware that she was inside, hiding under the seats.

Two more conversations with Casmarrans followed; for some reason, neither of the foul-smelling creatures quizzed her further about her credentials. *They must have some way of communicating*, she thought. Not for the first time, she considered that being one of the first Federation travelers to meet the Troika species was wasted on her. How much more would an exobiologist be seeing right now?

It didn't matter. Her mission was just as important, if not more. She stepped quickly toward the creature she'd been sent to. "Take me to *Jadama Rohn*," she said, smiling inwardly as she heard the words repeated in Casmarran. The level of difficulty for this routine had been extreme—but she might get high marks.

"I'll be damned," Georgiou whispered to herself, peeking around a corner in the Casmarran building at a wide floor covered with mothballed vehicles. "Looks like she found it." She couldn't believe it. Dax had been a nuisance, but she had also turned out to be someone to reckon with. *Who knew?*

The emperor had not wanted to chase after Dax, especially after seeing the trouble her own previous foray had caused for Quintilian. But the path to information about the blood devil led through *Jadama Rohn*, and while she'd contemplated not pursuing it just yet, the trail needed to remain in existence to be of any use later on. Georgiou had already taken a risk the day before by going to the Alien Region to ask about it; S'satah knew she was at least looking into it, and Quintilian had to suspect. All she needed was Dax blundering about looking for the impounded freighter; that would alert everyone, Casmarrans included, that it held some secret to be found.

Finding Dax, as it turned out, wasn't as hard. From the provided inventory manifest, Finnegan had determined that she had taken several gadgets from the equipment the Casmarrans had returned from *Boyington*, including a communicator. They'd been unable to raise her, as Dax had kept it switched off. But Georgiou had cracked open a Starfleet communicator before, and remembered seeing the transporter interlock circuit inside. Its antenna grid remained functional even when powered off. All that was needed was a transporter—and Quintilian had several for cargo in his warehouses.

Transporting Dax back to Tallacoe, however, had proven tricky given the makeup of the structure she was in. Pings came in only occasionally, and usually slightly delayed. It was then that Georgiou had decided to go herself, after first providing Quintilian a story covering her absence. She needed to see off Dax and Finnegan on their flight back to the Federation; newly busy trying to figure out who had stolen Phylla's aircar, he had bought that explanation.

"She's had three minutes to move from this point," someone behind her said.

"Yes, that's—" Georgiou's eyes bugged, as she had heard a voice that should not be there. She spun. "Finnegan! What are *you* doing here?"

"Helping you find Dax."

She dragged him farther into the corridor. "You're supposed to be at the warehouse, so you can transport us both back! I told you to stay!"

He shrugged. "Now, now. I know you said that, but I figured you might need a hand. And what's the big problem? We'll just use one of these fellows' transporters."

"The Casmarrans don't *have* transporters, fool. Quintilian got his by trading with the outside!"

"Huh." Finnegan tilted his head. "How'd you know that?"

"It was part of the tour. Yesterday—weren't you listening?"

"To be honest, a lot of that morning I was searching for the loo." He looked about. "You don't suppose the Casmarrans have one, do you?"

She clutched her hands in the air before him. "I would claw your eyes out but the screams might draw their attention!"

Another voice came from behind. "Business as usual, I see."

Finnegan looked over Georgiou's shoulder—and burst into a smile. "Daxie!"

Georgiou turned toward her. "You don't seem surprised to see us."

"I could hear you down the hall. You're kind of distinctive, especially around this place." Dax gestured to the area with parked vessels. "Well, what do you think?"

Georgiou was going to launch into a speech about how the Trill shouldn't have come—but her curiosity got the better of her. "*Jadama Rohn* is here?"

"This is where all the ships they have to disinfect wind up. But I don't know what the freighter looks like."

The emperor did—but only vaguely. The logs from *Archimedes* had included scans and images taken from a great distance. Seeing no Casmarrans on the floor of the impound area, she stepped out into it.

She and her companions were immediately lost within a maze of parked plunder. Some vehicles looked like recent arrivals; others were older. Quite a few escape pods sat about, representing many different cultures. The floor was a lesson in how the Alien Region had been populated.

They were only a third of the way across the floor when Georgiou saw a towering Casmarran up ahead, tending to a crystal column that rose to an even higher ceiling. She quickly held back the other two, whispering, "Get down!"

Dax resisted being held. "Don't worry." She stepped forward and approached the Casmarran, who paid no notice.

Worried, Finnegan hustled out to her side, and Georgiou hurried to flank her. "He's a big beastie," Finnegan said. "Stinks even worse than the rest. Can we take him?"

Georgiou tried to imagine what martial artistry might work on a three-meter-tall being with no head and thirty arms. "Find a weapon," she said.

"I'll just use this," Dax said, showing her universal translator.

"I'm supposed to throw it?" Georgiou looked disdainfully at it. "This isn't going to work. In any way."

The translator parroted, *"Object, Federation-type, speculative-ineffective."*

Georgiou looked at her. "Okay, I am impressed."

"You get full marks for this," Finnegan said.

"Glad you approve." Dax stepped before the others and faced the Casmarran, preparing to introduce herself.

But the titan spoke first, its voice box booming. *"Greeting-statement, Authorized-Visitor, Caitian-type."*

Finnegan whispered, "It thinks you're Caitian?"

"It thinks I work for S'satah. Identify," she said to the Casmarran.

"Archivist Ellgon."

"Greeting-statement, Archivist Ellgon." Dax then relied upon the translator to pose a more complicated interrogative, asking about the location of *Jadama Rohn*.

For a time, there was no response. The pillar before the Casmarran shimmered—and the giant moved around it to allow the visitors to see the image that had somehow taken shape on its surface. *"Jadama Rohn,"* Ellgon said.

"That's our freighter," Georgiou said. "But where in the room is it?"

"Misinterpretation. Query."

"We want to know which part of the room it's in," Georgiou said, gesturing to the wide mass of vehicles. "We could be looking all day. Tell us!"

"Response declined."

Dax frowned and identified herself again as a representative of S'satah. It elicited the same answer from Ellgon as before.

Georgiou felt her anger building. She wasn't going to be stopped by a walking stack of starfishes, but neither did she think she could operate whatever data system the pillar represented. "You will answer," she said.

"Response declined."

"You'll answer. You don't know who you're dealing with." She gritted her teeth. "I killed every member of your species."

"Georgie!" Finnegan said. Dax looked at her, shocked.

Ellgon's response: *"Misinterpretation. Query."*

"I killed all your people save one," Georgiou said. "I found out it was in league with my enemy. It had kept me from something I was searching for, allowed my enemy to destroy it." That information had been a consequence of her invasion; a Casmarran had tipped Lorca to S'satah's intent to deliver Whipsaw. "I didn't kill that one."

"Misinterpretation. Query."

"For thwarting me, I let it live, alone, forever. But I killed everyone else. You will help—or I will see you suffer."

Dax gasped with horror. "Why are you saying this?"

"Not for my health." She glared at the Trill. "What did you think would happen on this trip—that we'd never get information without threatening? I don't know what we can do to this thing, but damn it, I'll find a way—if it doesn't tell me where to find the ship on the pillar!"

"Response given," Ellgon said. *"Vehicle Orion-type designate* Jadama Rohn *column-visualized. Impound presence negative."* The Casmarran's limbs twirled and rose, almost as if making a point. *"Visitor-type Georgiou understood, minus two thousand six hundred seventy-four Casmarcycles."*

The words were understandable—but the translator could not provide their meaning. "What—what is it saying?"

Dax's eyes narrowed. "I'm not sure—but I think it's saying it already told you." She looked up to the archivist. *"Request record."*

As before, Ellgon moved to a different side of the great column—and as before, nothing happened for several moments. Dax shrugged. "I thought it was worth a—"

Georgiou interrupted her. Or rather, her image, appearing near the base of the pillar where the image of *Jadama Rohn* had been.

"—think I understand why we haven't been able to find the ship," the image said. This Georgiou appeared to be inside the pillar, looking out as if through a frosty window.

"That's you," Finnegan said, looking at the display.

"No," Georgiou said, her breath catching. "It's *her*. The captain."

31

"Twenty-six hundred cycles," Dax said. "That's what, five years? This is when you—I mean, when she—was here before!"

"Who was here before?" Finnegan asked, alternately pointing between the Georgious. "Her? Or *her*?"

"Hush," Dax and the emperor said in unison. They strained to listen.

"If I understand this, Michael, the Casmarrans seem to have traded the Jadama Rohn *away to get rid of it."*

A young woman she knew well appeared beside the captain. *"That's what I'm getting from these translations,"* Michael Burnham said, working at what appeared to be a data slate. *"They believed the freighter could not be disinfected—that it was permanently unclean because of what had happened upon it."*

"Cursed," the captain responded. *"That's about right."*

Georgiou blinked twice. She had seen imagery of her other self before, but it was a peculiar sensation seeing her counterpart in the same exact spot she was. "Dax, record this."

"Already on it." The Trill had her tricorder out.

The captain looked upward toward something out of sight. *"This data system is amazing. It's been well worth the time to decipher. Bring up the scans the Casmarrans made of the ship again."*

Burnham appeared to trace her fingers across the inside of the column. "What's she looking at?" Dax asked.

Georgiou looked up. "This column. The same thing we're looking at."

"So we can't see it," Finnegan said. "It's like they're trapped inside—or we are."

"*Look at that,*" Burnham said, pointing. "*What's the func- tion of that assembly in the cargo hold?*"

"*I don't know,*" the captain responded. After a moment, "*Oh, good eye, Michael. That shouldn't be there at all.*"

"What?" the emperor spouted. It was so frustrating, not seeing the same thing.

"*It looks like a large cargo unit,*" Burnham said. "*Only it's wired up to vents. A refrigeration system?*"

"*No,*" the captain replied, pointing at something. "*Those vents lead outside the ship, to the exhaust baffles.*"

"*But look where the vents are on the hull. They face forward.*"

"*You're right. Whatever* Jadama Rohn *was carrying in that container, it was scooping from space. Either that or—*"

Or what? the emperor wondered. But for whatever reason, the captain did not finish her sentence.

"*I've added it to the list of things to check out when we get to the ship,*" Burnham said, turning her data slate toward the cap- tain. "*I can see why the people in question wanted to look into it again.*"

"*That's too nice a term for them.*"

"*Well, we're here first. It looks like we're headed—*"

The recording abruptly ended. "What happened?" the em- peror asked. She faced Ellgon. "What people? Bring it back!"

The Casmarran moved in front of the display. "*Authoriza- tion revoked, Visitor Georgiou-type.*"

"Who says so?"

"*Manager Xornatta.*" As the lighting in the impound area went from warmly luminescent to an angry red-orange, Ellgon declared, "*Planetary expulsion order expanded. Enforcement im- minent.*"

Dax looked to her companions. "Planetary expulsion?"

"Actually, they'd already ordered it," Finnegan said. "I was on the way to tell you that. You and I have to leave Casmarra."

Georgiou's focus was still back on the message. "Casmarran, what was Burnham going to say? Where did your people send the *Jadama Rohni*?"

Ellgon said nothing. Instead, the archivist drew its limbs back, narrowing its diameter as it stepped behind the giant pillar. The peculiar data device went dark.

Georgiou took a last angry look at it—and remembered the device at her hip. She activated her comm unit, only to hear a familiar voice. *"Quintilian to Captain Georgiou. Come in, Captain. Philippa, if you're out there—"*

"I'm here," she said.

"Are you where I think you are?" he asked. *"Never mind. I already know. We traced the aircar to Vertex 22—and the Casmarrans said someone there was impersonating a member of S'satah's team. They're on the warpath."*

"What does that mean?"

"If you're in one of their sanctums without permission, they might use those limbs of theirs to tear off yours. They can get them going pretty fast."

"Use the cargo transport to beam me back," she said. "Target this communicator!"

"I can't do that. The Casmarran structures throw off interference—you probably found that out going in. But even if it worked, I still can't help. Two of you were already under an expulsion order. All three of you are now—and if I help, I may be too."

"I thought you cared."

"Of course I do—and I will help. But first, you're going to have to get out on your—"

Static replaced his voice—that, and thunder. Within seconds, the whole structure around them began to quake, with a distant rumbling sound coming from all directions but one.

Finnegan took several steps back, a sick look on his face. "Oh, I know what that is. It's the starfish on the march."

"And on the roll," Dax said, putting away her tricorder.

With so many vehicles parked in the facility, it was impossible to see far in any one direction. But the rumbling seemed to indicate Casmarrans advancing, both by rolling and their end-over-end walking. And after her interactions with S'satah, she didn't expect they would simply take her prisoner.

Georgiou gave a last angry look at the darkened pillar and made a command decision. She pointed up ahead. "That way!"

"Why there?" Finnegan asked.

"It's where we haven't been—and there's not as much noise coming from there." She had a hunch, but the only way to check it out was on the run.

They had passed another hundred meters' worth of parked derelicts when the first Casmarran came into view from the left, its limbs whirling too fast to be seen. Weaponless, Georgiou entered a defensive stance—only to realize as it approached that no martial artistry practiced by bipeds could deflect the attack of such a being.

"Dax!" she heard Finnegan call out.

She spun and saw the Trill gymnast scrambling nimbly up the slanted wing of one of the closely packed vehicles ahead of them. Georgiou got the idea and followed, shouting back to Finnegan, "Climb or die, fool!"

The three had reached the top of an alien shuttle when the wave hit. Charging Casmarrans, reeking of sulfur, slammed against the base of the vehicle, with other skittering specimens scuffling with one another to climb after the fugitives. The impact reverberated through the vessel, but Dax and Georgiou were no longer atop it, having leapt the narrow gap to the rooftop of the next vehicle over. Dax looked back to Finnegan and shouted, "Sean, come on!"

"Oh, I knew I'd regret all those meals," he said, bounding from one ship to the next. He didn't land nearly as gracefully, Georgiou saw, but she didn't care. The obstacle course had slowed down the Casmarran rampage just long enough for her to confirm her theory. Up ahead, over several more vehicles, was blackness.

The night.

Georgiou leapt to the next conveyance ahead. Of course, an indoor impound area would have an entrance—and the Casmarrans were so confident no one would trespass that they'd failed to include a door. And while she had not thought of the corollary earlier, it came to her as they worked their way ahead, clambering over a sea of alien guards: *Where else would the most recently impounded shuttle be?*

"*Boyington!*"

Georgiou didn't need to say the name; she had already bounded ahead. A backflip landed her on the floor outside its closed accessway. The hatch groaned open; the Casmarrans evidently hadn't drained the ship's power yet. She entered and prepared to shut the door.

"Wait!" Dax yelled. Georgiou saw that she had stopped to help Finnegan, who had evidently taken a spill; he was a jumper but no acrobat. The location of the Casmarran horde could be seen by the quaking vehicles in the distance.

Georgiou's impulse was to leave them. But there was no going back to Tallacoe for her now—and it had become apparent that, as flawed as her companions were, she'd gotten farther with them than without them.

She held the door.

"Thanks," Dax said, panting as she and Finnegan climbed inside. "I thought you were going to leave us."

"I wouldn't do that," Georgiou said, sealing the hatch. "You've still got the tricorder recording."

"Real sentimental," Finnegan said, settling into the copilot's seat. "Every day around Georgie I'm filled with the warmth of love and understanding."

Georgiou fired the thrusters, an act that, she could see from the external imagers, caused the Casmarrans to stop without coming closer. A pity, as she would have loved to have fried a few.

As *Boyington* pivoted and pointed outside, Finnegan looked to the skies, where the silhouettes of many flying vessels could be seen. "What's to stop those ships of theirs from just hauling us back?"

They didn't have long to wonder. The shuttle hadn't gone far when Quintilian hailed. *"Quintilian to* Boyington. *Are these my lost sheep?"*

"We're out," Georgiou said, "no thanks to you."

"You can thank me for this: I just threatened Xornatta that I'd forget to even pick up next season's harvest. It worked. You still have to leave, but you won't be followed."

Georgiou saw it was true. *Boyington* cleared the stratosphere and soared skyward, unmolested. "They kept their word," she said. "They respect you. Fear you."

"I wouldn't have put it that way, but—" Quintilian broke off before finishing. *"Ah, Philippa, we could have done so many things. Where will you go?"*

Behind the emperor, Dax had found something on her tricorder. She thrust it before Georgiou's eyes. Frozen on the small display was a close-up of the data slate that Burnham had turned in the direction of the Casmarran pillar, just before the interruption. Georgiou read aloud the name Burnham had written there, detailing where *Jadama Rohn* had been sent after its sale. "The Dromax system?"

"The Dromax system?" Quintilian echoed, having overheard. *"Is that where you're headed?"*

Georgiou said the name again. "I suppose so," she told Quintilian.

"Why do you want to go there?" He quickly followed it up with, *"Never mind. I've been trying to get you back here for five years. I'd rather you go next door than across the cosmos again."*

Georgiou tried to remember what she could from her invasion of the place. How much would have changed? But there was a matter to ask about first. "Are we expelled from all Troika space," she asked, "or just Casmarra?"

"The Dromax can be counted on to make up their own

minds," Quintilian said. *"Gnaeus can tell you where to find the leader of his tribe. I'll send that information along."*

Georgiou looked to her companions as *Boyington* ascended to orbit. Dax gave a thumbs-up. "I guess we're on our way," the emperor said. "Thank you for the hospitality."

"Bonne chance, Cherie. Au revoir."

"Wait a second," Finnegan said. "I have a question for Mister Quintilian."

"What is it?"

"This Dromax place. How's the food?"

Stage Four
DESTRUCTION

The evil that men do lives after them;
    To be immortal, learn that lesson well.

—MARC ANTONY,
    at the execution of Brutus
    The Revenge of Julius Caesar,
    William Shakespeare, 1599

32

"Incoming!"

Georgiou's shuttle had just barely dropped out of warp when Finnegan declared it was under attack. It was frightening news to Dax, who'd asked for some flying hours. "I thought Quintilian said they wouldn't fire on us!"

"It's not weapons fire," Georgiou said. She already knew what it was, from her conquests in her universe. "Retro thrusters, now!"

Dax activated them—and gulped as a hunk of rock, not present in her view before, hurtled by on a trajectory crossing *Boyington*'s path. "That asteroid wasn't on the scanners—or the star maps!"

"It's not an asteroid. It's ammo."

Dromax was a colossal gas giant, bloodred in a congested stretch of Troika space marked by star-on-star violence. So huge was the ringed world that it had more than a thousand moons: many misshapen heaps snagged as rogue bodies from passing stars, as well as a few dozen orbs that would have been M-Class planets had fusion ever ignited within Dromax.

The violence, Georgiou knew, wasn't limited to the stars.

"Look where that rock's heading!" Finnegan said as Dax turned *Boyington* hard about. The immense boulder soared directly toward a giant orange moon. Pizza-faced, it was much marred by its gravitic proximity to so many other large bodies—and now it received another blight, as the boulder entered its atmosphere and exploded.

"Direct hit!" Dax said.

"Of course," Georgiou said. "Someone was aiming."

Various tribes of Dromax had been battling with one another since time immemorial, she explained; on receiving the gift of spaceflight from early traders, they'd spread to all livable moons surrounding the gas giant. And many unlivable smaller ones, which the various Dromaxian forces used as platforms for mass drivers to launch still smaller bodies at their enemies.

Finnegan and Dax saw one of the launchers in action as an object in a higher orbit fired a hunk of rock in the direction of the source of the previous projectile. Watching ginormous bullets soar through space was a curious experience, Georgiou had found; they had none of the immediacy of energy weapons or even torpedoes. But while their transits might be relatively lazy, their impacts were immense.

"*Boom!*" Finnegan shouted as the stone, propelled into space by an electromagnetic launch system, slammed into a moonlet, pulverizing the installation that resided there.

"The Casmarrans manufacture the mass drivers," Georgiou said. "Quintilian ships those and other weapons and returns with raw materials."

Dax gawked at the destruction. "Isn't he worried about running out of customers?"

"I don't think so. He says the replacement rate for the Dromax is quite high."

"Good ol' Gnaeus," Finnegan said. "I was going to ask him what his people did for fun. Apparently they multiply."

"When they're not subtracting," Dax added.

Georgiou thought back. "They were nowhere near as prolific in my continuum. Their numbers declined after I pressed them into service." *The same as just about every other subject species*, she did not add. "I didn't give them a lot of freedom to replicate, however they do that, so maybe that's the difference."

"I know you're very proud," Dax said. "Where are we going?"

Finnegan referred to the screen before the copilot's seat.

"From the guide Quintilian sent us, the sun's called Dromax. The giant planet is called Dromax. And the moons—"

"Let me guess. All called Dromax."

"No, they're known by numbers."

"Oh, like stars in our star systems. Dromax I, II, and so forth."

"No, just the numbers. The first moon is just called One. The second, Two."

Dax sighed. " 'No points for artistry,' my old coach would say."

"Creative, they're not. That's why all their manufactured goods come from Casmarra," Georgiou said. "That, and they're too busy warring. You should like it, Finnegan. It's an endless brawl with no point and no end."

He shrugged. "It's been donkey's years. We'll be lucky if *Jadama Rohn* isn't smashed under a rock."

In fact, Georgiou didn't know where in the system it was—just that Michael and her captain had found some record of the trade. It had been plain to the emperor for some time that her counterpart had come to Troika space not to take up with Quintilian, but to investigate what had happened to the freighter. The fact that she'd brought Burnham along under-scored how important she felt the search to be.

Yet she'd never told Starfleet about it. About her visit to Casmarra, and Quintilian—or about any further venture to the realm of the Dromax. That had been plain from the long-distance contacts the emperor had made with Section 31 dur-ing their transit from Casmarra. In encrypted text exchanges, Leland had denied knowing anything about a past Georgiou visit; the only evidence of anything happening five years before was that time marked a change in the frequency and duration of contacts between the captain and the trader. "We're look-ing at her and Burnham's schedules during that time," he'd written.

Leland had also wanted to know what had happened on

Casmarra, and what else they'd learned. By mutual prior agreement, the trio had decided to claim signal interference and ignore his questions, lest words like "destroyed factory" and "expulsion" lead to their recall by Cornwell or some Federation official who cared more about the Prime Directive than finding *Jadama Rohn*. Nor had any mention been made of their voyage to Dromax territory; with any luck, they wouldn't stay long.

Dax, rattled by the boulders crisscrossing space, looked anxious to leave already. "Are we even in the right place?"

"Michael's notes said the Dromax system," Georgiou said, "and Gnaeus's general is on Thirty, which has the added benefit of a nitrogen-oxygen atmosphere. That's where we start."

Dax nodded—and looked to Finnegan in the seat beside her. "You want to—"

"New course laid in," he said, smiling. Then he looked back. "You're sure we can count on what Burnham wrote? Maybe she mistranslated something."

"If Michael told the captain about it, she was certain of it," Georgiou said. "And I believe her. She's brilliant—far too smart to have made such an error."

"Wow." Dax looked back at her, mouth open. "Listen to the big bad emperor being nice!"

"The child has gotten cheeky," Georgiou said to Finnegan.

"It's fine," Dax said. "I'm just not accustomed to hearing you compliment anyone. Was Burnham somebody to you in your world?"

"She was, until she wasn't." Georgiou crossed her arms behind her and looked to the side. "Here . . . it's more complicated."

It was indeed. This universe's Michael had experience with Captain Georgiou that was largely a mystery to the emperor. She'd been given to understand that the captain had taken Burnham under her wing; she figured the connection with the younger woman was more than a professional relationship, but less than a foster-daughter situation. It now seemed more than that. Burnham had tried briefly to befriend the emperor before Qo'noS, tried to show her a different path. How much of that was trying to force the emperor into filling the void left by the captain?

"Here we are," Dax said, pointing to a shabby world gray with clouds. "Moon Thirty dead ahead."

"Maybe more dead than not," Finnegan said, pointing out no fewer than three boulders on trajectories taking them toward the large moon.

Seeing the boulders soar past, Dax gripped the controls. "What should I do?"

"You're fine," he said. "Stay right on course. I'd just suggest not landing where they—"

Orange disruptor fire lanced upward from several locations on the cloud-cloaked moon. Several shots went wide, but two struck home, shattering the approaching boulders. This time, Dax did react, veering away from them—and toward the third projectile. It was a mistake. A powerful disruptor blast caught part of the rocky missile, releasing a spray of debris that struck *Boyington.*

The shuttle balked, jerking back and forth as it approached Thirty's atmosphere. In the cockpit, alarms sounded and indicators flashed as Dax struggled to regain control. "I think the thrusters are damaged!"

"Let me take this," Finnegan said, easing over.

Dax put up no argument. "I think you'd better." She surrendered the controls and the pilot seat quickly, and Georgiou quickly took Dax's spot.

She'd thought to take the command chair herself, but it immediately became apparent that experience and expertise would be of little help. *Boyington* handled sluggishly—and even more so as it pierced the upper reaches of the moon's envelope of air. Finnegan found himself fighting to keep the shuttle stable as the sky outside turned to friction fire.

"We're going to crash," Dax said.

"You can make stupid statements, or you can strap in," Georgiou said, punching commands that she hoped would improve the situation. She wasn't giving up just yet—but there was no returning to orbit now. *Boyington* was committed.

"Look on the bright side," Finnegan shouted over the ruckus of atmospheric entry. "At least they weren't shooting at *us*."

33

Moon Thirty
DROMAX SYSTEM

The thing about crash landings, any pilot understood, was that the medium mattered. Rock was helpful to neither vessel nor passenger. Water was kinder, depending on one's approach to it—but it had a way of swallowing what fell into it, particularly if the vehicle in question had been punctured in any way by, for example, fragments from a mass-driver-launched meteoroid. And then there was lava. While it had some give to it, it didn't always like to return the things it captured. Not intact, at least.

Finnegan had learned those simple aphorisms from one of Starfleet Academy's more experienced shuttle pilots, and while he had not internalized every lesson, this one had seemed simple enough. What he had failed to ask, however, was what to do in case of a forced landing that involved rock *and* water *and* lava—and on Moon Thirty, Finnegan had managed to find all three in close proximity.

Like most of its lunar cousins, Thirty was a mess of terrain types due to the pull exerted by its passing neighbors. Georgiou had managed to reroute enough power to send *Boyington* tumbling toward the polar area and its snowpack, as opposed to the distressed equatorial regions. Finnegan's former teacher would've endorsed that idea. Unfortunately, clouds hid the fact that the icecap was also rent by volcanic rifts, exposing rock in some places, and creating impromptu glacial lakes in others. Finnegan thought he should not be blamed for finding a three-kilometer-long skidway that crossed through all three, but he felt he could have done better on the order.

Georgiou apparently agreed. "Congratulations. We're in a volcano."

It wasn't exactly true, but Finnegan wasn't going to argue it. *Boyington*'s final bounce had brought it to rest in a lava bed about a kilometer from an active rift higher on a hill. He struggled to get the craft moving again. "Can't push off. Are we sinking?"

"Melting is more like it."

"Nacelles are damaged," he said. "Can't trust the retros." They were running out of options. Some Starfleet shuttles had transporters; *Pacifica*'s did not.

"Enough." Georgiou snatched at his shirt and pulled him from the pilot's chair. "Go aft and arm the hydro probes."

"Probes?"

"Show me," Dax said.

She followed him, but Finnegan was baffled as to what Georgiou had in mind. "What are we supposed to do, ride them? The launch doors are facing down!"

"Shut up and engage the locking mechanisms!" the emperor shouted from her seat in the pilot's chair.

Her command made no sense. "Locking the probes will keep the probes in the launch tubes!"

"Just do it."

He and Dax had to override several computer messages angrily warning the passengers that firing probes while their thrusters were still affixed to the shuttle might not be the best idea. He could feel from the shuttle's movement that Georgiou was urgently trying to rock *Boyington* back and forth, fighting to keep it from settling farther in the deadly morass.

"Locked!"

"Will the doors to the launch tubes open?"

Boyington's computer gave a report that was, at best, unsettling. "I don't think the doors will be a problem. They've just melted."

"Hold on!" Georgiou shouted—advice that would have been more helpful, Finnegan thought, if she'd given it a second or two earlier, instead of when she did: the very second that the impact probes, six of them, launched. Or tried to launch, still attached as they were to the shuttle's ventral tubes. Their thrust wouldn't have been enough to free *Boyington* even if they'd pointed in the right direction. As Finnegan and Dax tumbled, he saw every status display at the probe station go red—

—until Georgiou detonated the probes, at which point *everything* went topsy-turvy.

Hydro probes were part of the standard shuttlecraft research package. A typical model contained water under intense high pressure, for firing into regions to test for reactions. In case the shuttle encountered a cloud like the one *Farragut* had found, Section 31 had armed *Boyington* with several carrying various liquids—but all the solutions were water based. By deploying the probes' payloads while still attached to the shuttle, Georgiou created superheated jets of steam against the magma below, propelling the shuttle upward. She then ignited whatever thrusters still functioned at all.

Finnegan understood all that had happened—but only in retrospect, after *Boyington* ceased trying to knock his and Dax's guts out. The gyrations sent them against every bulkhead, until the vessel finally struck something solid. At last, it came to a stop, upside down and on a slant.

He got his bearings and fumbled about. "Daxie? Are you okay?"

Finnegan found her slumped against the overhead of the cargo hold. She was woozy, and bleeding from a knock to the forehead. "What . . . hit me?"

"We just got in a fight with a shuttle." He clambered backward—and saw out a side port what had happened. *Boyington* had found snow at last, having come to a skidding stop upside down on a mountainside.

He worked his way upward, having to climb to reach the fore of the vessel. "Dax is hurt!"

Georgiou, he saw, had problems of her own. She clung to the pilot's chair, kicking about for a place to land without plummeting the whole way aft. In the end, she let go, sliding along the inclined overhead until she reached Finnegan amidships.

"Cornwell won't be happy about her shuttle," she said, clearly winded.

Boyington quaked. "I don't think we're done moving," Finnegan said.

It wasn't clear to either of them whether they were just lodged on an incline leading down into a gully, or on the side of a mountain. The last thing either of them wanted to do was take their chances again in riding an avalanche. "Abandon ship," they said to each other at the same time. Hurriedly, she collected what few supplies she could reach while Finnegan returned to Dax's side.

"Hang on," he said, picking her up. "I'll go easy. You won't get hurt."

"Too . . . late," Dax said, clinging to his neck as he tried to ascend the sloped overhead.

Having opened the hatch, Georgiou straddled the doorway and offered her hand to Finnegan. "Quick, before I change my mind."

"I'll never . . . forget . . . your loving-kindness," Finnegan said, grasping for her hand. Catching it, he pulled himself and Dax upward, bringing the Trill within reach of Georgiou. The two disappeared outside the hatch. With a last doleful look around inside the shuttle, he followed.

This part of Thirty was in night, and while the air was breathable, as they'd expected, it was also exceptionally cold. *At least it beats the lava bed,* he thought. In the snow outside *Boyington,* he found Georgiou with the shoulder bag she'd collected, tending to Dax's injuries. Finnegan used a light from his belt to illuminate her.

Dax winced in pain, tears in her closed eyes. "It's . . . okay. I'll be . . . okay."

"You're not very convincing," Georgiou said. But she tended carefully to the younger woman, adjusting a cortical stimulator from the bag and placing it on her forehead.

Finnegan hadn't figured Georgiou out. She'd been advertised to him as a villain, and she'd certainly acted scurrilously a time or three in their acquaintance. She'd frequently insulted him, tried to abandon him, and, with the exception of the foundry aftermath, had never come close to thanking him. But she was being decent to Dax now.

Maybe she just thinks she'll need us, he thought. It wasn't clear that she would—but on a hillside on a strange planet, who knew?

A medical tricorder out, Georgiou ran it past Dax and squinted at the readings, backlit in the many-mooned night. She frowned. "That's odd."

"What?"

"The device must be damaged," she said. Dax moaned, prompting her to put the tricorder away.

Georgiou applied a hypospray. Dax's eyes fluttered. "There you go," the emperor said, replacing it in the bag. "Cursed with another day of survival."

Finnegan shone his light back at the shuttle, which had a mound of snow piled up at its lower end. "I think it's done moving," he said, turning back toward the hatch. "We might still use it for shelter, if nothing—"

He never completed his sentence. Light flashed on a hillside kilometers away. An explosion ripped into the ground and sent a pillar of fire high into the night. Georgiou snagged her satchel and threw it over her shoulder. She gestured for him to help lift Dax. "Quick, before—"

The sound from the explosion rang across the valley, setting the snow on the slope into motion. *Boyington*, which he was meters away from reentering, creaked and rocked. "Right!" he said, joining her beside Dax. The two got the Trill to her feet and moved with her across the incline, trying to get as much distance from the ship as possible.

Another blast on the horizon was followed by a third explosion, just a kilometer away in the valley below. That was it for *Boyington*'s perch: a chunk of their hillside started moving, taking the shuttle with it.

Finnegan couldn't afford another look back. Not when the whine of hoverjets announced new arrivals. Gunnery platforms borne on cushions of air crested one of the far hills, racing into the valley before them.

"Over there," Georgiou said, pointing to an outcrop rising from the snow. The pair crunched swiftly toward it, moving Dax toward a place of cover.

Dax looked to Finnegan, puzzled. "What's going on?"

"Just more fun with Georgie and Sean," he said.

"Let me down. You don't have to carry me."

"I'm just glad you weren't a weightlifter," Georgiou said. The two helped Dax to sit behind the boulders and then turned to study the new arrivals, who now numbered five.

The hovertanks—if that was what they were—didn't appear to Finnegan to be the source of the blasts they'd seen earlier. That became apparent when more shells landed, just missing two of the platforms before blowing a third to bits.

"There!" he said, pointing up. A pair of V-shaped aircraft soared down, crossing the battlefield and dropping more charges. Two more hovertanks were struck, sending some Dromax flying—and causing others to burst, shedding their innards across the ground. "That's disgusting."

"We killed quite a few in my realm. It's why they like armor."

"Whoever they are, they're not on the same side," he said.

Finnegan saw Georgiou peering through the night at the surviving pair of hovertanks. Given what they'd seen already, the vehicles, exposed under the night sky, had no hope against the fliers. If they stayed on the run, they could never bring their guns to bear.

The fourth hovertank suffered a glancing blow from an exploding shell and cartwheeled, sending its occupants flying in all directions. It slammed to a stop a hundred meters from their position. Faceup, its hover engines groaned hopelessly, bent rotors preventing it from rising again.

"This'll be over soon," he said to Dax.

"Will they come after us next?"

"I have no idea."

"I do," Georgiou said. She pointed to the crashed hovertank. "The symbol!"

Finnegan squinted at the marking on the side of the crashed vehicle. It was a pair of crescent moons, identical to the ones they'd seen on the midsection of Gnaeus, Quintilian's Dromax assistant. He began to turn to Georgiou. "What do you think of—"

She was already on the move, he saw, bolting from cover in a headlong run toward the grounded hovertank.

"Wait!" he called out.

Dax tried to rise to look. "What's she doing?"

"What she always does."

He started to rise to follow—only to decide to stay beside Dax, who needed him. But not only that. He got the chance to watch as the emperor closed the distance with the wreck. Above, one of the bombers turned about, while its partner continued to fire at the one Dromax platform still on the move.

Reaching the damaged vehicle, Georgiou hit the ground beside it, even as the first bomber lobbed a shell her way. Finnegan called out, but his voice was nothing at this distance, especially when the projectile slammed into the ground on the other side of the vehicle. Emperor and wreck disappeared in a cloud of raining snow and debris.

"Georgie!" Finnegan stood, wanting to do something,

yet powerless. The bomber ringed the valley and came in for a lower pass.

On her hands and knees beside him, Dax pointed. "Sean, look!" The dust clearing, the two beheld Georgiou alive and atop the gunnery platform of the fallen hovertank, standing at the controls of its sizable aft disruptor cannon. She fired it upward, winging the bomber and sending it careening into a ridge across the way.

It appeared to get the attention of the second bomber, which had been strafing the surviving hovertank. The flier's occupants paused firing—only to receive incoming fire from Georgiou. The bomber exploded in midair, showering debris across the battlefield.

Finnegan, mesmerized, didn't know what to say. Dax did. "I can walk." And she did, working her way with him at her side to the platform Georgiou was on.

He just stared at her when they reached it. Happy at her gun emplacement, the emperor grinned down at him. "I thought you were assigned to shadow me."

Before he could respond, the surviving hovertank approached. She turned her cannon toward it—only to raise it harmlessly to the sky as she saw its gunner doing the same. The vehicle slowed to a stop a dozen meters away.

The skiff carried at least half a dozen Dromax, but only one wore what appeared to be golden chain armor, draped across its gut. That individual trundled toward the fore of the vehicle—and looked down at Georgiou and her companions.

It turned and barked something incomprehensible. Moments later, someone brought the being a red box, which it affixed around its torso. *"I am Sergeant Garph of the Double Crescent,"* it said in modulated Federation Standard. *"Do you stand with us?"*

Georgiou responded in the affirmative. "I know your marking," she said, pointing to the symbol on the vehicle. "I come from Quintilian. Gnaeus sent me."

"Gnaeus! How is my old broodmate?" The Dromax lifted its mail armor, exposing an identical birthmark. *"We serve General Agamalon."*

Georgiou looked satisfied. "That's what I thought."

"You have our appreciation. What can we do for an ally?"

Finnegan crossed his arms and smiled—first at the situation, then at her. "Can I say it?"

"Be my guest," Georgiou responded.

Finnegan faced the Dromax and saluted. "Take us to your leader."

34

Moon Thirty
Dromax System

Georgiou had not lingered in the Dromax system during her first visit, in her universe, a few years before, and that was unusual. It had been the emperor's custom to tour the territories she conquered, seeing what was worth plundering and, on rare occasions, whether there was some title she could take for herself that would be of use. It was seldom fun to lay waste to places and move on.

The Dromax, on the other hand, had impressed her only as warriors—and nothing else. She had kept a portion of the species alive to serve her, but their works were of no concern. Based on the images her forces had provided her, there was nothing on any of their scrubby little moons worth getting her shoes dirty to inspect.

On traversing Thirty aboard Sergeant Garph's hovercraft, she had seen little to change her opinion. If anything, the sights had reinforced it. The moon appeared to be a lesser holding within the Dromax system, and Garph's general, Agamalon, controlled less than a third of it. Beyond the contested regions such as the one *Boyington* had landed in, Georgiou saw a battered landscape festooned with craters. Things that she'd imagined were permanent emplacements, like the disruptor batteries that had fired on the meteors and brought her shuttle down, were actually mobile units, larger versions of the hovertanks.

Then there were the ore mines. So many mines. The Dromax lived for war, with weapons from Casmarra and food from Oast, all delivered by Quintilian. The cost was minerals the Dromax carved from their moons, when they weren't firing chunks of them at one another. The mining wasn't performed in any orderly fashion, that she could tell: rather, when a space-fired projectile got through, the Dromax simply waited for the surface to cool and brought up what was uncovered. She wondered what would happen when the remaining leaders of the Dromax tribes—Garph said there were nine—were left alone squatting on the last mined-out pebbles in their system.

Spaceports were black maws in the ground, and Georgiou suspected the Dromax again let their enemies' munitions do the excavating. *All* buildings of consequence were under the surface, so far as she could tell. And not one of them had been designed for comfort. The warriors had no art, no music, no science; only war, and tales of war.

She had heard them all in the cavern fortress of General Agamalon, imperious leader of Garph and other Dromax serving under the banner of the Double Crescent. Quintilian had been right; little of the tribe's oral history seemed to stretch back very far. The legends were all of recent vintage—and now, it seemed, she had added to them.

"You're a damned wonder, Captain," Agamalon said, squatting in a tub of grain. *"None of those other stinking two-legs ever stood beside us. Nobody ever tried to help. Not before you."*

Georgiou suppressed the urge to vomit. Agamalon and company dined somehow by sitting on their food and grinding around, taking in nutrients via osmosis. She fought to remember what the general had just said. "Why has no one helped you?"

"To keep us down, of course." A wretched ripping sound came from someplace Georgiou couldn't see. *"Those disgusting Casmarrans need to sell weapons to keep themselves fed—where even is the mouth on those things? I'm sure they prop up our enemies on purpose!"*

How their lives were unfair: that was the other favorite topic of conversation among the Dromax, all of whom seemed, like Agamalon, not to have tuned their voice boxes to Gnaeus-levels of politeness. Indignation was all about. She tired to hear of it—but at least it took her mind off how the Dromax ate, and her own food. The human provisions the Dromax had shared were kept about for the use of the Veneti and other traders: drab survival rations. She was certain Quintilian carried his own larder with him whenever he visited to trade.

None of the Dromax stocks included anything remotely alcoholic, and that had contributed to a Finnegan who was both out of sorts and unusually able to participate in after-dinner conversation. "General," he asked, "what's the beef you fellows all have with each other?"

"Isn't it obvious?"

"You'll have to excuse Finnegan," Georgiou said. "He is what my species calls a buffoon. I'm hoping you can explain for him."

"A Dromax would know. The other tribes are filled with reeking pus-bags."

"And you consider yourself above them."

"No, we're reeking pus-bags too. But I'm damned if I'll let them say it about us." A wave of chortling came from the other Dromax in their food-tubs, a sound accompanied by the sickening grinding of grain.

The other tribes, Agamalon explained, had names ranging from the Three-Cross to the One-Star to the Jagged Spike, which was the outfit Georgiou had saved Garph from. Each name correctly described and corresponded to a marking on the guts of the member Dromax—not a birthmark or tattoo, as they'd guessed, but a brand.

"What do the slashes mean?" Finnegan asked, looking around. Several of the Dromax servers bore the moon symbols of the Double Crescent—but also painful-looking scars, canceling the icons.

Agamalon didn't seem that interested in answering. *"Indicators of rank, if you must know. Do I ask you uglies about the fronds of dead cells coming out of your heads?"*

Apart from the insult, Georgiou found that response curious. If the absence of a scar indicated higher rank, did no one ever get promoted? But it did seem true in practice that the scarred Dromax were orderlies. The only specimens outfitted with voice boxes belonged to the no-scar caste.

"There were other Dromax on Quintilian's estate," she said, trying to think back. "Their markings weren't like what Gnaeus had."

"The trader keeps a representative from each tribe in service— every stinking one of them. It allows him to maintain connections here. He keeps his options open."

Agamalon continued to rant for a while about the state of the war, which had gone on "forever." Leadership of the Double Crescent tribe had come from an old leader Agamalon had defeated in combat, a system of power transfer that Georgiou innately understood. There was no such thing as a home moon for each tribe; they had constantly been trading territory. Two years earlier, Agamalon's stronghold was on Moon Twenty-Four—and the year before that, Twenty-One.

"It sounds like you're going the wrong direction," she said.

"Clever animal. I'm sure remarks like that are what got you kicked off Casmarra."

But it was true, Agamalon said, that the less desirable moons were the smaller, more distant ones—and that he and his forces had been pushed from one to the next. "It doesn't matter. We'll recover. The Crescents have controlled One more than ninety different times. And we will again."

"Controlled one what?" Finnegan asked.

"The moon One," Georgiou interjected, trying to forestall another harangue. She tried to remember something, anything, about the system's largest satellite. "That moon is the best to control?"

"Of course. It holds our beloved. The prized place that gives our lives purpose: the Cascade."

Georgiou's eyes narrowed at the mention of the location. "A holy place? I didn't know you had a religion."

"We don't, and quit badgering me with questions. I swear, you creatures can't stand a minute without hearing your own squeaky voices." Hands against the side of the tub, Agamalon heaved, exposing a grain-encrusted lower section. Another push and the general was out of the vat. *"The Cascade sits at the exact center of the side of the world that always faces away from the gas giant. It is a place that . . ."*

The general's words trailed off. Georgiou stared, unwilling to interrupt again.

Agamalon trundled around the tub, the Dromax's undersides crunching on the stone floor. *"I was going to say it defies description. All the technology you offworlders have brought with you—your spaceships, your disruptors, your transporters—it all pales before the magic of the Cascade. I can't describe it."*

Georgiou had never heard of such a place, but the largest Dromax moon had been the target of such a bombing campaign by her people that Victoria Falls would have been reduced to rubble. The thought that the Dromax placed such value on a geographic feature was at once unsurprising and disappointing.

Dax, who had been quietly listening, looked to her. "Can we just flat out ask this time?"

Georgiou thought about it. *You know, I don't see why not.* There was no need to tiptoe with these people. "General, how long have you ruled?"

"Many cycles."

"Since before Quintilian began trading with you?"

"Heh. He's a child."

That was what she wanted to hear. "I'm interested in a freighter that was sold to the Dromax long ago."

"Which tribe?"

"I don't exactly know. But it's why we're here."

"If I ever meet this Starfleet you belong to, I'll be sure to tell them you go blundering about into other people's wars without any notion of where you're headed. Or is that what all their people do?"

"I've been known on occasion—" Finnegan started to say. This time, Dax shushed him. "The freighter."

"Yes, yes. What's so special about it?"

"I . . . boarded it once," Georgiou said, picking her words. "I liked it. And as you've heard, my own shuttle is in a mass of snow at the bottom of a hill." She went for it. "The freighter was named *Jadama Rohn*."

The name caused a stir among the voice-box-wearing Dromax. Agamalon laughed. *"Jadama Rohn? What kind of bad-brain would want that thing?"*

"Is something wrong with it?" Georgiou asked.

"Something wrong? It's notorious. I can't believe that imbecile Skove traded for it."

"Skove?"

"General of the Jagged Spikes. You should learn the name, you killed some of their pilots earlier. The Casmarrans made Skove the worst deal ever."

"Why was it such a bad deal?"

"The freighter was cursed!"

More rumbling from the Dromax, as Georgiou, Dax, and Finnegan looked at one another. That descriptor had come from the Casmarran video. "Cursed how?" Dax asked.

"The ghosts of the dead haunt it. It's said that the two-legs who ran it just dropped dead one day for no reason at all. Some even say they looked upon the face of an Oastling, and went mad. Their eyes rejected the sight."

Finnegan peered at him. "You do know there's no such thing as curses, right?"

"Talk down to me some more, two-legs. I haven't thrown anyone into the acid pool in a day and a half."

Georgiou ignored the byplay. She had never felt so close to her answers. "What did Skove do with it?"

"Skove couldn't trade it back—and the only way the Dromax trade is through conquest. The Spikes abandoned it to the Three-Crosses. Who lost it to the Whorls. Who lost it back."

"Sounds like a hot potato," Finnegan said.

Georgiou leered at him. "What are you babbling about?"

"A kids' game. Nobody wants to get stuck with it."

"Ah. We had that on Terra—but with live grenades."

Agamalon laughed. *"I knew I liked you, Captain."*

Dax interceded. "If the freighter is so horrible, why didn't someone destroy it? *Is* it in one piece?"

"Oh, it exists. I know that for a fact. And it exists for a very good reason."

"What reason?" Georgiou asked. "Where is it?"

"I'm tired of questions," Agamalon said, *"and the answers won't do you any good. Not now. But if you're as resourceful as you were back on the battlefield, Captain, you may just find out."* The general lumbered toward the exit.

35

Moon Twenty-Six
DROMAX SYSTEM

"Attack, you obscenities!" Standing atop one of Agamalon's hovertanks, Georgiou screamed at the Dromax infantry flanking the vehicle. "Get those disruptors firing—before I start firing at you!"

Wading through the muck of the swamp, Sergeant Garph called up to her. *"We should turn back, human. We're getting torn apart!"*

"Better there than here, where I can see it," Georgiou said. "Now go!"

She turned to face forward. Over the battered shield that served to protect her perch, she saw the enemy emplacements in the haze ahead. Toggling the communicator on her console, she called out coordinates. Seconds later, bombs from Agamalon's airships had the emplacements in flames.

"There's your opening! Go!" Ahead of her, the two Dromax on surface gunnery positions atop the platform fired their artillery pieces—while the hovertank itself launched a shell from its big gun. For good measure, she planted her disruptor rifle on the shielding and began laying down covering fire. *"Go, now!"*

Agamalon's Dromax, enlivened by her display, coursed ahead, moving more quickly through the guck than she would have thought their bodies would allow. They looked more like germs attacking a cell than valiant warriors—but there was no question they were fighters, just like the Dromax in her universe had been. No wonder they'd given her imperial forces such hell.

The emperor had personally led troops into battle many times, but never before had her army been an all-alien army.

Nor would she have ever considered herself likely to engage in some other species' civil war. Yet here she was, scarcely three days since agreeing to Agamalon's bargain, helping to invade a moon he had been driven from in shame months before.

Agamalon had appealed to her to address the Dromax's great problem: leadership. He had some promise—as much promise as a freakshow grotesque that talked through a box might—but he and his lieutenants were far outnumbered by the grunts, the beings whose bellies were marked. Finnegan had quipped that they were the "scars-on-thars," invoking some Earthly children's tale thankfully unknown to her. The lummoxes were dull in the extreme, capable of toting and firing a weapon but not much else.

To hear Agamalon tell it, no Dromax had ever employed alien mercenaries. Certainly neither of the other two Troika powers would get involved, and Quintilian and the rest of his merchant ilk only ever stuck around long enough to make their trades and depart. With giant boulders hurtling haphazardly about through space, that seemed a sensible response. But Agamalon's situation had grown ever more desperate, with his officer corps—who literally seemed to have superior brains—dwindling in number. Georgiou had shown more heroic individualism in her first hour on Thirty than most of his lieutenants ever had, and that had inspired Agamalon's unusual offer: leadership of a Double Crescent platoon.

With the promise of information about *Jadama Rohn* as the reward—and without many other options anyway—she had taken up the challenge. Before the unification of Terra, many decapitated regimes across history had invited great leaders to control them; it had even happened on this universe's Earth, when divided Slavic peoples invited the Varangians to rule over them, eventually creating the Kyivan Rus. Georgiou saw herself in that tradition, even if the forces she was called upon turned her stomach with their ugliness.

Hers was just a platoon. But in the first day, she had demolished Skove's strongpoint on Thirty, putting out of commission the launch site from which his airships threatened Agamalon's armor. That night, she'd found a way to upgrade the destructive power of the Double Crescent's Casmarran-built disruptor cannons—and before dawn the second morning, the Jagged Spikes were decamping from the moon altogether.

She'd then encouraged Agamalon not to rest on his gutsack, instead moving immediately to strike a neighboring moon currently in close proximity: Twenty-Six, sanctum of the One-Stars. The tribe's name, to human ears, sounded like it belonged to lesser lights; on Terra as on Earth, it indicated a poor score. But the One-Star Dromax tribe was mighty, so much so that Agamalon initially rejected the idea out of hand.

"You're thinking like a loser," she'd replied. "You live like one, you'll die like one. They're not expecting us. Use that."

It was working. As her hovertank circled behind an advancing column of Double Crescents, Georgiou smiled at the carnage the force—her force—was wreaking on the enemy. The smoke on the humid air was delicious, invigorating her. As good as it was to once again enjoy the spoils of rule in her brief time alongside Quintilian, there'd been something she'd been missing. The fighting, the killing, the striving that made those rewards seem earned.

She loved it.

A hatch in the vehicle opened, and Dax popped her head up. Seeing no disruptor fire about, she turned back to face Georgiou.

The emperor guffawed. Dax had rubbed black powder under her eyes, an awkward attempt at camouflage. "A lot of sniper fire coming at you down in the hull, my dear?"

Dax rolled her eyes, sullen. "Agamalon says he's putting two more companies under you. He wants us to head for Grid Five-Six-Oh."

That made sense to Georgiou. Another One-Star strongpoint, it meant that Agamalon wasn't letting go of the throttle.

"Down in a second." She called out commands to her sergeants in the swamp to disengage and follow—then she scrambled off her perch and made for the hatch.

Most of the armor Georgiou had ridden in involved low ceilings; the hovertank, constructed for the troll-like Dromax, was even more uncomfortable. It lacked any seating whatsoever; Finnegan, she saw, was sitting cross-legged at the front of the compartment, driving the vehicle and operating its forward turret.

He barely acknowledged her when she sat beside him. "We just spread goo everywhere," he said. He looked peaked. "It's a nightmare."

"Come now," she said. "Blackjack would have loved this place. It's a murder a minute."

"I'm just firing in self-defense, and I hate it," he said, scratching his fuzzy face. He hadn't shaved since aboard *Boyington*. "I don't know who these critters are. I don't know what they did to me."

"They're keeping you from your goal."

"What was that again? Why do I want it?"

Dax crawled forward to give both of them canteens. She looked at Finnegan with sympathy. "It's so we can make sure another cloud creature doesn't kill our friends."

"So to defeat that, we've got to kill a lot of these beasties." He shook his head. "This isn't what I signed up for."

Georgiou sighed. "Not you too."

Almost healed from her injury, Dax had refused from the beginning to do anything that would harm the opposing Dromax. That had prompted Georgiou to relegate her to communications and other nonlethal duties. It had also given Dax plenty of time to complain. She started again. "I didn't make it into Starfleet—"

"Here we go."

"—so I didn't learn all the rules and regulations. But I'm pretty sure that intervening in a civil war was on the list of *don'ts*."

"You're right there," Finnegan said. "Even I never did that one." He pursed his lips. "At least, I don't think I did."

"We're all getting such wonderful new experiences," Georgiou said. "I'm broadening your horizons."

Dax looked forlornly back at the comm panel. "I think we should call Leland."

The emperor chortled. "How well did that work when you tried it before?"

The Trill's eyes went wide. "I haven't tried to call—"

"Of course you have." She turned her head, showing Dax she was only mildly perturbed. "He's running silent outside the perimeter of Troika space—but the extremely low subspace-frequency unit we were using to contact him is back aboard *Boyington*. I highly doubt you can raise him on your handheld unit, or anything the Dromax have to offer." She shrugged. "But keep trying, though. It's time you're not complaining to me."

A hush fell, the only sound coming from the hovertank's engines. Finnegan rubbed his eyes and spoke, his voice uncharacteristically somber. "So how long do we have to do this?"

"Who's to say? Agamalon knows where *Jadama Rohn* is, and he's not telling. Not yet. Not until I've helped him take back a certain amount of territory."

Dax commiserated. "Nobody else among the Crescents will talk about the freighter. I've asked, believe me."

"If you'd like me to torture the general to find out, I'd be happy to," Georgiou said. "But I haven't got any idea how to make him hurt that won't spill his guts onto the deck. That leaves me out of options."

"Oh, I don't know," Finnegan said, "I think you found seduction worked with Quintilian."

Georgiou made a sour face. "Either of you want to try, be my guest. I'll be elsewhere, retching at the thought."

Finnegan finished his water. "All I can say is if we do much more of this, I'm going to need something a little stronger." Eyes on the canteen, he took a deep breath. "Maybe for a long time."

36

Dromax Troop Transport
DEPARTING MOON NINE

Another day, another moon—and another victory. Georgiou felt as she hadn't since she was aboard *Charon*, seeing one enemy after another fall before her.

Of course, none of the Dromax tribes she was scoring against had actually been eliminated; their forces were too scattered, too decentralized for that, and Agamalon's numbers remained small. What she had done, however, was execute the exact strategy necessary to permit a horde previously limited to the lunar hinterlands—*hinterlunes?*—to advance steadily closer to the gas giant.

"Ground forces report full control of big disruptor cannons on Nine," Sergeant Garph reported to her on the bridge. It had been the reason for the strike, guaranteeing that Agamalon's troop and material transports wouldn't be threatened by boulders hurled across space during their next hop.

"Well done," she said, going over the plans on her display. It depicted the motions of all the satellites of Dromax, real and artificial, and the ranges of the weaponry associated with each. Over the past week, she had wended her way through the system like a dervish, curling inward and spiraling outward to strike at as many enemy tribes as possible. Agamalon was, suddenly, a name to be feared, regardless of the true leader behind the victories. She hadn't even seen him for three days, always communicating remotely from wherever she was.

She'd done enough; it was time for her prize. She addressed Garph. "Where is your general?"

"Giving birth."

"Doing *what*?"

Acting like nothing was out of the ordinary at all, Garph simply directed her to a room two levels above on the transport.

The Dromax didn't use furniture, but they did have turbolifts. Dax and Finnegan were in the one she stepped into. Finnegan looked haggard; Dax, irate. "We want to talk with you," the latter said, her tone more shrill than Georgiou had heard from her.

"One moment. Come along—I think there's something you may both want to see."

No one stopped Georgiou and her companions from entering the general's quarters, though the squishing sounds gave all three pause. In a bowl-shaped depression at the center of the room, assisted only by a single Dromax, Agamalon was indeed amid some sort of . . . change. All armor removed, the general appeared to be excreting something large from flaps Georgiou had never noticed—or wanted to notice—before.

"Sorry," Georgiou said. "You want privacy."

"*Why? Stay, stay. I'll be just a minute,*" the general called out, a humdrum statement for such a bizarre spectacle. The voice box didn't express any strain—and neither did Agamalon appear to be in any discomfort.

Finnegan, on the other hand, cupped his hand to his mouth and ran out of the room.

"*There,*" Agamalon said, exertions finished. "*Brand the wretched thing.*"

The general's aide turned toward Georgiou holding a writhing being—a Dromax, perhaps a fifth the size of the adults. After placing the child on the deck, the aide activated a small device that soon glowed.

Dax, who Georgiou had noted seemed less put off by the event than Finnegan had been, reacted when the aide brought the white-hot implement closer to the child. "Wait! Don't!"

It was too late. The child howled as the aide seared it with a stamp, leaving two crescent moons on its glistening gut.

"*Another officer,*" Agamalon declared, exiting the bowl. "*Get it out of here. The next one better not come when I'm in the middle of a campaign.*"

Georgiou and Dax stepped aside for the departing aide. The prolific nature of the Dromax had been known to the emperor, but parthenogenesis wasn't something she'd considered. "How . . . often does this happen?" she asked.

"*Nosy, aren't you?*" The general crossed the room as if nothing had ever happened. "*A couple of times a month. Which is not as often as we need reinforcements.*"

Dax looked puzzled. "But I've never seen any of the soldiers go through this."

Agamalon snorted. "*Of course not. Only the officer caste can reproduce.*"

"A shame Finnegan didn't stay," Georgiou observed to Dax. "A self-replicating officer corps sounds like a Starfleet nightmare."

The Trill remained puzzled. "Gnaeus was your kind. Why aren't there more Dromax on Casmarra?"

"*Casmarra is at peace,*" the general said. "*Only Dromax in combat are moved to replicate. Now, did you come for something, or just to gawk?*"

"Nine is secured," Georgiou responded. "We're headed to the next waypoint."

"*Excellent. I'm putting the entire division in your hands.*"

"You might want to wait on that," she said, crossing her arms. "Tell me where *Jadama Rohn* is, or we're done."

Agamalon didn't miss a beat. "*I figured we were coming to that. It's all right—you've earned that much. It's on One.*"

She wasn't at all surprised. "Is this a deception? That's where your precious is, your Cascade, as you call it. You just want us to help you take it over."

"*Oh, we're going there. That's what this has all been leading to. But it's also where your death ship is.*"

Dax's eyes narrowed. "Is that a coincidence?"

"*It isn't, freckle-head. But first things first.*" Agamalon ascended a ramp to a portion of the room containing a screen. A map appeared on it, depicting two bodies of liquid nearly split by land. *"The place we need to conquer is a cataract connecting One's greatest lake with its largest ocean. The land it parts comes to points on the northern and southern sides."*

"A waterfall?" Georgiou asked. *"That's* what's so special?"

"What's special is within *the waterfall—in the cavern that runs behind it from north to south, a tunnel connecting both land-forms."* Agamalon regarded the map. *"We don't have to worry about the northern entrance."*

"Blocked?"

"You could say that. So we only have to take the southern entrance to enter."

"Who controls it now?"

"Who knows? It's always changing. We haven't controlled it in many cycles. I honestly never thought I'd get back there—but you may be the key. If you want your cursed ship, give us the Cascade." Agamalon turned away. *"Dismissed."*

Georgiou and Dax stepped into the hall, ducking the low overhead supports as they went. "He keeps stringing it out," Dax said. "Always one more stop."

The emperor agreed, but didn't want to seem dissuaded. "There is an end. In the meantime, we fight." She entered a strategic briefing room. Empty at the moment, it had ports facing outside—and multiple screens showing where various forces, friend and foe, were located.

"More war." The Trill sighed. "Sean and I were coming to tell you that this has to stop."

"What else is new?"

"Those last couple of battles were new," Dax said, stepping before a port. Several moons gleamed outside. "You've broken Finnegan, do you know that?"

Georgiou laughed. "Which bones this time?"

"I'm serious. Sean was holding it together when he was in the hovertank. But having us on the ground with the infantry—"

"He's the one who wants to shadow me. He's got to go where I go," Georgiou said, surveying the strategic maps. "The last two targets required commando tactics. Why are *you* upset? You only had to patch me and Finnegan up."

"Because Sean felt like he had to carry a disruptor and fight. But I don't think he ever wanted to fight a war."

"He worked security for Starfleet. What did he *think* he'd have to do?"

"He waited out the Klingon War playing bodyguard for merchants and barons. He's good for a barfight." Dax turned and gestured broadly to the strategic maps. "This—this *meat grinder* he never wanted at all."

"Not my Blackjack," Georgiou lamented.

"That's something else. You keep comparing him to someone he's not, and should never want to be." Dax looked back at her. "Yeah, he told me. He wants you to stop it."

Georgiou was amused. "He's certainly sharing a lot. Another fan gone sweet on you?"

Dax groaned. "You wouldn't understand people being nice to one another."

The emperor laughed. "You sound just like Michael Burnham."

"Good for her. What would she say about you now, running another killing machine?"

Georgiou turned and faced a screen. "I do wish you'd make up your mind. Back on Casmarra you were afraid I was going to try to stay with Quintilian. To hear you tell it, I was going to live the high life forever with him. Could you blame me if I did?"

"No, probably not. I mean, it was obvious you were missing how you got treated in your reality. But now you're here, and you're up to the same thing, only different. You're getting to lead. To conquer."

Georgiou turned abruptly and leered at her. "What's wrong with that? I was good at it. I *am* good at it. It's what I was born to do."

"Yeah, but that's just it." Dax waved again to the maps. "This isn't your empire. The Diomax aren't your army, and Quintilian's villa wasn't your palace. You're just borrowing these things."

Georgiou turned toward the port. She stepped before it and looked out at the moons beyond.

"I get it," Dax said, standing behind her. "By the lights of people in this universe, you're a bad person, from a bad place— and you don't see any reason to prove otherwise to anyone. The only person I've ever heard you speak of with any respect is Burnham. You don't want anyone to identify with you at all."

"I am the emperor. I am the empire. You could never understand."

"Well, maybe there is something I understand. You had it all, and then you lost it."

Georgiou looked back and smirked "Why, little Emony, are you *really* going to compare your hopping around for shiny medallions to my ruling the known portion of the galaxy? You *have* developed some cheek."

"I'm not saying we were the same. But the same on a different scale. I was trained from childhood to do one thing better than anyone. My whole world consisted of the gymnastics circuit. And I got treated really well, too, though I didn't get to eat like you did. But then it ended."

"So?"

"So I think between Section 31, Casmarra, and here, you've been raging against starting over. After all the time you put in becoming emperor, you don't want to go to the bottom rung of a different ladder."

"Oh, my. You see right through me." Georgiou rolled her eyes. "You should go see Finnegan next and read the bumps on his head. That ought to keep you busy."

"Make jokes if you want. It proves my point. I think you're afraid."

"Nonsense. There's nothing I can't do."

"Confidence is good. I sure didn't have it afterward. But you're not afraid you won't succeed. You're afraid it won't be worth the effort."

Georgiou looked back into space. "Oh?"

"I could have kept competing, but it wasn't worth it to me to beat children. My sport was mostly for the young. I mean, I had as much right to be there as anyone—but I'd done it."

"And you wept, like Alexander, 'Because there were no worlds left to conquer.' That's what you say here, isn't it?" Georgiou asked, turning toward her. "But nobody says that in my realm. Nobody would *ever* say that. They say '*Alexander cheered, for there were always worlds left to conquer.*'"

Dax lowered her head in sadness. From outside in the hall, the two heard the sound of a human, coughing. "I should see to Finnegan."

Before she could leave, Georgiou grabbed Dax by the wrist—and jabbed a finger at her own chest. "I wasn't done yet. There were star systems we hadn't found—to say nothing of other galaxies. So don't tell me about the pain of starting over, little Trill!"

She stared long at Dax before releasing her.

Dax stepped away—only to pause. She looked back, guarded. "My people know more about starting over than you could imagine," she said. "There's no pain in it. Only excitement. Adventure. The chance to live life again, as someone else. But you're not living it as someone else. You're trying to be the same person you were in a place that's not meant for her—and it's going to eat you up."

I'll be the judge of that, Georgiou thought.

37

Moon One
DROMAX SYSTEM

Burnham had once joked that the emperor had hailed from a place that was upside down. If that was the case, it was no wonder Georgiou had found herself at home in the realm of the Dromax: the place they considered heaven was a hell.

Georgiou had come to that conclusion earlier, while looking down on the Dromax's largest satellite from the Double Crescent invasion fleet. Tidally locked to the gas giant but not to its sun, Moon One still experienced phases of night and day—but other conditions had rendered its weather hellish. It spent a good deal of time in Dromax's shadow—and sat constantly under bombardment by its magnetosphere. Then there was the ground, which heaved and churned under tidal pressures from so many large neighbors. It still had a breathable atmosphere, but only just: it was like living in a house on fire.

As for the magnificent waterfall the general had talked so much about, it had proved to be a similar disappointment. Given the barely existent aesthetic standards of the Dromax, she'd never figured on it being towering falls. But a shallow lake spilling over a thirty-meter-high cliff only half a kilometer wide paled in comparison to a number of sites on her homeworld, which itself wasn't known for its topographical extremes when compared to other planets.

The site had, however, mesmerized Finnegan, who had been much relieved to realize this assault called for his skills as a pilot and not as a soldier. Georgiou had decided to go against the history of all previous assaults on the formation, which uniformly had taken land routes to either side; instead, she'd deployed Agamalon's hovertanks directly on the ocean for a naval approach.

"Feels like I'm running a Higgins boat on D-Day—only we're attacking a waterfall," he said. "And they had better weather and fewer aliens."

Georgiou didn't bother to ask him to explain his reference. She had only so much room in her head—and patience—for two sets of histories. And she had plenty to focus on.

The assaulting Double Crescents had been forced to operate their hovertanks from topside; the waves were far too high for occupants inside to see anything. Georgiou had designed a way to command the vehicles from atop their platforms. A simple innovation; the fact that nobody had yet considered it explained why no Dromax had attacked from the sea before. Amid roiling currents and raucous lightning, four-fifths of her flotilla advanced toward the lower southern approach to the falls from the sea, while the remainder had landed as a feint on the more placid lake to assault the higher shore.

The Dromax on deck were in awe of the falls, including Sergeant Garph. The officer she'd saved after her arrival on Thirty had become her principal liaison with the scar-bellied dunderheads she called troops. *"The Cascade is magical,"* Garph called out over the engines. *"Do you know why the lake is so small and the ocean so big?"*

"I haven't a clue," she replied.

"More water leaves the Cascade than enters it."

She sighed. *I thought you were one of the smart ones.*

The aerial assault began on schedule, as she'd planned it. The Jagged Spikes under General Skove held the southern approach; the fifth tribe to do so this year, she understood. The Spikes fully expected an assault from the stormy skies, and had turned their cannons upward—

—which proved a great mistake as her hovertanks, screened by spray and foam, erupted onto the shores, firing forward and disgorging Dromax warriors on either side.

Georgiou's craft would be the last to beach. "Dax, check in!" she yelled over her Starfleet comm.

Inside the hovertank, the Trill responded, reporting the various landings as the news came in. On top of the deck, Georgiou's gunners provided cover fire for the forces that had already landed.

The emperor did the math. Even with the element of surprise, she'd barely have enough forces to do the job. She'd need far more grunts to hold the place—and wondered where they could be found.

Georgiou had paid more attention to the Dromax life cycle since what she witnessed in the general's quarters. Something hadn't added up. Dax had been right; the emperor had also never seen any of the grunts replicating in the way that Agamalon had. The officers, yes. Even Sergeant Garph had been forced to remain aboard the transport to give birth during one of the operations. But she now perceived the officer reproduction rates to be at no more than replacement level, and probably less. How did any Dromax tribe keep its numbers high, when by all accounts nobody ever changed sides?

She dismissed the thoughts as the hovercraft bumped onto the shore. She promptly found something to shoot at—a pursuit that kept her busy for the better part of ten minutes, until she found a new sort of target.

It was a Jagged Spike vehicle like the others she'd shot at—but the different thing was where it was headed. It was in retreat, headed southward. And it wasn't alone. Surprise had been complete; no Dromax had indeed ever considered a naval assault from the ocean side. If the Dromax ever had their own book of stratagems, perhaps she would be remembered as the author of a few of those as well.

"Captain, we've done it!" Garph called out, jubilant.

Her hovertank grumbled to a stop and settled with a splat on the muddy surface. Georgiou stepped off the platform and surveyed the field of the brief battle. There were Jagged Spike vehicles ablaze, their black clouds adding to the angry mess above. And strewn all around were Dromax. Many with armor were dead; many without oozed from burst abdomens. Alarmingly, she noted a large number of her own forces among the fallen.

Dax climbed out of the hovertank hatch. On seeing the carnage, she fell to her knees, faint.

"Daxie!" Finnegan called out.

Georgiou looked up at them. "Now what?"

"I'm okay." Tears in her eyes, the Trill panted. "I just never thought—I never thought it would lead to this."

"Well, you're the one that wanted to find *Jadama Rohn*."

"She knows that, Georgie!" Finnegan snapped. He comforted the young woman. "It's okay," he said to Dax. "We'll make sure it's worth it."

"How?"

Finnegan was at a loss for words, for a change. "We just will."

Georgiou knew that not just the Spikes, but all the other tribes, had forces somewhere on or above the moon. They might not have long to work. She turned to Sergeant Garph. "Where's the entrance to this tunnel?"

"Up there," he said, pointing to a black hole in the escarpment, about halfway up the side of the adjacent falls.

Seeing that Dax and Finnegan had joined her on the ground, Georgiou nodded. "Sergeant, post the full force on the surface below the entrance. Guns arrayed in every direction—including the sea. We'll barely have enough troops to hold the position."

Garph laughed. *"That won't be a problem."*

"What do you mean?"

"Don't you know where we're at? The Cascade is inside!"

"I thought the falls *were* the Cascade."

"You'll see. You want more troops? Lead me in."

38

Moon One
DROMAX SYSTEM

The suggestion had made no sense to her—but she had soon realized that not just Garph, but nearly every officer intended to go inside. When a delighted Agamalon had landed in his shuttle, she'd protested. Yet he had fully supported his officers, overruling her and ordering only minimal supervision for the few grunts left behind.

It was foolish, she thought as she clambered up a well-worn pathway to the tunnel. *Such a risk, just for some kind of religious pilgrimage?* The Dromax would be picked off the southern approach in a hurry. Then again, she'd never seen their officers move so fast. None of them seemed built for climbing, but Agamalon was making marvelous time up the hill.

Inside, she understood even less.

The "tunnel" behind the cataract was only bounded by rock above, below, and to the left; water streaming over the falls shrouded its right-hand side. Spray from it made it hard to see far. Puddles were everywhere. The passage was wide and high, with no light coming from the other side; she couldn't tell if that was because the entrance was blocked or if the tunnel just arced out of sight.

"This is what you wanted," she said to Agamalon. "Now tell me where *Jadama Rohn* is."

"After."

"After what?"

Agamalon ignored her. *"Break out the lights."* Garph distributed handheld beacons, including to her and her companions.

"Wait here. Once we've got things started, I'll tell you where to go. Don't worry, it's close."

Georgiou watched Agamalon turn away, wondering when the betrayal was coming. There was always a betrayal in her world. Yet the general had seemed in earnest, his light-bearing pilgrims beginning to make their way into a void to the left.

Instead, the surprise came from Finnegan. "Where's the magic?"

Agamalon stopped. *"What?"*

"The magic. I want to see the magic."

Dax looked at him. "Sean, he didn't ask us—"

"Look," he said, "I've been through bloody blessed hell since I got here. And if there's magic around, then Sean Jacob Finnegan is going to see it!"

The general laughed. *"Follow us!"*

Georgiou watched as the Dromax headed to the left, farther away from the sheet of water representing the falls. Finnegan followed—and Dax, shrugging, seemed compelled to join him. At last, Georgiou threw up her hands and followed them into a side tunnel.

The other side opened onto a grotto. Lights weren't necessary here, she saw. Against the sweating far wall was a large shimmering pool, lit by the tall natural edifice that rose from it. Several meters across and enshrouded in luminescent crystals, the column was polished by shrouds of water pouring onto it from seams in the ceiling, high above.

Onto it—and into it, she realized as she listened.

"It's a lava pillar," she said. "Hollow inside."

"I've seen some tall mugs before, but that's the winner," Finnegan said, looking up. "Why doesn't it fill up?"

Georgiou squinted at a darkened area beneath where the base of the pillar met the surface. "Looks like one wall of it's given out, underwater. It's draining into the pool—then out to the waterfall and the sea." Looking up, she saw a ledge running along the cavern's rear wall, above it. Someone had placed a metal plank up there, bridging the gap to the shining tube.

"What are those crystals?" Dax asked.

"I'm not sure." Georgiou whipped out her tricorder. "This whole region was probably underwater once. Vulcanism plus erosion can do some strange things, but I've never—"

"Your kind would take the magic out of anything," Agamalon said. *"Watch—and learn."*

Garph remained behind as the group of Dromax officers parted into two groups, each bound for ramps hewn into the walls on either side. Like monks, the Dromax chanted until they reached the top. Finnegan followed, to the objection of no one.

Finnegan called down from the makeshift bridge. "It's hollow, all right. Fed by water coming in from the lake, I'd guess. Big enough for a fellow to dive right in."

Agamalon did exactly that. Georgiou heard a splash within the column, about two-thirds of the way down. Moments later, the Dromax appeared in the pool, having escaped through the column's underwater gap.

Garph helped the general out. *"I've got the blade ready."*

"Excellent, Soryowno. The miracle begins anew."

Georgiou stared at the dripping Agamalon. "Was that it? You took a dip?"

"Two-legs, for once, just shut up. And listen."

She turned her attention back to the column—and heard another splash. She looked up to Finnegan. "Who jumped that time?"

"Nobody."

That was plainly wrong, because a Dromax appeared from within the pool, water streaming off its hide. It looked just like Agamalon, to the extent that anyone could tell Dromax apart. Garph stepped toward it—

—and slashed it, cutting across the double crescent on the dripping creature's abdomen. *"You serve Agamalon of the Double Crescent,"* Garph said. *"Go out and join your troops."*

Above, another Dromax lieutenant jumped in. And emerged. Twenty seconds later, a second Dromax emerged, once again to be scarred and addressed by Garph.

Then it happened a third time.

Dax called up. "Sean, you're sure just three have jumped in?"

"You can see them up here, can't you? I can count!"

Georgiou stared at the gleaming column—and adjusted her tricorder. Something was fishy inside, for sure.

A fourth diver—and for the fourth time, a second Dromax emerged. "Where are these other ones coming from?" Dax asked. "They've got to be swimming in from somewhere."

Agamalon laughed. *"We don't swim unless we can help it. But this we'll gladly do. Don't you get it?"*

Finnegan was running out of companions on the upper level. "I'll dive in myself and take a look."

"*No!*" Georgiou yelled.

Above, Finnegan recovered his balance just in time. "Why not?"

She stared at the results on the tricorder. "There's a time warp in this column." She reconsidered. "No, not a warp. But a fracture."

"Call it what you want," Agamalon said. *"It's our miracle. Our savior."*

She ran the scan again and gawked at the results. "It's a plane of fractured time, cutting laterally through the column." Another Dromax jumped in; X-rays saw the creature plunge into the water within. Twenty seconds later, another Dromax appeared in midfall.

"Throw something in, Finnegan."

"What?"

"I don't know. Your disruptor!"

"I'll be glad to be rid of the damn thing." He made a show of chucking the weapon in, and a tiny splash followed. It could be seen moments later sinking into the glowing pool.

Dax looked to Agamalon. "Is it safe to reach in?"

"Of course."

"The warped space is in the column. Not the pool," Georgiou said.

Dax fished out the weapon—even as another splash could be heard. A second disruptor appeared below. She offered both weapons to Georgiou, who studied them with her tricorder. "It's amazing," she said. "The objects that pass through the temporal fissure are perfect replicas," she said. "All the experimentation that's been done with replicators? They've never created anything this accurate. The samples are equivalent to six decimal places." She looked up. "It's not really a duplicate. It's a time traveler, one whose existence here doesn't impact the original."

The emperor's mind raced. The portal seemed tied to the planet's geology, but it had something else at work—perhaps the crystals. Could there actually be something like a mineral with time-altering properties? It seemed too much to be believed. But if *Defiant* could pass through a temporal rift in space—and if *Discovery* could create its own passage sailing some interdimensional mushroom highway—was it too much to believe that time could be invested in crystals?

"The fracture is where your soldiers come from," she said to Agamalon. "They're replicas of you, arriving through the portal out of sync with time. That's why everyone wants to control the waterfall."

"*'Who holds the Cascade, holds the future,'*" Agamalon replied, speaking as reverently as she'd ever heard him. "*That's what the legend says—the only legend that matters. Those falls outside aren't the Cascade. This is. An endless shower of warriors, driving our tribe into tomorrow and beyond.*"

"More water leaves the falls than enters," Georgiou said, looking up at what was spilling in from above. "Of course."

"I've always wanted a twin brother," Finnegan called out. "Let me at it!"

"No!" It was Dax who shouted this time.

Finnegan again stopped and stood back. "What now? I could use a spare to send to work when I want to sleep."

"She's saying one of you is more than enough," Georgiou said. "Get down here."

As he descended, the processional continued. Dax stepped over to the pool's edge and brought forth her medical tricorder as a Dromax lieutenant emerged. "May I?" she asked.

"I don't care."

She ran a scan—and then, seconds later, addressed the Dromax's Cascade-spawned duplicate. "Do you mind if I scan you?"

"It can't talk without a voice box," Garph said. *"Or with one."*

Georgiou watched Dax as she activated her device and ran it over the new Dromax. At last, the emperor understood why the species' numbers had plummeted so much after she had invaded in her universe; the Dromax had either been cut off from the Cascade, or the crystalline structure had been destroyed under bombardment. But this one existed—and the potential for it was limitless.

It might even get her back to her own universe.

Dax deactivated her tricorder and beckoned for Georgiou and Finnegan to join her. She looked back up the passage they'd entered through. "This is something, but it's not what we were looking for."

"It's not what *you* were looking for. Quiet." Georgiou thought, desperately trying to figure out some other way that the column could be weaponized. "The Dromax have the power to duplicate anything with this—including a living being—and they choose to use it to create reinforcements. And only that. What a lack of imagination."

"No kidding," Finnegan said. "A fellow could run latinum through and be set for life."

Georgiou turned to face the column. *Forget blood devils, and the damn freighter. Forget Whipsaw.* This was the true secret weapon hidden within Troika space. She smiled. "It's perfect."

"It's not," Dax said.

Georgiou glowered. "What do you mean?"

"Look at these measurements." She showed the tricorder readings to the emperor. "This is something I was doing during my research project—comparing individuals versus their past baselines."

Georgiou studied—and frowned. She turned back to the edge of the pool, where Dax had placed the duplicate of Finnegan's disruptor pistol. She ran a scan on it with her own tricorder.

No.

In a quick motion, she snatched the weapon from the surface and pointed it at the column.

This time, it was Agamalon who said *"No!"* The general's voice resonated throughout the chamber—but as Georgiou pulled the trigger, that sound was all she heard.

The disruptor didn't work.

She looked back at her tricorder and reported the disappointing results. "The matter's fine," Georgiou added, "but there's something wrong with the energy. The phase variance is slightly out of kilter—unsurprising, if this thing is a natural phenomenon. It means that the second version is just a little bit off. In the case of the disruptor, it's off enough not to work."

"In the case of Dromax, it means the creation of a stupid, sterile fool," Agamalon said. *"One who can only follow, and who must be scarred so as not to be mistaken for a Dromax by birth—or accidentally sent through the Cascade, creating an abomination."*

"You sound like others have tried."

"They have. It wasn't pretty."

Dax's eyes were wide with wonder. "The Dromax are like all of us—bioelectric beings. The more complex the energy, the more out of whack it seems to get."

"Out of whack being a technical term," Finnegan said.

"That explains why the quality of the troops is so low," Georgiou said. "It's not that they're clones—it's that anything that walks out of the portal is going to be lesser. Officers are

born. The soldiers are reflections, echoes in space and time."
She looked keenly at the column. "Maybe it can be adjusted."

"You won't mess with it," Agamalon said. *"Our whole civilization has been based on this place since the beginning times, when Dromax first rose on this moon. We've been battling for control of it ever since. But so many want it that nobody can hold it for long."* The general passed Georgiou on the way back to the ramp. *"Get out of my way. I have a lot more dives to do!"*

Georgiou looked to Dax. "These errors in the duplicated Dromax. They are fatal?"

"Eventually, I'm sure."

"Everything is born dying. How long do they live?"

"It's a tricorder, not a crystal ball. Why don't you ask someone?"

"They don't have to live very long," Garph said, having overheard. *"They never get to, anyway."* The sergeant handed off the knife to another Dromax officer and made for the ramp. *"My turn!"*

Alone by the far wall, Finnegan looked unusually thoughtful. "Come to think of it, this thing could be abused. Imagine the Klingons getting it."

"It shouldn't even exist," Dax said.

"Just let me think," Georgiou said. "I need a minute."

It was one she was not to get. A low boom could be heard outside the chamber. Eyes wide, Georgiou and the others ran from the grotto into the main tunnel.

A battered Dromax lieutenant stopped them before they reached the end. *"We're under assault from the other tribes. They just started arriving."*

"Which ones?" Georgiou asked.

"The ones we struck over the last days."

Dax's eyes went wide. "But that's all of them."

"Yes. We're under siege."

39

Moon One
DROMAX SYSTEM

"The news just gets better and better," Finnegan said, returning inside.

"Now what?" After a night and day of siege, Georgiou had repaired back into the tunnel for a rest—and the few hours of sleep she'd caught hadn't made her feel any better. She rolled over on the rocks and squinted at him. "Why are you wet?"

"It's pouring out there again. Pretty bad."

She was relieved. She'd been afraid the lunkhead had gone through the Cascade, as he'd earlier wanted to. "Are we still holding?"

"Barely. Everybody's buckled down in the tanks and trying to keep moving."

"And the troops?"

"Agamalon's people are going through the Cascade as fast as they can and sending grunts outside." He scratched his growth of beard. "They're dying in under an hour sometimes."

Georgiou rose and worked the shoulder she'd slept on. She and Finnegan stepped to the entrance and surveyed the situation. Storms raged beyond. Below the precipice, the sloping trail to the southern approach remained intact—but much of that approach was pocked by craters from shells delivered aerially.

"When I last saw Garph, he was shriveled like a raisin," Finnegan said. "There's no way they can generate new troops fast enough. All they can use are the good weapons the dead have dropped."

She gestured. "The craters stop about a kilometer out."

"That's as close as the other tribes will bomb to the water-fall. I think they're afraid of damaging the Cascade."

Georgiou nodded. In countless years of fighting, nobody had ever dropped a meteor anywhere near the place. She remembered Agamalon saying the northern entrance wasn't an option; she wondered how it would have been blocked, if so many feared to bomb close by.

"Those are Skove's forces," Georgiou said, pointing to the vanguard engaging the Double Crescent's outer perimeter in the muck.

"Yeah, the Spikes let the other tribes send flanking assault waves, then they head up the middle." He looked to her. "I don't think we can hold out much longer. You think they'll care that we're not Dromax?"

"They know we've been helping Agamalon, so I doubt it." She eyed him. "We are in, sink or swim."

"I'm about ready to go make a bunch of copies of myself and have us all make a run for it. Maybe one of me will sneak through."

"You have an unusual and horrifying fixation on that concept," she said. "But I guess a bunch of dim-witted Finnegans wouldn't differ much from the original."

He looked back at her with tired eyes. "Oh, Georgie, I know you love me." He turned. "I'm going to find Dax."

Georgiou knelt in the opening. Night was falling, but the near-constant lightning kept the ground eerily lit. Even in the storm breaks, the night before, the spaces between the dark clouds had remained an eerie orange. The many moons saw to that, as did their proximity to the gas giant. Even with the bulk of the entire moon between their location and the planet, it made its presence known.

The emperor had wondered if the Cascade's position relative to the huge planet had contributed to its creation; doubtless, all the tugs from other moons had led to the feature's instability. She'd been unable to think of any use for it in the current situation. All she knew was that the Dromax were still willing to kill for it—and she was stuck inside.

A bolt of lightning struck nearby, sending booming thunder into the tunnel past her. She didn't move. Pelted with sheets of windswept rain, she considered that the entire enterprise had been a misadventure. Agamalon had been too busy to speak again of *Jadama Rohn*, and if it was anywhere on the moon, she had no hope of reaching it.

The only play she could imagine was escape—or perhaps treachery. Would Skove, who seemed the strongest of the rivals, take her on as an ally, as Agamalon had—or would he kill her on sight? And what would happen to Dax and Finnegan if she fled?

And why am I even thinking of them?

Battered by rain, she stood and straightened her uniform. *Captain Georgiou*'s accursed uniform. She was going to have to act on her own, and damn anyone who—

Light appeared before her feet. A transporter effect, resolving into a large briefcase.

It tipped over on the uneven surface, nearly tumbling out onto the sloping path. Georgiou snatched it and pulled it inside.

She looked about. No one was around. There was something wrapped around the handle to the case; a note, on some kind of paper she hadn't seen before. She squinted in the flickering light from outside and read:

MOST IMPRESSIVE.
TIME FOR A CLASSIC.
SEE YOU AT THE LAST STOP.

She read it twice—and then gawked as the paper burst into flames. She dropped it. It was gone in an instant, leaving no ash.

Time for a classic? What can that possibly mean?

She felt for the latches on the case. It opened easily—and what it revealed inside answered her question as well as any detailed briefing could have.

She closed it quickly and turned. A Dromax lieutenant was there, guiding a bunch of new soon-to-be-dead grunts out to the battlefield. "Go call Agamalon. I have a plan."

"To survive?"

"No. To win. Once and for all."

Georgiou had always suspected that the tribal chiefs of the Dromax had some means for contacting each other. No, the tribes never allied in groups with one another except as part of ad-hoc actions, like the one that had raged outside for a day and a half. But they did have ways to send threats besides simply hurling asteroids around.

Thanks to her, Agamalon had recently sent such a threat. And it had prompted an immediate cease-fire, with the warlords of eight of the other tribes presenting themselves at the front lines. Some, like Skove, were already on the scene; others had to descend in shuttles. To avert a brawl, Georgiou had ordered the Double Crescent lines re-formed to screen the leaders from one another as they were led, one at a time, up toward their holiest of places.

Last to arrive in the grotto, General Jorza of the Whorls reacted as all the others had: with revulsion at the sight of Finnegan standing, shoulder deep, in the pool before the crystal column that was the Cascade. *"Get out of there, you filthy beast!"*

"I know, I know," Georgiou said, sauntering past. "You're afraid he dove in from above. I'd never do that to you. I just wanted him to make a little adjustment."

Finnegan moved aside—revealing, on the portion of the Cascade just above the water line, an oblong device adhering to the crystal surface.

"It's like Agamalon told you," she said, stepping to the outside of the pool and facing the device. "A bomb. It's strong enough not just to annihilate this room, but also to blow the whole front of the cataract out into the ocean. Your lake up there will drain into the sea in a day." She stopped before the pool. "And it will definitely destroy your precious Cascade."

Jorza was horrified. *"Agamalon, how could you let her do this?"*

"I didn't want to," the general replied. *"But then she gave me one of these."* The Dromax displayed a communicator that had also been sent in the case. *"I don't know where she got it from—but everything changes. Now."*

A classic. Georgiou had understood what it meant as soon as she'd seen the bomb. She'd been given a much more powerful device weeks earlier by Starfleet to end the Klingon War. Intended to devastate Qo'noS, the bomb had gone unused, thanks to the meddling of Burnham. She had given control of it to L'Rell, who had used it to blackmail the other Klingon houses into backing her.

At the time, it hadn't seemed to Georgiou to be a practical solution. First, and most obviously, it left the Klingons alive and undamaged. The second problem related to the so-called honor that the Klingons who visited her bar often prattled about. Would a planetful of raging, self-righteous zealots really consider kneeling before any blackmail, even one that threatened to annihilate their world? Many Klingons she'd met would have gladly taken planetary death over that.

But the Dromax, knowing they'd be limited to reproducing the slow, messy, old-fashioned way?

They would deal.

She made sure of it. "Right now, with you all here, Agamalon will detonate this bomb." An unsettled stir went through the gathered Dromax. "The general accepts martyrdom now, knowing that you all lost too." She turned. "Or perhaps the general will use it later, after hearing any of you have gotten out of line. And the Double Crescent will deal, just as you, with never having any more shock troops again."

The generals went silent. She'd expected such a change to the status quo would be hard to contemplate. Georgiou began to pace. "But every day that Agamalon doesn't detonate it, the Double Crescent will be churning out more and more warriors. And the general will do favors, as well, for those tribes that are cooperative."

General Skove, who'd been more disagreeable than any since entering, responded predictably. *"What you're saying is inconceivable. You'd make us all Agamalon's vassals!"*

Georgiou strutted toward Skove and put her hands on her hips. "That is *exactly* what I'm doing, Lieutenant."

"I'm a general, you freakish fool!" Skove shouted.

"There's only one general." She gestured to Agamalon, still holding the remote detonator. "And if you'd like to address your general's guests more politely, those voice boxes of yours have nicer settings." She smiled. "I have a feeling we may get the chance to use them."

40

Moon One
DROMAX SYSTEM

The haggling went on long into the night, though it was only haggling in the sense that the other tribes were vying with one another to decide what to offer Agamalon. This starship, that moon, total political control. Finnegan, once dry, had suggested something called "pool passes," which might result in some kind of economy of its own.

Dax had predictably objected, saying the Cascade-spawned Dromax were essentially slaves, bereft of the right to choose for themselves. Georgiou had countered that they likely couldn't do that in any event. Regardless, Dax had, also characteristically, remained silent about her objections before the Dromax. She saved her crusading comments for her companions.

Georgiou still had no idea who her benefactor was. Only a very few people within the Federation knew about the bomb plot on Qo'noS, as did the leaders of the Klingon houses. Her best guess was that Section 31 had sent the device; the burning message was a silly flourish worthy of Leland. She knew he had certain capabilities for knowing where they were, but how he would have known exactly what was going on and what she needed remained a mystery.

Agamalon finally broke free from his clutch of new admirers and joined Georgiou and her companions in the main tunnel. *"This is an amazing thing you've done, Two-Legs."*

"Oh, it's nothing," Georgiou said. "Just bringing an end to countless years of stagnation and pointless infighting." She smirked. "The price for that ought to be a lot higher, but I'm willing to settle for what I asked. Maybe I *am* a freakish fool."

Agamalon laughed. *"You'll feel even more like one when I tell you this. The freighter you want is farther up the tunnel."*

Dax gawked. "What?"

"The one time I had control of the Jadama Rohn, *I also controlled the Cascade. But the two approaches to the falls had always made it difficult to hold—we had to cover two fronts at once."* Agamalon gestured to the north. *"So I hired one of the traders, some idiot willing to fly it, to move the ship to the antechamber inside the northern approach. Nobody dared come in that way again!"*

Georgiou scowled. "You mean just because of superstition, people gave up on the northern entrance entirely?"

"I changed the strategic map. I thought that's what you've been encouraging me to do these past few days. And as you've seen with the Cascade, some unbelievable things are quite true."

"Fair enough." Georgiou turned to see Dax and Finnegan, as flabbergasted as she was. "It's been right here! We never even looked."

Finnegan gestured up the side corridor. "To be fair, there was a magic pool that way."

"I don't know why you want the damned ship," Agamalon said. *"Perhaps its proximity to the Cascade will have sanctified it. In any event, my thanks to you all. If you need anything—a flight out, a meal—just ask."*

"Go," she said to Dax and Finnegan. Satchels of supplies slung over their shoulders and portable lights in hand, the two headed up the tunnel, the rumbling of the waterfall covering their jubilant voices.

Once they were gone, she turned back to Agamalon. "Come to think of it, I may need something after all, General . . ."

The sun had risen outside, but the storms had not stopped. Georgiou could see the sky now, outside the abandoned northern entrance of the tunnel. And before her, across a wet black floor, sat the cargo ship she had seen in images taken by *Archimedes*, twenty-five years before.

"*Jadama Rohn*," she said.

It was an old Orion freighter, like the one in her universe, and it had the external-vent modifications that Captain Georgiou and Burnham had noted in the surveillance video recorded in the Casmarran impound station. The ramp was down; apparently it was still working. Dax lingered outside, staring up inside it.

"Where's Finnegan?" Georgiou asked.

"He went inside," Dax mumbled. The Trill's eyes were fixed. "I don't—"

Georgiou snorted. "You mean you've come all this way, gone through everything to find this ship—and now you're afraid to set foot in it?"

"The Cloud," Dax said, snapping out of it. "If the Cloud that struck *Farragut* came from it—"

"Then it's no longer here. There was no relapse aboard *Farragut* after it left, was there?"

"No."

"Then you're being silly." Georgiou marched up the ramp. Glancing over her shoulder, she saw Dax had not moved. She turned. "Fine. Go tell Agamalon you'll accept his flight out of here. Tell Leland everything you've seen. I'm sure he will consider that a successful mission."

Dax looked up—and reluctantly turned.

Good enough, Georgiou thought. *One down.*

She walked halls filled with musty, stale air. It was clearly a death ship, but someone had hauled off the bodies. Black markings from some kind of indelible ink could be seen on the deck, noting where crewmembers had fallen. They were everywhere, in every pose. If a blood devil visited here, it had stricken quickly, and without mercy.

Even more markings awaited her on the bridge—as did Finnegan. He looked back to her. "Where's Daxie?"

"Nature called."

He seemed to accept that. "At least Agamalon's guest quarters for 'two-legs' had plumbing. This cave, not so much."

She advanced to the control stations. "What's the status?"

"Ship seems nominal—someone flew it here, after all. But the controls are locked under an external encryption program. I had to cycle the landing ramp by hand—and hot-wire the consoles here just to get a prompt."

"You sound like you've had to steal an Orion ship before."

"I don't put everything on my résumé."

Georgiou studied a screen. "Someone tried to erase the logs, as well. It didn't work—so they locked up the whole ship."

Finnegan pointed to another screen. "There's a Starfleet log-in program that's been added on top of the system."

"*Starfleet?*"

"Surprised me, too. It wants a captain or higher."

"Verbal command interlock?"

"Aye."

The emperor moved to that station. "I was given Georgiou's codes when they gave me control of *Discovery*. I'm sure they changed them the instant I got off the ship—but they wouldn't have been changed here." She said Captain Georgiou's name and rank and cited a numeric code.

Within seconds, the log-in attempt worked—and all systems aboard *Jadama Rohn* hummed to life. The emperor found it amusing. "No wonder Section 31 needs a computer to imagine security threats. These people never plan for anything."

Finnegan pointed to the screen he was standing before. "There's a message with the Starfleet program."

"Open it."

On the large forward viewscreen, Georgiou saw a familiar face—five years younger than the one belonging to the woman responsible for her exile:

My name is Michael Burnham. I serve with Starfleet aboard Shenzhou, *with Captain Georgiou. She's outside now, dealing with one of the Dromax tribal leaders. We beamed in from our shuttle once we figured out where this freighter was, but we're not supposed to be in this place, and we're going to have to leave.*

This recording is to inform whichever Starfleet officer finds it that the Jadama Rohn*'s fate was not drug-related. Rather, it may have been something more sinister.*

Since the captain first saw the ship, she believed there was something unusual about it; earlier this week at Casmarra, we began to believe the vents on the hull might have related to a collection device, targeting an interstellar antigen. We believe this antigen was not secured properly, killing the crew.

We expected the logs of this vessel would lead to the source of the antigen, and they have. But we urge you not to go, for the same reasons we were reluctant to inform Starfleet about this trip. We think Captain Vercer may have been seeking to weaponize the antigen—and Captain Georgiou and I share grave concerns that someone else could do the same, should this information leak. In fact, it was concern about that very eventuality that prompted us—

—never mind. I won't get into that now. My captain believes the thing which struck Jadama Rohn *is so dangerous, so hostile to life, that the only responsible course is to prevent others from searching for more. Whether this decision is right or wrong, she is prepared to accept the consequences, and so am I. We cannot live with what may happen should we fail. Burnham out.*

Georgiou stared at the screen, now blank. *So that was it,* she thought. Little Captain Georgiou was so frightened of opportunity that she'd not only broken Starfleet regulations to lock away the secrets of the blood devils, but she'd dragged Michael into it as a willing accomplice.

"I've got the logs going," Finnegan said. "There they be." He read. " 'Twenty-five years ago, immediately before the *Archimedes* encounter'—huh."

"What?"

"It came from Oast." He looked back—

—and into the heel of Georgiou's boot. Finnegan slammed backward against the console, giving her an open shot to deliver a knockout blow with the back of her hand. His body collapsed across the markings on the floor where others had fallen, so many years ago.

She took a long breath as she looked down at his fallen form. "You would get useful only here at the end." She grabbed his wrists and began dragging.

She was in the corridor outside the bridge when his unconscious form rolled across something. She paused and knelt, fishing for the thing lodged beneath Finnegan's body. It was a black marker, probably the one that had been used on the decks. The markings of manufacture were Orion. She was not surprised by that, nor by the fact that when she shook it, its ink was still liquid. Nobody could beat the Orions for making quality implements that few people really used anymore.

Thinking again, she realized it might have a use after all.

Having resumed her exertions a couple of minutes later, she finally got Finnegan out onto the landing ramp. Agamalon and several armed Dromax were outside, waiting at its base. "Take him," she said, gesturing. "Do you have Dax?"

"She was on her way down the tunnel," Agamalon said. *"When she saw us, she turned and ran. We'll find her."*

She didn't pass me, Georgiou thought. It didn't matter. "I'm leaving. I don't want any trouble from either of them."

Agamalon snorted. *"I guess two-leg leaders have to put down insurrections the same way I do."*

"They do in my world."

"Should we vaporize them?"

The question jarred Georgiou. After a pause, she said, "No. Just make sure they never leave—and that they don't call anyone." She thumbed back at *Jadama Rohn*. "If you don't mind, I'll get this plague ship out of your way."

"There really is no end to your good deeds. Farewell."

Stage Five
VENGEANCE

Terrans wallow in their past. It's their great weakness. They say our Alliance would never have defeated them had, say, Emperor Georgiou survived. Rank nonsense. When one human more or less barely makes a difference to the mining quotas, I think the fate of the universe is safe!

—SUPREME LEGATE DUKAT
Speech at Cardassian Central
Command, 2377

41

Freighter *Jadama Rohn*
Troika Space

Fear, Lela Dax had once said before other Trill legislators, was a thing of variable utility. In proper quantities, it prevented people from making the wrong decisions; when overactive, it stopped them from making the right ones. Those effects scaled, impacting individuals and entire states alike. Good government, she'd said, required telling the difference between the two.

Fear had prevented Emony Dax from setting foot on *Jadama Rohn*. It was, as Georgiou had said, irrational — but as soon as she'd approached the freighter in the tunnel, she'd felt as if she were with Eagan and her other colleagues, walking the halls of *Farragut* while the cloud creature was still active. No matter that she had faced risks since then from Casmarrans, Dromax, her own piloting skills, and the odd ex-emperor. The Cascade wasn't the only time machine behind the falls.

She had turned back, thinking that, as Georgiou had said, she had done her part for Eagan, *Farragut*, and Starfleet. But something about the advance of Agamalon and the other Dromax, weapons drawn, seemed less than welcoming. That left *Jadama Rohn*, which she still had no desire to hide in. She'd crawled beneath the landing ramp then. That was where she was when Georgiou emerged with Finnegan's body, along with her orders to hold him and Dax indefinitely.

Dax had no desire to leave Finnegan behind—but also no expectation of being able to evade the Dromax. Where might she go? When *Jadama Rohn* suddenly lifted off, she decided. Grabbing onto the bottom of the still-closing gangplank, she did her best parallel-bar act to get on top of it and squeeze into the ship.

The Orion vessel terrorized her with its remembrances of the fallen, marked in black everywhere on the decks. Georgiou frightened her more.

She'd thought at times she was coming to understand the woman; most recently, when they were aboard Agamalon's transport. But something inside the emperor kept her veering off the path of decent behavior. Yes, Dax understood that Georgiou saw her and Finnegan as anchors around her neck. But why would she wait until they found *Jadama Rohn* to run off? There were many better ships to abscond with, for certain.

There had to be something else.

She'd waited hours trying to figure out her next steps, all while hiding in a chilly closet. She wasn't about to seek sanctuary in the cargo hold; that was where Captain Georgiou and Burnham had found that strange container attached to the exterior vents. But there really was no sanctuary anywhere: the freighter shuddered like a ghost, its long-dormant engines setting off creaks and groans that terrified her.

Then she had reached up to the garments in the closet—and felt the disruptor pistol in the pocket of one of the jackets.

She searched for a smaller jacket, figuring the one thing she didn't want to do was carry the weapon openly. She wasn't even sure why she wanted it. *Farragut*'s shot, had it come in time, might not have done anything to the cloud. How much damage was a handheld weapon likely to do? And she couldn't see herself shooting at Georgiou, except maybe to stun. But toting the disruptor about freely would surely result in the emperor trying to disarm her. Better to wait until she needed it.

After calculating how long Georgiou had already been awake, Dax took a chance and slipped from the closet, jacket on and fastened and pistol hidden in the pocket inside. Her reconnaissance then began—

—and ended, sooner than she expected, on the bridge. The ship was in interstellar space, she saw, headed somewhere—and Georgiou was nowhere to be seen. Dax approached the control station and thought. She'd been able to get Eagan's shuttle, *Leizu*, back to Starbase 23, but that route had been among the preprogrammed ones, and everything she needed to read had been helpfully written in Federation Standard. All she could see in that language on the screens was a message waiting to be played.

After first turning down the volume—that much she could figure out—she played it, beholding Michael Burnham on the larger screen above. Spellbound, Dax stepped closer to hear it.

She was still standing there when the message snapped off. It had ended—but that was not the only reason. She turned to see the emperor at the control station. "Hear anything interesting?"

Dax looked at her, wide-eyed. "You know what I heard."

Georgiou pointed to the jacket. "Cold?"

"Freezing."

"Almost certainly a dead man's jacket," Georgiou said, stalking around the console. Dax took several steps to the side. "I didn't think you wanted to be on this ship."

"I want to know why *you* want to be on it. I want to know why you came this far. Why you came at all."

Georgiou smiled primly. "You told me your opinion. I came to be pampered by Quintilian—and to play general again with Agamalon."

"But that's not why you want to be on this ship."

"No." Georgiou stared at her for a long moment—and then gestured with her hands. "*Boo!*"

Dax jumped a step back—but did not go for the gun.

Georgiou laughed. "You're too much fun, Dax." She stepped back around to the command consoles and checked the vessel's heading. "If you must know, I'm following the leads, just like I was asked to. Before *Jadama Rohn* encountered *Archimedes*, she'd come from Oast."

"The third part of the Troika?" Dax looked at the viewport. "That's where we're going?"

"Following the leads. Do try to keep up."

Dax stared. "But you're not doing this for Leland. For Section 31."

"Maybe I am, maybe I'm not."

"Why would you go if you weren't?"

Georgiou looked up from the console—and exhaled deeply. "Okay," she said, pacing. "Say the dikironium cloud creature existed in my universe."

Dax had always wondered about that. "Did it?"

"This is a thought experiment, darling. I don't think your poor heart could take anything else." Georgiou knelt by the black markings on the deck. "Say there was a *Jadama Rohn* in my universe, delivering me what I expected would be a cloud creature. Oh, let's just use the name I knew them by—a *blood devil*."

Dax seemed to remember hearing it from her before. It fit, she thought. "Why would you want something like that?"

"For the reason Burnham there didn't want anyone to know about it. Power. You just saw it back there with the Cascade. Something unique, something special, has great value to the possessor. It's worth killing for, even here."

"So it can kill *for you*."

"Sometimes. Sometimes so I can prevent others from killing *me* with it." She stood and crossed her arms. "That's how I lost it. *Jadama Rohn* was destroyed by a traitor who didn't want me using it. A little pissant named Eagan."

Dax did a double take. "Not Rodolfo Eagan!"

"I have no idea. He was Dead Eagan by the time Finnegan—er, Blackjack got done with him."

"He's dead here too. He was Lieutenant Georgiou's captain when she first encountered the ship—and who I was working under at the *Farragut*. He's the one who sent me to warn Section 31 about the cloud."

Georgiou looked genuinely surprised. "The name was redacted in Section 31's briefing. But then Leland hadn't intended to tell me anything about why we were going."

"Until I opened my mouth." Feeling sick, Dax shrank back against the bulkhead. "Now I guess you want a blood devil for yourself, here in my universe. Is that it?"

"I haven't decided. Quintilian keeps his romantic options open; I do the same, but with everything."

"But how could you even think of using something so—so wretched? The thing kills randomly." Dax waved about the bridge. "It killed the very people who were carrying it!"

"Because they didn't know how to handle it. Did you know the first people in my universe to deploy a sodium bomb killed everyone within thirty kilometers of the test site, including themselves? But that doesn't mean you stop trying."

"It does if there's no safe use for something. It's a damned cloud!"

"You haven't convinced me."

The console chimed. Outside, the hurtling stars vanished and slowed—revealing an inky spot of blackness ahead.

Georgiou stepped back to the navigation station, seemingly unsurprised. "Oast is in an absorption nebula. One little star in there in a tiny pocket—only traders like Quintilian knew the best route in. And Vereer was one of them." She moved to the helm and activated the impulse drive. "Course is set. We're heading in."

Dax looked at the comm station. It had been her other option, besides rerouting the freighter. Georgiou caught her expression. "Don't be tiresome, Dax. You're unlikely to reach Leland even if you tried—and I'd rather not have to hurt you."

The Trill looked up. "Why not?"

Georgiou had no answer. "I don't really know. But I think you are as curious as I am to see what's ahead."

Dax had to admit that she was. She fixed her eyes on the viewscreen—and watched as blackness replaced everything else.

42

Moon One
Dromax System

Finnegan had awakened in prisons before, but seldom a cage. Yet that was all the Dromax had handy: a latticed metal container, evidently for restraining one of their own kind.

After the first time he woke up in it—sitting against the bars cross-legged with an angry welt on his forehead and no idea what had happened—he'd overheard that his captors had gone to great difficulty to bring the cage up the hill and into the tunnel. It now sat, Finnegan inside it, exactly where *Jadama Rohn* had rested for years. Apparently whatever superstitions the Dromax had about the freighter departed when it did—though Finnegan had no recollection of the vessel leaving, or what had happened to his friends.

He just knew he felt miserable. Beyond the knock to the head, he'd suffered from being in the wet draft from the waterfall that curtained one wall of the tunnel. Spray ran freely across the cave floor, meaning he was often sitting in a puddle; he had a raging rash. And sneezing hurt his lungs awfully.

He'd gone in and out of consciousness enough that he'd lost track of time. The Dromax had mostly been busy through all of it, appearing infrequently to toss him food. Sometimes it was for humans. He wanted medication—but most of all, he wanted to know what had happened to Georgiou and Dax.

The whole adventure had gone wrong somehow. He assumed it was his fault; most everything usually was. But the current turn was a complete surprise. Hadn't they just found their goal?

A Dromax entered. Bleary eyed, Finnegan looked up. "Who's there?"

"*Can't you tell us apart yet?*" the Dromax declared. "*Georgiou was right about you. You are an oaf.*"

"General Agamalon. Grand." He stopped to cough. "I'd shake your hand, but I've got a bad dose of it. That—and, well, I'm in a cage."

"*It happened that way. I haven't been a kilometer from the Cascade since everything happened—and I promised not to let you out of my sight.*"

"Who'd you promise?"

"*Your commanding officer, before she left in the ship. I don't know what you did to irritate her, but count yourself lucky. Were you my subordinate, I'd have had you killed by now.*"

Finnegan rubbed his head. Part of it was coming back, but the message from Burnham aboard the ship was the last thing he remembered. Georgiou had tried to ditch him before; she'd finally succeeded. "Did Dax go with her?"

"*We're still searching. We think she may have gone out the northern entrance, into unclaimed territory. There's a lot of jungle there.*"

Good for her, then. Finnegan could see her, gymnastically swinging from branch to branch over the heads of the shorter Dromax. "I've seen all of you running about. I don't suppose you're willing to tell me what's going on?"

"*Everything's changed,*" Agamalon said, squat body jittering with excitement. "*Now that the Double Crescent rules the Dromax, the Casmarran economy is collapsing. Some of them fear we won't need to buy their weapons anymore. Some of them fear we'll be turning our sights on them next.*"

"Reason to be worried, have they?"

"*We'll see. There may be other forces in play. And speaking of . . .*"

Agamalon turned to see Garph approach. The two Dromax

retired to a space farther away to confer. The discussion, Finnegan saw, was animated.

After a long wait, he watched as both of them approached. *"Sergeant Garph tells me we've just gotten word of a new situation,"* Agamalon said. *"Apparently there is no end to the wonders of the past few days."*

"Can't wait to see them."

"Afraid you won't," the general responded. Garph drew a disruptor and pointed it at Finnegan.

He could only summon an exhausted sigh. "Ah, Sergeant. I thought we were friends. We saved you, remember?"

"Your captain saved me."

"Did 'my captain' order this?"

Neither Dromax responded.

Finnegan straightened himself as best he could in the cage. "Well, crack on. Don't leave me here waiting."

He steeled himself. A burst of energy washed over his body—

—and he found himself in a bright, antiseptic room.

The afterlife is duller looking than I expected, he thought. The cage was gone, he noticed; only after his eyes adjusted did he realize he was sitting on a transporter pad.

The side doors whooshed open, admitting Leland. "We have him," Sydia said from the control station.

"Leland!" Finnegan raised his hand for the spymaster to help him up—only to draw it back and sneeze into it. Then he offered it again. "Where am I?"

"*NCIA-93*," Leland said, taking care to grab Finnegan by the sleeve rather than his dripping hand. "Sydia, medical team at once. Bridge, get us out of orbit before the Dromax see us."

"I thought you couldn't come here," Finnegan said. "The treaty."

"We're Section 31, Sean. We don't ask permission, and we rarely ask forgiveness."

"Is that your motto?"

"That's classified." He helped Finnegan stand. "We knew they were about to shoot you. We acted. You're complaining?"

"No. I mean—yes, that's not good enough." Finnegan frowned. "Georgiou said you were outside the edge of Troika space—that you might not even know where we were. How'd you know where I was? Or what was happening?"

"That's classified."

Finnegan felt another burst of energy: this one, righteous rage. He grabbed Leland by the collar. "I've been through hell, you stupid eejit! Tell me or I'll sneeze in your face!"

Leland looked at him—then to Sydia—and chuckled. "Pipe the sound down here," he said.

Sydia touched a control. Then, over the room's public address system, Finnegan heard his own voice: *"Reason to be worried, have they?"*

And then another: *"We'll see. There may be other forces in play. And speaking of . . ."*

"That's me and Agamalon, a minute ago." He released Leland. "How in the hell?"

Leland pointed to Finnegan's mouth. "The tooth you lost on *Pacifica*. We replaced it, remember?"

Finnegan froze. "Yeah?"

"It's a transmitter. Works in combination with a very classified substance called viridium. It decays in the subspace spectrum—a starship can home in on it from systems away."

Finnegan's finger went immediately to his mouth. "You mean," he said after removing it, "you've been listening to my every word all this time?"

"No, not all. The transmitter's range is limited. But when we didn't hear from your team, we homed in on the viridium—and once we got close enough, heard your conversation. Sounds like we got you out just in time."

Finnegan stepped to the wall and sagged against it, exhausted. "It's just as well. I don't have the energy to explain everything."

He had slid down to sit on the deck again when the medic entered. She was immediately startled by Finnegan's ragged condition. "You look rough," she said, opening her bag. "Where do you want me to start?"

"I could murder a drink."

"Georgiou and Dax," Leland said. "Where are they?"

Finnegan looked up at him, pained. "Dax is on the ground."

Sydia responded. "That is not what our life-sign readings say. Every being on the moon is Dromax."

"Then she's with Georgiou," Finnegan said. "She took *Jadama Rohn.*"

"She found it!" Leland said, brightening. "We heard a bit of that, but didn't believe it."

"Believe it. She found out where the killer clouds came from."

The medic finished running a scan of the wound to his face. "This injury of yours—did you run into something?" She shook her head as she examined the readings. "It's like you were kicked in the face with a high-heeled boot."

Finnegan winced. "Well, that's it. Your emperor. She's cutting you people out."

Leland's smile faded. "She's gone bad?"

He tried to laugh, but could only cough. And coughing made him rock about on the deck, and that made his backside hurt even more. He tried to stand. "I've got this rash," he said, pawing at his pants. "I've been sitting in water for I don't know how long."

"We'll get to that in sickbay," the medic said.

"It's burning like hell!" He pulled at the trousers, even as the medic backed away.

Leland blanched. "Sean, buddy, we'd really rather you didn't—"

Then, everyone went silent—expressions going from horror to astonishment to puzzlement.

"What is it?" Finnegan asked. "A Dromax leech gnawing on me?"

"Somebody's written something on your ass," Leland said. Startled, Finnegan looked back and down. "Huh."

"Swollen," the medic said, running her tricorder past. "Some kind of indelible ink. You're allergic to it. It's—er, extensive."

"Must have been while I was knocked out," Finnegan said.

"I sure hope so," Leland said, staring.

"Come on, what's it say?" Finnegan started to pull his pants farther down.

"Stop! Read it in sickbay," Leland said. "That's a hell of a way for someone to send a message."

"Definitely where the Dromax wouldn't look," Finnegan said, buttoning up.

Regarding him as he headed for the doorway, Leland chuckled. "You don't seem very surprised. You were expecting someone to do something like this?"

"Yeah—but years ago," He scratched his head. "Cadet Kirk always said he'd get his revenge. I just didn't expect it now."

43

In her continuum, Emperor Georgiou had taken one look at the absorption nebula surrounding Oast and had decided not to subject *Hephaestus* to its hazards. A flagship was as much a showpiece as it was a platform for waging war. There was no sense in having its exterior marred by whatever the hell was blackening that stretch of sky. She'd sent in her battle cruisers instead in an operation coordinated by Maddox; within half a day of firing into the nebula, they had turned the surface of the mystery world to glass.

It had taken substantially longer than that for *Jadama Rohn* to make its way across the cosmic structure to the pocket that held Oast's sun. The Orion ship was of an older vintage, and while the course Georgiou had found in its systems was an easier way in, much had changed in the active nebula in twenty-five years. In-flight maintenance was also required, and that took time.

Fortunately, Finnegan had brought aboard his and Dax's shoulder bags containing their food, water, and instruments; Georgiou had found them soon after knocking him out. The emperor had surrendered some of the comestibles to her companion on seeing how lowly the Trill looked.

"Let them eat field rations," Georgiou had quipped upon her act of largesse.

"Do what?"

"General Antoinette didn't say that in this universe?"

"I don't know Earth's history." Dax was not in the mood for banter.

The delay had permitted something else: active scans of the

nebula itself. If Vercer had used *Jadama Rohn* to collect a blood devil—or if S'satah had, in her universe—it was quite possible the Cloud had come from the cloud, so to speak. Certainly many nebulae were rich with organic elements. But she could find no trace of dikironium, or any of the other compounds the protean mass had been said to transform into.

Dax had refused to help in those scans, but she had been happy to agree that nothing was out there. If her goal was to make Georgiou give up and turn around—and the emperor was certain it was—the Trill had failed. Georgiou simply finished her repairs and got back underway.

The nebular envelope finally pierced, the two had beheld a baby star with a single world orbiting round. The planet Oast was a golden pearl, a bauble nested deep within the darkness. Massive, grain-covered steppes stretched out across its lightly clouded surface. But for the lack of large oceans or forests, it would have been the closest thing to Earth that either had seen in Troika space. It looked peaceful.

The approach was their smoothest since arriving in the region, as well. Did the Oastlings have any forces to stop an incursion, beyond the superstitions of their neighbors? It hadn't seemed so. Georgiou had brought the *Jadama Rohn* to a soft landing on what its maps—and her sensor readings—said was the commercial landing zone. She had found the field half-covered with Veneti freighters, all more modern than *Jadama Rohn*. The vehicles sat, sealed, around a large cluster of silos and attendant supply huts. One storage tower was capped with a transmitter, two others with directional receiving dishes. Floodlights, inactive, pointed down from the heights.

And that was it. Nothing met them at the foot of the landing ramp but a light, warm, breathable air. No Oastlings, no traders. The freighters were locked up, but tricorder scans suggested nobody was home.

"This is strange," Dax said. "These are Quintilian's ships. Why does he keep them here? I thought the harvest was over."

"Quintilian is sharp," Georgiou said, completing a scan of the silos and finding them full. "If any of his rivals start ramping up food sales to the Dromax and Casmarrans, he can flood the market in a heartbeat and depress the prices."

"He told you this?"

"I have a brain." Georgiou stepped around a freighter and ran her hand along its surface. "And look at how pristine the hulls of these ships are. He's rarely had to send them through that nebula, if at all. I'll bet he put these here as just a threat, and has never had to use them once."

She could see Quintilian doing that, perhaps even inviting the other traders to tour his landing field here. She grinned inwardly at his shrewdness. No wonder the Vercers of the region had been forced to look for other opportunities. Quintilian was no warrior, but he knew how to run an empire.

Dax stepped off the landing area onto the grass. Tan in color, it matched what was in the surrounding grain fields. "We read massive life signs from orbit. Where are they?"

Georgiou struck out in a different direction, tricorder in hand—and stopped. She knelt. "No buildings. No anything. Who's he been trading with?"

Dax snapped her fingers. "Dinner."

The emperor looked back. "We just ate breakfast!"

"No," Dax said, stepping toward her. "Back at Quintilian's. We only saw the two Oastlings, what's their names—"

"Pyramis and Thisbe."

"Right. We only saw them at dinner, or right before it. Maybe they're nocturnal."

"We were inside then," Georgiou said, ready to dismiss the notion—until she took it more seriously. "But they never left the villa, and he always kept the lighting low." She was willing to give the idea a chance. There wasn't any other viable explanation. And they'd landed so close to the planetary terminator that they wouldn't have long to wait.

Oast lost only a little of its warmth when the sun went

down. Georgiou had, by that point, run out of scans to perform. The natives weren't aboveground, and they weren't under it either.

"It's a dead end," Dax said—almost too readily, the emperor thought. "Let's go, while we can still see our way to the ship."

"No," Georgiou said, lifting a finger to the air. "Wait."

It was the faintest of zephyrs, at first. A chill that ended as quickly as it began, barely tousling her hair. But as the landscape vanished, the wind picked up—and all around, the tall yellow stalks of grain went into motion. Soon, it was at a low roar, an ocean of foliage on the move.

"There!" Dax called out, grabbing her arm.

It appeared first as just a flash—something within the tall stalks. But more light appeared, and soon Georgiou realized what she was looking at: an Oastling, stepping out of the field toward them.

The oval, gas-filled bubble perched sideways on the creature's shoulders looked just like what they'd seen before, with the heads of Pyramis and Thisbe. But in the night, with the creature's brain emitting what little light there was to be seen, the electrostatic activity within the Oastling's transparent brain—if that was what it even was—gave off a macabre glow.

The creature stepped forward into the open, a ghoul from the fields—only to pause before Georgiou and Dax. The emperor had never been able to tell whether the Oastlings in Quintilian's house had visual receptors—but it became apparent that she had been sensed somehow when a visual of her face coalesced inside the being's gas-filled head.

"Yes, it's me," the emperor said. She'd been beaten to the last two locations by her counterpart; she fully expected the captain to have visited here as well. "I am Philippa Georgiou. I take it you know me."

The Oastling did not move—but the face within its head grew cloudy and dark as bioelectric storms corrupted the picture. *"You are her,"* declared a voice in Georgiou's head. It sounded not much different from the whistling wind. *"You are her, and you are* not *her."*

Dax blurted, "Did you hear that?"

"I did. Our friend is a telepath," Georgiou said. That explained why there were no voice boxes for them like the other Troika species had.

"I am Umyda, keeper of the garden." The Oastling gestured to the fields. Four more Oastlings appeared from between the grain stalks, pushing the plants back to make a path lit by their luminescent heads. *"You may follow,"* Umyda projected to the visitors. *"But you must disarm."*

Georgiou expected that might happen. She reached into her boot and dropped the knife she'd concealed onto the soil. When the Oastling did not move, she put her hands on her hips. "There's nothing else. I swear."

"Not your weapon. Hers," the Oastling replied, indicating Dax.

Georgiou looked to Dax, who took a couple of steps back. "Why, Little Emony—"

"Stop calling me that," Dax said, partially unzipping her jacket. "And don't come near me." Half fumbling, she drew forth the disruptor and pointed it.

"You would really shoot me?" Georgiou asked, amused.

"Emony has been considering shooting you to prevent you from taking what is here," Umyda said. *"But Dax hasn't been so sure."*

Georgiou was confused by that. "What do you mean? She's Emony Dax."

"She is Emony—and she is also Dax."

Dax froze, eyes wide in the flickering light. "It's just nonsense."

Georgiou stared at her. "Is it?" Several of Dax's recent accidental statements combined with the things she'd always wondered about Trills. "Umyda, is she two beings?"

"Emony the Trill contains a long-lived symbiont. It has an independent intelligence, but they also act in unison."

Dax shrunk back. "That's crazy."

"It is the greatest secret of her people. It is a threat to her that you know." Umyda gestured to the younger woman. *"And now Dax is reconsidering whether to shoot you."*

"For what reason do they conceal this secret?" Georgiou asked, anger rising at the news. "Are they spies? Invaders, who mean to infest the rest of us?"

"No!" Dax cried out, anguished.

"Her people do not wish to make others uncomfortable."

"Uncomfortable!" Georgiou stared at Dax—and then doubled over with laughter.

"Georgiou-Emperor finds this amusing," Umyda observed to Dax.

"I get that."

Wiping tears from her eyes, Georgiou looked again into the barrel of the disruptor, which shook in her companion's hand. "You have a problem, dear. If you don't shoot, you will always have to worry that I would tell your people's secret. To Leland, perhaps." She gestured toward the field. "And if you don't shoot, I will follow these creatures—and possibly find the secret you so fear." She looked to Umyda. *"Is what I seek here?"*

"Yes."

Georgiou faced Dax again. "But if you're not going to shoot, the only way that you can join us is to drop the weapon. It's not me saying so. It's the Oastlings."

Umyda bowed to Dax. *"Georgiou-Emperor speaks truthfully."*

Still clutching the disruptor, Dax looked fretfully at the Oastlings. "You can't give her what she wants. You've got to swear not to!"

"We cannot give that which cannot be owned. But ours is not the final word."

"Whose is?" Georgiou asked.

"Follow and learn."

Umyda turned and stepped toward the passage between the

stalks her companions had opened. Georgiou took a long look at the motionless Dax—then turned to follow the Oastling. She paused to look back at Emony Dax, now to her both Emony and Dax. "Hear that, you two? Follow and learn."

Georgiou did not look back to see whether the weapon had been dropped. But some people simply didn't have it in them to kill, and the emperor didn't need a mind reader handy to be able to identify them.

44

The Fields

Oast

For an hour, Georgiou walked through the croplands, with only the light from the Oastlings' heads to guide her. At least, it had felt like an hour—and she felt like she was still in the fields.

But more than anything, she felt as if she were asleep. Asleep, back in Quintilian's luxurious bed. Where she should have stayed, if she were the least bit sane—

—and where she had also had a dream, attended by Oastlings.

She spoke up. "I'm not really walking, Umyda, am I?"

No response came from up ahead.

She continued to follow the light. "This final word you speak of. To reach the blood devils. It's a password, right? Someone has locked the door, secured it against invaders."

She had no clue where she had gotten that idea. But there was again no response. And this time, the lights ahead seemed to drift away. She struggled to keep up.

"You won't lose me this easily. Take me there—I don't care who guards the way!" She shouted again at the waning lights. "I am Emperor Philippa Georgiou Augustus Iaponius Centarius!"

Darkness enveloped her.

"Mother of the Fatherland! Overlord of Vulcan!"

She looked about, not knowing which way to turn.

"Dominus of Qo'noS! Regina Andor!"

She strained to hear even the slightest echo. A trace of her own voice.

Her own voice.

An echo—but only in her mind. The emperor turned. "I know you're here. Of course. If anyone would be the guard, you would."

"I wondered if you'd figure it out." A woman stepped from the darkness, wearing the same Starfleet uniform. Her very image—save one thing: Captain Georgiou was five years younger. *"That's an awful lot of names you have. It must get tiresome."*

"Tests are what I find tiresome," the emperor replied. "And this is another. I know you're not really here. You never even knew that I existed."

"Don't be so sure. Interdimensional physics would have predicted you," the captain said, looking her up and down as she circled. *"Well, maybe not you."*

"Cutting." Georgiou leered at her. "That's probably the most hurt you ever delivered anyone, Captain."

"I thought you just said I wasn't Captain Georgiou."

"Of course. This is the Oastling speaking, in my mind."

"A funny thing happens when you look deeply at an Oastling," her counterpart said. *"They see you—and know you, who you are and how you would react. I came with a mission, to prevent others from releasing and exploiting the blood devils—"*

The emperor brightened. "Ah! There *is* more than one!"

"Be less predictable for just a moment," the captain said. She gestured into the nothingness. *"Umyda and the others don't really understand much about who we are, and how the clouds threaten our physical bodies. But they saw into my mind and recognized my desire."*

"You never acted on your desires in your life."

"Again, don't be so sure. Though I'll admit my standards are higher than yours."

"We have the same body," the emperor said. "You can't imagine what you've missed, being the way you are—living in this universe among these people."

"I see exactly what you've done—and I see exactly where it's gotten you."

"Do you? Then you already know." The emperor's lips curled. "In a few years, Captain, you're going to die. Die, pointlessly, killed by an attack you should have seen coming. *Would* have seen coming, had you listened to Burnham. Or listened to—"

"To my better self? Is that what you think you are?"

"I'm better than you, that's for certain." The emperor shrugged. "I was going to say you should have listened to the intelligence coming from Starfleet."

"You mean, from Section 31?"

"For want of anything adequate, yes. At least they seem sensible enough to spy on their neighbors. To head off threats coming their way."

"I don't trust them. And I certainly don't trust them with knowledge of the blood devils." She stared. *"Haven't you figured it out? That's why I came here."*

"Wait." The emperor's brow furrowed. "You mean with Michael? Five years ago? Why then?"

"When Michael, aboard Shenzhou, *detected that Section 31 had hacked my private messages with Quintilian, we also found they'd been looking again at my tricorder readings from* Jadama Rohn. *They'd concluded, as we had, that it was no drug, but some kind of biological weapon. It was only a matter of time before they sent an expedition to do what we did, to find this place."*

"And now they have sent me."

"Imagine the irony. Tell me you at least know that Section 31 wouldn't be satisfied with simply protecting others from the blood devils, right?"

"Of course. I understand who they are very well."

"But it didn't matter who wanted it. Once I got here and learned the devils' power, I had to prevent anyone from making the same trip. I want to do the right thing."

"The right thing." The emperor walked past the captain and sneered. Then she looked back, having noticed something. "You're terrified."

"Of the blood devils? Of course."

"That's not all. There's something else. It's obvious. I see your face. I see your mind. This works both ways, you know. You're scared as hell."

"What, because you said I'm going to die? You already said it: this isn't me. It's my mind as of the joining, five years ago. I will not fear what I will not experience."

"No. You were experiencing fear *then*."

"Because I know what the blood devils can do."

"That's not it. You're frightened because you're alone. You've gone off on your own, without the permission of your precious Starfleet. You took Michael most of the way, but you sent her back after you found *Jadama Rohn*, didn't you?"

"To protect her. We'd already broken enough regulations—and I didn't want to endanger her. I had to come here alone."

"And you don't know how to do that, do you? To exist without that structure, those people, all those rules backing you up."

"I don't exist at all."

"Not now, no. Maybe not ever."

The captain's image began to fade. Then it brightened. *"I exist in you."*

"Now you're fighting dirty."

"But I am fighting. I desired to seal the shrine. That desire is the lock—the Oastlings have seen to it. Only Philippa Georgiou can open the lock, and only if she wants it opened more than Philippa Georgiou wanted it closed."

The emperor smiled. The game was given away, the truth known. "Then there's nothing more to discuss."

The captain spoke more urgently. *"Listen to your friends, Philippa."*

"Friends are a luxury I have never had."

"That's not true. You did have a friend. San."

"I lost him. Early, and in time to learn to live without."

"But you have friends here—and they have wisdom. Listen to Burnham. To Dax. To Finnegan."

The emperor chortled. "You really haven't met these people, have you?"

"You're afraid too—afraid of starting over. But you are not alone. Ask yourself what your friends have done. I see it in your mind." The captain's shape blurred—

—and transformed into the image of another. *"I lost my family,"* Michael Burnham said. *"I went to prison for six months. To a starship where nobody wanted me. Each time, I had to start anew in a strange place. But I persevered."*

Her shape shifted again, into Emony Dax's form. *"I've died twice,"* she said. *"But each new start is a challenge. A blessing. A joy."*

A final transformation yielded the grinning image of Sean Finnegan—who launched into misquoting an old barroom song. *"Knock me down! I'll get right back up!"*

The emperor buried her face in her hands. "Please stop."

"That's what I'm asking you."

She looked up to see the captain's image had returned. *"This* is how I start again," the emperor said. She started walking forward. "Go sell Cornwell your sorry psychologist act—I'm sure she'll love it. I know what I'm looking for. Where is it?"

The captain hurried along beside her, grasping at her. *"You're right, Philippa, I was scared. But you're stronger with people than alone."*

The emperor turned abruptly, reaching in another direction. "The game is up. You've already told me."

"You don't have to do this alone." The captain stepped forward and confronted her, looking into her eyes. *"You don't need this."*

"No. I *want* this." The emperor looked over her shoulder. "The time for playacting is over. There was only ever one way this was going to end. Umyda, open the door."

Captain Georgiou faded away, to be replaced by the shining visage of the Oastling. The emperor saw where she was—in a circular clearing in the grain fields, lit by a ring of luminescent orbs on posts. Dax stood to her right, her hands on her mouth.

And before the emperor: a stone shrine. Its door, open.

Dax stammered, "W-what just happened? She was standing there for a long time—and then it opened."

"*We sealed the structure to outsiders because Georgiou-Captain greatly desired it,*" Umyda communicated. "*Only an equal or greater opposite desire from Philippa Georgiou could compel us to open it.*"

"But she's not the same person."

"*By your definitions. The Oastlings are satisfied.*" Umyda gestured to the building: small and serene, a gatehouse to something. "*The House of the Lost Traveler.*"

"Is it safe?" Georgiou asked.

"*No. But neither will you be harmed, so long as you step with surety.*"

"Always." She winked at Dax and walked inside.

45

The House of the Lost Traveler
OAST

Georgiou had thought the small building was a shrine, but it was no such thing. The building held only a staircase, spiraling down into the depths of Oast. As she descended, small globes on the walls came to life, luminescing; apparently Oastlings sometimes needed to see where they were going too.

The bottom steps led out to a dank place. Stone walls defined a large, domed room, forty meters across. Its major feature: a large circular pool, taking up much of the space. Lonely Oastlings walked the area ringing the pool, not so much standing guard as participating in some kind of vigil. None of them took note of her.

Georgiou stepped closer to the pool. Black and placid, and of uncertain depth. Remembering her satchel, she removed the light she'd brought from the Dromax moon and activated it.

As soon as its rays hit the surface of the liquid, something within stirred—and in the same moment, the Oastlings stopped walking. She could hear their faint chants in her mind. Edging closer to the pool, she knelt.

Something had moved beneath the surface, and was still moving. But it wasn't solid. Rather, it appeared as a haze— much like the result of some chemical experiment, some cloudy substance that would not dissolve.

She moved the light about. The thing responded to the rays, separating and subdividing only to combine again into new shapes. As she stared, she grasped the enormity of what was below. Was she looking at one being, or many?

Or many-as-one?

She heard footsteps leave the stairs. Without looking back, she said, "If you intend to push me in, do it."

"We've already had that conversation," Dax said.

Georgiou looked back at her. "I'm surprised to see you in here."

"They wouldn't let me stay out there alone." The Trill looked bereft. "For better or worse, I'm with you."

"Be useful," Georgiou said, gesturing to her tricorder. The emperor drew forth her own. "There's our blood devil. Or devils."

Dax stared at it, frozen with fear. "How—how is the liquid restraining it?"

"I don't know. It doesn't look like it's just water." She pointed out the red ring around the pool near the surface. "A lot of copper."

"It's the same thing that *Farragut* encountered, all right," Dax said, reading her instrument. "What did they call this place?"

"*House of the Lost Traveler.*"

"How could a lost traveler have a house?"

Georgiou thought about it. "I don't know—but I think they mean *house* as in a place built to house it. Not a home."

Dax seemed to relax—but only a little—as she realized the cloud was restrained. "It's almost peaceful."

"At the moment."

"Among my people, symbionts come from pools tended by guardians." She looked back to the Oastlings. "Maybe they're doing something to restrain it too."

"Maybe." She stared, wondering what the real value of the find was.

After several silent minutes, Dax, who would come no closer to the pool, called to her. "So you've found it. What are you going to do?"

She made her decision—and rose. "Vercer discovered the hard way what it meant to mishandle one of these. There's nothing I can do, unless I learn more about it." She faced one of the Oastlings. "Will you tell me of these creatures?"

There was no response, mental or otherwise.

Weapons were not good or evil—they just were. But something about this one made her unsure. Too much had gone into hiding it, protecting it. "That's that," she said, walking around the pool. "I just don't know enough about it."

"Look!" Dax said, pointing. Georgiou turned her head to see a tall figure materializing near the pool's edge. She cast her light upward—

—and across the armored form of Quintilian. He held a walking stick, again, but this one tipped by a golden eagle. He wore a dark metallic breastplate, but one that still reflected the light; it gave him much the appearance of a Roman centurion.

Or emperor.

He stepped around the pool and faced her. Georgiou thought of a dozen things to say—but went with, "You mean we could have just beamed in here?"

He smiled, that broad infectious smile she'd found something to like in. "No. Nobody could. Not until you opened the door." He reached forward and embraced her.

She patted the soft metal. "Not much of an armor. Costume party?"

"Precaution," he said. "The devils don't like copper."

"You knew about them!" Dax said from across the pool.

"I like history," he said, breaking the embrace. "The Oastlings don't write theirs down anywhere—but once I got to know Pyramis and Thisbe, I learned a lot."

Georgiou stared at him. She wasn't completely surprised to see him—so little happened in Troika space that he wasn't aware of—but she needed to understand the reason for his presence. She knelt again beside the pool and looked at the phenomenon below. "Tell me."

"It's almost mythological," Quintilian said, gesturing with the walking stick. "His name was Anowath. An Oastling, just like those you see here. Long before the Troika closed its borders, long before any of us traders were around, he was an explorer. He visited the Casmarrans—he may have even journeyed beyond Troika space. But he also visited the Dromax."

"I can't see them liking that," Georgiou said.

"I don't know if their dislike for Oastlings had developed yet. But it sure did while he was there."

"Because he found the Cascade."

"Found it—and used it, trying to figure out what it was. The true mark of an explorer." He smiled at her. "You are one, too, it seems."

She frowned. "You knew the Cascade existed? What it was?"

"There isn't much Gnaeus doesn't tell me."

"Yes, but why didn't you tell *me*?"

"You didn't ask. Besides, you left in a bit of a hurry." He began pacing the circumference of the pool. "An Oastling is a curious thing, bundling so much mental energy. Going through the Cascade, he came out normal. But his duplicate, inside, was shattered."

Georgiou nodded. "The scarred Dromax have deficits."

"This was several orders beyond that. Where Anowath had communicated peaceably with his Dromax guides, his twin's mind-touch drove them mad. Anowath fled, taking his 'brother' with him—and that was the end of any further contact between the Dromax and the Oastlings."

"How did Anowath feel about it?" Dax asked.

"Oh, he was horrified. Anyone would be. But he was also sympathetic to a being he had, himself, created. So he brought his duplicate back to the clerics of Oast."

Quintilian paused his walk and looked up, reverently. "When an Oastling dies, its mental membrane ruptures, releasing his or her intellect to the wind. The Oastlings spend their days walking about through the fields, communing, literally, with the fallen." He lowered his head. "But Anowath's duplicate was broken, in more ways than one."

Quintilian stepped to the edge and knelt. "He insisted on living in water, immersed as much of the time as possible. His body ultimately failed. Anowath sat in this pool, cradling him as he expired. And when his membrane burst—"

"It killed Anowath too," Georgiou said.

"Yes—but not before it did something astonishing, as if all that wasn't amazing enough. Contact with the temporal fissure had infected the duplicated Oastling's mind, imbuing it somehow with the ability to ignore physical limitations. And it subdivided into many 'spirits,' if you will—all equally lethal." He gestured to the pool. "The blood devils."

"How are they contained here?" Dax asked. "It sounds like they can go anywhere, do anything. I saw one pass through the hull of a starship."

"That's right. As I said, they don't like copper—my people have learned that but to actually control them, they need to be immersed, as here. Under the constant mental control of the minders." He gestured to the Oastlings.

"The minders don't seem to care that we're here," Georgiou said.

"They know we're supposed to be here. We're allowed to do whatever we want. The guardian, for want of a better term, was above, on the surface: Captain Georgiou, mentally imprinted on the Oastling gatekeepers. That block is removed, thanks to you."

Dax's eyes remained focused on the pool. "If the minders watch them, how did they escape into space? One struck the *Farragut*—and before that, *Jadama Rohn* had captured one."

"Eh?" Quintilian looked back at her. "No, that's not quite right." He stood. "But I'm not sure how much more I'm willing to share with you." He touched a control strapped below his copper wrist guard. "Gnaeus, bring Emony Dax to the surface, please. She's four meters ahead of me."

"Yes, sir."

Dax's eyes went wide. "Wait. I don't—" she started, only to vanish in a whirl of transporter energy.

As Quintilian turned back toward her, Georgiou stood. "How much more are you willing to share with *me*?" she asked.

"What do you mean?"

"We never told you about the *Farragut*. What happened to it is classified." She walked around the pool toward him. "I'll ask again. *How much are you willing to share with me?*"

"Everything—*Imperial Majesty*."

Georgiou stared. "What?"

Quintilian bowed—and spoke words she had heard from him before in another continuum. "Hail, Emperor Philippa Georgiou Augustus Iaponius Centarius! Mother of the Fatherland, Overlord of Vulcan, Dominus of Qo'noS, Regina Andor!"

She froze. "You know who I am?"

"I didn't. But after that night—such a wonderful night!— when you talked to me about emperors and empire, I got to wondering about the change in you. So when you slept—"

"Pyramis and Thisbe read my mind." She looked back at the Oastling minders and frowned. "That was the dream."

"Sorry about that—but I needed to know if I could trust you." He rose and smiled. "You are really amazing, you know that? I could listen to your stories for days."

"I take it that you already have. Who needs me when you can download my brain?"

"Oh, I definitely need you," he said, raising his arm toward the stairs. "And if you'll join me above, I'll show you exactly why."

46

Quintilian had an army.

That was the only way to describe it, Georgiou thought, even though it matched no force she'd ever known in appearance. And she saw it all, because the floodlights she'd seen earlier on the silos were now operational.

She'd never known any planet to have a darker night than Oast, but Quintilian had utterly defeated it.

And he clearly seemed on the way to conquering something else. A dozen Veneti freighters had landed beside the pristine ones she'd seen earlier; Quintilian's employees were all about, readying the new ships for flight. Beyond those, she saw several vessels of a sort she had gotten to know well: Dromax troop and equipment transports. Finally, several of the peculiar Casmarran fliers sat on a rise nearby, their pilots out but keeping their distance from the crowd.

The crowd in question: Dromax, by the hundreds. Having unloaded from their transports, the creatures gathered in packs beneath banners featuring icons denoting their tribes—tribes until recently at war with Agamalon, now his vassals. And keeping them in line: a host of Cascade-created warriors of the Double Crescent, led by none other than Agamalon.

The emperor had seen more impressive forces gathered, of course, including her own. But Quintilian seemed to want to put on a show for her, and she'd decided to let him. "You were going to tell me how all this happened."

"It started when you ran out on me," he said, walking

alongside her. "Leaving abruptly seems to happen with all you Georgious."

She didn't like the joke much, but she offered no objection. "Go on."

"The night you left Casmarra, I'd already learned from Pyramis and Thisbe you were the emperor, and what you were after. I knew Captain Georgiou and the Oastlings had installed their psychic lock sealing the blood devils' lair, but I couldn't just send you to Oast. There was too much chance your companions might tell Starfleet."

Quintilian strolled past rows of Dromax like a general on review. "That's why I suggested you start with Agamalon, one of my oldest customers. I knew he'd do what I asked—and was delighted to hear the progress you'd made with him. That's when I boarded one of my Veneti ships, which was making a weapons delivery to the system."

"Then it was you," she said, eyes widening. "Leland didn't transport that bomb to me at the Cascade. *You* did—because you'd learned that tactic when they riffled through my mind."

He grinned. "History doesn't repeat, but it sometimes rhymes. I don't think Twain said that, but it's true." He looked to her. "Did that really work with the Klingons?"

"One warrior race at a time."

"I guess you're right. The important thing is you gave me something I was going to need, anyway: the Dromax, under one leader, and control of the Cascade." He looked up ahead and waved. "General!"

Agamalon turned to face them. *"Greetings, trader—and to you,"* he said, indicating Georgiou. *"If you'd told me you two were in league, Quintilian, I'd have treated her better."*

"I couldn't give up the game yet," Quintilian said. "How are the troops, General?"

"None of them like being here. But we are—for you."

"Don't worry. My Oastling aides are back aboard ship, and all the natives are off in the fields doing whatever they do at night." He gestured to crates, just unloaded from his freighters. "You'll find special armor for the troops there—manufactured for the occasion. There was a reason S'satah wasn't able to get enough copper to keep her smelter open—we had it. Get everyone outfitted and we'll leave, soon enough."

"The sooner, the better."

The human couple resumed walking. "Leave?" she asked. "For where?"

"It's all happened so fast—but more or less how I expected it. The Casmarrans went into immediate panic when the war ended. No market for their weapons—the Dromax aren't about to start buying consumer goods. It put me into a position to—"

Quintilian stopped as he noticed Agamalon's return. "Forget something?"

"Yeah. With everything I had to prepare, I forgot to ask about the two-legs. You know, the giggling fool."

"The—" Quintilian started. "You mean Finnegan?"

Georgiou wasn't sure who else fit that description. "The one you imprisoned."

"We held him, yes—but someone transported him away. I assumed it was you," he said, gesturing to Quintilian. *"You'd just called us to execute him, and nobody else has that technology. I figured you wanted to do the job yourself. How did he die?"*

"We didn't transport him," Quintilian said, alarmed. "My freighter was out of range by then."

Georgiou's eyes went wide, and not only because Quintilian had ordered Finnegan's death. Someone else had transported him, and she had a good idea who it was.

"Hot night, darling," she said, turning away.

"Philippa?" he asked, while her back was to him.

"Just a moment," she said, adjusting her cuffs. "It was cooler before. I think it's all these engines running." She faced him again. "I wouldn't worry about Finnegan. You know I was here for Section 31. Perhaps they found him."

"I don't know how they could have." Quintilian scratched

his head. It was the first time she'd seen him thrown by anything. "Did Finnegan know you were headed to Oast?"

"He's an idiot. I don't think he could find his own ass with a map."

"Well, it'd take them a long while to discover where this planet is." He looked back to his forces. "We can redouble our preparations and leave them nothing but an empty landing zone."

"Then maybe you'd better finish explaining." She reached for his hand. It felt unusually cold. "I can't help you without knowing what's next."

Quintilian pulled his hand away. "Just a second. Gnaeus!"

She saw Quintilian's assistant exiting a freighter. Dax followed behind, prodded along by a disruptor-wielding Dromax. *"How may I assist, sir?"* Gnaeus asked.

"Hypospray."

Gnaeus had one at the ready. Quintilian applied it to his own neck. "Steroidal. A little arthritis from the old injury," he said to Georgiou. He passed the device back to Gnaeus. "We're speeding up the clock. Spread the word."

"Very good." Gnaeus gestured to Dax. *"What's to be done with your guest?"*

Quintilian started to say something—only to look to Georgiou. "Dax isn't going to approve of any of this," he said. "I was going to deal with her the same way as Finnegan."

"What happened to Finnegan?" Dax asked. She looked to the emperor. "What's going on?"

"You may wish to dissect rather than disintegrate her, sir," Gnaeus said. *"I noticed something unusual during her transport."*

Dax's eyes went wide at that. "What?" Quintilian asked. "Does she have a weapon?"

Georgiou quickly interceded. "Dax had to disarm before the Oastlings would take us to the shrine." She tugged at Quintilian's arm. "You just said Gnaeus has much to do, darling. Other things can come later."

Quintilian studied the Trill, unsure. "I don't know—"

"Will someone tell me what's going on?" Dax asked.

Georgiou took a step toward her. She stared at her intently, speaking slowly and choosing her words with care. "Emony, something very big is happening—and I need Quintilian to tell me about it. Do you understand that? If you want to stay safe, you'll let us talk."

"But—"

"I'm talking to *you*, Dax," Georgiou said, a little louder. "You know what it's like to want to keep a secret. Quintilian is concerned you'll tell. I need him to know that you won't talk. Just listen."

Their eyes locked for a couple of seconds. Then Dax put her head down, resigned. "I'll do what you say."

Georgiou looked to Quintilian. "She won't cause any trouble. I guarantee it."

He accepted that. "The guard will follow us, just in case. Gnaeus, make the rounds."

"Very good, sir."

Georgiou shot Dax a quick look before stepping closer to the armored Quintilian. She wrapped her arm around his. "Now, before we were interrupted. You were saying?"

NCIA-93
Oast Nebula

As messages on one's arse went, Finnegan had found his to be disappointing reading. It was just a bunch of numbers and letters, and even Section 31's finest hadn't figured it out. Their doctor was still working on how to remove the ink, some Orion variety that had thus far defied erasure.

At least she'd been able to cure his sniffles—and, most importantly, provide him with fresh clothes. Often during his various exiles from service he'd longed to be in an official Starfleet uniform again. Just not for days on end, as had happened in Dromax space.

The Section 31 vessel had left that region. When Finnegan walked onto the bridge, he saw a dusky mass filling the screen ahead: they'd entered the nebula Oast was supposed to be in. But listening to Leland, Finnegan quickly got the sense that nobody quite knew where they should be headed.

"This is ridiculous. There's no sign of the system?" Leland asked his crew.

"We've scanned as much as we can under silent running," said the officer at the helm. "If there's a pocket in here, we can't find it."

"What about all the vessels we detected entering the nebula a while ago? Didn't we get headings?"

"Some were Casmarran vessels of the sort Finnegan described," Sydia replied. "We were reluctant to close in, given how he said they responded to *Boyington*."

Finnegan stepped into the command well. "You said there were other vessels entering?"

"Dromax, Casmarran, Veneti," Leland said, not budging from his stance near the helm. "It's a big parade."

"I don't get it." Finnegan scratched his new beard— something he'd started to like, now that he'd had a chance to groom it a little. "The Dromies and the Casmarrans hate the Oastlings. It's the whole reason the traders have jobs."

"We know, Sean. You covered it in the briefing." Leland looked back with impatience. "Is there anything else?"

"Come to think of it, I had a question." He pointed inside his mouth. "This viridium stuff in my tooth. Is it going to kill me?"

"Well, we really don't know."

"The doc doesn't know?"

"The doctor doesn't know the stuff exists. And I'd rather you not talk about it here."

Finnegan was incredulous. "You folks put it in without

knowing?" He grew enraged. "I want it out. Or some other people will lose some teeth."

"Calm down. We'll get to it." Leland gestured to an empty chair at a console away from the action. "Just take a seat, all right?"

Finnegan looked back at the unattended console and frowned. He'd forgotten why he was here. Georgiou and Dax may have been recruited by Section 31, but he was representing the Federation and Kitty Cornwell. And with no Georgiou to shadow, he had nothing left to do.

He sat, happy that some of the tenderness was gone. It was a communications console, he saw—but the screen at its center was running programs he couldn't recognize at all. Jumbles of characters identified channels.

Idly, he picked one and turned up the volume to listen. "Nothing," he said—

—only to hear his own voice amid a screaming snarl of feedback that nearly deafened the bridge crew.

Sydia stepped quickly over and silenced the noise. "That is the feed from the sensor in your tooth."

"Great," he said, glad the ear-splitting clamor was gone. It was another reason to get the dental work. Even if the Section 31 ship was out of range most of the time, he felt squeamish knowing his every utterance and belch had been broadcast across space.

He was about to leave the console behind when something on the comm screen caught his eye: a series of numbers followed by a series of letters, divided by a slash. "Hey, what's this?"

Leland called back, "Sean, we really don't have time."

"No, I'm serious. What are these characters?"

Responding to Leland's aggravated gaze, Sydia stepped beside Finnegan and looked. "That is the frequency on which the particular viridium in your mouth appliance decays. It is unique to that transponder. The characters that follow are the decryption key."

"Doesn't that look like—" He shifted in the chair. "Well, like what I'm sitting on?"

"Impossible. There are no other viridium beacons currently in use in this region."

"Why don't we just see?" Finnegan asked. "Does anyone have the message handy? I'd rather not try to look at the moment."

Sydia turned back to Leland, who shrugged. "Try it," he said. The Vulcan called up the character string and entered it into the receiver interface.

"There is a signal," Sydia said. "Very weak."

Leland stepped over. "Boost it!"

Over the comm, they heard static resolve into recognizable words. *"—won't cause any trouble. I guarantee it."*

"That's Georgiou!" Leland said.

"The guard will follow us, just in case," said another voice. *"Gnaeus, make the rounds."*

"That's Quintilian," Finnegan said. "Gnaeus is his Dromax-about-the-house."

"Yeah," Leland said, "but the range is limited. What are they doing out here?"

"Did you do some dental work on Georgiou too?"

"She'd have bitten off someone's hand." Leland seemed bewildered. "She shouldn't have access to something like this at all."

"The identifier in the encryption key says it is of our manufacture—but we did not deploy it," Sydia said.

"Amplify that signal—and track it." Leland jabbed Finnegan in the shoulder. "Good catch."

Hands behind his head, Finnegan stretched his legs out and proceeded to listen. *Looks like I'm back in the shadowing business.*

47

Commercial Landing Zone
Oast

Quintilian walked the bridge of the *Jadama Rohn*, his every halting step filled with reverence. "This takes me back."

His plans proceeding apace outside, he had made time for the detour as soon as he saw the freighter parked near his unused ones. Georgiou had followed him, with Dax and her guard in tow, as the tycoon boarded and walked the old ship's corridors, careful not to step on any of the markings on the deck.

She knew that he'd been here before, with her other self, when the bodies were fresh in those positions, twenty-five years earlier. "It seems a strange thing to be nostalgic about," she said.

"Oh, *Jadama* and I go much further back. When I was a refugee, Vercer was flying her even then and when he took me on, the ship was my first home." He ran his fingers gently over the helm console. "It was on this ship, in fact, that I first visited Oast." He turned and regarded the captain's chair. "He was a good man. My mentor. He first showed me the way to Oast—and introduced me to Pyramis and Thisbe, who handled the grain trade on this end."

"Then you hired them."

"It's the rare Oastling who'll travel. As I said, they told me about Anowath and the blood devils." He turned to look out the forward viewport. "In those days, Umyda and the others hadn't barred entry to the place. I saw the devils—and realized what they could do. How valuable they could be." Checking the time, Quintilian cut his moment short. "We'd better go."

Once on the ground outside, he gazed up at the freighter

again, taking it in. Georgiou looked back to Dax—and asked a question she suspected they were both thinking. "There's something I don't understand. If the blood devils come from the underground pool, how did Vercer collect one from space?"

He looked back. "I'm not sure what you mean."

Georgiou walked until the three could see the dorsal hull of *Jadama Rohn*. "Those vents atop the cargo area, ahead of the warp manifold. They're collectors."

"Oh," Quintilian said. He crossed his arms and looked back at the ship. "That's right. You two thought he collected the blood devil through those."

So did Captain Georgiou. "He didn't?"

Quintilian chuckled. "It's an interesting concept, scooping up evil clouds from space. I don't think it would work."

"Then what—" Dax said, momentarily forgetting her promise.

Georgiou stared at the freighter—and at once, all became clear. "Those aren't collector vents. They're part of a *delivery system.*"

"That's my emperor," Quintilian said. He looked to Dax. "She's amazing, isn't she? I envy the time you've had with her."

"The freighter was carrying a blood devil, collected from the pool," Georgiou said, walking through the steps in her mind out loud. "But the shipboard containment breached."

"The rest you know."

"I'm not sure I do. Why was *Jadama Rohn* heading out of Troika space? Where was it taking it? Who was it going to deploy the devil against?"

Quintilian just looked at her.

Of course.

"*Jadama Rohn* was heading to attack *Archimedes!*"

He grinned. "You are brilliant."

"Vercer was carrying it for you," Georgiou said. "You had never fired him."

"I would never have done that. But at the time, attacking a

Starfleet ship would have been very controversial with my other customers here, especially the Casmarrans. I couldn't be seen to be involved." He let out a deep breath. "After the inquest, I couldn't help his family either. A shame."

Georgiou looked to Dax, who could no longer control herself. "Vercer was going to kill you," she said. "I mean, your double!"

"Every system needs a test," Quintilian said. "And Starfleet had definitely earned being a part of it."

"What?" Dax blurted. "Why?"

"Wait," Georgiou said, waving her off. "Is that why you reached out to Captain Georgiou, to keep tabs on her? To see what she'd figured out?"

"At first, yes. We couldn't kill her when she boarded—not when we knew the test had failed and *Archimedes* was out there. The Veneti couldn't have beaten that firepower. I'd hoped she hadn't figured out anything. I had hold of her tricorder for a few moments; I tried to delete some of the readings. But she was just too dogged. She never let it go."

He stepped toward her. "I'm sorry," he said, touching her shoulder. "I didn't know her or you then. Don't take it personally."

"That's all right. If your lackeys read my mind, you already know: I killed your double."

He withdrew his hand quickly, only to make a show of dusting his armor off. "They did tell me something," he said in even tones, "but I didn't understand it."

"It involved this very ship," Georgiou said, indicating *Jadama Rohn*. "S'satah was delivering me a blood devil in my universe, just a few years ago. She'd code-named it Whipsaw."

Quintilian nodded. "They did mention that. Go on."

"It was in a containment system. She was going to beam it to me. Unless—" She stopped abruptly—and felt her blood beginning to boil. "That little rat was going to test it on *me*, wasn't she?"

"I don't know. I don't know that S'satah."

"I thought I did. I certainly got to know yours." She stalked about, thinking hard. "Captain Georgiou broke the two of you up. But if you and the captain had never met, you still could have been together." She looked to him. "When your other self came out to confront me, he was buying time until S'satah could reach me!"

He put up his hands. "Again, not me."

"You know what this means?" Georgiou spun and addressed Dax. "This means that little traitor Eagan actually saved my life. And the lives of everyone aboard *Hephaestus*!"

"An empire could have fallen right there," Quintilian said, clearly eager to calm her. "But I'm much happier that it didn't." He approached her. "What matters isn't what we did to one another in some other life. What matters is what we're going to do now."

She regarded him coolly—up until the moment that two glowing newcomers emerged from one of the other freighters.

Her two least favorite people.

"Pyramis! Thisbe!" Quintilian advanced toward them. In each hand, his Oastling aides gripped several chains. Copper-coated cylinders dangled from each. "Excellent. The traps are prepared."

He took one from Thisbe and manipulated it. A little over half a meter in length, the drum featured two parts. The external sheath, serving as the trap, and a crimson-colored rod. "A hemoglobin equivalent," he said. "Just as I used, years ago, to collect Vercer's devil."

"So small," Georgiou said.

"It doesn't take much. Remember, part of the cloud doesn't exist in this dimension." He turned. "Ah. Looks like the wait's over."

Georgiou followed his gaze to the brand-new freighters. Each disgorged a single passenger. Coming together in a group, the humans and Orions in Veneti uniforms presented themselves to Quintilian. Among them: Phylla, the kindly pilot from Tallacoc.

"Freighters are all functional and ready for cargo," she said. She cast a disapproving eye at Dax, thief of her aircar. "Orders?"

"Deployment check," Quintilian said.

Phylla turned back to the freighters they'd just left and gave a hand signal. In unison, doors on the hulls of each vehicle opened, revealing delivery-system vents similar, but not identical, to the ones on *Jadama Rohn.*

"Excellent. Take your traps and assemble on the northern perimeter. Pyramis and Thisbe will join you shortly to lead you to and from the pool. We're not sure how the specimens will react to transporters." Quintilian stood back as his Oastling aides distributed the containment units. Phylla smiled as she took hers.

"She seemed so nice," Dax muttered as the woman marched away.

"The Veneti believe as I do. And they'll do as I ask." He gestured to the remote field where the Casmarrans were parked. "You've set it in motion, both of you. The Casmarrans know they're finished without new markets. Xornatta agreed today to allow me to open trade beyond Troika borders. Those ships are part of our greeting to the rest of the galaxy."

"What about the treaty?" Georgiou asked.

"As of this morning, the treaty is null and void. The Dromax will do as I say—and the Oastlings never vote. Troika space is open for business."

"Some business," Dax said. "You're not just taking merchandise! You're delivering death!"

He gestured to Georgiou. "She said it to me at the villa. To take on the Federation and the Klingons, I will need more than conventional arms."

"Your wealth isn't enough. You're going to start your own empire," Dax said.

"Empire . . . ?" Quintilian froze. After a moment, he looked back at her, his face gripped with hatred. "You Federation people. You're unbelievable."

"The Trills are nonaligned."

"*So was my colony!*"

Georgiou had never heard Quintilian shout before. But now he was looming over Dax, yelling.

"Federation, Klingons, Romulans, Gorn—all of you, with your states and empires, always butting up against one another. Testing one another. And who gets crushed?"

"Do you care?" Georgiou asked.

"Of course I do." He looked back to her. "Don't you remember the proverb? *'When elephants battle, it is the grass that suffers.'*"

"We don't have that one."

"From what I know of your reality, I'm not surprised." Stalking the landing field in his armor, he gestured to the gathering forces. "I don't want to be an emperor. If there's one thing I've learned in all my studies, it's this: Empires fall. Everyone else gets sick of them and rises up. Sometimes they fall to barbarians—and sometimes to plague."

Georgiou looked about—and saw the rest. "You're planning both."

"*That's* the whipsaw. It may even be what my counterpart had in mind: a one-two punch. The clouds strike. And then, before the enemy can recover—the deluge." He gestured to his army. "Or rather, the Cascade. An endless stream of Dromax, armed with Casmarran-built weapons. We'll need them in any event: forces to strike those who are immune to the devils."

"Intriguing."

He rushed back toward Georgiou, taking her hands. "You can be a part of it, Philippa. With me. I can't do this alone—I don't have your talent for it."

"You seem to be doing pretty well!"

"As a first stage. But with what you know, you can help me plan the rest. You can be a kingbreaker. Make sure that no alliance of more than two dust motes ever lasts in this universe!"

"It won't work," Dax said. "What happens after the devils hit their targets? They stay alive. They stay hungry." She pointed back at the freighter she arrived in. "You've said they can travel across space in an instant. What if the one that hit *Farragut* is the same one that left *Jadama Rohn*?"

"It may be. I don't care." He pulled away from Georgiou. "We know more than we did then. There's no hemoglobin in Casmarrans; they're safe. And we know copper is a defense. My people and the Dromax will be outfitted. And while their people won't leave the planet, much less help—Pyramis and Thisbe will be along to help control the devils. They, and some like-minded Oastlings whom they think they can convince today. I could never have done any of this without them."

A wind swept across the surrounding fields, causing the grains to rustle. Momentarily, Georgiou thought dawn was approaching—

—and then a sound caused her to think otherwise. The lightest of hums, accompanied by a glimpse of light, well beyond Quintilian's back. No Oastling in the field had looked like that.

It's about damned time. She took a few steps away from the others, raised her wrist to her mouth, and whispered to the item secured inside the seam of her sleeve. "The freighters."

If Quintilian heard, he did not react. "And with that," he said, facing Dax, "we have to say good-bye." He addressed the Dromax guard, still waiting patiently nearby. "Sergeant?"

Georgiou saw the Dromax lift its disruptor toward the Trill. Tears of anger in her eyes, Dax didn't move. "You won't get away with this."

"Of course I will. I've been planning since before you were born."

Quintilian started to gesture to the guard—but the emperor quickly stepped in front. "No," she said. "Let *me* do it."

The magnate's head tilted. "*You* want to?"

"Killing is nothing to me—and neither is she." Georgiou

smiled primly at him. "Besides, everyone seems to want to test me."

"To your loyalty, then," Quintilian said. He took the weapon from the Dromax and passed it to Georgiou. "Sorry we can't toast to it, but there's a fine vintage on my ship we can have, later after we've lifted—"

The device on his wrist beeped. He tapped it. "Yes?"

It was Gnaeus. *"You're needed on the command freighter, sir. It's urgent."*

The interruption seemed to fluster him—but only a little. "So many details." He looked back at Pyramis and Thisbe. "Join the collectors. Lead them to the shrine. And then recruit your friends. We'll leave when you return."

The Oastlings bowed.

"Gnaeus, bring me to you." A second later, Quintilian vanished in a transporter effect.

Georgiou stepped several paces from Dax and pointed the disruptor in her direction. Dax, tears dry, snarled at her. "Well, what are you waiting for?"

"It."

"What?"

Georgiou glanced upward. "That."

From several places within the fields, targeted phaser fire lanced out, striking the camp's towering portable lights. As those sources blinked out, something big and dark screamed past overhead, laying down fire of its own. One of the freighters burst into flames.

In successive swift moves, Georgiou shot the Dromax guard—then pivoted to target Pyramis with a shot in the back. Thisbe received the next an instant later. The incinerating Oastlings briefly lit the night before vanishing from existence.

Dax gawked. *"What are you doing?"*

"Keeping my options open."

48

Oast was as peaceful a place as Georgiou had ever seen. Yet inside of a minute, it had become like the largest moon of Dromax all over again. Energy weapons fire lanced between snipers in the grain fields and Quintilian's forces in his staging area. Meanwhile, in place of lightning from above, disruptor fire came from below, searching for the stalker in the sky.

As Georgiou ran between freighters, the dark vessel rocketed over again, delivering a phaser barrage that struck the ship to her right. Its landing supports gave way, and it tipped with an angry groan, forcing her to tumble to avoid being crushed.

Scrambling to her feet, she saw Dax running through the now-firelit night, cutting around burning hazards. Georgiou had to catch up. She plowed through, hopping across debris in a desperate attempt to gain ground. The tactic helped—but as fast as the emperor was, she was no Olympic athlete. Dax ran like a jackrabbit.

Georgiou decided to take a chance, and did so, hurling her disruptor pistol ahead of her. Dax looked down as it careened past—a mistake, as the step she lost doing so gave the emperor the chance to tackle her. The two rolled near the landing gear of one of Quintilian's freighters. It was hardly the safest place to be with an attacker in the air, but the emperor couldn't be choosy.

"Get away!" Dax yelled over the din as they struggled. "I don't want anything to do with you!"

Georgiou pinned her. "Didn't you see what I just did back there?"

"I never know *what* you're going to do. You killed Pyramis and Thisbe!"

"They read my mind without asking. And Quintilian was going to use them in his plan."

"*His* plan!" Dax spurted. "You talked like you were going to join him!"

Georgiou grabbed the younger woman by the shoulders and pushed her down. Not to harm her, but so she could look directly at her. "Dax. Emony. Either of you—both of you—listen! I had to keep him talking!"

"Why?"

"Because I had something up my sleeve!" Georgiou let go of Dax and demonstrated exactly that: the left sleeve of her uniform. She slipped her finger into a hole and withdrew something small and white.

"A *tooth*?"

"It's the one Cornwell had her medic put in Finnegan's mouth, replacing the one I knocked out on Thionoga." She held the incisor between her fingers. "It's a transmitter so the Federation could keep tabs on him—and me. Remember when I was trying to escape *Pacifica* and I hit him again? It fell onto the deck."

Dax looked at her in bafflement. "You picked up his tooth? And kept it?"

That'd be an odd fetish even for me, she thought. But she had done so—another part of keeping her options open.

Around the time of her romp through *NCIA-93*'s Pandora's Box, Georgiou had come across a file on the Viridium Integrated Dental Surveillance System. Beyond noting the usual Section 31 attempt at obfuscation—that a system abbreviated VIDSS had no vid component at all—she'd learned enough then to identify one, and also the spoken code words to turn it on and off and access its housekeeping file.

Boarding *Jadama Rohn* on the Dromax moon, she'd known there was a possibility not just that the blood devil lead wouldn't pan out, but that the creaky old ship would fail, requiring a way to contact Section 31 for an evac. She'd doubted either her communicator or the ship's comm would be of much help by the time she got to wherever Oast was.

That had led to her brainstorm. Finnegan was too incompetent to be anything but Cornwell's plant; Leland certainly would have used him the same way, as a walking homing beacon and bug. She'd even overheard him offering to replace Finnegan's tooth. But with the Federation and Section 31 at cross-purposes—even as they shared the same secret technology!—there was a good chance Leland didn't know Cornwell's earlier bug existed at all. He would need the proper frequency and decryption key, information she'd gotten from the tooth using the tiny voice that served as its interface.

Getting that data to Leland had required quick thinking. The spymaster would almost certainly have wanted to recover Finnegan, dead or alive, once Georgiou went missing, if for no other reason than to recover the second VIDSS appliance. The emperor had then picked a method sure to convey her message, so long as the Dromax didn't incinerate Finnegan's body. The method of sending that message was unpleasant, to be sure, though she did note that the young brawler had kept in shape.

It was a true trick up her sleeve, deactivated and waiting, until she desired to be found. On seeing the blood devils, she'd decided that might be necessary. Quintilian's mad plan had cinched it, even before she'd heard it all. As soon as she'd learned Finnegan had been transported from prison, she'd activated the unit while pretending to adjust her cuffs, adding voice transmissions to its viridium homing system. Section 31 would find her—and receive tactical information.

All due to her code words, spoken right in front of Quintilian's face: *"Hot night, darling."*

There would be time to tell Dax later, perhaps, when they were not huddling for safety amidst a firefight. "You'll just have to take my word. That's Leland up there shooting. I called him."

"*You* called—?" Dax looked away. "You and Quintilian are both deranged. You're a great couple."

"Maybe we are." Motion to the left caught her eye. One by one, Phylla and the other freighter pilots dashed into the grain fields to the north, devil traps clutched in their hands. No longer having Pyramis and Thisbe to guide them, the battle—or perhaps orders from Quintilian—had convinced them to make their own way.

Georgiou spoke emphatically. "Dax, there's no time. I need you to do something—the most important thing you've ever done in your life. In any of your lives."

"What—what do you want?"

She stood and stepped over to recover her disruptor. "Listen closely. And then—I need you to run!"

"Come on, cadets! To the obstacle course!"

The black-clad Section 31 security forces weren't cadets, Finnegan knew, but he didn't have a better war cry. And the landing zone was certainly an obstacle course. Quintilian's Veneti were afoot, taking tactical positions and firing back with the aptitude of a group that knew something about fending off pirates—or competitors. Whirling Casmarrans were on the move, mostly trying to get back to their vessels and take to the air. And copper-armored Dromax were everywhere, firing randomly either into the fields or up in the air.

He'd almost not gotten to join the party. Leland had objected that Finnegan had only been out of sickbay a short while. That didn't wash. Finnegan had finally realized the truth. The spymaster had no faith in his abilities, using him instead as a bulwark against meddling by the Federation Council, and then, literally, as a listening device planted in Georgiou's party.

But on reaching Oast, Leland understood the sheer size of the task ahead. Every able-bodied crewmember was on the ground, fighting, while *NCIA-93* contributed what it could from the air.

Finnegan finally found a firefight he was happy to take part in.

"Over there," Finnegan called out as his squad gathered at a point of relative safety. "Those tall shadows. The Dromax are raising their portable artillery pieces."

"You've seen them?"

"Seen them? Boyo, I've *fired* them." He switched the setting on his phaser to something more devastating. "Let's give it a lash. Go!"

Georgiou ran back through the encampment. Quintilian had transported to his flagship, she knew, but the freighters looked alike even in broad daylight, and she couldn't remember which one she'd seen Gnaeus emerge from earlier. Some parked vehicles were aflame, while others were serving as fortresses on the ground, firing their disruptor turrets upward as impromptu antiaircraft batteries.

One of them struck pay dirt, winging the marauder overhead. It dipped and slowed for a moment, allowing her to confirm what she'd already suspected: it was either *NCIA-93* or another of the same class of Section 31 vehicles. It hadn't appeared to her to be particularly well suited for strafing runs; she suspected it would now be even less effective, putting more burden on the commandos.

She saw a group of them dash past, fleeing something. She found cover behind a cargo container—and then opened up on the pursuers. Four Dromax warriors vanished in swift succession.

"Halt!" A shot burned past her, nearly singeing her elbow. *"Drop it!"*

Georgiou considered spinning to fire—but couldn't tell how close her assailant was. She let the weapon fall from her hand, figuring an enemy intent on killing her would already have done so.

She turned to see a single Dromax, alone in a makeshift alleyway between freighters. She recognized its ornate armor from earlier. "Hello again, General."

"*You!*" Agamalon said, stunned. "*I thought you were with Quintilian. Why are you shooting my people?*"

"That's . . . a complicated question," she said, fervently thinking on a better response. None came.

"*I should never have messed with two-legs. If I didn't owe the trader for the Cascade, I'd leave in an instant.*"

"You owed *me* for that."

"*He said you were working for him. It doesn't matter. He provided the bomb for the Cascade; I'm sure he could activate it himself if I didn't obey.*"

"Some ally."

"*Dromax don't like alliances, even with each other. But I've made my bargain. Good-bye.*"

On seeing Agamalon's weapon in motion again, Georgiou had considered a last-ditch pounce—but it proved unnecessary, when a metal bar struck the general from behind. The Dromax tumbled forward, revealing his attacker.

"How's *that* for Blackjack, Georgie?" Finnegan said.

"Good enough," she said, swiftly gathering her disruptor, as well as Agamalon's. "You were expected."

"I should be mad at you for the note you left—and for leaving me—but I didn't mind giving this one a smack. I've always wanted to belt a general."

Georgiou went over Agamalon's body, searching. The general stirred—and looked back on Finnegan. "*Oh.*"

"That's how I usually react," Georgiou said.

Finnegan stepped past her and peered around a cargo container. "Have you got this? I'd better get back to my squad."

She gave a thumbs-up. Then, seeing him about to leave, she called out, "Hey, Finnegan."

He looked back. "Yes?"

She tossed him one of the disruptors.

"Thanks," he said. "My phaser was spent."

"And lose the crowbar. Not much use in a firefight."

Finnegan smiled—and then laughed. He chucked the implement on the ground and dashed into action.

She turned back to see Agamalon, reeling but trying to get upright. *"Well, get on with it,"* the general said, noticing her. *"Kill me."*

The emperor had other ideas. "You'd leave if you didn't owe Quintilian."

"I said that. What of it?"

"Just making sure." She revealed the item in her hand, retrieved from Agamalon's body: the remote control she'd been provided days earlier on Moon One. "There," she said, pushing a button.

Agamalon struggled to get upright. *"What did you just do?"*

She pointed upward. "It depends on whether the Veneti's transmitter relay on that silo is still powered and networked to their ships in your region. If it isn't, then nothing happened." A light blinked on the control. "Then again, I could get a message back telling me the deed is done, like this one." She showed it to Agamalon. "The Cascade is no more."

The Dromax general shook for several moments, with only unintelligible sounds coming from its voice box. The first recognizable words were of fury. *"Oh, you insipid fool. You stupid, stupid alien. You have no idea what you've done!"*

"I think I do."

"You've killed my race! Do you have any idea what will happen to us now?"

"Actually, I do," she said, recalling her experience in her own post-Cascade universe. "Your species will be limited to reproducing the normal way—and if you battle, your numbers will dwindle." She threw away the remote. "Whether you fight for Quintilian or with one another, you'll speed the end. Frankly, I don't care what happens to any of you. But if you have any intelligence at all . . ."

The Dromax stared at her. *"We're leaving."*

"That's sensible." As she heard the firefight continuing to rage, her lip curled upward. "Unless you'd like to speed up extinction just a little more for some retribution."

"What? You're the one who pushed the button!"

"It wasn't my bomb—and I never blackmailed you. I just suggested you blackmail others. Quintilian's your manipulator."

Agamalon ruminated. *"I don't know—"*

"Come on, General. We always saw eye to . . . well, whatever you have." She gestured in the direction of the battle. "Really, does it matter *which* two-legs you kill?"

49

The Fields
OAST

It didn't matter what ships were burning, what ordnance was exploding, what hell was breaking loose in the staging area. Out in the fields, the night seemed as deep as before, as if the Oastlings themselves had the ability to shut out the universe beyond.

Maybe they have, Georgiou thought as she materialized in the clearing outside the House of the Lost Traveler. There was a reason she thought so.

With her recruitment of Agamalon, the Dromax started to turn the tide against the remaining Veneti employees. She'd boarded Quintilian's flagship, the general in tow. Gnaeus, it turned out, owed more fealty to his former general than to the master on whose estate he'd served for years. It served Quintilian right for setting his voice box to speak so politely.

Gnaeus reported that, on learning that none of his pilots had reached the blood devils' lair, Quintilian had attempted to beam there. The attempt had failed. So, too, did his attempt to transport outside the shrine—until he took the step of abandoning his disruptor. No weapons had been allowed in the fields when she'd approached earlier; somehow, the Oastlings had enforced that prohibition.

The emperor, too, was unarmed when she walked into the clearing—lit, as it was before, by the glow globes ringing the area. Quintilian stood quarreling with an Oastling outside the shrine.

Its door was closed.

Quintilian noticed her approach. "You're here."

"I'm glad I found you." She approached with care, wondering how much, if anything, he knew about her recent activities.

"Maybe you can talk sense into Umyda. The house is sealed again."

"Your people couldn't get in?"

"None of them even found the place. I don't know what happened to Pyramis and Thisbe." He lifted his hands—and showed that he was gripping the chains for two devil traps. "I couldn't bring a weapon. But with these, I won't need one." He beckoned for Georgiou to approach. "You opened the house the last time. Maybe it'll open again for you."

Georgiou stepped closer, concerned that might actually happen. But nothing did. She suspected she knew why.

"Tell us, Umyda," she said. "Am I the guardian?"

"No," came the psychic response.

"Is Captain Georgiou the guardian?"

"No longer."

"Is there a guardian at all?"

"Yes."

"Show us."

The light inside Umyda's mental membrane flickered. Georgiou stared deeply at the hypnotic light—

—until she was back in darkness again, able only to see Quintilian beside her.

He looked to her. "What's going on?"

"You call for the guardian," she said.

"I don't have time for this." He turned his head and shouted. "Show yourself!"

"Hello."

The two turned. "Dax!" Quintilian said, flabbergasted. He looked to Georgiou. "You said you were going to kill her!"

"It's not her," Georgiou said. "That's her spirit, imprinted onto the Oastling gatekeeper."

Quintilian reached out to grab Dax. His hand passed straight through her arm.

"*Tickles,*" Dax said.

"Where are you really?"

"*I'm inside the shrine right now, waiting.*"

"How—" Quintilian frowned. "Open the door!"

"*Let me think about that.*" Half a second. "*Yeah, that'll be a no.*"

"No?"

"*N-O,*" she spelled. "*You shall not pass. You don't have a ticket, you don't get in. We're all booked up.*"

Georgiou marveled. She'd sent Dax here, reasoning that what Captain Georgiou had done, Dax could do too, providing she got there before Quintilian and his minions. Apparently, she had.

"This is ridiculous," Quintilian said, stalking around her. "I've been inside many times before. I beamed inside just tonight!"

"*That was then. There's a new guardian at the gate.*"

He shouted. "*I want in!*"

"*Want all you want. Decisions of the judges are final.*"

"Umyda!" Quintilian called into the void. "I'm not going to go through this again. My people are lost out there—bring them here. They all need access. I want it now!"

Dax's body transformed into the visage of an Oastling—but her face remained the same. "*You want access, but Dax does not. Her word commands. You could have brought no one here, including Philippa Georgiou, who more wants the House sealed forever.*"

"You mean she's just got to *want* it?" Quintilian blurted. "That's ridiculous. Someone else can want it opened more. I can!"

"*No. Emony Dax is Emony—but she is also Dax. She is also Lela.*"

"Lela? Who's Lela?"

"*She is. I am,*" said another Oastling, materializing from the darkness. This one had the face of an older Trill woman. "*She is also Tobin.*"

An Oastling with the face of an older male arrived from the void opposite. *"I am Tobin. And she is us."*

The Emony-faced Oastling stood between the new arrivals, all facing Quintilian. They spoke in unison. *"Four minds, four souls, four wills speaking as one. Their/her/his/its desire outweighs yours."*

"Who are these people? What are you talking about?"

"It is right," the Emony Oastling said, *"that the spiritual gatekeeper of the House of the Lost Traveler should be one who is divided, yet seeking to be one. Perhaps our tenders below can, like the Trill Guardians, help the broken aspects of Anowath's brother heal."*

Baffled by the turn of events, Quintilian looked about— until his eyes landed on Georgiou. "What about her and me? We're two people."

"You do not speak with one voice. And if you did—the emperor does not want inside. She does not want the creatures within."

He looked to Georgiou, eyes wide. "You don't?"

The emperor was choosing her words when the Emony-faced Oastling declared, *"She has acted in support of your enemies. Your force is in tatters, your plans on the precipice."*

The emperor swore. "You have got to stop reading my damn mind!"

Quintilian took several steps away from her, a vain act in a place where physical space had little meaning. He stared at the nothingness. "You did this. You sent Dax here. You're why Pyramis and Thisbe haven't arrived."

"Georgiou-Emperor ended them."

"Ended—?" Mouth open, he looked on her in horror. "I can't believe you'd do that!" Then his eyes turned on the Oastlings. "I can't believe you'd *allow* her to do that!"

"Pyramis and Thisbe left our people—and our ways—long ago. Like Anowath, their path was theirs alone."

He focused again on Georgiou. "How?"

"Quickly," she replied. "If it matters, they knew fully who I was. You made sure of that."

"But why did you have to kill them?"

"Your plan required them." Georgiou stared at him. "I could either contribute to your success—or your failure. In that moment, I had to choose."

"I thought you *had* chosen. Before, back on Casmarra!"

"I kept—"

"—your options open," he said. His tone grew icy. "I should've expected it. An emperor, against empires. Like you would ever turn."

"You did expect it," the Emony Oastling said. *"You chanced to bring her in anyway, because of how you felt about her."*

He frowned—and nodded. "And how did she feel?"

"She found your offer intriguing," the Emony Oastling said. *"But she—"*

"I can do this myself!" Georgiou stepped in front of the glowing figure. "I liked your estate. How you look at things. Parts of your world reminded me of mine. And you—" She spoke plainly, knowing that the words would be spoken for her anyway. "I haven't met anyone like you on this side."

He stared at her. "But?"

"But I don't take on lost causes. Your power base here is too small. It will take too much time, even with the blood devils and a waterfall that produces soldiers. If you'd brought me in earlier—a lot earlier—it might have worked. But in my universe, we met too late. And in this universe—you met the wrong me."

"There would have been time," he said.

"There wouldn't. It's why you've sped up your timetable now, isn't it? You're not well."

"I'm fine!"

She looked to the Emony Oastling. "Do I have to ask her?"

Quintilian stared—and lowered his head, resigned. "No." As he stepped back, his shoulders slackened. "The weakness, the medication—it's not arthritis. Not only." He looked toward the void. "Getting that first sample for *Jadama Rohn*—the traps weren't perfect. I must have gotten too close. I developed aplastic anemia."

The cold hands. The rouge, to color his skin. It all made sense. "The medications."

"They help. I've imported the best medical minds I can find—they've helped stem the tide. But eventually I won't produce hemoglobin fast enough. That's why I've got to go. And go now." He looked to her. "You're really not with me?"

Georgiou shook her head.

He watched her for a moment—and averted his gaze downward. "Okay," he finally said. "If that's the way it has to be." Traps still in his hands, Quintilian looked up and stepped back over to the Emony Oastling. "I was originally welcome inside— and I have served your people for twenty-five years, keeping intruders away."

"Until today."

"No matter. I ask you to respect my claim."

Georgiou crossed her arms. "I told you, the cause is lost. What's happening outside—"

"Isn't happening here. I'm still standing." He gritted his teeth. "*Respect my claim!*"

For several moments, nothing happened.

Then, from the Oastling: *"We recognize your claim, to a point. Those who have entered before may do so again. No others. Ever."*

Quintilian bolted through the blackness—which resolved into the open doorway of the House of the Lost Traveler. He bounded down the staircase, startling the real Dax, who sat on the upper step, as far away from what lay below as possible.

Georgiou quickly followed, passing the Trill. "Come on!"

Dax stood. "What happened? They said only I could go in or out!"

Georgiou had no time to explain what a complicated, strange, and capricious people the Oastlings were. Quintilian had turned his head start into a lead down the spiral staircase.

She hurried to catch up—only to see him lose his footing on the moldy stones near the bottom. He stumbled, rolling in his armor down the final dozen steps. He lost hold of the traps. One bounced away and splashed into the pool; the other was crushed beneath his body as he slammed into the floor.

Georgiou reached the bottom to find Quintilian moaning in pain, on his hands and knees. The trap beneath him, she saw, was bent and broken; so was its owner. He reached in vain for the trap bobbing momentarily in the water—only to see it sink into the murky, cloud-filled liquid.

She stepped to his side, keeping him between her and the pool in case he attacked. But the fight had gone out of him, and the older man seemed in no physical shape to resist anyway.

"Damn knee," he muttered. "Of all the times . . ."

The knee, she saw, was just one of his problems now—but she made no motion to tend to his injuries. Nor did he ask her to do so.

Instead, he asked, "Is it . . . really over? Outside?"

"Yes." Out of the corner of her eye, she saw Dax arrive at the bottom step. The Trill waited there. "Agamalon will not let you live. And if he doesn't take you, the Federation will not let you live free."

"There's no third way?"

"Not with me."

"I came close," he said, trying to stand up. He clutched his side, pawing at bones obviously broken. "No . . . time for a . . . second try, I don't guess."

"Not in this universe."

"Forgot to pack a spare one," he said. He started to laugh—but nearly doubled over. She caught him—and caught the look in his eye.

"How?" she simply asked.

He gritted his teeth. "In this universe . . . Vespasian said . . . an emperor should die standing."

"That one I've heard." Georgiou helped him upright—and

brought him into an embrace. But it was not simply that. She unhooked the straps securing his copper breastplate. It clattered to the floor between them.

He gazed at her. "Sorry there was just one night."

"It was a good night." She gestured to the left. "Your bath, Your Highness."

Quintilian smiled—and turned, stepping one shaky foot at a time down the recessed steps that led into the pool. Beneath the surface, the clouds swirled about, and grew angry. He took more steps and stood, surrounded by the swirling mists of the blood devils.

"Something smells sweet," he said, shivering. "I guess as last words go, those aren't—"

He vanished into the depths. Georgiou waited—and watched. No creature broke to the surface. Human, or otherwise.

"Wow," Dax said, mesmerized. After a few moments, she asked, "Was Vespasian a great warrior?"

"Vespasian died of diarrhea," Georgiou said. "Come on, Guardian. Let's get out of here."

50

"Debriefings, debriefings, debriefings," Georgiou said. "They're never as fun as they sound."

She put her boots up on the admiral's desk and stretched. The office was a loaner, but that wasn't why Cornwell didn't object. The woman was too engrossed in reading reports from the past eight hours of meetings.

In Georgiou's continuum, after a battle, the victors took the spoils. Then came the scavengers, provided scorched-Terra tactics hadn't been called for. In the Federation's realm, triumphs were apparently celebrated by the dispatch of hordes of investigators, sometimes outnumbering those who'd fought, picking over the evidence and trying to reconstruct, millisecond by millisecond, what had happened. All so a completely different legion of eggheads could debate the whys and wherefores until they had completely neutered even the most heroic acts of any hint of accomplishment.

She'd never sought parades as emperor, preferring to achieve what she could while she could, leaving the laurels for later. There would clearly be no parades for this episode, she'd learned. A blood devil from Oast was indeed the source of *Farragut*'s woes; there was a fair chance it was the one from *Jadama Rohn*. But the Oastlings had the pool locked down, perhaps forever, and with Troika space opened to trade—the one, immutable deed of Quintilian's—the Casmarrans and Dromax were able to look elsewhere for food. No one ever needed to approach Oast again, and Section 31 surveillance would ensure no one did.

To make certain of that, the words "blood devil" were

never to be said. Starfleet vessels were to be provided no more than the knowledge that the *Farragut* attack had happened. There was no proof that copper-based beings were immune. That would never be put to the test. The Federation's scientists thought Quintilian's researchers were deluded, like ancients wearing copper bracelets to ward off arthritis.

Georgiou found it peculiar that whole bits of history could go redacted in a supposedly open society, but apparently the Federation had done similar things before. Such a strange people.

She looked up after a yawn. "Can we—?"

"Shh," Cornwell said, eyes locked on the slate. "I'm just up to Casmarra."

As much as it pained Georgiou to see it happen, control of Quintilian's industries in the Alien Region on Casmarra fell to S'satah and her son. The Veneti had spread to the winds, many leaving Troika space. Others fell in with P'rou, running a much-reduced trade between Casmarra and the Dromax moons. Georgiou gave up any hope that S'satah could ever evolve into the ferocious and fun pirate friend she'd had in her universe.

The Dromax peace fell apart long before General Agamalon got his forces home from Oast. The Cascade had indeed exploded, the blast punching a hole through the middle of the cataract. Any nearby Dromax who weren't killed in the explosion were carried away when the lake above poured violently into the ocean.

And while Federation science investigators had found no trace of the temporal anomaly—so much for a doorway home—the Dromax elected to keep acting as though the moon was worth fighting for. Fueled by new recriminations, battles in the system continued. Georgiou expected that to begin winding down once it became clear that only the officers, and their young, remained to do the fighting.

Her operation, to her eyes, was a success. The blood devils had been found; that no one wanted to risk their containment by studying them further wasn't her concern. A forbidden zone had been opened, partially, to trade—and a potential threat to interstellar security had been put down.

And still, they nagged her.

"The Federation Security Agency suspects you of double-dealing in this affair," Cornwell said, putting down the slate at last. "You assaulted Finnegan, their agent, on the Dromax moon."

"And I wrote on his butt. Don't forget that part."

"I tried to tell them that was just the sort of thing you did," the admiral said. "The double-dealing part, not the butt part." She blanched. "I don't know what they do over in your universe."

"I suppose there'll be a boring inquest now. More boring than this one, I mean."

"There would," she said, referring to a data slate. "But Finnegan came forward and said the two of you were just wrestling, and things got out of hand." She looked up at Georgiou, incredulous. "Given his record, they believe him."

"It pays to have one's idiocies documented."

Cornwell put the slate down and muttered, "Well, it seems to work in this universe." She took a deep breath and plowed ahead. "It amazes me to say this, but as far as the Federation is concerned, they have no further reason to object to your working with Section 31."

"And you have one?"

"I've met you." She put the data slate away. "Don't assume that because things worked out that you can get away with whatever you want. I know what you are—and I'm pretty sure you went on this mission hoping you could recover what you lost."

"What a thing to say, Doctor." Georgiou tut-tutted. "Doubting the sincerity of my journey to self-improvement? You could undermine my personal growth."

"Uh-huh. If I hear you're making the slightest bit of trouble, you'll be on a journey back to my brig."

"Can I bring my own chef this time?"

"Feet off the desk," Cornwell said. "I mean, dismissed."

"I don't know that I work for you."

"Just get out of here," the admiral said, waving with the back of her hand. "Go. Shoo." She paused. "Be free."

Georgiou walked out, down a corridor, and into a festive lounge. Several starships could be seen in spacedock through the observation port. Dax was by the window, looking out proudly at one of the smaller ones.

"That's the *Leizu*," Dax said. "I found out that's the name of an empress."

Georgiou knew. "The legends—both your world and mine—call her one of the first scientists. She discovered silk."

"That fits. It's the shuttle for my research project."

"You mean the boring one where you run around studying whether walking on other planets causes the fingernails to grow a fraction faster?"

"That's the one. I'll take boring." She gestured to a group of researchers at the other side of the lounge. "Picking up where I left off—but I'll be assistant lead."

"You do assist."

Dax smiled. "Only when you listen."

Georgiou rolled her eyes. "I don't know what I'll do without my self-appointed conscience about."

"Maybe you should try to go see Michael Burnham," Dax said. "The way you talked about her, it sounds like she could have a good influence on you."

"You think I need influencing."

"You're acclimating. It doesn't hurt to have a friend." Dax looked off to the side—and then back. "So, are *we* friends?"

"I don't know," Georgiou said. "This not-using-people thing is new to me."

"Good luck with it." Seeing lounge patrons looking at her, she said, "I'd better go to my team before someone tells them I'm famous. They'll want backflips or something."

"Such a difficult life." Georgiou smiled gently at her—only to call out before she left earshot. "Dax!"

The Trill returned. "What?"

Georgiou drew her close and spoke quietly. "This business of hiding what your people really are—the symbionts."

Dax's eyes went wide. "You won't mention that to—"

"No, I won't mention it to anyone, especially not Leland. He'd just use it against you, and I don't want his smug self to have leverage over anyone if I can help it."

"*Thank you.*"

"But here's a piece of advice. If there's no reason to keep it a secret, come clean. Someone will use it as a weapon against you—someone besides me, that is."

Dax agreed. "And besides, people don't like being lied to."

"I haven't heard that." She watched Dax join her companions.

From the bar side of the lounge, familiar laughter. Finnegan approached her with a frothing mug and smiled, displaying his third new front lower incisor of the month. "Fancy a pint, Georgie? I'll get you one."

She seized his from him—and drank it completely in seconds while his eyes bulged. "Fair play!" he said, grinning broadly.

"It was me drinking it or you." She wiped her face with the back of her hand and passed the mug back to him. "Besides, I've been in meetings all day."

"Ah!" He leaned against the window. "I know that feeling."

"I heard you stuck up for me. Why'd you do it?"

He raised his hands and spoke as a philosopher might. "Well, I figured as your shadow—or your henchman—my job was to stay with you, keeping an eye on you. I was thinking that might be a bit hard to do if you were in Thionoga, and I was out running around with the FSA."

"Federation Security Agency? Cornwell's gotten you a regular job."

"*I* got it—we'll see if I can keep it."

"Well, if you're ever in trouble with a supervisor, just tell them that in my universe, you clubbed five superiors to death. That ought to shut them up."

"Not Mary Finnegan's little boy. He wouldn't hurt a flea." He smiled. "Besides, I don't start right away. They're giving me a year, first, to serve as pilot for a mission in the name of health research."

Georgiou followed the direction of Finnegan's gaze. "What, with Dax?"

"I've flown for her before. We seemed to get on."

"I know where your mind is." She rolled her eyes. "She doesn't know you're alive."

"What can I say? Some people want impossible things." He turned over the empty mug in his hand. "For now I'll settle for getting another drink." He looked over to Dax. "Maybe I'll bring a spare."

She watched as he left—and smiled in spite of herself. The people of this continuum were different from the residents of hers; many, she still thought, were much inferior. But a current of hope ran through this universe, encouraging lightweights to seek responsibility—and giving those with dark pasts a shot at something other than incarceration.

She would never get her revenge on those who had ended her rule over the Terran Empire. The conspirators were dead, disintegrated—with no graves to mark them, and a universe away. But she could avenge herself: her different self. Philippa Georgiou of this universe had fallen. And while she once hadn't wanted to claim her, to cross one Georgiou was to cross them all. What better way to scream defiance at fate than to live and work in this universe as Philippa Georgiou, the woman death could not stop?

She turned—and saw Leland approach.

"Damn. And I was just starting to feel good."

"Nice to see you too. I had one more briefing than you did."

"That's how you died in my universe, you know. Drank poison and keeled over at the conference table. You just couldn't take inflicting one more senseless meeting on anyone."

"You've finally come up with one I can live with." He shrugged. "Actually, today wasn't that bad. Because we had audio of Quintilian saying the treaty was kaput before he got to Oast, we were able to argue we weren't abrogating Troika space when we came to extract you."

"And you're going to keep reminding me of it until I offer thanks."

"No—in fact, I'm here to offer *you* something." He waved a data slate in front of her. "Now that you're no longer under house arrest, we're off to Qo'noS."

Her eyes widened. "You're not dumping me back there?" She looked about. "Granted, the bar's a lot more exciting—"

"Relax. It's a mission—should you choose to accept it." He shrugged. "Sorry, I heard that someplace." He passed her the data slate.

Klingons. Politics. Compromises. Conniving. She looked up. "Tell me again why this is important?"

"We put L'Rell in charge, but her rule's shaky. You were right about the bomb trick. We may need to do some maneuvering to stave off a negative result."

"*A negative result.* Such a fine phrase for a potential war, killing billions. You're talking like Control again."

"Are you ready?" Leland took the slate back. "I figured you'd like this. You'll be changing the course of history."

"I've changed history before."

"Your history. This time it's ours."

"What's yours is mine." She smiled politely. "Shall we begin?"

Georgiou's adventures on Qo'noS continue in Season Two of *Star Trek: Discovery*.

Acknowledgments

I took some time away from writing novels after the enormous project that was my *Prey* trilogy; what drew me back—and back to *Star Trek*—was the Mirror Universe arc in the first season of *Star Trek: Discovery*. I considered it one of the finest *Trek* stories in years, and found the concept of Emperor Georgiou loose in the Prime Universe brilliant, sparking lots of ideas. So when my editor Margaret Clark suggested I could follow up my *Enterprise War* novel with one covering Georgiou's adjustment to life without an empire, I jumped at the chance.

I worked with Kirsten Beyer of the *Discovery* writers' room to develop a story that synced up with Georgiou's adventures thus far and into the future; I again owe her a debt of thanks. Fellow author Dayton Ward, working in a support role between Kirsten and the authors, joined her and Margaret in suggesting several ideas that ultimately found a home in this book. Appreciation, as always, goes to John Van Citters at CBS, Ed Schlesinger at Simon & Schuster, and copyeditor Scott Pearson.

Thanks go as well to my local proofreaders, including Meredith Miller, number one on my bridge, and Brent Frankenhoff, who won't know this book is dedicated to him until he gets the printed copy. Like the emperor, I can be sneaky when the situation calls for it!

About the Author

John Jackson Miller is the *New York Times* bestselling author of *Star Trek: Discovery—The Enterprise War*, the acclaimed *Star Trek: Prey* trilogy (*Hell's Heart*, *The Jackal's Trick*, and *The Hall of Heroes*), and the novels *Star Trek: The Next Generation—Takedown*, *Star Wars: A New Dawn*, *Star Wars: Kenobi*, *Star Wars: Knight Errant*, *Star Wars: Lost Tribe of the Sith—The Collected Stories*, and fifteen *Star Wars* graphic novels, as well as the original work *Overdraft: The Orion Offensive*. He has also written the eNovella *Star Trek: Titan—Absent Enemies*. He has written for franchises including *Halo*, *Conan*, *Iron Man*, *Indiana Jones*, *Battlestar Galactica*, *Mass Effect*, and *The Simpsons*. A longtime comics industry historian and analyst, he operates the Comichron research website. He lives in Wisconsin with his wife, two children, and far too many comic books.